Praise for *The C...*

"*The Cutting Room* is a well-written, [...]
will keep you on the edge of your se[...]
serial killer. Margaret Murphy and Helen Pepper, who write as a team
under the name Ashley Dyer, have constructed another intriguing
police procedural that is full of tension and misdirection. There's
enough of Edgar Allan Poe, Peter James, and Michael Connelly in
The Cutting Room to make every mystery reader's heart beat faster.
Highly recommended."   —Joseph Badal, bestselling author of the
Danforth Saga series, for *Suspense Magazine*

"The beauty of *The Cutting Room* is Dyer's easy writing style. . . .
The result is another highly effective crime novel filled with extremely
complex, real characters who keep the pace at high-stepping speed
from start to finish. Jump on in with Lake and Carver, and make sure
you have several hours blocked out in your schedule. You're going to
need them once you're absorbed inside this well-constructed thriller."
                                                    —Bookreporter.com

"Disturbing and wickedly entertaining."   —*People*

"Refreshing. . . creative. . . . If you're a fan of in-depth crime procedurals, this is hands down a book for you."   —Criminal Element

"A riveting investigation. . . . A grimly authentic narrative and deeply
defined characters."   —*Booklist*

"Addictive. . . . The material is fresh enough to keep readers turning the
pages. Fans of British police procedurals will be well satisfied."
                                                    —*Publishers Weekly*

"The latest exploration of 'murder as art' comes from Ashley Dyer's *The Cutting Room*. . . . The authors weave in a number of additional, internationally hot topics, such as society's addiction to true crime and social media. . . . Relationship dynamics will continue to grow and evolve as the series progresses. . . . We can't wait."   —The Big Thrill

"Another intriguing tale and a good follow-up to the first story *Splinter in the Blood*. The characters of Lake and Carver are well-written and have good chemistry together. The story is intense with twists and turns that keep the reader engaged right up to the end."
—Red Carpet Crash

"The endearing characters, a truly horrifying crime, and the forensic details make *The Cutting Room* a standout."   —Murder and Moore

"*The Cutting Room* is well-written and full of suspense. The authors combine their knowledge and skill into one seamlessly written novel that I couldn't put down. Carver and Lake are well drawn, interesting characters whose demons I enjoyed exploring. The killer's work is complex and horrifying, and I was on the edge of my seat as I read."
—Mysteryplayground.net

"The Ashley Dyer team delivers a *'skin crawling'* realistic British crime drama in this latest work."   —*Iron Mountain Daily News*

Praise for *Splinter in the Blood*

"A taut and compelling thriller, as sharp as the thorns that feature in the plot."   —Ann Cleeves, internationally bestselling author
of the Vera Stanhope and Shetland series

"[An] enthralling debut. . . . The skillfully constructed plot complements the intriguing characters, including a deliciously creepy killer who lurks in the background. Dyer is definitely a crime writer to watch."   —*Publishers Weekly* (starred review)

"One of the boldest, most inventive serial-killer thrillers since *The Silence of the Lambs*. Packed with forensic detail, anchored by a protagonist as complicated as she is compelling, this ferocious novel is perfect for fans of Jeffery Deaver and Lisa Gardner."
—A. J. Finn, #1 *New York Times* bestselling
author of *Woman in the Window*

"This debut spins to a breathless conclusion. Solid suspense fiction by a knowledgeable duo."   —*Booklist*

"Compelling, clever. Packed with macabre and fascinating forensic details. A stunning debut."   —Mo Hayder, bestselling author of *Gone*

"With complicated leads and a ruthless killer whose method is barbaric enough to be frightening without shading into the grotesque, this is a debut worthy of sequels."   —*Kirkus Reviews*

"This novel starts off with a bang of a puzzler and keeps surprising all the way through. . . . Very nice start to a new series."
—*Deadly Pleasures Mystery Magazine*

ALSO BY ASHLEY DYER

Splinter in the Blood

THE CUTTING ROOM

A NOVEL

ASHLEY DYER

WILLIAM MORROW
An Imprint of HarperCollinsPublishers

THE CUTTING ROOM. Copyright © 2019 by Ashley Dyer. All rights reserved. Printed in the United States of America. No part of this book may be used or reproduced in any manner whatsoever without written permission except in the case of brief quotations embodied in critical articles and reviews. For information, address HarperCollins Publishers, 195 Broadway, New York, NY 10007.

HarperCollins books may be purchased for educational, business, or sales promotional use. For information, please email the Special Markets Department at SPsales@harpercollins.com.

A hardcover edition of this book was published in 2019 by William Morrow, an imprint of HarperCollins Publishers.

FIRST WILLIAM MORROW PAPERBACK EDITION PUBLISHED 2020.

Designed by William Ruoto

Library of Congress Cataloging-in-Publication Data has been applied for.

ISBN 978-0-06-279772-8

20 21 22 23 24   LSC   10 9 8 7 6 5 4 3 2 1

For Murf

PROLOGUE

A man strides down a moonlit alley, his heels echoing like stones dropped on cobbles. He is twenty-two or twenty-three, young enough to take his invulnerability for granted, perhaps. He is yet to learn that a lone male walking the backstreets of Liverpool is never as safe as he imagines. The cocksure swagger that shields him from hard cases and shadow-creepers this side of night cannot protect him from the hooded figure who waits, unseen, in a doorway.

He senses the presence and in a practiced glance that would serve as warning in the bars of better lit, more populous streets, he sees the figure, and a tremor of uncertainty passes quickly over his face.

Is it the stillness of the strange apparition that makes him miss his stride, or perhaps the facelessness of the threat? Darkness seems to fold in on itself in this quarter, at this hour, and neither eyes, nor a face, are visible under the hood.

The figure steps out into a thin slice of moonlight, and the young man's shoulders twitch as if a finger has traced the length of his spine. He takes his hands from his pockets and readies himself to fight or flee. He is not afraid of face-to-face confrontation, but this threat is sly, insinuating. It matches his footfalls, echoes the echoes of every step he takes. Fear seeps into his heart.

He quickens his pace, but the hooded figure casts a long shadow. Darkness seems to ooze from it like evil intent. The shadow creeps closer and closer, flowing like poured smoke.

He half turns as the shadow catches his heel and his eyes flash with fear.

The shadow engulfs him; darkness falls.

The lights go up. A man stands on a semicircular stage. The camera pulls back to reveal a studio audience. It switches to an overhead view. A second camera swoops in on a wire, focusing on the man, as the screen behind him becomes awash with binary code, running down the screen like water.

"I am Professor Mick Tennent, and this is *Fact or Fable?*"

The presenter is tall and lean, his gray hair at odds with the youthful energy that seems to crackle off him. A ticker tape crawls along the bottom of the screen, revealing the episode title: "Statistical Uncertainty— Learn to Think Outside the Box."

"Liverpool is a city in fear," he says over the audience's applause. "In just six months, twelve men aged between twenty-two and twenty-eight have vanished without a trace."

The backscreen lights up and images of the missing appear in succession, their faces expanding on the screen for a brief, bright moment before vanishing again into the darkness.

"Theories abound," Tennent says. "A 'time slip,' which transports the missing back in time . . ."

As if the audience couldn't possibly imagine this preposterous scenario, the screen runs a clip of a male actor, his back to the audience, walking toward a busy street corner in the Liverpool city center. As he reaches the intersection, his image fractures in lines of interference, and he vanishes.

"Criminal gangs who prey on the vulnerable, stealing their valuables and disposing of the bodies."

As this second reconstruction fades, Tennent pauses.

"Now, a new contender: a sinister figure locals call 'The Ferryman.'"

An image of the faceless, hooded figure looms like a threat on the screen behind him.

"*Is* a serial killer *really* stalking the streets of Liverpool?" He gestures over his shoulder to the dark, hooded male. "Is Liverpool's 'Ferryman' Fact . . . or Fable?"

Staring straight into the camera, he says, "You decide."

1

Ruth Lake was working at her desk when DCI Carver appeared at the door. He had lost weight in the last few months—signed off as unfit for duty for the first two. A serious head injury and a bullet in the chest had put his return to work in serious doubt for a time, yet here he was. And on the whole, he was doing okay.

"What's up?" Ruth said.

Carver frowned. "Not sure."

Ruth lifted her chin in acknowledgment but didn't comment. With no clarification forthcoming, she said, "Want a lift home?"

Carver was on a phased return to work, and not yet declared fit to drive.

"No . . ." He had an *otherworldly* look since his injuries—a dreamy, slightly unfocused gaze, as if he permanently had something on his mind. But looks can deceive—and Ruth was one of very few who knew that in some ways Carver was sharper than he'd ever been.

"So it's case related?" Ruth prompted, after he'd remained silent for another half minute.

"You could say that."

She rested her chin on her hand. "Oh, you're going to make me guess. Tell me it's another urban myth—I *like* those, they're fun."

Carver had brought Ruth in to help with a Missing Persons case review. Of the twelve men who had vanished from Liverpool over the last six months, four were last seen around Bold Street and Central

Station, an area of the city that had a reputation for "time slips"—at least among *Twilight Zone* enthusiasts. One local hack had even written a book on it.

Carver handed her a printout of an e-mail. The message read: "The Ferryman is no fable."

"Urban myth it is," she said.

"Sign out a fleet car, would you?" he said. "Nothing too flash."

"Okay." She turned the sheet over. "I don't see any directions—where are we going?"

He handed her a second e-mail. It read, "Await instructions."

She lifted the page to her nose and sniffed.

"I know," he said. "Smells like bullshit. But look at the subject line."

It read: "Statistical Uncertainty: Learn to Think Outside the Box"—the title of a *Fact or Fable?* TV program about the disappearances.

"Digitally signed *F*," she said. "Nice dramatic touch. Obvious windup." She handed the sheets back.

"Maybe. Did you watch the program?"

"Yeah." Of course she had—Ruth was a former CSI—science programs were her go-to TV fix at the end of a long day. Plus, Mick Tennent was a prominent statistician: she'd wanted to hear his take on their case.

"What did you think?" Carver asked.

"He rubbished the speculation, which is helpful," she said. "His main argument was that people drop out for all kinds of reasons, and the numbers of missing males were about what you would expect in a city of nine hundred thousand souls."

"I meant what did you think of *him*?"

"He was convincing. His tone's a bit snarky—but that's Tennent's trademark."

Carver nodded, still thoughtful, and she realized he'd used the past tense.

"Has something happened to him?"

"The day after the program went out, Tennent presented a lunchtime lecture at the Wellcome Trust in London," Carver said. "He called his secretary at King's College in the Strand to let her know he'd just finished. Told her that he'd be making a short stop to meet someone on his way in, but he'd be back in time for a meeting at the university later that afternoon. He hasn't been seen or heard from since."

"I'll have the car ready in five minutes," she said.

Ruth Lake watched in the rearview mirror as her boss tried to walk a straight line across the police headquarters car park. It was a valiant effort, and he almost made it, but by six in the evening Greg Carver had usually exhausted his reserves of energy, and twice she saw him brush his fingers lightly along the bodywork of a parked car to steady himself. She waited in silence while he eased himself into the passenger seat and buckled up.

"Do you know where we're going yet?" she said.

"Stone Street. D'you know it? It's near Stanley Dock."

"I can get us thereabouts."

The last week in March—officially springtime—but it was already dark, and a sleety rain spattered the windscreen as they turned right, joining a slow-moving stream of commuters heading home. The first mile along the riverfront was travel-brochure glossy, lit in a carefully chosen palette of blues, orange, and gold. But just past the honey-lit façade of the Liver Buildings, the road darkened, their view of the water barred by a fifteen-foot wall. A mile farther on, Ruth glanced across at her boss; his eyes were closed.

"It must be coming up soon," she said.

Detective Chief Inspector Carver checked his smartphone and directed her into a narrow, unlit street, hemmed in on both sides by crumbling nineteenth-century light-industry units. A large storage warehouse loomed at the easterly end. Crossing a busy arterial road, they dipped down into Stone Street. A brand-new commercial unit took up a sizable plot on the corner, the rest was a huddle of ancient lockups in danger of collapse. They trundled toward a railway arch, passing an abandoned car. Every window had been smashed, the wheels stolen, the roof caved in by a chunk of concrete, no doubt dumped off the railway bridge.

"You sure about this?" she said.

He frowned. "Yes."

"Any clue what we're looking for?"

"The message said follow the lights."

Ruth noticed the slight evasiveness in his words. Carver didn't want to preempt the facts, but he was expecting something bad. She ducked her head, trying to squint up at the buildings, but the street was too narrow to see beyond the ground floor, and sleet blurred the view. "I'll have to park," she said, glad she'd used a fleet car—and one of the low-end models, too. Even so, she rolled forward until they were under the railway arch. No point in taking chances.

They walked on for twenty yards, collars turned up against a biting northeasterly.

"See that?" Carver asked.

"I see it," Ruth said.

Colored lights pulsed up ahead.

Twenty yards on, they came upon a three-story 1960s commercial building. Set back from the road behind aluminum fencing, it was braced by scaffolding and swathed in plastic and tarps. Behind the sheeting, the lights phased from red to green, through blue, to purple.

On the first stage of scaffolding, a twelve-by-ten-foot section of tarp had been cut down to reveal a large wooden packing crate, open at the front. Inside the crate, they saw that the source of the light was a continuous strip of colored LEDs. Suspended from thin wires attached to the roof of the casing, three gleaming disks of plexiglass twisted in the wind.

"Gate's open," Ruth said.

They moved inside the perimeter fence and took a closer look.

Embedded in each disk was a flat, oval shape, convoluted at the outer edges, with a void shaped like a cat snout in the center.

Carver said, "Jesus—is that—?"

"Sections of brain—human, I think."

"Is it real?"

"I don't know . . ." Lake blinked against the disorientating flicker of the lights and the icy sting of sleet. The sections looked ominously organic. "Yeah," she said. "I think it's real."

Carver called out, announcing their presence. No reply. He started toward a stepladder at the end of the scaffolding.

"Greg," Ruth said.

His shoulders tensed and he turned a little too loosely, compensating with a slight sideways step to right himself. "I'm fine," he said.

That was debatable, but she let it go. "If it *is* real, the victim is way past help," she said. "We need to preserve the scene."

The tension in his shoulders relaxed a little. "Okay."

While Carver called in Scientific Support, Ruth Lake headed back to the car to pick up a roll of crime scene tape. Ahead, a figure appeared out of the shadows of the railway arch and Ruth felt a prickle of unease. This was the kind of street that would be quiet even during the day; at night, it became a no-man's-land, where only the foolhardy and the wicked would venture. Her first thought was a local scally, sizing up their car for salable items to scavenge.

"Police," she yelled. A second figure joined the first, then another. She glanced over her shoulder toward the easterly end of the street. Five or six were heading toward her from that direction. Two more rounded the corner, and Ruth called to Carver, "Boss, you might want to draft in some uniforms. We've got company."

"Police!" she yelled again. "Stay where you are."

They kept coming. Both ends of the street, at least twenty of them now.

The first lot had reached the car. If she moved toward them, the others would reach the gate before she could stop them. She did the only thing she could do: retreated to the crime scene, barring entry through the gate.

Carver joined her. "Where the hell did they come from?" he murmured.

"I do *not* know," she breathed.

He yelled, "Stay back!" and the crowd halted six feet away.

Casco baton in hand, Ruth picked on a tall guy in a beanie hat. "This is a crime scene," she said. "You need to *move back*."

He gave way by half a pace.

Carver spoke quietly into his phone.

"Hey, *I* know you." Beanie Hat turned to the others. "I *know* him—he's the one that got shot." The rest of the crowd paid no attention; they were watching the light show.

"What *is* that?" someone asked.

"Looks like bits of brain," another said.

Exclamations of disgust, a burst of nervous laughter. Someone swore. But the shock didn't dampen their enthusiasm for long: in an instant, it seemed that every one of them had a mobile phone in their hands. They got busy, enlarging, photographing, and video-recording the scene.

A sudden flash. The audience flinched as one. Ruth turned.

A line of text began streaming in LEDs across the bottom of the crate: "Statistical Uncertainty: Learn to Think Outside the Box."

Ruth Lake glanced at Carver.

With the sound of police sirens approaching, she turned on her phone video app to record the crowd: some of the onlookers would vanish into the night as soon as the uniforms arrived on the scene. If the perpetrator was among them, they might just catch him on camera.

2

They ran a trailer for that episode of *Fact or Fable?* for three solid weeks. Watching it now, I have to admit it is beautifully shot. The city cast in shadow and light is reminiscent of the chiaroscuro techniques of film noir. Does the program maker have any notion that the technique is borrowed from Renaissance art, I wonder?

Perhaps not. But he/she/it caught the mood: dark alleys, reflections of light on water.

"Six months . . ."

The rich bass notes of the voice-over is backed by suspenseful string music.

". . . Twelve men."

A lone male figure enters the frame. Let's call him Dillon. Although it could be John, or Tyler, or any one of another half dozen. For the sake of illustration, we'll stick with Dillon. I watched him walk his plump girlfriend home. They cooed like doves, kissed like virgins, and then he did the gentlemanly thing: he headed toward his cold bachelor pad—and fell off the cliff edge between life and death. All because he decided to hoof it home, instead of getting jiggy with Miss Piggy, his fat *amore*.

The double irony is this: *she* was perfectly safe—from me, anyway. And if he'd been less the gentleman with his porky princess, he might still be alive today.

On-screen, a young man strides down a moonlit alley, his footsteps ringing out. Behind him, a hooded figure casts a long shadow; it creeps closer and closer, finally overtaking him. He begins to turn, horror-movie-victim style, and his eyes flash, wide with fear. The shadow engulfs him and the screen fades to black.

Very dramatic. But in reality, they never saw me coming.

Tennent introduces the theme, and for the next few minutes the narrator recaps the story: the disappearances; photographs and sound bites from anxious families; tearful encomiums from the friends left behind. Fear stalking the streets of Liverpool; hysteria and paranoia among young males in the city. They deal with time slips first, needing to get that nonsense off the slate fast—this *is* supposed to be a serious scientific program, after all.

Then Tennent talks through the stats of assaults, stabbings, and shootings in the city during the past five years, listing alongside the victims of violent crime impressive numbers who've died of drug overdoses, or alcoholic poisoning, or been dragged under buses, or mangled in car crashes. *Fact or Fable?* is all about balance.

Smug and disparaging, he tells his rapt audience how many men aged twenty to thirty-five go missing every year, how they are found, the duration of time missing. Reasons for disappearance: drunken binges; the call of the wild; escape from relationships and responsibilities; depression; drugs (somber face); and suicide.

He concludes that there is no evidence that the so-called Ferryman exists.

I cut him off midsnarl, click to a recording of my exhibit on Stone Street just before the police arrived. Three disks, three slices of life—irrefutable evidence that the Ferryman is no fable.

3

DCI Greg Carver had called together a team of detectives and support staff and would draft in more when he'd assessed the scale of the inquiry. He left his office, closed the door behind him, and leaned against it for a moment. Okay. Time to get back in the saddle.

Boosting himself from the door, he strode down the corridor to the seminar room they were using as a temporary base.

The room fell silent as he entered, and he felt every pair of eyes on him. Most would be pondering on what had happened to him only a few months earlier, many assessing his fitness, a few no doubt speculating on how long he would last in the job.

He picked up the projector remote and clicked to the first Power-Point slide: an enlarged image of the macabre scene he and Ruth Lake had been directed to the night before.

"The pathologist's preliminary examination confirms those *are* sections of human brain." He located Crime Scene Manager John Hughes. "John, what are the chances of getting viable DNA samples?"

"It depends on how much preservative he used and how deep it penetrated the tissues." The CSM had the craggy features of a born outdoorsman. He was calm and unshowy, but thorough. "These are fairly thick slices, so there's a chance the chemicals didn't get all the way through," Hughes finished.

"Which is good news?"

"It'd leave more of the DNA intact, so potentially, yes."

Carver clicked to the next slide. This photograph had been taken in natural light, each disk laid flat against a white background. To Carver, they looked like inkblot butterflies. The first two had a slightly pink wash, although there was a hint of blue toward the edge of the lobes in the second section. The third section was paler than the other two. "Presumably he used some kind of stain to make them that color?"

Hughes nodded. "And that won't help the DNA profiling. But we'll ask the lab for low template analysis, just to be sure."

"Prints? Trace?"

"Nothing from the disk surfaces," Hughes said. "There's a chance we'll get something off the lighting equipment he used, or the scaffolding, but I wouldn't hold out too much hope: rain is bad enough, but it was sleeting last night. Sleet sticks, then slides off, taking any useful trace with it."

"What about the storage box and the gantry he hung the disks from?" Carver asked. "They were protected from the weather."

"They are a better bet," Hughes conceded.

Carver nodded. The message was clear: they would just have to wait until the evidence was processed. "Did the techs have any luck tracing the tip-off e-mails sent to my account?"

Hughes shook his head. "They were routed through an anonymous server."

"Interesting that he sent them direct to your e-mail account, and not to the Contact Center."

Heads turned. Carver introduced Doctor Kris Yi, forensic psychologist, senior lecturer at the University of Liverpool, consultant to Ashworth Hospital. Ashworth had a notoriety of its own as a secure psychiatric hospital that had housed some of the UK's most dangerous and violent killers, including child killer Ian Brady, and Carver saw curiosity on the faces of his team.

Yi, a trim, besuited figure of around forty, acknowledged the police and forensics specialists in the room with a courteous nod. "Go to the Merseyside Police website, you're directed to a generic 'contact us' page," he said. "Google 'contact Merseyside Police' you get the Contact Center e-mail address. Yet the e-mails were directed to you, personally."

He's saying I was targeted.

"I must've handed out scores of business cards during the previous inquiry; every one of them carried my direct e-mail and work mobile." Carver saw a flare of light and color around the seated detectives and blinked to try and shift it. Auras, the neurologist called these light shows; one of many aftereffects of the brain injury he'd sustained during that case, and he knew the colors represented his colleagues' complicated emotions.

He glanced down at his notes, intending to move to the next point. But he couldn't see the words on the page. When he looked up to address the room again, an afterimage of light persisted in the center of his field of view; his light show had morphed into a migraine. Alarmed, Carver realized he couldn't see the faces of his team and felt his brow and neck break out in a cold sweat.

Ruth Lake said, "Thanks, boss," as though he'd given her the nod. "Can you click to the next slide?" Carver obliged. Dizzy and nauseated, he didn't risk looking at the screen, but he recalled that Ruth had supplied a still from her video recording of the onlookers: upward of thirty people, all holding phones up to record the scene.

"They came around the corner like something out of *The Walking Dead*," Ruth said. "And that street isn't likely to be on any list of ten cool places to visit in Liverpool. So where did they come from?"

"Social media," Hughes said. "Last night, someone created new accounts on Instagram, Facebook, and Twitter using the name 'The Ferryman.' He posted the same messages exactly fifteen minutes after he e-mailed them to DCI Carver. And he uploaded an image of the scene that was clearly taken before you or *The Walking Dead* got there."

Carver was relieved to see that Ruth was beginning to emerge out of the blodge of green light in the center of his vision; the blind spot was shrinking.

"He's getting most hits on Instagram," Hughes went on. "Calls himself @FerrymanArt."

"Do we know it's the same person?" Carver asked.

"There's no way of telling. But he uploaded a one-minute video that must have been recorded before anyone got there. He hashtagged you, Merseyside Police"—he glanced at Dr. Yi—"and your last case."

By now, Carver's vision had completely cleared, and he saw that Yi was frowning.

"Problem, Doctor?" he asked.

"This person seems to court notoriety, yet he timed his posts so that you would arrive at the scene before he posted the image to his followers. He wanted you to get there first."

Another hint that the killer's targeting me. Best to meet it head-on.

"You're saying he's got some kind of fixation on me?"

"I wouldn't put it that strongly." Yi glanced down at his mobile phone. "But you *are* mentioned on every one of FerrymanArt's Instagram postings: it's fairly obvious he's piggybacking on your media profile to build his following."

Dr. Yi's message was clear: if he was a target, he was a liability.

Well, sod that, Carver thought. "Did you see the text streamer under his nasty little exhibit?"

"Text streamer?"

" 'Learn to Think Outside the Box,' " Carver said. "It's the episode title of a *Fact or Fable?* program that ran several nights ago; caused quite a stir."

"I'm not sure I follow," Yi said.

"You said yourself he wants notoriety—he used me, *and* the TV program, *and* 'The Ferryman' moniker because they had ready-made hype he could clip like a badge to his virtual lapel." Carver shrugged. "He's media-savvy, that's all."

Dr. Yi leaned back in his chair. He didn't seem convinced. Perhaps he'd noticed that Carver had left out one important detail: that the presenter of "Learn to Think Outside the Box" was currently missing.

Ruth Lake came to his rescue again: "Okay, so the Web-based stuff doesn't look promising, as yet, but let's look at the disks again," she said, turning to the CSM. "Are there traces of him, or his location, inside the plexiglass?"

"We're looking into that," Hughes said. "If fibers or dust got into the mix, it would be fixed there. And we'll do an HPLC analysis on the stains; if they're medical stains, he would've had to have sourced them through specialist suppliers."

Relieved that he could rejoin the discussion with attention off him, Carver said, "As soon as we have the analysis, we can start canvassing them."

Yi said, "Do we have a cause of death, yet?"

"The postmortem is slated for later today," Carver said.

"A note of caution on that," Hughes said. "With such a small amount of tissue, it's going to be hard to determine cause of death."

They seemed to be butting up against the need to wait for forensic results at every turn. It was Carver's job to ensure his team made productive use of that downtime, but he detected a sludgy gray darkness beginning to shroud the heads and faces of a few in the room: they were defeated before they'd even got started.

"All right," he said. "What do we have that we can work with *right now*?"

Ruth lifted her chin, indicating the crowd of ghouls at the scene. "Potential witnesses," she said. "We can start tracking down the ones who got away."

"Good." Carver pointed to the screen. "The perpetrator would've had to have transported a heavy box, batteries, and lighting equipment to the scene. So we look at traffic and security cameras in the area."

"It'd take a while to set the display up," a ginger-haired detective constable offered. This was DC Tom Ivey. "We should talk to business owners, find out if there was any unusual activity in the street in the last week or so."

"Excellent," Carver said, and the young detective flushed brick red.

Carver looked around the room; typically, the variations of light and color were elusive, best caught from the corner of the eye, as you might catch a glimpse of a star cluster in the night sky. But when the mood was strong, Carver's auras lingered. Right now, he was pleased to see that the gray mantle was lifting.

"Who's doing the work on the building demolition?" someone asked. "We need to talk to them."

Carver gave a nod of approval. "And anyone who's been working at the site as well. DS Lake will act as task manager on this."

With his squad motivated, Carver felt strong enough to bring Dr. Yi back into the conversation. "You said this individual wants attention," he said. "He's obviously willing to go to some lengths to make sure he gets it. Does the scene tell you anything that might help us find him?"

Yi took a moment to consider before answering. "The means of presentation is artistic," he said.

That got a few mumbles of protest.

"At least to *his* way of thinking," Yi added with an apologetic dip of his chin. "And judging by the Instagram name, he *does* seem to want people to regard this as art." He studied the screen for a few moments. "A few questions you might consider: Why did he choose to exhibit the brain, and not some other part of the body, like the heart, for instance? Does he see himself as an intellectual? Or is he making a sly reference to some aspect of the victim's life? Did he exhibit those parts of the brain for a particular reason?"

"Meaning?" Carver said.

"I'm not a neurologist," Yi said, "but we all know that different parts of the brain have different functions."

Carver glanced at the screen with a queasy familiarity: he had seen images just like it, many times during the course of his treatment.

"And there are three disks," Yi was saying, "three parts to the . . . exhibit, for want of a better word. The number three has powerful cultural and mystical meaning—from the Three Graces in Greek mythology, to the Holy Trinity in the Christian tradition. There are parallels in Judaism, in Norse mythology, in Taoism, in Wicca, too—the triple goddess: Maiden, Mother, and Crone."

"Bad luck comes in threes, and all . . ." someone muttered.

A ripple of uneasy laughter followed.

"It's our job to make sure it doesn't in this instance," Carver said firmly.

4

Stone Street is closed to traffic. The razzmatazz of flashing lights and emergency vehicles from the previous night is a distant memory, and just two uniform police guard the crime scene tape at either end of the scene. A single Scientific Support Unit van is parked a couple of yards inside the outer cordon.

The mood is quiet, businesslike; CSIs come and go, carrying plastic tote boxes. Of course, they will find nothing.

The scene is flat and gray in daylight; so much of the glamour of the piece was dependent on the contrast of light and dark.

Two TV crews and a few newspaper journalists shiver at the boundary, and I am grateful for the warmth of my car. I'm in the Toyota this morning; the van safely hidden close by, but where they will never think to look. Occasionally the reporters turn to gesture down the street toward my exhibit. For now, it's only local news coverage, but that will change.

I take a moment to check my Instagram account: comments are coming in at the rate of one every thirty seconds. My followers have surged from zero to seven thousand in twelve hours, with more following me, and "liking" and "sharing" the story, all the time. I check the profiles of the particularly vocal and find the usual: wild enthusiasm and energy coupled with ignorance. Worshippers of the weird, who have no respect for the history and provenance of the work. I take a breath and let it go. Irritating though they are, they will direct others to my art and must be tolerated.

A CSI pauses at the back of the police van, dragging the hood of her disposable oversuit down and lowering her mask. She takes a grateful gasp of cool air before lifting one foot to peel off an overshoe. She freezes, just for a second, then straightens and turns away. The police constable at the cordon glances in my direction and my heart begins to thud.

Time to go. I pull away from the street corner and slide into the steady stream of morning traffic, blending in with the anonymous and the invisible.

5

Carver sat in his office, watching a video of the crime scene recorded by the Scientific Support Unit the previous night. The footage started at the outer cordon; keeping to the common approach path marked out by a member of the team who had gone ahead of her, the CSI swept slowly left and right before panning upward to the exhibit. She'd zoomed in on the storage box with its grim cargo of disks, jangling in the wind off the bay. The display lights transitioned from red to green, to blue, to purple. Newly sensitized to color and light by his brain injury, Carver wondered briefly if the colors meant anything to the killer.

Spinning on their wires, the disks seemed to disappear as they turned edge-on, then reappear as the light shone on their faces. The brain tissue, fixed in plexiglass, like inkblots in a nightmarish Rorschach test, and their constant motion made him slightly queasy. The image blurred as spots of sleet hit the camera lens, and the CSI gave it a quick wipe, then focused in on one of the disks. At that instant, the LEDs cut out, and Carver saw his own face reflected by the disk; trapped, it seemed, *inside* it.

Darkness.

Something skulks in the shadows just beyond his field of view.

He can't see; can't move.

Turn your head. He tries, fails.

He's paralyzed, unable to fend off the malevolent force, knowing it is close enough to touch, but is powerless to act.

Sleep paralysis, he tells himself. *Wake up!*

A rap on the door.

The darkness lifts. He blinks, his eyes watering with the sudden influx of light, and he feels a slight tingling in his fingertips.

Another sharp rap, then Ruth Lake poked her head around the door.

"Greg?"

It was just a dream. But he didn't really believe he had been asleep, and if what he'd just experienced wasn't sleep paralysis, then what the hell was it?

"You okay?" Ruth said.

"Fine. Must have nodded off." Ruth had seen him at his worst; he could admit minor weaknesses to her, knowing they would go no further. He closed his laptop without looking at the screen. "What's up?"

Ruth didn't answer at first, but her brown eyes fixed on him, and he met her gaze. She was reading him—a default position with her, reading people—a reflex, like breathing.

"The pathologist rang," she said at last. "His written report will take a day, but he's ready to talk someone through his findings. Should I head over there?"

Carver stood, reaching to take his jacket from the chair. "I'll go with you."

The room tilted hard left, and he put a hand out to steady himself, scattering papers and pens from his desk to the floor.

Ruth stepped smartly inside and shut the door behind her, scooping up the mess in one smooth and graceful action.

Carver left his jacket where it was and lowered himself back into the chair.

"Maybe I'll sit this one out," he said.

"Sure."

He was grateful not to see concern or anxiety in Ruth's eyes. "Still keeping up with the physio?" she asked.

Physiotherapy was a required segment of the agreed rehab plan that the neurosciences center and Merseyside Police Human Resources and

Occupational Health departments had put together as a condition of his phased return to work.

She was entitled to ask the question, under the circumstances, but he countered with a question of his own: "How about you—finished with the laser therapy?"

"Three down, two to go," she said.

Again, she gave him nothing. He knew the procedure was painful, but in almost three months of treatment, she had never once complained—never even mentioned it unless he'd asked.

"Well, it's been nice having this heart-to-heart," he said, pleased to catch a brief flash of amusement in her eyes.

Two hours later, Ruth Lake was typing up a report of her visit to the hospital mortuary. The fabric of her blouse chafed in the angle between her forearm and biceps, wakening a nagging burn caused by laser treatment to remove inkings drilled into her skin—her own legacy of the last case she'd worked with Greg Carver.

The brain tissue was in good condition, the pathologist told her: their killer had used formalin on the first two, but not the third. As CSM Hughes had speculated, the formalin hadn't penetrated into the center of the tissue, so the pathologist was confident that the plugs they'd taken as samples would yield intact tissue for DNA testing. The slices were cut smoothly, he'd said, with none of the "saw marks" you might expect from a standard kitchen knife. That suggested two things: their killer used a butchers'-quality knife—and he'd had practice. The dye was yet to be identified, but he thought it more likely to be food colorant than a biological stain; the chromatographic analysis would tell them more.

When Ruth asked where the killer might have got the plexiglass, he had demurred—it was not his area of expertise. But he did add that it looked like good quality—clear and colorless.

There weren't many air bubbles, either, Ruth had noticed.

"He's good with his hands," she murmured, adding a note to her report.

She scratched the skin of her forearm absently, thinking about the plexiglass. She'd found companies online that specialized in "embedding" services—anything from books to tins of Spam, frozen in blocks of clear plexiglass. But the Ferryman wasn't likely to send his trophy slices of brain for mounting, so he had to've made the stuff himself.

She knew that plexiglass was a form of acrylic. To make it, you needed to persuade a lot of simple, single molecules called monomers to link together to form a long-chain chemical called a polymer. Once the polymer was made, it set, so if you wanted to shape it, or embed something inside it—like, for instance, brain tissue—you had to do it while the stuff was still liquid.

But how hard would it be to get hold of the right chemicals in sufficient quantities?

A quick Google search told her that the syrupy liquid monomer base was available by the gallon. All you had to do was add an enzyme activator, stir, and pour. And you could use ordinary domestic silicone food molds. Amazon even had a helpful algorithm to ensure buyers found everything they needed for their craft project. But there must be tens of thousands of crafters across the UK, using kits to make paperweights of flowers or dandelion clocks; finding the one sicko who set human remains in acrylic would not be an easy task.

She called John Hughes to relay the pathologist's findings and let him know her thoughts on how the Ferryman was sourcing the acrylic.

"The mortuary sent the disks back after they finished extracting tissue samples," he said. "We could sample the material, do some chemistry on it. If it *is* quality acrylic, it might help your lot to identify the manufacturer."

"That'd be great," Ruth said. "According to the technical specs I found online, this stuff can take twelve to twenty-four hours to cure, so unless he used an air purifier with a HEPA filter, it's likely something got caught in there."

"We'll start processing for trace today," he said.

She thanked him and hung up, pausing to print out her report notes to take to Carver's office.

He was on the phone. He waved her in and pushed a button on his desk phone.

"DCI Solen," he said, "DS Lake has just come into my office. I've put you on speakerphone. DCI Solen is from SCD1," he added, for Ruth's benefit. "He's the SIO investigating Professor Tennent's disappearance."

SCD1 was Serious Crime Directorate 1—an operational command unit tasked with investigating homicides and other serious crimes in London. It seemed they were taking the professor's disappearance very seriously.

"DCI Solen was just saying his team has pinpointed the professor's last location," Carver said.

"Well, we think so," Solen said, his accent authentic East End. "I sent you a sequence of CCTV clips."

Carver opened the e-mail attachment on his laptop.

As it played, Solen talked them through: "The professor used his Oyster card at Warren Street Underground Station at 2:15 P.M. on the day he disappeared."

Two short clips showed the professor passing through a ticket barrier on the underground, then boarding a train. He wore a black waterproof jacket over a gray wool suit and had a laptop shoulder bag looped over one shoulder.

"We've got him on CCTV disembarking at Charing Cross underground from a Northern line train at 2:31 P.M.," Solen went on, as the action unfolded on-screen. "The CCTV shows him turning left out of the station, then he cuts through an alley called York Place."

Suddenly, the screen went white. At first, Ruth thought that the footage had ended, but then she saw a blur of gray bird's wings as a pigeon flew past the security camera.

"What are we looking at?" Carver asked.

"The white 'nothing' you can see is a Ford Transit van, parked outside a loading bay on Buckingham Street, at the back of the Theodore Bullfrog pub."

"The professor called his secretary to say he was meeting someone on his way back to work after his lecture across town," Ruth said. "He could have set the meeting up at the pub."

"It's possible."

"Is the alley an obvious shortcut?" Carver asked.

"Not *obvious*," Solen said. "But locals would know it, and Tennent lectured at King's College's Strand Campus, about ten minutes' walk from Charing Cross Station, so . . ."

"It's likely he knew the alley as a cut-through," Ruth finished for him. "May I?" Carver leaned back to let her take the controls and she rewound the recording to point out two CCTV cameras were mounted on the loading bay on the other side of the alley—one either side of the loading doors. Neither would be high enough to give them a view over the top of the van.

"No security cameras on the opposite wall?" she asked.

" 'Fraid not," Solen said.

Whatever was happening on the other side of the van in those minutes was lost to them.

Ruth played the recording on and the white side of the van began slipping past the lens as it pulled away from the curb, revealing a gray wall that had been hidden behind it.

Carver leaned back, and even closed his eyes briefly as the motion started. *Vertigo*, Ruth guessed.

The wall sloped upward, left to right, and was topped by black iron railings. There was no sign of Professor Tennent.

"The van just turned left at the junction," Carver said.

"That's John Adam Street," Solen said. "The professor's last mobile phone signal pinged off a tower near Charing Cross Station. Our dog trackers found it smashed up about a minute's walk from there— probably chucked out the van window."

The footage jerked through a series of shots of the van in traffic for a few seconds and the chief inspector said, "We got him on cameras all the way to Embankment."

"Probably making his way toward the M40, to head north," Carver commented.

"My thoughts exactly."

Ruth heard surprise in Solen's voice.

Then, "Oh, yeah . . . You were on Operation Trident at the Met, weren't you?"

"Long time ago," Carver said, cutting the conversation off before it got started. "Did you get any shots of the driver?"

A slight hesitation, then Solen said, "Fast-forward five minutes."

He gave an exact time stamp to look for, and Ruth zipped through the sequence while Carver looked away.

"Got it?" Solen asked.

Ruth froze the screen on a perfect shot of the front of the van in good light. The number plate was clear, but the windscreen reflected light in a rainbow of colors, the driver no more than a bulky gray shadow behind it.

"He's used a reflective film," she said.

"On the windscreen and side windows, yeah," Solen said. "That stuff is called 'chameleon film'—the colors constantly shift. The bad news is, the techs say the shimmer effect you see there is a bugger to deal with."

"But they can clean it up," Carver said, a question in his tone.

Ruth shook her head. "The image behind the flare just wouldn't exist. It'd be like trying to remove the door from a picture so you can see who's behind it."

"Into photography, are you?" Solen asked.

"Not particularly," Ruth said, not feeling the need to explain. "But there is a faint image of the driver, so they might be able to improve the contrast."

Solen grunted. "Click forward to the next frame, you'll see the cleaned-up version."

The driver's shape was more clearly defined. He was probably tall, judging by his head height behind the wheel, but his facial features were no more than a smudge.

"We've got teams scouring CCTV and ANPR from the scene onward," he went on. "I'll let you know if they find anything."

"What about the number plates?" Carver asked.

"Stolen off a van in Liverpool the night before."

Carver glanced at Ruth.

"We'll check CCTV at our end," Carver said. "See if we can locate the van on its way into or out of the city. What about the professor's credit cards? Some of the missing here had items bought on their cards for weeks after they disappeared."

"Sorry," Solen said. "We got nothing."

"Makes sense," Ruth said. "Foul play wasn't suspected in our cases—at least not at first—he's not likely to take that kind of risk, knowing we'd be on the lookout for it."

"Any chance of getting something from Tennent's phone?" Carver asked.

"It got crushed under car wheels, but we retrieved the SIM card," Solen said. "The techs are doing their best to work their magic on it as we speak."

"He knew the shortcut through the alley," Ruth said. "He knew how to block the CCTV cameras with the van; he took the most efficient route out of London, so either he had local knowledge, or he did some recon on the area in the days before."

"We'll look out for that on the recordings," Solen said. "Anything else?"

"Could you send through a list of evidence gathered at the scene?" Carver asked.

"I'll get the Evidence Recovery Unit to send it through," Solen said. "But you know how it is: London alley . . ."

Ruth did. As a CSI, she'd picked up, bagged, and logged an awful lot of unsavory rubbish that had nothing to do with the cases they were investigating. Added to which, it was three days since Tennent disappeared—hundreds of people must have passed through that alley since then.

Solen signed off shortly after, and Ruth kept her eyes on Carver. His hand trembled a little when he reached for the mouse to close the video sequence.

Carver seemed to sense her attention and looked up. He lifted his chin, indicating the folder in her hand. "Is that the pathologist's preliminary findings?"

"Yeah," she said. "D'you want me to run through them with you?"

"Just leave the report—I'll take a look later."

Ruth was one of very few who knew about the peculiar aftereffects of Greg's injuries, and she'd learned to accept it. But whatever had happened this morning was far more than simply seeing auras—and he still seemed to be struggling with the aftereffects.

"Is it Emma—is she okay?"

He stared at her, distracted. "What? No—I haven't seen Emma in three weeks."

It was beginning to look like Carver's marriage had become a permanent casualty of his drink-fueled spiral into obsession during their last case.

"Was there something else, Sergeant?" Carver asked, his tone a little too sharp.

"I don't know," Ruth said. "Is there?"

He sighed. "I had a migraine. I'm fine now."

She nodded. "I'll get someone on tracking that number plate." She muted the sharpness in her tone but kept enough edge in it to let him know that she wouldn't take any crap from him.

He exhaled. "Yeah. Yes—thanks, Ruth."

Not an apology, but as close as she'd get, and it was enough. She gave a quick nod, then left, closing the door softly behind her.

6

If I've learned one thing in life, it's the importance of timing. The *tick-tick* swing of the metronome that separates good moment from bad moment is largely misunderstood by artists. Those who consider themselves on a higher moral plane than the rest of humanity might say that even *thinking* about timing is monstrous, that taking a business approach to aesthetic creativity is tacky. But would they try to mount an exhibition of fine art outside a football stadium on a wet Saturday afternoon in November? Of course not—it's all about catching the wave.

I'll admit, I've been through my share of personal wipeouts; I've even missed the wave entirely because of bad timing. So, while I am impatient, I can wait for the surf to swell beneath me.

Which is why I am watching the news updates hourly, listening to the *tick-tick* of the metronome, waiting for the announcement that will signal a change in pace, and launch the next phase of my campaign.

So far, the press releases have been unforthcoming. Apparently the postmortem examination is "complex and delicate."

It pains me to contemplate what they will do to my art: dismantle, dissect, slice, macerate, analyze the component parts as though they were no more than sliced meat. And all this in a fruitless search to discover hints of my presence. No matter: as Gustav Metzger once said, "Destroy, and you create." I must think of this as artistic process, constructive destruction.

My followers continue to grow, which is consolation—fifteen thousand at the last count, and no sign of a slowdown. They reach out to me, flattering, trying to coax me into a response. But timing is of the essence in this, too, and I will not be rushed. I monitor, and I wait.

Tick-tick, tick-tick, tick-tick.

7

DAY 3, MORNING BRIEFING

Greg Carver stood at the front of the room. The projector screen to his left was lit with the Merseyside Police logo, and the mood was tense: they knew something important was coming, they just didn't know what, yet.

"DNA analysis of the brain sections came through overnight," he said. "We have not one, but three victims."

A buzz of murmured conversation. The case had evolved from a Missing Persons review to a serial murder inquiry in under three days.

Carver waited for silence.

"The victims, all male, have been identified." He looked into every face in the room. "Their names will be released by the Press Office after the relatives have been informed; I don't want that information to come from any member of this team." He saw nods of agreement. "And I don't want any speculation about a serial killer."

"That won't stop the press, boss," someone said.

"I know," Carver said. "They've already got a name to hang on him, and once this is in the public domain, it's going to feed public anxiety." He waited until every pair of eyes were raised to his. "So no one talks to press—on or off the record—okay?"

When he was sure that message had gotten across, Carver clicked to an image of a dark-haired man of slight build.

"John Eddings, twenty-three. He went missing six months ago—

September of last year. Walked out of a bar on the Albert Dock and vanished." He clicked to the next image. "Dillon Martin, twenty-five." Martin was fair-haired and muscular. "He disappeared in October of last year. He saw his girlfriend back to her flat in Wood Street after a night out in the center of town. Never made it home. Martin owned an apartment in Kings Dock Mill, Tabley Street. That's a ten-minute walk from his girlfriend's place."

He called up the final slide—a lean, gray-haired man, with a fiercely inquisitive gaze.

"Professor Mick Tennent," he said, over gasps of recognition. "Aged fifty-two."

He clicked to a short clip of the professor presenting *Fact or Fable?*

"Liverpool, a city in fear," Tennent said. "In just six months, twelve men aged between twenty-two and twenty-eight have vanished without trace. Many believe that a sinister figure they call 'The Ferryman' has lured these young men to their deaths.

"Could a serial killer really be stalking the streets?" He gestured over his shoulder to a dark, hooded male. "Is the Ferryman fact or fable?" Staring straight into the camera, he said, "You decide."

"That program ran just under a week ago," Carver said, closing the frame. "The episode title was 'Statistical Evidence: Learn to Think Outside the Box.' And in case anyone is in any doubt, Tennent rubbished the Ferryman theory, so while John Eddings and Dillon Martin might have been taken at random, it's clear that Professor Tennent was deliberately targeted. London Met is talking to his family, the TV producer, and his university colleagues."

He glanced at Ruth Lake. "DS Lake will organize teams to interview friends and colleagues of the two Liverpool victims. Family liaison officers will talk to the immediate family. But before you speak to anyone, familiarize yourselves with the original witness statements." Carver went on. "Try to clear up any discrepancies, establish a reliable timeline. We need to know if there were links between the victims, so ask about their habits, hobbies, likes, and dislikes. Who did they associate with? What were their favorite haunts? Was there something going on between Martin and his girlfriend? Did they have an argument or dispute before he disappeared; did she have a problem with ex-partners?"

He watched them scribble down notes.

"Who's on the search for the van?"

Ruth Lake had tasked three detectives to search traffic cam and CCTV footage for the Ford van that had probably been used in the professor's abduction.

A paunchy, middle-aged cop in a crumpled suit raised his hand.

"Where are we with that?" Carver experienced a slight discomfort that he couldn't remember the detective's name.

"Nothing so far, boss," the detective said. "But there's a hell of a lot to get through, and, you know, white vans—" He shrugged. "Like searching for a snowflake in a blizzard."

Carver didn't like the man's slouch. The Liverpool victims were effectively cold cases, but the professor was very much a hot investigation, and as such, their best chance of finding new leads. He needed sharp eyes and keen minds committed to treating even the most tedious jobs in the inquiry as potential leads.

"We know the professor disappeared midafternoon, four days ago," he said. "London Met have a first sighting of the van on the M40, heading into the city at eleven A.M. that day. We know the plates were stolen from Liverpool the night before, from—" With a dull thud, Carver realized he couldn't remember the time, or place.

"Merlin Street in Toxteth," Ruth supplied. "Between midnight and four A.M."

"The most likely route would be to take the M62 east, then head south on the M6," Carver went on. He pulled up an image of the van parked at the side of the Theodore Bullfrog pub in London. "Look for this white Ford Transit at junctions one to six of the M62 between those hours on the day Professor Tennent disappeared."

Ruth Lake spoke up again: "Professor Tennent disappeared between Charing Cross Station and Embankment, just after two thirty that afternoon," she said. "Assuming the same travel time of four to six hours to drive back to Liverpool, you're looking for the van to appear here in Liverpool on the return leg of the journey, any time from six thirty P.M. until about nine."

"Yeah," the detective said with another dismissive shrug, "and what if he parked up for a few hours in London after he snatched the professor, waited till after dark to make his way back?"

You always got one doomsayer in any investigation: someone you could rely on to make a mountain from a speck of dust, just so he could say how hard it would be to get over. Carver would've liked to give the detective a verbal slapping, but he still couldn't remember the man's name, and for some reason his healing brain couldn't get past that. He felt his skin break out in a sheen of sweat and he couldn't find the words to answer.

"You keep looking till you see him," Ruth said, in her usual, imperturbable manner. "But we know that the plexiglass our killer used to make the disks takes up to twenty-four hours to harden, so he'd be pushed for time. Remember, he had to extract the brain and slice it before he could even start to set it in the plexiglass." Carver saw a few winces, but Ruth carried on as if she hadn't noticed: "The disk would need to be properly hardened before he could drill it and thread the wire through, ready for hanging. Our man is a planner; he'd've thought of that. He'd drive straight back." She looked at the detective, her gaze steady and implacable. "Get on with the job." It wasn't entirely clear if she was making an observation about the killer or issuing an order to her griping colleague. "DC Gorman, isn't it?"

Gorman—of course. Carver felt the coil of anxiety loosen around his chest.

Ruth went on: "If you want to make life easy for yourself, you might look into traffic conditions that day, adjust the ETA, *then* scour CCTV for the license plate."

Carver saw a smudge around Gorman's eyes, a shadow, tinged with burnt orange. The man was angry, but embarrassed, too, that he hadn't thought of this himself.

"While you're on a roll, DS Lake," Carver said, "d'you want to tell us what the pathologist said?"

Ruth Lake walked swiftly to the front of the room, drawing the eye of every straight male. She moved with the effortless grace of an athlete, aware of her body, yet unselfconscious. Carver saw a dull glow to the left of the gathering and identified the source as DC Gorman. His gaze was a little too intense to be respectful. They made momentary eye contact, which Gorman broke first. But Carver kept his eyes on the detective until he picked up a pen and started taking notes.

"The killer used formalin to preserve Eddings's and Martin's brain tissue," Ruth said, "so establishing their cause of death will be difficult if not impossible, but he didn't mess with Tennent's—his was fresh when it was set in the acrylic . . . The pathologist is fairly sure that he was asphyxiated."

A brownish fog misted around DC Ivey's face.

"Petechiae," Ruth said, addressing him as though he'd voiced the question forming in his head. "Small pinpoints of red in the brain tissue. Burst blood vessels," she explained. "Given the circumstances of the professor's disappearance, it could be he was either suffocated— plastic bag over the head, say—or else strangled."

"Wait a minute." CSM Hughes riffled through some papers stacked on the table in front of him. "I've been looking at the scene record the Met's Evidence Recovery Unit sent through." He carried on talking while he found the right page and skimmed the list: "This is stuff they picked up from the alley near Charing Cross Station . . ."

Carver had seen the list: thirty cigarette butts, spent matches, various sweet and food wrappers, trodden gum, three beer bottles, and two used condoms scooped up from the probable abduction location.

"We've been examining the plexiglass for physical trace," Hughes went on, ". . . and found a few unusual orange synthetic fibers . . ." Another pause as he turned the page. "Got it. Item one-three-seven: a sixty-centimeter length of orange nylon cord. It could be the murder weapon."

"I'll request a sample for comparison," Carver said.

"We also need to get it checked for DNA—if the professor's is on there, then maybe the killer's is too," Hughes said.

Carver made a note.

Ruth spoke up: "Did you find any other trace in the disks, John?"

"A brown, powdery particulate," Hughes said. "We haven't finished the analysis, but I'll let you know when we have an idea what it might be."

"How much specialist skill would the killer need to do the dissections and make the disks?" Carver asked.

Ruth said, "The pathologist reckons he could be using a butcher's knife to slice through the brain tissue; I found craft kits online that would make acrylic of the right grade. The path lab will run the dye through HPLC, but the pathologist thinks our guy just dropped the brain sections in a container of food dye, left them to steep for a couple of days. As for skill, he said a reasonably competent first-year biomed student could remove and slice the brain, fix, stain, and embed it with comparable results."

Hughes said, "Maybe, but I had a CSI make some disks using slices of pig brain. The base comes as a gloopy liquid; all you do is add a small quantity of enzyme and mix to get the solid acrylic. But you need to measure the liquid base and the enzyme precisely, mix them thoroughly, pour the stuff carefully into the molds. Even then, you can get bubbles ruining the set. And don't forget, he would've had to create the disk in at least two stages—one layer on top of the other. He might not be an expert, but he's got skills—and he's had practice—plenty of it."

A rustle of unease ran through the gathering.

"The pathologist said the same thing." Ruth paused. "Would the first layer have to be hardened before he poured the second?"

"Hardened, but not completely set."

"I'm just wondering how he managed two lots of pouring and

setting—or partial set—for Professor Tennent," Ruth explained. "He had the drive back from London; time must've been tight. Can you speed up the process? Using specialist equipment, maybe?"

Specialist equipment meant a narrower search.

"You *can* . . ." Hughes gave an apologetic grimace. "But all you need is gentle heat from a household oven or a space heater."

If she was disappointed, Carver couldn't see it in her face.

"Okay," she said. "Craft kits and space heaters aren't going to lead us to this toe-rag. We need something more specific and specialized." She looked around the room. "Any suggestions?"

"Would he need a special kit to get the brain out of the skull?" DC Ivey asked.

"If he didn't want to make a mess of it," she said, with an appreciative nod. "A sagittal saw would be the best tool for the job—that's the gadget they use to remove the brain cap during postmortems. But this is a good news/bad news scenario. Bad news: you could probably pick one up on eBay for a few hundred quid. *Good* news: I doubt if they're big sellers, so if we're *really* lucky, you'll find one among the victims' credit card purchases."

"Where are you on card use?" Carver asked. DC Ivey had been tasked with checking purchases for the missing.

"Mostly food and booze from small convenience stores," Ivey said. "I plan to start visiting them today. And I did find a couple of online electrical goods suppliers on the statements as well—I'll ring them this morning."

"Good. Ask if anything was delivered to the card holders' addresses. If it was, we might find trace. Focus on the two confirmed victims, for now."

Carver asked for Dr. Yi's observations.

He pursed his lips. "There's no physical similarity between the victims."

"Do you think that the professor's *Fact or Fable?* show was the trigger for his abduction?" Carver asked.

"I do . . ." Yi said carefully. "But I believe his reasons for taking the professor are not as straightforward as they might first appear."

Carver waited for the psychologist to gather his thoughts.

"It's tempting to think that this was an act of rage. A narcissistic killer, injured by the dismissive tone of the TV program, murdered Tennent and included him in his exhibit as proof of his power over life and death."

"Tempting, but not convincing?" Carver said.

"He has been active for at least six months, yet the Ferryman handle has only emerged in the past few weeks—and seems to've been spontaneous.

"The timing is also important," he went on. "As Sergeant Lake says, he plans ahead, and he's disciplined. He waited half a year before staging this 'exhibit'—why rush it after all that time and preparation?"

Carver nodded. "Good point. He found one of the few places in London where he could snatch the professor out of security camera range. He had to've planned ahead—so it does seem odd that he didn't take more time over Tennent."

"On the other hand, the Ferryman rumors have had a lot of press," Dr. Yi said. "And the *Fact or Fable?* program drew four million viewers—as high as some TV dramas. Added to which, the killer used the program title as the name of his exhibit."

This was exactly what Carver had suggested yesterday. "You're saying it *was* about publicity after all?" he asked.

The forensic psychologist's dark eyes met Carver's, a hint of rueful amusement in them, but he didn't answer immediately.

"Do we know how many followers FerrymanArt's Instagram account has gained since the program aired?" he asked.

"Sixteen thousand and counting," Ruth replied.

"Well, then. Yes, it seems you were right, Chief Inspector," Yi said. "He's media-savvy and opportunistic."

"So he *didn't* hold a grudge against the professor?" Carver said.

"He may have resented the disparaging tone of the program," Dr.

Yi said. "But that wasn't his primary motivation, in my opinion. Your two Liverpool victims will provide the most clues to the killer's home base—even serial killers have a comfort zone. And that's likely to be close to where he lives or works."

Carver nodded. This was basic geographical profiling. "Can you give us some more insights into the man, based on what we have?"

Yi considered the question, taking a sip of water before answering.

"He has resources—some stolen from his victims, clearly. And he has time, which suggests he's not in regular employment. This is a man who is driven, and focused. The degree of planning, the care in execution, the ability to remain unnoticed until a time of his choosing suggests a mature, intelligent person, in full control of his faculties. He is also a sociopath who will kill without hesitation, or regret, to achieve his goals."

"Which are?"

"In the short term, it would seem that he craves power and notoriety," Dr. Yi concluded. "But there is never enough of either to satisfy that kind of hunger."

8

Carver's mobile rang as he reached his office. Number unknown.

He answered briskly, ready to cut off any telesales chancer before they launched into their script.

"Mr. Carver, it's Doctor Thomas."

His neurologist. Carver had asked for a phone consultation after the weird waking-dream he'd experienced the morning before. He ducked into his office, thanking the doctor for making the time.

"I wanted to ask—are vivid dreams associated with migraines?"

"They can be. Have you had any change in symptoms—pain, for instance?"

"No." Although Carver experienced visual disturbances during migraines, he'd never had any pain.

"Are they more frequent? Severe?"

Both, Carver thought. He admitted to more frequent.

"Hm . . . if your symptoms are worsening—"

"I wouldn't say that," Carver interrupted, trying not to sound too defensive; Dr. Thomas was one of the team charged with managing his return to work.

"All right. Could you describe the nature of these dreams?" Dr. Thomas asked.

"As I said—they're vivid. Surreal."

"I wouldn't place you in the category of the 'worried well,' Mr. Carver—so I imagine you called me because you find them disturbing."

"Yes," Carver said, hearing the tightness in his voice.

"Like the hallucinations you experienced in the beginning?"

"More like replays of things that happen in the day," Carver said, falling back on his own small knowledge of the psychology of dreams, wishing he'd googled his symptoms instead.

"So, not hallucinatory episodes?"

The episode had happened during the day—he'd *thought* he was awake, but he couldn't admit to that, so he answered with a firm "No," adding, "I am still experiencing the synesthesia, though."

"Interesting," Thomas said, although he had the good grace not to sound too excited by the prospect.

Carver had resisted becoming the neurologist's pet project. But Dr. Thomas had the power to have him consigned to sick leave, so he added, "D'you think the auras will stay with me for life?"

It was a cynical ploy to deflect the neurologist from turning the phone consult into a monitoring session.

"As your brain recovered, it had to reroute nerve pathways around the damaged tissue," Thomas said, slipping into teaching mode. "It seems to have forged novel—even unique—ways around the lesions via your visual cortex. Which explains the unusual associations you have between color perception, mood, and body language. It's *entirely* possible that the new nerve pathways are a permanent feature." He paused. "Does that prospect trouble you?"

"It can be tiring trying to make sense of what I see," Carver said. "But I'm learning to live with it."

"These dreams, on the other hand, *do* bother you." Like the good doctor he was, Thomas had circled back to the real subject of the call. "How're you sleeping?"

"Not well," Carver had to admit.

"That could certainly be a factor," the neurologist said. "Napping at work?"

"No."

"You're sure?"

"I think I'd know," Carver said, evading a direct answer.

"Well, if you do, take it seriously."

"I will." Focusing on the topic of migraines seemed a safer option than exploring the possibility that he was taking microsleeps during the working day, so Carver added, "I really just wanted to know about dreams and migraines."

The doctor seemed to debate for a moment whether to push harder, but after an agonizing pause, he said, "When the sleep cycle is disrupted, dreams can become intrusive. Added to which, disturbed sleep often causes the neck muscles to tighten. The occipital nerves can become irritated and inflamed. Result: migraine. Stress, too, can affect sleep—and you're heading up the inquiry into the missing men, aren't you? There's been a development in the case, hasn't there?"

This was dangerous territory: in all his dealings with the neurologist, he'd seemed curiously ignorant of what was happening in the world beyond neurosciences. Dr. Thomas had definitely been briefed.

"I am heading the inquiry, yes, and yes, there has been a development," he said.

"Which makes me think—"

"Overstimulation," Carver said, putting words in Thomas's mouth. "That's probably it. I need to work harder on my relaxation techniques."

"I can arrange for you to see a neuropsychologist, if you're concerned—"

Sweat broke out on Carver's brow. "There's really no need." The last thing he needed right now was greater supervision.

"Well, keep it in mind," the consultant said. "And you should mention this to your therapist."

"I will." He made an effort not to hang up too hurriedly, thanking the doctor for his time, telling the neurologist that he felt reassured. As for the Review Board shrink—of *course* he'd divulge that he was having trouble sorting reality from dreams, micronapping, and suffering sleep paralysis in the middle of the day.

On the very day hell froze over.

9

I have five screens streaming news items twenty-four/seven. I've set up Google alerts for the keywords "Tennent," "John Eddings, "Dillon Martin," "Fact or Fiction," and, of course, "Ferryman." I have BBC Radio Merseyside playing at a low volume while I work on an exhibit—not artwork 2, which is ready and waiting for the green light. Nor is it artwork 3, which is already edited and ready to roll. What I hold in my hands is artwork 4; I have a title for it already: *Art for Art's Sake*.

I like to plan ahead, and this one is special. This is Marcus: smug, privileged, blithely ignorant of the damage he wrought. Although he was very clear at the end. When I looked into his eyes, he knew me.

My inner metronome counts time, and my heart *tick-tick-ticks* to the rhythm.

Soon. It must be soon. My hand trembles slightly and I consciously slow the speed of the metronome. It will take as long as it takes; the important thing is to be ready.

Even so, it's a challenge, curbing my impatience, trying not to be too distracted by the movement and the gabble of voices on-screen. But thirty minutes later, I have completed the first stage of artwork 4 and returned it to cold storage.

At three o' clock, I sit at my bench, watching the news on all five screens simultaneously. They rehash old footage, play a short loop of CSIs at *Think Outside the Box*, and recite the official press release that police are "working on strong leads."

Tick, tick, tick.

I will not rush this, despite the agony of waiting. Ask a moderately well-educated nonartistic type what "pop art" means to them, they'll probably trot out "the Marilyn picture" or "Campbell's soup tins." Everyone knows Andy Warhol. And I'd bet a month's salary none of them mention Eduardo Paolozzi, even though it was Paolozzi's *I Was a Rich Man's Plaything* that first used the word "pop" in an artwork. It predates Warhol's *Marilyn Diptych* by fifteen years. Yet who, outside of the art world, has even heard of him? Who gives a damn? And why do we care about Warhol, with his mass-produced, throwaway art, anyway? Because Andy Warhol saw the commercial and—let's not be shy—*financial* benefits of timing his product release to the demands of the market.

So I can wait.

As a distraction, I pick up my phone and trawl social media.

Lots on Twitter. Which is encouraging.

I open my Instagram app: two thousand new followers since six this morning. Comments keep coming in on my exhibit photos, and I can't resist scrolling through, playing a kind of roulette game.

Scroll, stop.

"OMG, @FerrymanArt." Dull.

Scroll, stop.

"@FerrymanArt, you are #thebest." How sweet.

Scroll, stop.

"You are one sick fuck @FerrymanArt." That's had a lot of negative replies. Ooh . . . I would *not* like to be in @mr.kdpics's virtual shoes—there's a *big* outpouring of hate for him.

Scroll, stop.

"Respect to you @FerrymanArt. I've created a photomontage of *Think Outside the Box*. Would be honored to hear what you think."

Another invitation to connect. But this one shows a little more learning than the rest; it includes the hashtags #UrbanArt #EphemeralArt #FleetingArt #GuerillaArt. And then there's the choice of Instagram handle: @kharon, after Kharon—sometimes "Charon"—the ferryman of Greek mythology, who carried souls across the river Styx from the land of the living, to the land of the dead.

I click the hyperlink to @Kharon's account, slightly irritated to have my identity hijacked in this sly way.

Kharon has put together a series of crowd shots with *Think Outside the Box* as the backdrop. The cascade of light passing through the disks is stunning; I have the peculiar experience of seeing the exhibit through the eyes of the audience and feel a thrill of newness and excitement.

Kharon has made the observers part of the exhibit, reminding me of Martha Cooper's photographs of New York street art. Flecks of sleet add a hint of van Gogh's *Starry Night* to the ensemble. He's done a good job of balancing darkness and light—not easy when you're trying to capture figures in front of a lit exhibit, shot in the dark. Beanie hats and backs of heads, mostly, but one has been taken from above.

In this image, you see dozens of hands raised, each holding a phone. He must have climbed up the side of the building opposite to get the perspective. On each phone, a tiny image of *Think Outside the Box*, and beyond these miniature replicates, the real thing, full-size, washed in mauve light at the instant the camera shutter closed. A kind of picture-in-picture representation of the piece. Quite clever. He signs every image #FerrymanFan and links to my own account.

All in all, it's a pleasing *homage*. I won't reply, but this could be someone worth returning to at a later date.

The words "Breaking news" rise above the mumble from the computers ranged on my bench, and my heart skips a beat. I locate the screen and focus in on it. A panning shot of Stone Street, police tape, a lone officer in uniform on guard.

"Remains discovered near Liverpool's North Docks three days ago are human," the newsreader says.

Remains, he says. As if I dumped them like offal.

"Merseyside Police revealed today that Detective Chief Inspector Carver was directed to the macabre display by an anonymous tip-off."

The newsreader gives some background on Carver and his previous murder inquiry, talking over a short video of my exhibit. They've blurred the disks—to protect delicate sensibilities, no doubt.

More *blah* about the previous case, which is useful from a PR point of view, but only up to a point. The newsreader is making far too much of the chief inspector's past tribulations.

Tick, tick, tick.

"Come on, come *on* . . ." I lean forward, willing him to say the words that will trigger the release of my next exhibit.

He frowns at the camera, and it's almost as if he is speaking directly to me: "In a shocking development, police have revealed that one of the disks contained the remains of Professor Mick Tennent, who disappeared shortly after he presented a popular science program on the so-called Ferryman disappearances in Liverpool just six days ago. That episode was called 'Learn to Think Outside the Box,' and it has been widely speculated that police were investigating the possibility of a link between his abduction and the Ferryman."

From "so-called Ferryman" to "Ferryman" in under a minute. I check my phone—my follower numbers are clocking up like the digits on a gas station fuel pump. *Good, but not enough. I need two more names.* It's vital to the impact of the next exhibit that the public knows there are three contributors to *Think Outside the Box.*

As if he's heard me, the newsreader says the words I've been waiting for: "Two other victims have been named as local men John Eddings and Dillon Martin." Their photographs appear, side by side on-screen.

The metronome freezes, midswing. That's the green light. *It's a go.*

The equipment is ready: checked, packed in boxes, color coded for ease of assembly. Gloves, overalls, climbing equipment, mask are bagged separately, ready to be packed in the van. But I skim through the inventory one final time—there will be no coming back to pick up a forgotten item.

On-screen, the news has shifted to a press conference: Carver, flanked by the chief constable and another man in uniform—presumably his superintendent. They have a picture of my van—or more accurately, one very like it. They give the number plate. Which I ditched as soon as I got back to Liverpool, of course.

Final checks are complete. Okay, this is it. Drive the van round, then move the boxes to the service entrance. Sliding them into the van, I prepare myself for a slight correction in follower numbers. This exhibit will be difficult for some of them: less visceral, more cerebral. It makes demands on the audience. They won't be able to passively absorb the message—if they want to appreciate it fully, they'll have to do some thinking. But I will make it worth their while: those who see the deeper meaning of the work will receive personal invitations to my third exhibit, which is visual and visceral in a way they will never have experienced before.

10

Carver sat at his desk, updating his decision log.

London Met had sent samples of the nylon rope, which was now being examined by the forensics team. He had briefed the family liaison officers who would be attached to the families of the two victims in his jurisdiction; London Met would take care of Professor Tennent's family. The FLOs' job was never easy: the bereaved always wanted more than they as investigators could give without compromising the investigation. Added to which, those dealing with John Eddings's and Dillon Martin's families were in a particularly hostile situation, given the delay in beginning the inquiry. The media interest wasn't helping, either: it was hard to reassure those struggling with loss that everything was being done to bring the killer to justice, while press and social media were screaming police incompetence.

The press conference had been a drain—so much animal passion in the room it seemed awash with light and color. He'd had to focus on a police tech who seemed shut off from the emotion around him, all his attention fixed on his role as sound engineer for the session.

Carver rubbed a spot on the right side of his skull, just above his ear, where a slow, throbbing headache had started. It was six thirty; he'd been at work for nearly twelve hours. Under the terms of his restricted duties he should be at home, resting, by now, but he had an evening debriefing to manage, and his log to finish, so he remained at his desk, feeling spaced out, on the point of exhaustion.

His desk phone rang, jolting him out of drowsiness.

"Sergeant Farrow," the caller said. "Contact Center." What used to be called the Calls and Response Unit, renamed under the new consumer model of policing.

"Go ahead," Carver said.

"We got a call from someone claiming to be the Ferryman. Said he had information about a new exhibit."

"Put him through."

"There must be thirty or more cranks out there, claiming to be him—"

"That's okay, put him through," Carver said again.

Farrow cleared his throat. "I can't."

"What d'you mean, you can't?"

Farrow cleared his throat again. "He hung up."

"You mean he left a message and hung up?" Carver said, dreading opening his e-mail account to check for another message.

"Not exactly."

"What is this, twenty bloody questions? Give me a straight answer, man—did he leave any instructions—a location?"

"The adviser asked for one, but like I say, the caller hung up—"

"Did the operator refuse to put the caller through to me?" Carver interrupted.

A pause.

"Look, Chief Inspector, this is a newbie. He—"

Carver swore under his breath. "I want the original recording in my inbox in ten minutes."

He ended the call, as a new e-mail message notification popped up like a speech bubble in the bottom right corner of his computer screen.

No subject heading.

The message read "ANSWER YOUR FUCKING PHONE. ~ *F*" The same address as the Ferryman's first contact.

He steadied himself and headed to the Major Incident Room. He rapped hard on the first desk he came to and everyone stopped what they were doing.

"We've got another, incoming," he said. "And we don't know the location." He spotted DC Ivey standing next to Ruth Lake. "Ivey, see if you can find anything on social media. Ruth, call John Hughes, tell him I'm about to send him a voice recording from Calls and Response—Contact Center—whatever the hell we're calling it now. I need him to clear his desk, focus on it as priority. Everyone else—" He took a moment to get his temper under control. They were hanging on his every word, and he needed to keep it together. "Be ready to move as soon as we know where this is happening."

Ruth Lake closed her phone. "John is ready when you are," she said, businesslike and calm, as always.

Carver nodded. "Put a call through to the Matrix team—we're going to need crowd control." He glanced at DC Ivey. "What's taking so long, Tom?"

"I'm looking on Instagram," the young detective said, his eyes fixed on his laptop monitor. "He hasn't given a location this time, boss."

"Come *on*—anyone?" Carver said.

Phones appeared out of pockets, heads went down as people started scrolling.

"Got it!" Ivey shouted. He turned the monitor so that Carver could see it.

He had multiple tabs open: Instagram, Vimeo, Tumblr, Twitter, YouTube. Thumbnail images, all of which seemed to be showing the same thing: different views of a wall built into a sandstone escarpment. Massive, arched doorways punctuated the wall every ten or fifteen yards, and at the top of the wall, a ledge, on which three lit oblongs were perched. A crowd of thirty or more had already gathered below it, many of the spectators holding phones and tablets up to record the scene.

"Can we get in closer?" Carver said.

Ivey enlarged one of the thumbnails and clicked to full screen. The lit oblongs resolved into a row of laptop computers, propped open on the ledge. "This is being streamed live by someone calling themselves 'Kharon,'" he said.

Each laptop screen was split into two images, one above the other. Both showed some kind of wave trace, one a pale blue sequence of blips of varying height and wavelength, the other a vivid red, against a black background, and Carver was transported back to the hospital room where he'd spent over a week hooked up to heart and blood pressure monitors after he was shot.

"What is that?" someone asked.

"Some kind of medical trace, I think," Ruth said. "ECG? EEG?"

"The lower one is a cardio," Carver said. "Does anyone know where this is?"

There wasn't enough room for everyone to huddle around the monitor, so Ivey zipped to the front of the room and hooked his laptop up to the data projector. Seconds later the video was playing on the big screen.

As he clicked the mouse to turn up the volume, there was a sudden flash. The crowd—and everyone in the incident room—flinched as one. Yelps of excitement from the spectators were followed by relieved laughter, as a dazzling array of LEDs illuminated the stone wall below the monitors.

The lights flashed up a message three times: "Statistical Uncertainty #2." It repeated three times, then began spelling out more words, ticker-tape style: "Catch . . . the . . . gamma wave," Ruth read aloud.

"Jesus," Ivey exclaimed. "Has he released some kind of radioactive substance?"

"Gamma waves are a type of brain wave," Ruth said, her voice still sounding calm, though Carver saw a steel-gray shimmer of light around her face—a rare sign of anxiety. "I think the trace at the top of the screens must be an EEG."

The cardio trace, which had been bumping across the screen the entire time they had been talking, stopped abruptly on the first monitor, then the second, then the third, and the red trace drew a ruler-straight line across the bottom of all three screens.

"They're flatlining," Carver breathed.

The blue trace of the gamma brain waves continued, however, the peaks becoming more intense and regular in pattern. Then all the laptops went out, plunging the gathering into darkness.

The ticker tape burst into life again, spelling out a name: "J-o-h-n E—"

Whoops of appreciation rose up from the crowd, followed by applause.

"John Eddings," Ruth said. "He's spelling out the names of the victims."

Someone in the room murmured, "What the hell . . . ?"

"The bastard had them hooked up to monitors as they died," Carver said.

A chant rose from the crowd: "*Fer-ry-man, Fer-ry-man, Fer-ry-man!*" They began to stamp in time as they chanted, then as one, they began to move forward.

"What are they doing?" Ivey asked.

"My guess is they're looking to take a little piece of history home with them," Ruth said. "And that ledge can't be more than about fifteen or twenty feet high." It would be the work of a moment for the crowd to dismantle the computers, effectively destroying the evidence. "We need to get to those laptops before the crowd does."

"DC Ivey," Carver said. "Does this Kharon give a location?"

The detective exited full screen to check the video details. "Nothing, boss, but it's already had two hundred comments. I could scroll through, see if anyone mentions it?"

"It'd take too long. We need context—another landmark. Try to find images taken from farther away."

The young detective minimized the screen and clicked through a few more thumbnails.

Carver dialed the Contact Center and Farrow answered. "Have you had any reports of a crowd causing a disturbance or nuisance?"

"Nothing," Farrow said.

"Call me with a location as soon as you do."

He turned his attention to the rest of his team. "Has anyone got *anything*?" he demanded.

A few glanced up, shook their heads, but most kept their eyes on their phone screens.

"*Nobody* is naming the location," Ruth Lake said.

"So how did they know where to go? There must be a hundred people there now—they couldn't all just happened to've been passing."

"Private messaging," Ruth said.

Carver closed his eyes for a second. This was punishment for not taking the Ferryman's call.

"Sir." Ivey pinged a wide-angle shot of the scene up on-screen. Above the ledge to the left end of the escarpment was what looked like an old sandstone railway arch.

Carver squinted at the screen, trying to make out lettering etched into the stonework of the bridge. "L.O.R.," he said. "The name of a railway?"

"Yeah." Ruth moved closer to the screen. "Liverpool Overhead."

"I didn't know Liverpool *had* an overhead railway."

"It doesn't—not anymore. Closed in the nineteen fifties, I think," Ruth said. "It ran along the docks from Dingle to Seaforth—can't have been more than five or six miles long, and there's not much of it left, so it should be easy to find this section. Get googling, everyone."

She started searching on her own phone, and the rest of the team followed suit.

A minute later, one of the younger detectives said, "I know it! It's down the Dingle, sir—near the go-kart track."

"Which is *where*, exactly?"

"Sorry, sir. Sefton Street, the big roundabout by the Royal Mail depot."

"Someone locate it on a map," Carver said. "I want a post code or grid reference."

11

The police convoy sliced through rush-hour traffic under the banshee howl of the sirens. Lights blazing and horns blaring, it took less than three minutes from headquarters to the scene.

Ruth Lake had snatched the keys to a patrol car from the board, and with red and blue grille lights blazing and siren whooping, she matched every maneuver of the bright yellow Matrix Mercedes Sprinter van as it steered and swerved and braked, diving from one lane to another at nerve-jangling speed, Greg Carver clinging grimly to the passenger-door grab handle.

The crowd had gathered in a car park adjacent to a health and fitness center, and Lake risked sliding a single look Carver's way as they swung into it seconds behind the Matrix van. The strobing police lights alternately gave his skin a deathly blue cast and a hectic glow.

The Matrix team's Serious and Organized Crime Unit was highly trained in managing public disorder incidents; they would take the lead here. Ten officers in body armor piled out, muscling through the crowd to get between them and the wall, and moments later a second police van screamed to a halt on the road above the archway. This was a specialist crew trained in rope access, the plan being to drop a few officers down to the ledge to secure the scene.

"I underestimated the height of the ledge," Ruth commented.

That should work to their advantage: the sheer face of the wall and the overhang of the ledge above the arched steel doors would act as a deterrent, holding the spectators at bay. The laptops still rested in place, strips of unlit LEDs strung beneath them, like windblown party streamers.

A second later, the place was flooded with powerful light from the Matrix van on the car park and portable "Night Owl" floodlights from the street sixty feet above.

Carver's detectives, bolstered by the arrival of uniform police, managed the outer perimeter.

The police presence, and perhaps seeing the words "Caught on camera—mobile CCTV" blazoned on the side of the Matrix van, were enough to encourage some of the crowd to disperse. The Matrix team leader addressed the crowd from the van's PA system, advising them to stay put—they would need to question everyone present—but the area was open on three sides, impossible to contain them all without a greater police presence, and spectators continued to slink away.

Carver nodded to his left. "Over there." Two of the men had split off from the crowd and were running to the far side of the wall, where the natural bedrock extended all the way to the level of the car park. Cracks in the stone, and shrubby trees growing up the escarpment, would give them hand and footholds.

"They need to be stopped."

His tone, and his reluctance to meet her eye, told her that Carver wasn't going to be able to help.

The first of them, a lanky youth, had already started to climb the rock face, making for the ledge as Ruth sprinted from the car, dragging her police ID out of her pocket.

A Matrix cop turned away from the crowd, bellowing, "YOU, STOP!"

Ruth held her ID aloft, pointing to the two idiots about to risk their lives and breach the crime scene. She didn't turn back after that, but kept running, satisfied to hear the heavy clump of size twelve boots gaining on her.

The second runner was shorter and less athletic; he had just begun to climb when Ruth caught up with him. She yelled for him to stop, but he kept going, laughing hysterically like he was high on something. She leapt, hooked her hand through the back of his trouser belt, and yanked him off the rock face.

He fell backward with a cry of dismay, catching her a glancing blow above her right eye, but she held on to him, shoving him to the ground and whipping her cuffs from her belt as the Matrix cop powered past her to the rock face.

He yelled for the climber to stay where he was, that help was coming.

The lanky male laughed, and from the base of the cliff his friend yelled, "Go 'head, Robbo. Lob 'em down."

Jeez, he's planning to throw the laptops down to the mob.

"Robbo" edged right, finding purchase in the rock above the ledge with his fingertips and the toes of his Nike trainers, cheered on by the spectators. He reached the first laptop to whistling and applause, wedged his left hand into a crack in the rock face to anchor himself, and bent to retrieve the laptop.

He snapped it closed, one-handed, and flung it.

The crowd yelled, "*Woooo-OH!*," heads turning to watch the laptop skim like a frisbee over the heads of the Matrix cops. Whoever caught the thing must have regretted it a second after his moment of triumph, because the crowd surged inward like prop forwards in a rugby scrum. Officers moved in to break it up.

Simultaneously, several shouts of "Rope!" from above, then a whistle of air as rappelling ropes snaked over the escarpment from the street above.

Robbo continued to work his way, inch by inch, along the grass-clogged guttering attached to the ledge. He reached the second laptop as a Matrix officer rappelled down the cliff, heading directly toward him.

Robbo reached, straining for the second laptop. Overreached—

The guttering gave way under his weight; he scrabbled for something to hold. Stones, twigs, and dirt came away in his hands, and Ruth saw his wide-eyed gape of horror as he toppled forward, off the cliff.

Ruth's prisoner shouted, "Robbo!"

Someone screamed.

He fell headfirst. Instinctively the crowd splashed backward. There was nothing between Robbo and the concrete below.

He swung face-first with a clang into the steel door under the ledge.

And dangled, held by one ankle.

A Matrix team rappeler had caught him just in time.

Robbo groaned, dripping blood from a serious nosebleed, and the rappeler gently lowered him to police waiting in the car park below.

12

Carver found an e-mail from the Ferryman waiting in his inbox when he returned to base.

Under the subject heading "You missed the wave," the killer had written: "People get hurt when you don't pay attention. You need to PAY ATTENTION."

Carver checked the date stamp; it was sent moments after Robbo fell from the ledge.

He looked up and saw Ruth at his desk. He hadn't heard her come in, and she was looking at him as if she was waiting for an answer to a question.

"Take a look," he said, turning the laptop for her to read. "He was there, Ruth."

"I'll get a copy of the CCTV recording from the Matrix vans," she said. "Cross-ref them with the Stone Street scene. Hughes is coordinating evidence collection at Dingle Station. If this bastard left any trace, they'll find it."

"Thanks. Anything else?"

"The super wants to see both of us," she said.

He nodded.

"As of five minutes ago," she added.

Carver hauled himself out of his chair, feeling a hundred years old.

Detective Superintendent Wilshire made Ruth Lake wait outside his office while he spoke to Carver.

"The injured onlooker is exercising the media," he said without preamble. "The press office has been fielding suggestions that you were slow on the uptake, that we at Merseyside Police aren't taking the threat to public safety seriously enough."

"There was a miscommunication in the Contact Center," Carver said. "I've already spoken to the team leader, and the contact adviser. We'll work on a protocol to ensure it doesn't happen again."

"Be sure you do," Wilshire said. "And brief the Press Office, too."

Carver nodded, waiting to be dismissed, but Wilshire seemed in no hurry.

"Look," he said. "As it turns out, this case hasn't exactly been the gentle ease-in to work that we intended."

Carver hated the thought that others had sat around a table discussing his welfare, deciding what they could give the invalid to make him feel useful without taxing his delicate constitution.

He groped for something to say that wouldn't sound defensive and came up with, "It's been a good motivator."

"You never lacked *motivation*, Greg," Wilshire said, with a rare flash of humor. "But this is a high-pressure investigation—"

"Nothing I can't handle," Carver said quickly, preempting what he feared would be an offer to relieve him of the burden.

Wilshire didn't look convinced. "You always were your own worst enemy." He sighed. "All right, you can call DS Lake in."

Ruth entered with her shoulders back and a quiet calm emanating from her that soothed Carver but seemed to exasperate Wilshire.

"That's a nasty-looking bruise, DS Lake," he said, gathering his brows as if accusing her of recklessly head-butting a wall.

Most people would have touched the sore spot, but Ruth kept her hands relaxed at her sides. "It looks worse than it is, sir," she said.

This seemed to irritate Wilshire further. "For God's *sake*, Carver," he growled. "Sit down before you fall down."

Carver would normally have politely refused, but he didn't want to make things worse for Ruth, so he took a chair and waited to see how the storm would progress.

"I wanted both of you to hear this," Wilshire said. "So there is no confusion about where we stand. 'Robbo'—real name Wayne Roberts—suffered serious injuries. Broken nose, fractured cheekbone, and a dislocated knee. He'll need reconstructive surgery on his face."

Wilshire was a big bear of a man, not good at hiding his feelings, and it didn't take any special skills to know that right now, he was royally pissed off. Carver just wasn't sure who with. He glanced sideways at Ruth for guidance, but she seemed to be accepting the proffered facts as helpful information with no emotion or accusation attached to them.

"Mr. Roberts's solicitor," Wilshire went on, "is complaining that an overzealous police reaction to the situation caused his injuries."

"He was interfering with a crime scene, destroying evidence," Ruth said, her tone mild, but firm.

"You can add inciting a riot to that," Carver said, remembering the laptop sailing over the heads of the Matrix team officers.

"And endangering the lives of others," Ruth agreed.

Wilshire didn't comment.

"Mr. Roberts's accomplice, Daryl Smith, whom DS Lake prevented from climbing the rock face, has additionally threatened to sue for assault," he said, flatly.

Ruth's only response was a slight lift of her eyebrows.

"She probably saved the pillock's miserable *life*," Carver said.

Wilshire scowled at the interruption. "The incident has been referred to the IPCC."

Carver groaned inwardly: this was the Independent Police Complaints Commission—and would be a huge pain in the backside.

"But those two bozos won't have it all their own way."

Carver had to run the last sentence through again before he realized that Wilshire was effectively backing them.

"Mr. Smith was three times over the legal limit for alcohol," Wilshire went on, "and saliva tests suggest that both he and Mr. Roberts had been smoking cannabis. Blood tests have been taken to confirm the levels, but Mr. Roberts admitted he had been smoking weed all afternoon."

"It's a wonder he didn't *float* up there," Ruth said, deadpan.

Carver smiled; Wilshire did not. "The bruise over your eye is evidence that Smith resisted arrest," he said. "He could be charged with assaulting a police officer in the execution of duty."

"He fell backward, caught me with his elbow in the fall," Ruth said.

"Merseyside Police has a no-tolerance policy on violence against its officers," Wilshire countered.

"Like I said, he wasn't violent, just uncoordinated—I wouldn't want to press charges."

"That will not be your decision, DS Lake," Wilshire said.

Carver shot her a warning look and Ruth fell back on a well-worn strategy: she gave Wilshire her wide-eyed stare and an ambiguous, "Sir."

"Will that be all, sir?" Carver said.

"For now." He dismissed them with a wave of his hand.

Carver waited until they were in the elevator heading down to the incident room before he said, "Wilshire's doing you a favor."

"He's covering his backside," Ruth said.

"No doubt. But he's covering yours, too—so let him."

13

I watch Robbo dive headfirst off the ledge for the twentieth time. I've been replaying that moment on video at my studio. That's got to deserve a nomination for a Darwin Award—pity it was a near miss. From my perspective, his near-fatal nosedive could not have been timelier or turned out better. Far from *losing* followers who failed to understand the message behind *Catch the Gamma Wave*, the *gains* have, in fact, been phenomenal. Social media loves to scream police brutality, and Robbo's spectacular fall has been played over and over, shared, tweeted, retweeted, and screen-grabbed on thousands of phones worldwide. All the main news broadcasters used it in their bulletins; someone even made it into a GIF. It went viral.

Kharon was very helpful in getting word out after the police switchboard refused to forward my call to Chief Inspector Carver. I decided right then not to spread the news publicly, and when I private-messaged Kharon, he was eager to be involved. He PM'd his followers, giving strict instructions to keep the exhibit under the radar. They private-messaged others. My own video upload netted seven thousand new followers.

All in all, a good day.

14

Ruth Lake drove Carver in sleepy silence. Twilight was paling to sullen dawn, and low clouds promised rain later. She had worked well into the night and would have liked another half hour in bed, but Carver had scheduled a seven A.M. meeting with their forensic psychologist, Dr. Yi.

The streets outside the city center were quiet, and Ruth took advantage of the empty roads, pushing the car to the speed limit, zipping around slow-moving traffic. They didn't stop for a single traffic light from Carver's place to the turn into Upper Parliament Street that would take them on the downhill curve to the waterfront.

A half mile on, at the church of St. James in the City, Ruth slowed for the first time.

"What?" Carver said.

"Nothing," she said. "Tiredness." She thought she'd seen a gray silhouette, a misty shadow on the brick perimeter wall of the church. She dismissed it as a trick of the dawn half-light and four hours of troubled sleep. But then she saw it again—or one like it—on a broadband street cabinet: a gray, hooded figure, the face obscured in darker shadow. She flicked on the hazards and pulled over to the curb.

Moments later, Carver stood next to her, staring at the figure, spray-stenciled in two shades of gray on the narrow end of the cabinet. "Are you thinking what I'm thinking?" he asked.

"Depends," Ruth said, snapping a few pictures on her mobile phone.

"Are you thinking it looks a hell of a lot like the hooded bogeyman in Tennent's *Fact or Fable?* TV program?"

They saw four more of the graffiti figures between the church and their destination: images of the gray, monklike figure ghosting around corners, lurking on the gray walls of Wapping Dock, fading into the stone on which it was painted. Finally, on a reconstructed stone arch—a monument to the history of the dock—its arm raised, a finger pointing toward the police headquarters a couple hundred yards north of them.

Ruth glanced across to Carver. "Are *you* thinking what *I'm* thinking?"

Echoing her earlier reply, Carver said, "Depends whether you're thinking this bastard is taking the piss."

With half an hour to spare before the meeting, Carver went to his office, while Ruth Lake went in search of coffee. They convened in his office on the hour.

"Let's start with the Ferryman's response to being denied access," Dr. Yi said.

He was sitting in a chair to Ruth's left, looking fresh and rested. She tried not to hold it against him.

"As I understand it, he shut down all lines of communication with you?"

"Even social media went silent for the first fifteen minutes," Carver said.

"We think he direct-messaged a few followers and even they kept it between themselves," Ruth added.

"So *you're* difficult to reach, and *he* withdraws entirely."

"Classic passive-aggressive," Ruth said. That drew a sharp look from Yi.

"It certainly indicates a fragile ego," he said. "This is a dangerous personality."

"We know that," Carver said. "We had a near riot on our hands last night. The question is, do we give him the access he wants?"

Yi looked doubtful. "Appeasing him could have serious repercussions."

"The repercussions of *not* appeasing him have been fairly serious," Ruth said, immediately regretting her sarcasm.

Yi dipped his head, accepting it with good grace.

"Even so, I would advise restraint. Direct dialogue with you could cause him to shift focus, and that carries its own risks." He left the rest unsaid, but she and Carver both knew the dangers of becoming the target of a psychopath.

"I hear what you're saying," Carver said. "But I won't endanger the public, playing games with this man, so why don't I tell you what we've done already, and then you can tell us if there's anything else we can do."

Yi folded his arms and looked at his feet.

In some, Ruth would read his closed posture as defensive—even obstructive. But in Dr. Yi it was a sign of concentration.

"Calls through to the police are routinely recorded," Carver said, "and as of today, every switchboard operator will have heard a recording of the Ferryman. He's disguising his voice, but he isn't using a voice changer, and so far, he's stuck to the same tone and fake Midlands accent. Our techs are using yesterday's recording as a baseline and they'll be able to match it to any calls recorded from here on in. As soon as we can get the right software, they will be able to establish as it comes in whether a call is genuinely from the killer. The problem is, setting it up could take a few days, and we can't risk a repeat of last night."

He directed his slightly unfocused gaze toward Ruth, and she realized he was gauging her reaction by the play of lights and colors he saw around her. "So, until we have the live voice analysis up and running," he said, "*any* caller claiming to be the Ferryman will be routed through the switchboard to either me or DS Lake."

Yi's head came up: this was in direct opposition to his advice, and Ruth saw annoyance in the creases around the psychologist's mouth.

Ruth shrugged. "Fine by me."

Carver twitched an eyebrow. "Wait till you hear the whole plan. As I said, calls to the switchboard are routinely recorded, but work-issue mobiles are not. From today, however, our phones will also be adapted to automatically record every call, and we will be allowed to keep them with us off-duty."

"Effectively, you'll be available night and day," Yi said. "I would strongly urge you to reconsider."

"As far as I'm concerned, it's nonnegotiable," Carver said. "But I can't speak for Ruth."

Ruth looked him in the eye. "Like I said, it's fine."

Carver's brow cleared, but Yi blinked, his eyelids closing a fraction of a second longer than was normal: he didn't like what Carver had said, and he didn't like what she'd said.

Even so, he uncrossed his arms and offered a small smile. "I suspect I'm not going to be able to change your minds."

"Not a chance," Carver said, returning the smile.

"Well, then, I won't argue."

But Ruth saw a tiny microshake of Yi's head, which gave the lie to his words.

He paused. "You said he was faking an accent?"

"Midlands," Carver said. "Is that significant?"

"It might be, from a geographical profiler's perspective," Yi said.

"Given that serial offenders often start close to home, you mean?"

"It's also close enough to a Liverpool accent, if he was trying to disguise the fact that he's local," Ruth said.

"I'll see if we can get a dialect expert to listen to it," Carver said. He turned again to Ruth. "How's the scene analysis going?"

"It's a difficult site," she said. "They got footwear marks. Those will be compared with the trainers Robbo was wearing. We'll know later today, or maybe tomorrow, if there's any trace on the laptops and the rest of the kit left on the rock."

She hesitated, and Carver gazed at the space around her head.

"What?" he said.

Ruth knew that Carver had learned to read emotions like anger and guilt accurately, but complex emotions were trickier, and anyway she wasn't sure if there was a color for freaked out.

"I did some background reading on gamma brain waves overnight," she said. "They're typical of the brain state associated with Eureka moments—you know, sudden, unexpected sparks of insight or knowledge."

Yi nodded. "There's quite a lot in the literature about gamma brain waves and the 'A-ha!' moment."

"Okay," Carver said. "And the brain waves on the laptop screens— were they *actually* gamma waves?"

"I couldn't tell a gamma wave from a microwave," Ruth admitted. "Doctor Yi?"

The psychologist leafed through the notes and printouts he'd brought with him. "Yes," he said. "In my opinion they are."

They looked to Ruth to take up the story again.

How to explain it? "If you drop a stone in a pond, you'd expect the ripples to get weaker and shallower as the energy dissipates, wouldn't you?"

Carver nodded.

"Brain waves should behave in the same way," Ruth said. "So, when the heart stops, brain activity weakens, brain waves slow down, and finally, they stop."

"Flatlining," Carver said.

"Kind of . . . An academic study on rats found that a type of brain wave called 'low gamma waves' got *stronger*—for up to thirty seconds *after* the animals were technically dead."

"I recall the study," Yi said. "They thought it might explain so-called near-death experiences."

"I'm not following," Carver said.

"Low gamma waves are linked to heightened, organized, focused consciousness. Moments of exceptional clarity," Ruth explained. "He wanted us to know the victims were aware even after he killed them."

Carver looked sick.

"I don't know that we can assume that was the case," Yi said. "The significance of the increase in low gamma waves has been widely contested. It may be that—"

"Doesn't matter," Ruth interrupted, before he could warm to his theme. "The *killer* believed it. The people banging the drum for him believe it, too."

"And it's gaining him more support," Carver said. "Did you notice the graffiti on your way here?"

"The Ferryman symbols . . . yes," Yi said. "Hangers-on, wanting to be part of the Ferryman phenomenon."

"Really?" Carver said. "They want to be part of sadistic murder?"

"I'm not sure that's it," Yi said. "Thousands of people take part in zombie walks—it doesn't mean they aspire to be flesh-eating undead. In my opinion, the people attending these events range from the intellectually curious, at one end of the scale, to those for whom the exhibits resonate with their sense of personal dissatisfaction, their alienation from society. The danger is that there's also an unreal quality to the works. Add to that the destructive impulses resulting from mob anonymity— you're almost guaranteed the behaviors we've witnessed so far."

"We need to persuade them to stay away."

"I'm not sure you can do that by appealing to their sense of justice: many who turned out will be troublemakers, known to the police," Ruth said. "The type who will turn out to a riot because it gives them an opportunity to kick in a few heads."

"A graphic example," Yi said, "but largely accurate. In a crowd, guilt is shared, diluted, if you will—allowing people extremes of behavior they would never dream of as individuals."

"So what do we do to dissuade people from turning out?" Carver asked. "It was pure luck no one died last night."

Yi thought about it. "You could probably scare the less criminally minded into staying away by emphasizing the dangers."

Carver nodded. "Can you brief the Press Office on that?"

"Sure," Yi said.

"Going back to your zombie analogy," Ruth said. "Should we be worried about wannabes?"

"Ferryman copycats, you mean?" Yi seemed surprised by the question.

Ruth waited.

A quick frown. "If these were simple murders and body dumps, I might share your concern," the psychologist said. "But the Ferryman's artwork is far more complex and difficult to replicate."

"So there's no immediate danger?" Carver said.

Ruth saw a slight glassy look in Yi's eye as he turned his thoughts inward to rummage through the possibilities, testing what he was about to say before he spoke.

A fractional nod, more to himself than to anybody else in the room, then: "At this time, I think copycat killings are unlikely."

Until that moment, Carver had seemed almost *coiled* with tension. Now Ruth saw relief flood through him, releasing the tightened sinews and muscles of his shoulders and neck.

"You've seen the pathologist's report," he said. "There was a slight difference in the brain sections—the staining was a smidgen darker on the right side. Is that telling us anything?"

"Ah, the question of right-brain creativity versus left-brain logic," Yi said. "Maybe, if there were anything in the theory. The fact is, it's a myth. But as Sergeant Lake points out, if the perpetrator *thinks* there's something in it, then we should be able to infer something from it."

"That he values creativity," Ruth said.

"Precisely."

"Could our killer be an actual artist?" Carver asked.

Yi answered the question indirectly. "He defines himself as such and expresses himself through his art."

Carver nodded slowly, absorbing the information. "Tox screen found traces of GHB in Eddings's and Martin's brains, but there were no drugs in samples taken from the professor."

"GHB is commonly used as a recreational drug," Yi said. "My guess is this is about availability: GHB is still quite easy to get hold of, and as you know, it can have powerful anesthetic effects. Both Eddings and Martin were young and fit; he may have used it to subdue them."

Carver nodded.

"Why is he targeting men?" Ruth asked. "Friends and family of both Eddings and Martin are convinced they were straight, so it's unlikely he's targeting gay men. Is he homosexual himself, or in denial of his sexuality?"

"Could be either," Yi said. "Or this series of murders may not be sexually motivated at all. It could simply be about power, or fame, or a twisted sense of what art is."

"Okay, thanks, Doctor Yi," Carver said, and Ruth heard the sigh in his words. "Is there anything else you wanted to mention?"

Yi thumbed through the report. "No, I think—" He checked himself, turning back to the printouts of brain waves that were displayed on the laptop monitors.

"A problem?" Carver asked.

"No . . . it's nothing, really. Just a duplicated set of printouts of the gamma waves."

Ruth felt the hairs on her neck prickle. Those words, "it's nothing," so often led to something important. She flicked through to her own copy, finding the trace of gamma waves for all three victims blocked one above the other and printed in landscape orientation on a sheet of A4 paper.

"No," she said, protective of the integrity of the unit she had once managed. "They're all correctly labeled. There's no duplicate."

The psychologist tugged the sheet of paper from his file and folded it so that Eddings's gamma wave trace sat directly above Professor Tennent's. "See?" he said.

"Those are from two different monitors." Ruth pointed to the evidence labels for each. "See? Scientific Support doesn't make mistakes like sticking the same label on two different pieces of evidence. But . . ." She took her own sheet and tore it in two, then laid Eddings's wave trace over the top of Tennent's and held it up to the light.

"They are identical," Carver breathed. "If the SSU didn't duplicate the evidence, then the killer must have."

"The killer couldn't risk bringing Professor Tennent alive all the way from London to Liverpool," Ruth said. "So he improvised, using Eddings's wave trace because *Catch the Gamma Wave* wouldn't be complete without it."

A few people have worked out the meaning of *Catch the Gamma Wave*. Good for them. Interesting to note that Kharon is among them. He really is keen. Makes me almost nostalgic for the indentured apprentice system of the fifteenth century: the master painters of Bruges put dozens of eager pupils to work on the more mundane aspects of their creations—perhaps I should do the same with Kharon.

But would he have the stomach for the messier aspects of my craft? Preparing the components of my works is physically and mentally challenging. Would Kharon have what it takes to create a *Catch the Gamma Wave*? Not only the abductions—recording the heartbeats and brain waves of dying men takes a bold spirit and a steadfast mind. I'm no sadist; it wasn't easy to watch John Eddings and Dillon Martin suffer. I shaved their heads for better contact with the sensors in the EEG cap, hoping that I'd get what I needed on the first take. I taped their mouths—not needing to hear them scream. I'll confess it was distressing having to make several attempts before it came right, and I prolonged their deaths only for as long as it took to get good EEG traces.

By the third attempt, I swear John Eddings was the very image of Titian's *The Penitent Magdalene*. Those eyes! Their look of supplication made me want to take a few digital images for the album. But it wouldn't be true to the nature of the artwork, so I didn't—I'm a purist on that point.

The Major Incident Room was almost empty. Now that they had two crime scenes to investigate, available staff were stretched thin. DCI Carver had requested extra help for house-to-house inquiries around the old Dingle Station, but budget cuts meant they simply didn't have the capacity to pull in the number of officers they needed. As divisional commander, Superintendent Wilshire had begun drafting in volunteers. One of them—a new face—had been flitting in and out of the office all morning, picking up any spare keys from the board, fulfilling the mundane task of checking on supplies of evidence bags and scene kits in the pool cars. Many volunteers had day jobs, though, and it would take a day or so to set up rotas.

While others knocked on doors, Detective Sergeant Ruth Lake sat in front of two computer screens, scanning the crowd at *Think Outside the Box*, comparing it with events at the defunct Dingle Station the night before. They were still waiting on the Matrix team's videos, so she had to rely on video clips and photographs posted on social media, flipping between screens and clicking through multiple tabs.

Arsonists and murderers were two categories of serial offenders known to linger at crime scenes. House blazes, dump sites, graveyards were haunted by the perpetrators, and many police forces routinely maintained covert surveillance on such places long after fires were extinguished, bodies removed, and mourners gone. So, mind-cramping though it was, Ruth gave her full attention to the work.

But psychopathic serial offenders are never easy to spot: like chameleons, they mimic the humans around them, blending in with the pack, and while Ruth had plenty of material available, it was mostly poor quality and focused on the exhibit, making a difficult job almost impossible.

An hour in, Ruth became vaguely aware of someone hovering in the doorway. She glanced up, expecting to see the volunteer: he'd been trying to catch her eye for the past hour.

She recognized immediately the tall, fair-haired man at the door.

"Looking for DS Lake?" he said.

"You found her."

She paused the recording and he strode to her desk in easy, fluid strides. A runner, like herself, she guessed. His eyes flicked from whiteboards to desks, sucking up information on the case. Not that she blamed him; she'd done the same, often—it was just something cops did. Like noticing that he carried a bagged DVD in his big mitt of a hand: the CCTV from last night's crime scene.

"Good of you to bring this in person. Sergeant Rayburn, isn't it?" she said, although she was in no doubt at all.

That drew a quizzical look. "Have we met?" he asked.

"No." Ruth remembered Rayburn from an internal memo that had gone the rounds a month ago. It announced Rayburn's relocation from Greater Manchester Police and his appointment as head of the Matrix team.

His eyebrow quirked at the lack of explanation. "You seem sure." He spoke in flat, slightly nasal Mancunian tones.

"I am," she said, not wanting to give the more honest, and more loaded, "I would remember," because Rayburn was handsome, and he knew it, just as surely as Ruth knew he was chatting her up.

"This is great, thanks," she added, and meant it.

"Don't suppose the car park cameras gave you anything?" he said.

Ruth shook her head. "The cams were shot out with an air rifle just before dark."

He jerked his chin in acknowledgment. "You could try canvassing the businesses that use the casemates," he said. "They might have security cams."

"We already thought of that," she said. Tunneled into the bedrock and fronted by solid steel doorways, the "casemates"—fortified storage units—were practically bombproof.

"You don't sound hopeful."

"They survived two world wars; it's not likely the owners would feel the need for security cams." She shrugged. "But we'll try."

"You *are* going to search them, though?" he said.

Ruth gave him a blank stare; Rayburn was expecting far too many answers for his one small, courteous act.

His smile somehow managed to convey both apology and mischief.

Her phone rang and she picked up, thinking Rayburn would take the hint and clear off.

It was Sergeant Naylor, who was in charge of house-to-house. "We've got an eyewitness," he said. "He was visiting the gym last night. Says he saw a man in black climbing the rock."

"Did he get a look at the face?"

"Sorry, Ruth. Climber was wearing a hoodie."

"Didn't challenge him?" she said, aware of Rayburn at her elbow.

"He was properly kitted out—rope, harness, and whatnot—and being just outside the gym, the witness thought he was getting a bit of practice on a real wall."

Ruth thought the ninja clothing might have given him pause. "Could you double-check contact details before you let him go?" she asked. "I might want him to take a look at anything we get off the video clips."

As she hung up, she leveled her cool gaze at Rayburn, still by her side, peering at the frozen image on her computer screen. "Did you forget something, Sergeant?"

"Rob," he corrected.

She waited calmly, relying on silence to unnerve him.

After a pause that seemed reflective rather than rattled, he said, "Is it true what they say about you?"

"I don't know," Ruth returned, draining her tone of any emotion that might suggest that she in any way cared. "What do they say?"

"You know—that thing with the faces."

He wanted her to say "super-recognizer," but she wasn't going to fall into that trap. Saying you're better than 98 percent of the population at remembering faces was too much like bragging, and "braggart" was not a label you wanted pinned to your lapel in any cop shop.

So she tilted her head, said, "That 'thing'?"

"They say you know everyone in this building."

"Not true," she said.

He smiled, and she saw he was enjoying himself. "My mistake." He took a moment to rephrase. "They say that you know everyone in this building *by sight*."

It would be churlish to deny it outright.

"Maybe," she said.

"Cool."

That surprised her: most men thought it freaky, rather than cool.

"A lot of cops are good with faces," she said aloud.

"Not me," he said. "Half the time I can't recognize my own reflection in the shaving mirror."

"You want to lay off the juice, Rob," she said.

He surprised her again, this time with a laugh. Most men would have taken offense.

"Well," he said, "I can see you're busy . . ."

"Yeah," she said.

The speculative look in his eye, the quick glance away, the sharp intake of breath all told her what was coming.

"I don't suppose—"

"No," she said.

"You don't know what I was going to say."

"Yes, I do." He was going to ask her out. She saw it, just as clearly as she saw the three stripes of rank on his epaulettes.

He lifted his chin and stared at her for a second, then he huffed a laugh. "Okay, I'll let you get back to it," he said.

"Thanks for this, though," she said, to his retreating back. Rob Rayburn was a good sport, she had to give him that. But work relationships were always a bad idea, and that went double for a woman.

The Matrix van's superior CCTV technology produced much better-quality footage than the mobile phone videos she had been watching, and within minutes of Rayburn leaving, Ruth had worked out an efficient strategy. It was easier to work backward from the Matrix video of the crowd gathered on the gymnasium car park, retro-matching individuals to faces recorded at the first crime scene, scouring the footage for anyone who seemed unnaturally focused or still, or who seemed to be relishing the crowd's appreciation of the show.

A good number of groupies appeared in both recordings. She made a note of the time stamp on each, screen-grabbing the relevant images ready for printing and distribution. Alongside the simply curious and thrill seekers were the usual proportion of troublemakers, petty thieves, and drug peddlers you'd expect to see at any public gathering. Ruth's exceptional ability meant she could recognize faces even if she'd seen them only once—months, or even years, before. She'd spotted some wolves among the sheep at the second scene: a couple of bail absconders, a pickpocket, and a man wanted for sexual assault. She made a note to send officers to the pickpocket's house. The absconders would be trickier, but with luck, they would turn up at another scene, and this time, the police would have their photos to hand. If nothing else, they would clear up a few outstanding crimes.

The majority of the crowd were there for the thrill of it, though—the young and trendy in their designer gear stood alongside graffiti artists wearing paint splashes on their street clothes like badges of honor. Ruth wondered if their stencil graffitist was among them. A few entrepreneurs were plying a more honest trade: she saw someone selling selfie sticks and another had an armful of T-shirts emblazoned with the *F* logo.

Carver appeared at the door, and Ruth gave him a nod.

"Got a minute?" he asked.

"Sure."

He checked the room. They were alone except for the one detective who was still grinding through hours of recordings and traffic cam stills, hoping to find the white Ford Transit used to abduct the professor.

Even so, she saw Carver decide that they needed greater privacy.

"My office in five?" he said.

"I'll come now." She glanced at the screen, ready to note the time stamp before logging out, and her eye snagged on a face in the crowd. Her heart stopped.

It can't be.

From across the room Carver said, "Ruth?" She heard concern in his voice. "Are you all right?"

Ruth doubted if Carver would make sense of the storm of emotion she felt right now, but he would recognize a lie. Carver read lies in shades of bile green.

She said, "Nauseated, that's all."

That much was true: her heart thrummed in her chest and she fought a wave of nausea.

"Watching those things for a few hours would give you travel sickness," she went on, listening to herself burble when he of all people knew that she was usually laconic; explaining, when she never explained.

Carver locked gazes with her, but she switched her attention to the computer, took a screen grab, and saved the image, trying to make it look like a normal log-out.

A moment later, he was at her shoulder. He stared at the screen, a slight furrow between his brows, but she'd already shut down.

"So what's the news?" she asked, a little too brightly.

His eyes flicked to hers. His troubled expression told Ruth that he had seen right through her attempt at distraction.

"Let's finish this in my office," he said.

17

Carver didn't say a word all the way from the MIR to his office.

He closed the door after Ruth and asked her to sit, moving behind the desk, leaning across it, his fingertips braced on the desktop. "What's going on?"

"I . . . don't—"

"Stop, Ruth. I can see you're lying."

He seemed to look past her, but Ruth knew that he was staring at the air around her head, seeking out stray gleams of Judas light that would tell him she was concealing a lie behind a truth. She slowed her breathing, relaxed her shoulders, and said nothing.

He sighed. "You're not going to tell me, are you?"

"Nothing to tell," she said.

He shook his head and lowered himself into his chair. Carver was pushing himself beyond the limits of his delicate state of health, and Ruth suppressed a pang of guilt that she was adding to his troubles. "So," she said. "What's this about?"

"What?"

"The news," she said.

"Oh." He passed a hand over his eyes. "Blood analysis shows the scall you arrested last night was *five times* over the legal limit for THC."

"We already knew those two had been at the weed," she said.

"But we didn't know that your arrestee was half man, half kite."

He paused and she had the sense that words had passed between Carver and her rock-climbing toker. That a deal had been struck. "I'm guessing he won't be pursuing the civil prosecution?"

"You're in the clear," Carver said. "On that point. But—"

His phone rang. He answered, and a moment later he gave her a sharp look.

Ruth stood, ready to leave, but Carver raised a finger to stay her.

"John." His voice was taut. "I'm putting you on speakerphone—Ruth Lake is with me—can you repeat what you just said?"

The crime scene manager launched straight into the reason for his call. "We got a hit on IDENT1 from one of the laptops," he said. "Tyler Matlock. He's got a record for assault, ABH and GBH."

The Matrix team did the door-knock, taking no chances with a man convicted of both actual *and* grievous bodily harm. Matlock lived on the second floor of an ex-council block, four miles east of the waterfront. The "Enforcer" battered the door off its hinges on the second swing. Five officers in body armor piled in and cleared the one-bedroom flat in under two minutes.

"Matlock isn't here." Sergeant Rayburn gave Ruth Lake an apologetic shrug. "He could be at work."

"He's on disability," Ruth said. Preliminary checks said the man had been receiving personal independence payments since a car crash two years earlier.

"When did that ever stop any self-respecting Scouser from earning a dishonest crust?" Rayburn winked. "We'll leave the CSU to do their stuff, then."

Ruth watched him go, taking the time to give Matlock's small sitting room a final once-over. Crime scenes weren't her job anymore, but with three years of study and eight in the field, it was hard to break the habit of scene analysis.

It was midmorning, and sun streamed through the open curtains. Motes of dust sparkled in the wake of the assault on the place, but the flat had an atmosphere of long absence. In a room to her left, a tap dripped, ploshing into a mug or a full bowl.

A sixty-five-inch Sony Bravia took up half of one wall, and the cabinet beneath it was stacked with a Sky box, Xbox One console, and a Bose sound system that must have been the envy of his friends and the bane of his neighbors.

In the unforgiving light, she saw that a fine dust had settled on every surface, even the TV remote, and judging by the sizable dip in the seat cushion of his La-Z-Boy sofa, Matlock watched a lot of TV. A top-of-the-line gaming chair to the right of it crowded one corner, while a barbell and a stack of weight plates took up the space beneath the window. A pair of dumbbells sat next to the sofa, also lightly filmed with dust. No one had been in the place for a while.

On one wall, a full-length mirror. Arrayed around it, posters on weight training.

Ruth gave her stab vest a sharp tug, then hooked her fingers over the top to pull it away from her chest, listening to the heavy tread of the Matrix crew clomping down the stairs, delaying for a few more moments until she was sure Rayburn had gone. She said a quick hello to the CSIs logging in with the constable on duty and stepped into the hall to make way for them.

As she signed herself out of the scene, the door opposite opened. A sixtysomething woman sized her up from the doorway. Her hair was worn loose to the shoulders, dyed brown, and her face was fully made up, including ruby red lipstick and false eyelashes.

"Hi," Ruth said. "Do you know Mr. Matlock?"

"What's he done now?" the woman asked.

"You first," Ruth said, softening the rebuff with a smile.

The woman folded her arms and tapped her elbow lightly with one finger, as if considering how much she was willing to say. "I wouldn't say I *know* him," she said, at last. "But I know the type."

"Which is?"

"Let's see some ID."

Ruth's police stab vest identified her as police, but she dug out her warrant card anyway and waited while the woman scrutinized it.

Handing it back, the woman opened her front door wide and tilted her head, inviting Ruth in. "This could take a bit," she explained. "And Tyler's a man who comes and goes—wouldn't want him to catch me talking to the police outside his bashed-in front door."

Her name was Maria Reilly. Ruth stood in the doorway to her tiny galley kitchen while Maria brewed an excellent dark roast and filled in some of the background on Tyler Matlock's "type."

"Bane of the block, he is," she said. "When he isn't boozing, he's brawling. He'd steal the newspaper out your letterbox to save him a fifty-yard walk to the corner shop."

"He lives alone, then?"

The woman looked over her shoulder. "What makes you think that?"

"All that boozing and brawling," Ruth said. "And his flat has a definite whiff of bachelor about it."

Maria left the coffee to drip while she warmed a jug of milk in the microwave. "Fact is, *she* never had much say in what went on."

"Oh yeah?" Ruth said.

"*You* know the story, girl—feller thinks he's got God-given privileges just because he's got the right equipment in his trousers."

"So where's Mrs. Matlock now?"

"Walked out six months after the car crash."

Ruth heard a note of triumph in the woman's voice.

"What d'you know about that?"

"What d'you mean, what do *I* know?" Now she sounded defensive. *Afraid she'd get Matlock's wife into trouble, perhaps?*

"Here—" The woman shoved a mug of coffee into Ruth's hand. "Help yourself to milk and sugar."

Ruth added a dash of milk and breathed the nutty aroma before taking a grateful sip, giving Maria time to calm down.

"First decent cup of coffee I've had all day," she said.

Maria gave a satisfied nod, lifting her own cup to her lips.

"We're investigating a series of murders, Maria," Ruth said.

The woman's eyes widened. "And you think he—?"

"We just need to locate him. And I need to know that Mrs. Matlock is okay, so anything you can tell me . . ."

Maria gazed at Ruth over the rim of her coffee cup, drumming her perfectly manicured fingernails musically on the porcelain.

"I don't want to get her in any bother."

Ruth didn't respond to that, not wanting to make promises she couldn't keep.

After a moment, Maria sighed. "What d'you wanna know?"

"Tell me about the car crash." Ruth sensed this would be the easiest place for her to start.

"Shelly—Mrs. Matlock—was driving. He'd had a skinful—*as per*. Phoned her to come and fetch him from a pub out Aigburth way. This was half eleven at night. It was icy, she skidded. Nothing serious, just a bit of a fishtail, you know. He punched her in the face to remind her to pay attention. She crashed the car."

"Mr. Matlock received compensation for his injuries," Ruth said.

Marie arched an eyebrow. "Oh, he got compo, all right. Claimed it off her insurance. Didn't mention the fact he'd knocked her silly a split second before they hit a lamppost. Made sure *she* didn't, either." She smiled bitterly. "She had the last laugh, though. Packed her things, cleaned out their bank account, and done a flit the day the compensation come through. The exact same week he was due to get out of hospital."

"His flat's well kitted out for a man on benefits," Ruth said.

"That'll be the compo he got off the council. That was the winter they run low on grit—*he* claimed they hadn't salted the road right."

Ruth did a quick calculation. "This'd be, what, eighteen months ago?"

"About that."

"Has Shelly been home since?"

"This was never a *home* for her, love. And no, she hasn't been back; her own mother doesn't know where she is. Took herself out of harm's way."

"So you've no idea where she is?"

"I get the odd postcard; not signed, but they're from Shelly all right." Her face softened into a smile. "Always nice places."

"It's an extreme move, breaking ties with her family . . ." Ruth let the comment hang; an observation often yielded more than a direct question.

"Safer for her, safer for them."

"Did he ever threaten *you*?"

Marie took a sip of coffee, and Ruth saw a shadow flicker behind her eyes.

"I knocked on his door, one time. He had his music blasting and him and his mates were giving it some welly after Liverpool had won a big match. Now, I was a barmaid—worked bars and pubs round here for thirty years before I retired—so I'm used to dealing with drunks and dickheads. But when I asked him, nice like, if they wouldn't mind keeping the noise down, he stepped outside, told me he'd do whatever he effing wanted. And if I bothered him again, he'd break every finger in both my hands."

"What a charmer."

"Oh, that was only for starters. Said if I ever so much as *looked* his way he'd cut my cat into tiny pieces and post him to me in a jiffy bag."

18

DC Ivey knocked on Carver's office door just as Ruth Lake had finished bringing him up to date on Matlock. The young constable carried a Samsung tablet in one hand.

"Matlock bought all three laptops on eBay six months ago," Ivey said. "Delivered to his address, paid for on his PayPal account, which is linked to his bank account."

"Any other purchases?" Carver asked.

"A commercial-grade meat locker."

"Delivered where?" Not that it was likely the Ferryman would have the thing delivered anywhere that would reveal his true identity.

"An empty shop in Walton." The north end of the city. "The landlord says a charity calling itself Community Art rented it for a week, last October, as a pop-up gallery."

"I'm guessing the community exhibition never happened."

Ivey shook his head. "I canvassed the shop owners on the street. One of them remembered a large item being delivered—it stuck in his head because within a couple of hours, two guys in a white van rolled up and took the package away again."

"Description?"

"That's it: 'two guys, white van.'"

"Well, someone must've been there to take the original delivery," Ruth suggested. "And to let the removals men into the shop to take it away again."

"Nobody saw them," Ivey said. "The manufacturer put me in

touch with the firm who made the delivery, and I spoke to the driver. He makes twenty or thirty deliveries a day, and this was six months ago—he couldn't even remember the *shop*, never mind who signed for it." Ivey's light blue eyes shone with excitement. "Is Matlock our man?"

"Not necessarily," Carver said. "We can't rule him out as a victim yet."

"But he isn't on our missing persons list," Ivey said. "He hasn't even been reported missing."

"Even so, he hasn't been seen for months," Ruth said.

"His fingerprint's on one of the laptops."

Ruth shook her head. "You can't age a fingerprint."

Ivey's high forehead wrinkled; he still wasn't getting it.

"Tom," Carver said, "we know the Ferryman keeps body parts . . ."

Carver saw him reevaluating.

"Oh, so the fingerprints . . ." Ivey blanched, and he closed his own hands into fists.

"Any activity on his credit cards?" Carver asked.

"His PIP benefits are still being paid, and his bank account was accessed five times after he dropped off the radar. I could find out where he withdrew the money."

"Okay, good." Carver turned to Ruth. "If he *is* still alive, do we have any idea where Matlock might lie low?"

"His neighbors don't know and they don't care. It's been quiet with him off the block; they're in no hurry to bring him back. And his family haven't heard from him since last autumn. They don't seem too broken up about it."

Carver tugged one ear. "Let's face it: Tyler Matlock hasn't been reported missing because he will not be missed."

Ivey's tablet buzzed, and he glanced at it, his eyes widening. "I think you should see this, sir."

The young detective enlarged the frame and the three of them huddled around the screen.

"This is Instagram; I've been following Kharon—the fan who put together the video of *Think Outside the Box*. He just posted a new video, put together from last night's scene."

They watched as Kharon's new "appreciation" of the Ferryman's *Catch the Gamma Wave* unfolded on screen.

It began with an image of the three laptops viewed over the heads of the crowd. The camera pulled back to get an overview of the crowd itself; the video was steady and the focus sharp.

"He couldn't get that kind of clarity using a smartphone," Carver said. A glance at Ruth told him she understood completely.

"I'll take another look at the Matrix team's recording," she said.

If Kharon was using a portable camcorder, he would be easier to identify in the crowd.

The footage segued to an archive recording of the Liverpool Overhead Railway: trains approached the screen in faded black and white. Spliced between these short passages, close-ups of the ECG and EEG traces recording the victims' deaths. The video faded to black, and for a moment, Carver thought it had finished. Then a pinpoint of light appeared. It grew bigger and brighter, and he became aware of variations at the edges of the screen: tunnel walls, rushing past.

The camera accelerated toward the light, interspersed by microsecond bursts of the victims' gamma wave EEGs.

Carver became aware of a high, thin whistle. The light became unbearable and, simultaneously, the whistle rose to a scream. Then, a blinding white flash.

Carver winced, shutting his eyes against a nauseating disorientation.

"His version of 'going into the light,' I suppose," Ivey said.

His heart hammering, Carver worked on controlling his breathing and stilling the jittery need to escape the room, but the scream lived on in his head.

Ruth looked at him, a question in her eyes. Did he want her to step in?

Carver gave a minute shake of his head.

"This Kharon calls himself a fan," Carver said. "But what if his links with the Ferryman are stronger than that? What if Kharon is helping directly?"

"Well, if he is, he's not doing such a good job," Ivey said. He was scrolling down the screen as comments came in from Kharon's followers. "This post is getting a lot of negative comments . . ." He read out a few: "The Ferryman is a FAKE"; "Photoshopped phony." Another had written, "Recording 1 and 3 are identical. I'm unfollowing. Bye, suckers!"

"They've worked out that Professor Tennent's heart and EEG trace were a duplicate of Eddings's," Ruth said.

Carver nodded. "That could be useful. If his followers turn against him, somebody might be willing to turn him in."

19

Well, this is fun. Four thousand followers lost overnight—which is not a major issue. What I *do* have a problem with is that, apparently, I'm supposed to sit here and listen to useless tossers who never created anything of worth in their sorry lives telling *me* I don't have artistic integrity.

Circumstance *forced* the compromise over Tennent's encephalographs. If they had anything between their ears, they would appreciate that.

Would I have preferred to bring Tennent back alive? Ideally, yes.

If the option to create an authentic gamma wave trace for him was there, would I have taken it? Of *course* I would.

Was I disappointed? Again, yes. But art, like life, sometimes requires compromise. If I'm guilty of anything, it's perfectionism—I set myself the highest standards. And, yet, watching Kharon's montage, I truly *cannot* understand their objections. *Catch the Gamma Wave* does exactly what I intended. The effect—the impact—is just as strong as if there really had been three different traces.

Just how many of those four thousand actually *noticed* the duplicate? Five? Ten, maybe? Less than a dozen train-spotting nerds with nothing better to do all day than sit in front of their computers fiddling with themselves. Obviously, they just *had* to share their nitpicking, shit-for-brains observations with the virtual world. Naturally, the herd followed, bleating about having been "lied to." Do they not know that ALL Art is a lie? Call it artifice, or illusion, trick, trompe l'oeil or whatever the hell you want, Art is a lie. The beauty of it is that it's the lie that brings us closer to the real truth.

20

DAY 4, EVENING DEBRIEF

Chief Inspector Carver asked the sergeant leading house-to-house inquiries at the Dingle scene to speak first. The apartment blocks nearby mostly had their backs to the escarpment, to take advantage of the views over the riverfront, and many of the occupants were young professionals who were still at work at the time the fun began, so the team had had a frustrating time of it.

"We're hauling PCSOs in to handle back-office duties as of tomorrow," Carver reassured him. "That'll free up some bobbies to help out. And we've got callouts ongoing to specials." He located Mick Driscoll, the shift sergeant, who was lurking at the back of the room. "How's that going?"

"We've got five on their way here, one who looks doubtful," Driscoll said. Being volunteer police, special constables were not required to drop everything and head for the nearest cop shop. "Still waiting to hear from a few."

A man at the back of the room sat up tall, a rainbow of color flashing around his head and shoulders and Carver was distracted for a moment. Then he saw Dr. Yi in the doorway, and he asked Ruth Lake to bring the meeting up to speed on inquiries into Matlock, their missing suspect.

Yi listened intently, and when DS Lake had finished, Carver said, "Any comments, Doctor Yi?"

The psychologist looked from Ruth to Carver. "You're wondering if Matlock could be your killer?"

"Or another victim," Carver said.

Yi folded his arms and mused a moment, his chin cupped in one hand. "He is thirty years old, which is in the right age range for this type of killer," Yi said. "And he doesn't have a regular job, which would leave him free to plan the abductions and murders. But he's also violent and impulsive—an alcoholic, judging by his neighbors' comments—which doesn't fit with the calculated planner we've encountered so far." He glanced again at Ruth Lake. "Is there any indication he has an interest in art?"

Ruth said, "His reading material seemed to consist of porno magazines; the closest I saw to art were a few bodybuilding posters on the wall of his sitting room."

"And his web searches are mostly porn related," Hughes added.

"Which, again, doesn't fit the profile," Yi said. "On the other hand, Matlock doesn't fit the victim profile too well, either."

"We have a victim profile?" Ruth asked.

"I misspoke," Yi said. "However, there are some common factors: John Eddings and Dillon Martin were twenty-three and twenty-five, respectively. Both were in heterosexual relationships. Both were healthy—mentally and physically—which follows the pattern for other missing males within the scope of this inquiry. In addition, several of the missing, including Eddings, had talked about dropping out to travel."

"To be fair, a lot of early- to midtwenties males talk about taking time out to travel," Ruth said.

Carver scratched his brow. "Who spoke to Eddings's family?"

A couple of hands went up—one was the FLO.

"Did anything pop?"

"He bought a flash apartment for cash two months before he vanished," the first detective said. "And it's not like he comes from money—his mum and dad live in a council flat in Netherfield."

"Lottery win," the FLO said. "He won two hundred K, decided to do the sensible thing and invest the bulk of it in property. It was in the *Liverpool Echo*—his mum showed me a cutting."

"Martin put his engagement on hold a week before he disappeared," DC Ivey said. "But his girlfriend seemed fine with that. He'd got a degree in engineering, after leaving the army, and was working for Phillip Jackson Group—they specialize in building engineering. They offered to half fund him for a master's—it looked like he was going places."

"All right," Carver said. "Let's see if we can find out more about Matlock. Track down his drinking buddies. Did he have a favorite pub? He was a football supporter—did he have a season ticket? Who did he go to matches with? We need to establish exactly when he disappeared."

"He's been missing for months, boss—that's not going to be easy."

This came from the gloomy detective who had made a big deal of tracing the suspect van.

Carver quelled an urge to snap back: intimidating the team would not get the job done. "Even so—" He racked his brain, trying desperately to recall his name again, gave up on it, and turned instead to the crime scene manager.

"What about the footwear marks on the rock ledge?" he asked.

"One belonged to the pothead arrested at the scene," Hughes said. "We got two partials we haven't been able to match, but according to the footwear database it's a right Adidas trail running outsole."

"Sorry to be such a ray of sunshine today," Ruth said. "But that's in the top fifty most popular sports shoes."

"On the positive side, we got some unique features on it," Hughes said. "So find us someone to match it to and"—he lifted one shoulder—"Bob's your uncle."

This gave rise to cynical laughter, which at least provided some relief from a bad news situation. But the bad news wasn't over.

Teams had searched and cleared all sixty-three storage units under the escarpment, and found just one casemate, which, to the embarrassment of the registered owner, was being used by a lessee to store stolen goods. Other than that, nothing.

Carver was beginning to sympathize with the gloomy detective; it felt like they were playing catch-up with the killer. He had put time and physical distance between himself and his victims, and he could set up his "exhibitions" at leisure, knowing he was ahead of their inquiries by many months.

"Has the Met had better luck with Professor Tennent, boss?" Ruth asked, and Carver realized he'd flipped out for a moment.

"They managed to extract a brief voice memo from Tennent's damaged smartphone," he said, trying not to sound too downbeat. "Tennent said he was going to meet a man called Charoneau." He spelled the word out, watching the detectives write it down.

"The first part of the name: C-H-A-R-O-N, is an alternative spelling of Kharon," he went on.

"So, this Kharon is helping the killer?" someone said.

It was a question Carver had asked himself, but he said, "Let's not jump to conclusions. 'Charon' is just an alternative name for the mythological Ferryman—a joke at Tennent's expense, maybe. For now, our Instagram Kharon is a person of interest, that's all."

He picked up where he'd left off. "In his voice memo, Tennent said the mystery caller named our two victims, Eddings and Martin, and claimed to have definitive proof of what happened to them. The professor agreed to meet in a public place, and they settled on the Theodore Bullfrog Pub.

"The original call was made on a burner phone," he added. "And the only DNA on the cord they found at the scene was Prof. Tennent's." Which reminded him—"Why is it taking so long to track the suspect van down?"

"We've only got one pair of eyes on that now, boss," Ruth said.

The glum detective, Gorman (Carver finally remembered his name again), spoke up: "He's not on ANPR, so he must have switched plates. I'm going cross-eyed searching CCTV for white vans with reflective windows now."

Hard not to see the day as a complete bust, but morale was as much Carver's job as were management decisions. So he told everyone that they had done a good job eliminating false leads; the footwear impression had given them physical evidence that could link their perpetrator to one of the scenes; and they now had two persons of interest they needed to trace, interview, and eliminate.

There was little else he could do, and he'd already exceeded his allowed hours for the second day running, so he left Ruth Lake at the helm and caught a taxi home.

21

Ruth Lake sifted through a stack of video stills she'd screen-grabbed from the Matrix team's CCTV recording. Buried beneath the others was one that she had kept to herself.

The man had been standing in a group with three others: two men and a woman. Unlike the rest, he hadn't been recording the scene. Hands in his pockets, shoulders hunched, back toward her, this man should have looked like any other dark figure on the video, but seeing him, she'd felt a prickling of uncertainty in the lizard part of her brain.

Ruth had learned to trust the primal instincts of fight or flight; the limbic system could trigger evasive action before the conscious brain was even aware of threat. So she'd paid attention. A second later, the man had turned to one of his companions, and, *Oh, jeez . . .*

And when Carver asked was she all right, her secondary survival instincts had straightaway kicked in: show no weakness; hide the truth.

Now, knowing that she was safe from curious eyes, she stared at that face frozen in profile. Dark hair, buzz-cut sides, with a knife-sharp parting just above the ear; a longer hank tied in a topknot. Vandyke goatee and a nose ring. *God, he's changed so much!* But scrutinizing his face, she saw that he still had the same intensity of expression.

The same anger, too? she wondered.

Adam Black, nine years on.

What the hell is he doing with this rabble? Ruth knew the answer to the question even as she posed it: Adam was with the rabble because he had always been drawn to trouble.

Should have told Greg Carver.

But the explanations that must follow, the memories that would rekindle, the emotions—and, yes, the guilt—were excellent reasons to keep her mouth shut. Better to deal with this herself.

She remembered with painful clarity the last time she'd seen Adam Black, the look of hate on his face, the rage in his voice as he screamed at her to get out. She had convinced herself that he would calm down—was so sure of it that she had rung the next day. He'd hung up. She'd waited until the next week and tried again, and the week later, and the week after that. He hung up every time. She left it two weeks before ringing again, then three. After a couple of months, Shauna answered the phone. She was kind but said that Adam didn't want to speak to her. Every month for a year Ruth had dialed his number. He never forgave her, and he never spoke to her again.

At the end of that year, just before her final exams, and after yet another rejected call, Ruth had been summoned to her personal tutor's office. Shauna sat across from him, and she looked close to tears.

The room seemed to close in from the edges, and sudden fear scrabbled at her insides.

"Is something wrong? Is Adam—?"

"Adam's fine," her tutor said.

"He asked me to come and speak to you, Ruth." Shauna was a big woman, and she had a heart as big and soft as her size twenty frame. Ruth could see this was hurting her.

"You know how to reach me," she said, confused by the woman's formality, by her grim looks.

"Yes," Shauna said. "But—"

"Why didn't you ring me—why put me through *this*?"

"Adam wants you to stop," the older woman blurted out.

"Stop what?" Ruth glanced at her tutor. He avoided her gaze.

"You *know* what."

Shauna's voice had a sharp rasp she'd never heard before, and Ruth stared at her, surprised.

"The phone calls," Shauna said. "He wants you to leave him alone."

Ruth felt a muscle jump in her face.

She looked again at her tutor, but he was staring at his hands, clasped in front of him on the desktop.

"He doesn't mean that."

Shauna sighed, and Ruth blundered on, unable to stop herself: "Look, if we could just sit down, face-to-face, I think we could straighten this out. He's built a wall between us, that's all. I understand why, but—"

"For God's *sake*, Ruth!"

Ruth flinched; Shauna never raised her voice.

"I'm sorry," Shauna said, "but this harassment has to *stop*."

"I h-haven't been harassing him," she stammered. "I just—I . . . I want him to understand."

"You're *harassing* him—and if you persist, he *will* take this to the courts."

"He can't."

"Yes, he can. And I will do everything in my power to help him."

Ruth stared at Shauna, trying to hear what she was saying over the booming in her ears.

"I know you want to work with the police after your degree," Shauna said. "And I don't want to put that in jeopardy. Which is why *I'm* here, and not the police. But if you call Adam just *one more time*, we *will* take it further."

Ruth had responded with a sarcasm it embarrassed her to recall.

"Let's get it over with," she'd sneered, pulling back her sleeves and offering her wrists, ready for the cuffs. "Arrest me. 'Coz I *won't* stop caring for him just because he's too bloody-minded to have a sensible conversation!"

"Listen to yourself!" Shauna said. "Can't you see it's *not right*, what you're doing?"

"No," Ruth said. "No, I can't." She began shaking. She couldn't control it.

"Well, I've tried, and I'm too tired to keep on trying," Shauna said. "You're not *listening*. I can't keep explaining if you won't listen." After a moment, she seemed to reconsider and went on in a gentler tone, "I'm sorry, love. I didn't come here to upset you. But you *have* to leave him *alone*."

"I can't," Ruth said again. She was crying now, tears streaming down her face; and she was angry that she was crying in front of her tutor; angry that he was hearing things she had tried to keep secret from her university life; furious with Shauna and Adam for putting her in this position.

She wiped her face with both hands and clenched them into fists at her sides.

"I love him," she said, her voice choked with emotion, but she regained control by digging her nails into her palms. "He's all I've got."

"Nevertheless," Shauna said, and Ruth saw steeliness in the set of the older woman's jaw, in her steady gaze. "He's a child—"

"Oh, come *on*—"

"A 'looked after' *child*, in local authority care," Shauna said, speaking over her protestations. "And as his legally appointed carer, it's my responsibility to keep him safe."

"*Safe*? What d'you think I'm going to do to him?"

"You're already doing it," Shauna said quietly.

They stared at each other in hostile silence for a few moments, then Shauna spoke again. "Your tutor is witness," she said, and Ruth saw a flash of alarm in his eyes. "You have been warned. If you try to contact Adam in any way: by phone, e-mail, social media, or letter, he will go to the police. If you call the house to speak to me, I will construe that as an infraction. If you happen to see him on the street, turn around and walk away—" Ruth shook her head. "Or he *will* prosecute, and he *will* win."

Ruth clasped her arms across her chest to still the shaking; her knees threatened to buckle under her.

Her tutor cleared his throat and spoke for the first time since Ruth's outburst.

Practically whispering, as if he was afraid she would blow up again, he said, "Even if the harassment isn't proved, Adam could get a restraining order. But it wouldn't look good, having something like that on your record."

Shauna nodded in grim satisfaction. "Did you hear that? I'm telling you this for your own good," she went on, relentless. "If you care about your future . . ." She left the rest unsaid.

Ruth took a breath and looked around her. The office was deathly quiet; everyone else had gone home or was out knocking on doors. Nine years ago, yet thinking about that day still had the power to send shock waves through her. That was the last time she had spoken to Shauna. She picked up her mobile, selected the phone icon, and stared at it until the numbers blurred.

Uttering a gasp of disgust, she flipped the phone over and slapped it facedown on the photograph. *Nine years, and not a word.* She didn't owe Adam a thing. *And what if he makes good on his threat? Complains of harassment even after all these years?*

She would take this to Carver, say she'd just found him in her latest trawl-through—he wouldn't suspect a thing. Adam would be picked up and brought in for questioning like any other lowlife.

But a second later, she was keying in Shauna's number from memory. One final hesitation, then she thumbed the dial icon.

Shauna answered immediately.

"Shauna, it's Ruth Lake."

"Ruth?"

"Please, don't hang up."

"Of *course* I won't, love," Shauna said. "What's the matter?"

"Adam," Ruth said, reaching for the calm that she was known for as a cop, had believed was an immutable part of her nature. "D'you know how I can reach him?"

A pause.

"I'm police now," Ruth said, silently cursing the clumsiness of her phrasing. "I mean this is police business. I don't want to hassle him, but I do need to ask him a few questions."

"Oh, love . . ." Shauna said, and the ground seemed to drop away.

He's dead, Ruth thought. *I got it wrong. This man isn't Adam at all. Adam is dead, and no one told me.*

Shauna was speaking and she forced herself to listen: "He moved out years ago. Six . . . seven, was it?"

"He didn't keep in touch?"

"For a while," Shauna said. "But you know how it is."

"He didn't say where he was living?"

"No . . . See, he just sent birthday and Christmas cards. Handmade, though," she added, with a hint of pride. "He always was good at art."

"So you've no idea how I could contact him?"

"Sorry, Ruth, love," Shauna said. "He never gave a return address."

Ruth thanked her and hung up. She'd done all she could; now would be a good time to tell Greg Carver what she'd found.

Instead of which, she began typing Adam Black's name into the PNC database.

22

Greg Carver lay on his bed, waiting for sleep to claim him. An hour later, he was wide awake, staring at the ceiling. He decided he would count backward from one hundred; if he hadn't dropped off by then, he would abandon the attempt. Ten minutes later, he sat up, feeling simultaneously exhausted and wired. This wasn't getting any easier.

His eyes slid to the two sleeping pills lying next to a half glass of water on his nightstand. He would regret it in the morning, but what the hell.

He swallowed both at once, grimacing against the bitterness, wishing for the millionth time that he could find oblivion in a quart bottle of whisky, like he used to. But that was out of the question—even the smell of the stuff gave him wild flashbacks and hallucinations.

"Christ," he murmured, closing his eyes and waiting for the drugs to kick in.

The bed began to rock, and his eyes flew open. The ceiling seemed to grind down in shuddering motions, then recede again.

Vertigo. It'll pass.

The rocking increased. He screwed his eyes shut and held on to the sides of the mattress to steady himself.

He thought he caught a faint whiff of whisky, though he hadn't had the stuff in his flat in three months. The aroma asserted itself, despite his rationalization. Damp hay, honey, a hint of caramel. His favorite single malt—

The bed tilted alarmingly, and, startled, he opened his eyes again. He was in his sitting room. Now the reek of whisky was overpowering, choking. He had a bottle in his hand; he felt it slip through his fingers, heard the dull *thunk* as it fell to the rug.

He opened his eyes.

Gun!

A flash of flame.

PAIN.

Silence . . . Shadows.

Ruth stared into his eyes.

You're dreaming. That's over—finished with. Wake up.

Bzzzziiiippp! He recognized the auditory hallucinations he often experienced after sleep.

The realization summoned him back to a kind of reality. He was in his own bed, in his apartment.

You need to move.

Even before he tried, he knew he could not. *Sleep paralysis.* He knew what would follow: his half-aware state would fail him, and he would be dragged back to that night; to the dark presence, oozing malice like an evil stench. To terrifying vulnerability, and powerlessness.

The room seemed to darken.

It's happening. For God's sake, MOVE.

His heart was hammering, but his limbs refused to obey him. He drove every ounce of his strength into the muscles of his right arm. And felt his finger twitch. *Really* felt it.

Wake up, wake up, wake up.

But he felt himself slipping back into sleep. He made one final effort. His right hand jerked and it felt as if he were tearing his real self from his dream self. He could swear he heard the ripping sound as the two separated.

He swung his legs over the side of the bed, despite his dizziness and disorientation, terrified that otherwise he would be clawed back, paralyzed and defenseless, into that nightmarish state.

His phone lay on the bedside table. He picked it up and thumbed to the phone log. A dozen outgoing calls to Emma, his wife. She hadn't been near since his release from the hospital or replied to a single call—hadn't even texted. He tried one more time.

23

Ruth Lake logged out of her computer and checked the time. With the evening briefing wrapped up, Greg Carver would be waiting for his lift home. Checks on Matlock had confirmed that he had been working part time as a security guard at a pub in the city center, was known to be handy with his fists, and was miraculously free of the debilitating health problems he'd manifested during a Department of Work & Pensions benefits assessment last summer. His place of work had not seen him since the previous autumn.

The pickpocket working the crowd at the gymnasium car park had been charged with theft and possession of stolen goods, and house-to-house officers had found a witness who saw a white van with "shiny windows" parked on the pavement of Grafton Street, which overlooked the sandstone cliff, forty minutes before *Catch the Gamma Wave* lit up. She'd been on her way to do some shopping; her return home was delayed by the police road blocks and all the "hoo-ha" as she called it, so she couldn't say when the van had driven away, but it was gone when she was finally allowed through an hour later. The witness didn't get a plate number, but a detective would start checking CCTV in the area first thing.

Just another dull day at the office.

Ruth's desk phone rang and she scooped up the receiver, trapping the earpiece against her shoulder as she shrugged on her jacket. The caller announced himself as a "contact resolution officer"—a call handler in the old system. "What's up?" Ruth said.

"I've got someone on the line, wants to speak to DCI Carver, but I can't raise him."

"Okay," Ruth said, raising her voice over a murmur of conversation and shuffling of chairs. "You can put them through to me."

"Sarge," he said, "I think it's your guy."

Ruth covered the mouthpiece with one hand and rapped on the desk with the other. People stopped midaction, all eyes on her. "You might need to cancel your evening, folks."

She didn't hear one groan of complaint.

Locating Ivey, she said, "Tom—see if the boss is in his office."

The young detective left at a run. A special constable—the new face she'd noticed the day before—jumped to his feet, eagerness in every muscle. She sent him in the other direction, then spoke into the phone: "Okay, put him through to my mobile, and get a trace on it."

Her mobile phone rang a few seconds later, and Ruth ducked out of the incident room to check on Ivey's progress. He stood halfway down the corridor, at Carver's door. He shook his head.

Hell.

Ruth exhaled, hit the answer icon, and announced herself.

"I know who you are," he said. "And I asked to speak to DCI Carver." His nasal Midlands tones were definitely overdone. Their dialect expert had established that the real accent underlying the fake was local to the Merseyside region, quite likely Liverpool.

"He's not in his office," she said, calm and polite.

"I warned him about not paying attention."

"And he listened to that." She waved Ivey over to her, miming "phone" as she continued to talk to the killer. He handed over his work handset, as Ruth continued:

"If you dial the emergency number, day or night, you will be put through to me, or the chief inspector."

By now, she had dialed Carver's number on Ivey's phone. It was switched off. "I've tried his mobile and can't get through," she told the caller.

"Looks like he *didn't* listen, then, doesn't it?"

"That's not the case," Ruth said. "Some parts of this building have signal blocking for security reasons." She was improvising. It was true that they had Wi-Fi blocking in some rooms—but there was no reason why Carver would be near one just now. "He could be consulting with senior ranks . . ."

The lie had the desired effect. "He should be," the killer said, and she heard a note of satisfaction in his tone.

"We're trying to locate him," she said.

The special constable appeared at the end of the corridor, shrugged his shoulders.

"As soon as we do locate him, I'll put him on the line," Ruth went on.

She mouthed *Keep looking* to the special, and he vanished through a doorway.

Ivey had stopped a PCSO coming the other way and was speaking softly to her. He looked over the woman's shoulder and pointed farther down the corridor.

"Stand by," Ruth said, hurrying toward him.

Ivey opened the door to the men's room. "Sir, we've had a call," he said. "Uh, sir?"

Ruth brushed past him; Carver was standing at one of the sinks, holding on to it like he was afraid to let go.

"Wait outside," she told Ivey. "Watch the door."

Ivey stepped outside, and the door swung closed behind him.

Carver lifted his gaze to hers in the mirror, his face gray, and she held up her phone.

"Him?" Carver said.

She nodded, then mouthed, *Are you okay?*

He nodded wearily, taking the phone.

Carver repeated the Ferryman's instructions aloud, naming the location. Ruth knew that the call handler would be listening in, and the Operational Command Center would already have dispatched rapid response units, but everyone on the murder inquiry needed to know the situation. She cracked the door and relayed the information to Ivey. "Tell the team to get moving," she said.

This done, she gestured to Carver to keep the conversation rolling, but by now he looked as gray as the vinyl flooring.

She held out her hand for the phone, and he managed to gasp, "Hang on a second, Detective Sergeant Lake wants to speak to you."

Ruth took the handset, but the Ferryman was gone.

"Contact Center, are you still on the line?" she asked.

"Still here," the calm, implacable voice said.

"Did you trace it?"

"He pinged off two towers, but it's not enough to triangulate. Sorry, Sarge."

Ruth glanced over to see Carver's reaction. He was leaning with his back against the wall, and he looked near collapse. She peeked outside and saw Ivey leading the pack as they piled out of the Major Incident Room. Some would inevitably make a pit stop at the men's room, and they did *not* need to see Carver like this.

She held up both hands, palms out. Ivey nodded, showing he understood, and promptly dropped a stack of files, swearing, apologizing, arguing, creating exactly the kind of commotion she needed to get Carver out of the men's room and into the nearest stairwell. She half carried her boss up a flight to the turn in the stairs and sat him down.

"Don't move," she ordered, although she doubted he would be able to stand unaided, let alone go anywhere.

She poked her head around the fire exit door and there was Ivey, still holding back the horde, face cherry red, cops cursing him for being in the way. He glanced up and she gave him the thumbs-up. With an agility that belied his earlier clumsiness, he scooped up the files and stepped aside. Ruth held the door, ushering the cops down the stairwell, shouting words of encouragement and instruction, but she stayed Ivey with a look.

When the last booted echo faded to silence, Ruth posted Ivey to guard the fire escape door and returned to Carver. He was sitting exactly where she'd left him, his head bowed, his elbows resting on his knees.

"What can I do?" Ruth asked.

"Nothing," he said. "I'm fine."

"Yeah," she said, "you look great." He gave her a sharp look, and she added, "boss."

He huffed a laugh. "One of these days, Ruth . . ." He stopped to take a breath.

"I'll go too far?" She raised an eyebrow. "We both know that ship sailed *long* ago. Do you need to go home?"

"No. It was just . . ."

"What?" she said. "A flashback?"

He didn't answer but hauled himself to his feet, using the banister. His color was a little better.

"Let's go," he said.

"Okay," she said. "Where?"

He kept hold of the banister with both hands and jerked his chin, indicating the direction his team had just taken.

"You're kidding," she said. "You can't go to a crime scene, the state you're in."

"Ruth—"

"You really want Wilshire to see you like this? Greg, I can't keep covering for you."

"I didn't know you were keeping a tally." The cold look in his eyes told her that he resented her help as much as he needed it.

"C'mon, now," she said. "There are things I can do inside this building, but out there, I have no control—everyone with a mobile phone will be recording us as soon as we turn up."

He held her gaze, and after a few seconds, he nodded. "What d'you suggest?"

"Go to your office," Ruth said.

"What am I supposed to do when I get there?"

"I dunno," she said. "Do what SIOs do—make a few calls, push some paper around." That drew another sharp look. "Sorry, boss, you really can't intimidate me looking like"—she couldn't think of a simile that didn't include the word "shit," so she gestured to his face and finished—"like . . . that."

He managed a bitter smile, and she softened.

"Give yourself space to breathe, huh?"

He hesitated, ran a hand over his face, but she knew he'd seen sense.

"I'll call you when I get there." She started down the stairs then turned back. "I get that you don't want to talk. But people are asking questions. For now, it's just a few sideways glances and mutterings over coffee, but you know how it can escalate."

He lifted his chin—a tiny gesture, barely a nod—but acknowledgment enough.

She tapped the stair rail lightly with the fingers of one hand, wondering how far she could push him, how far he would let her go.

To hell with it—if he doesn't hear it from me, he'll hear it from Wilshire, and by then it'll be too late.

"You need help, Greg. You need to open up to someone sometime."

She left him on the stairs, relieved Ivey of his guard duties, and they headed down to the car park together.

24

Ruth Lake flung the wheel left, then right at a dogleg; it was rush hour, and fully dark and—just to add a shot of adrenaline—it was beginning to rain. She was driving a patrol car, DC Ivey alongside her.

Every set of keys was gone from the board by the time they'd gotten to it. Cursing, Ruth had shoved through the fire doors onto the car park, hoping to hitch a ride, and saw the eager volunteer waiting for them. He held up a set of keys to a 3-series BMW—one of the relatively new fleet—very high-powered, very sleek.

"I swiped these before the lot went," he said. "Thought you might be needing something with a bit of poke."

"I like a man who shows initiative," Ruth said, and he grinned, handing her the fob. "What's your name again?"

He positively preened. "Parr, Sarge. Jason Parr."

Ruth nodded, letting him know she wouldn't forget, though she didn't offer him the chance to ride along: she needed to talk to Tom Ivey about what he'd just witnessed. She drove at speed, lights ablaze and sirens blaring, and traffic parted ahead of them. She wouldn't broach the subject, herself—but she knew that Ivey would eventually.

At the next set of traffic lights, she hit the strobe light and yelp button, forcing stationary traffic out of the way. From here they had a clear view for half a mile ahead, and she just caught the blues of another squad car disappearing around a kink in the road.

It was a twenty-five-minute drive from headquarters, but at this rate, they'd be there in half the time.

A message came through on the dashboard radio: three double-crewed units were on their way, and the Matrix team had been scrambled to take charge of managing the crowd.

This was a main arterial road to all points east of the city, densely populated, and bristling with shops and side streets.

"Is the boss all right?" Ivey had one hand braced against the dashboard, and the strained tone of his voice told her he was distracting himself from the driving conditions.

"He's fine," Ruth said, adding a blast of white noise as they hit a busy junction.

"He looked sick."

"Yeah, well, he isn't." She kept her eyes on the road. "And I don't want to hear any locker room gossip otherwise."

"I don't gossip," he said.

Ruth slid him a quick, appraising glance. Ivey was gay and still firmly in the closet at work; she believed him. "Well, that's okay, then."

"Even so, he did look sick."

Ivey was also dogged.

"Tell me about Parr."

Ivey shot her a look. "What's there to tell—Hobby Bobby, wannabe . . . ?" He shrugged.

"Yeah, well, we're going to be relying heavily on specials during this investigation, so you might want to rethink the attitude."

He shuffled in his seat. "Sorry, Sarge."

"I meant, what do you know about his background?"

"Nothing. Doesn't go much for small talk."

Ruth approved of that. "He's around a lot—does he have a job?"

"He said he's taking time out—he's applied to be real police, but they said he needs more experience."

"He's certainly getting that," she said, thinking he'd matched her hours over the last couple of days.

Ruth drove on for a few minutes, concentrating on the traffic, pedestrian crossings, two bikers playing tag, weaving in and out of the lanes in the wake of the squad cars ahead. Terraced rows of houses gave way to large detached properties set behind high walls; passing Liverpool Cricket Club, they skimmed the edge of the once-gated, private village at Cressington Park.

Less than a mile on from there, the road changed abruptly; the tree-lined central reservation, thick with daffodils, dwindled to a narrow strip of tussocky grass and finally disappeared altogether. Houses gave way to light-industry estates and retail parks, and still they blasted on, maneuvering at speed through the traffic.

"Okay, it should be coming up any second," Ivey said, consulting his mobile phone. "Just after the bend, there's a roundabout. Go right."

"What?" Ruth said.

"It's a right turn," he said.

"I heard you." She made the turn. "But you do know we're heading straight for the Operational Command Center?" The OCC was the recently opened complex that housed MSOC—which had brought together under one roof for the first time all the specialist Matrix Serious and Organized Crime units from across Merseyside.

"The bastard's taking the piss," Ivey said.

Ruth lifted one shoulder in acknowledgment. Hard to see another reason for the Ferryman to take his freak show to a location that was a twenty-five-minute drive outside of the city.

She slowed down, but seeing no sign that their killer had set out his stall at the OCC, she drove on. A couple of minutes later, turning a bend, she saw a uniform cop standing at the end of a coned-off road. She drew to a halt alongside him and saw to her left the jarring strobe of out-of-sync emergency vehicle light bars. Multiple emergency vehicles had converged in the cordoned-off section of roadway.

The constable directed them to a layby fifty yards distant. Ruth pulled in behind another patrol car, and they returned at a jog, logged in with the constable, and ducked under the police tape at the cordon.

Both sides of the narrow street were fenced off with rusting chain link. It wouldn't present much of a barrier, but it would at least discourage people from trying to evade them by cutting across the fields. This was brownfield land. Small light-industrial units that had thrived in the '50s and '60s had lost out to bigger firms in successive economic recessions, giving way to the leaner, more modern developments that were springing up in the area.

Lake jogged ahead of Ivey, squeezing through the cluster of police and private vehicles, passing empty, crumbling buildings. One plot had been razed to the ground; in the damp air, she could smell the sooty remains.

Why had the Ferryman come to this desolate place? Despite its proximity to the new Operational Command Center, it was very much out of the way for a man obsessed with publicizing his "art."

Turning a corner, she jolted to a halt.

On one giant concrete wall of a disused factory, a film was playing. It seemed to show a beating heart in an open chest. A crowd had already gathered, but the rain was coming down hard now, and many of them had retreated to their cars, parked on the raddled concrete in front of the building, watching the spectacle as if they were in a giant outdoor movie theater.

DS Rayburn was standing next to a Matrix van, and Ruth knew that one of his crew would be recording every face in the crowd.

"Hey, Rob," she said, sidling up to him, but keeping her eyes on the crowd. "Looks like we got lucky with the location."

"Yeah," he said. "This lot's kettled themselves good and proper. Nobody goes home tonight till we've had a good chat."

Ruth turned, tracking the projector beam, and located the projector in an adjacent building, third window along. Something moved behind the light.

"Is someone up there?" she said.

He handed her a pair of binoculars from his pocket. "Two of 'em."

The men were wearing *F*-logo T-shirts.

"They've barricaded themselves in, but we've got six men standing by. Soon as we've got enough warm bodies to contain this lot, we'll make a move."

Ruth handed the binoculars to him. "Looks like you've got half of Merseyside police already," she said, then did a double take. "Wait—are those Manchester Police uniforms I see?"

He laughed. "We've just finished a consultation and training exercise at the OCC," he said. "They were up for it, and it seemed rude to refuse."

Ruth smiled.

It was unlikely that the Ferryman would barricade himself in with the projector, but they would take no chances: the two projectionists would be arrested and questioned about any special knowledge of the Ferryman.

Someone called, "Sarge!" and both DS Lake and the Matrix team leader turned around.

On the wall behind them, the heart had begun to pulse fiercely. It continued for a few moments, then began to beat erratically. Finally, it slowed and stopped. The screen went black, and the crowd began to whistle, some getting out of their cars, applauding and whooping their approval.

"Jesus wept," Rayburn muttered.

Under normal circumstances, a derelict building like this would be the haunt of homeless people looking for a bed for the night, maybe thieves out to steal whatever metal was left in the place, but tonight, it was populated by the young and trendy. And they were applauding the death of another human being. Ruth wondered if Adam Black was among them.

Suddenly, the screen rekindled and the film began again.

"It's playing on continuous loop," Ruth said. She'd missed the titles, first time around. Now she read, "*Life Passes in a Heartbeat—the Death of Hope.*"

"You ready?" Rayburn said.

Ruth nodded. "Let's shut this horror show down."

25

Greg Carver waited for the last of the stragglers to come in and find a seat. The Matrix team and six members of his squad, together with uniform police and volunteers, were still interviewing members of the public corralled at the scene, so only seven detectives and one uniform cop were present. Dr. Yi was sitting quietly, a little apart from the rest, a notebook perched on his lap.

Carver hadn't allowed himself to think about what had happened in the men's room until he got to his office and closed the door. Ruth was right: he'd had a flashback. Emma had finally seen fit to return one of his calls—but only to tell him to stop bothering her with them. One minute he was arguing with her; the next, he was throwing up in a cubicle of the men's room. He hallucinated the smell of whisky again— was overwhelmed by the reek; it seemed his nightmares had begun to seep into his waking hours.

Mostly, the sequence of images faded as soon as he came to—it did feel like a coming to—as if he'd been absent, transported during those terrifying minutes to another place. He was grateful that those images faded—most of them, anyway. But one remained, vivid and terrifying—it was a lake of fire, and Ruth was drowning in it.

He was feeling better now; a few hours alone, thinking through what they had, writing up his decision log, had been oddly restful, and he felt he had greater clarity and was more in control than he had been since day one. Staring over the heads of the small gathering he saw two things: an orange afterglow—the adrenaline and aggression that had built up dealing with the crowd; and, faintly, a pale blue shimmer.

As soon as the murmurs died down, he got to business: "Tomorrow is going to be busy," he said. "News of tonight's events are already all over social media, and I expect the press will be baying at our door by the morning. So, while we have a quiet moment to think, I'd like opinions and ideas from everyone who feels they have something to say. Doesn't matter how wacky—speak up."

"Could there be a geographical connection?" This came from Ruth Lake. "He started at the north end of the docks and seems to have taken a line heading south and east of the city."

Carver looked to Dr. Yi. "Too soon to say," he said. "Although we should keep it in mind." He left the rest unsaid, but everyone knew that geographical profiling relied upon statistics: the bigger the number, the more reliable the data.

Carver was about to move on, when DC Ivey spoke up: "Don't you think he's just sticking two fingers up at us, sir? I mean, tonight's scene is only about half a mile from the new MSOC complex."

"Good point." Carver looked to Dr. Yi again. "One worth considering?"

Yi nodded thoughtfully. "Yes . . . your perpetrator could certainly be mocking you."

"Brain and heart," Carver said. "Mind and emotion . . . Is that some kind of message?"

"It'd be a first," a gray-haired detective said. "He hasn't said anything at all so far—sets up his 'exhibits' and lets his followers do the chat."

"It's not strictly true that he hasn't said anything," Dr. Yi said. "He communicates through the titles of his works. Which, as far as I can tell, are focused on his ability to take lives sadistically, to make the terror his victims experience a matter for public display, and his freedom to treat their bodies as objects to be taken apart and then rearranged as entertainment—or 'art' as he would term it."

Yi might have been reading a shopping list, for all the emotion surrounding his words.

"Okay," Carver said. "Does that help us in any way?"

This time he did see a hint of regret in the light around the psychologist. "Unfortunately, it only confirms that this really is all about the offender—to him, we are mere shadows."

26

Ruth Lake had been at her desk early: Carver had texted her to say he would be in at nine thirty; she was relieved that he was finally seeing sense, taking rest when he needed it.

With the briefing set for ten o' clock, the office was quiet, and she took the opportunity to run through the list of onlookers interviewed at the scene. Adam Black was not among them. But of course, names could be changed.

She had already searched the database of County Court Judgments, looking for debts against his name. He was in the clear, and he had no criminal prosecutions. She tried the online database "People Tracer" but could find no debt relief orders, independent voluntary arrangements, or registered bankruptcies. No marriages in the General Records Office database, either—at least not around Liverpool.

The electoral register listed eight Adam Blacks in the Merseyside area—none under his full name, Adam Saul Black—but to be certain, she would pay each plain "Adam Black" a visit. A name change was looking more and more likely; certainly, it wouldn't be the first time for Adam. Finding him was not going to be easy.

A message popped up in her inbox: John Hughes. There was plenty of trace at Tyler Matlock's flat, including fingerprints belonging to a wanted criminal—a scumbag who'd absconded while on bail for aggravated assault—but nothing that could help them right now.

Ruth skimmed the house-to-house inquiries team's report: nobody had been seen near Matlock's place for the last fortnight, though neighbors had seen a man—not Matlock—coming and going in the early days. They didn't see his face—and some had confessed they didn't want to. Better to stay out of any business that involved Matlock and his dodgy associates. It could be their absconder, could be the Ferryman, but in reality, it looked like another dead end.

The white Ford Transit van used to abduct Professor Tennent continued to elude them, although London Met had tracked it on the Automatic Number Plate Recognition system all the way through London on its way back to Liverpool the night of the kidnap, lost it for a bit around Fulham, then picked it up again forty minutes later, and had it in view all the way to Watford, about twenty-five miles from the abduction site. Then it vanished. ANPR on the route to the Ferryman's last exhibit was a bust, too. He must have switched plates again.

Ruth's desk phone rang. It was her contact at the Missing Persons Bureau.

"Hi, Terry," she said. "What've you got for me?"

"Ah, no, Ruth," he said. "This isn't about Adam Black."

She had flagged up his name with Terry the day before.

"Okay." She picked up a pen and dragged her notebook over.

"It's a new report," Terry said. "Just in, fits your criteria. And it's bang in the middle of your area."

"Go ahead," she said.

"Steve Norris." He spelled out the surname. "He's been missing for four days."

Putting his disappearance on the day after the first exhibit.

"He failed to show for a wedding anniversary party at his parents' house. They couldn't rouse him at his apartment, and when they checked, he hasn't been to work, but didn't call in sick; work colleagues can't reach him on his mobile or by e-mail, and friends haven't been able to raise him on social media, either."

"Thanks, Terry." DC Ivey had arrived, and she noticed him watching her, his thin face tense with anticipation. "What's his address?" she said into the phone; then, to Ivey: "Tom, find out if DCI Carver's in yet."

She jotted down Norris's address and was on her way out as Ivey reappeared from down the corridor.

"His door's still locked, Sarge," Ivey said.

It had been a very late night for the troops, and the office was still sparsely staffed, but the volunteer special, Parr, was there, as always. He seemed to haunt the MIR, ghosting down the corridors, lingering in the canteen.

He caught her eye, and the eager light in them said, *Pick me! Pick me!*, but Ruth wanted this done fast, so she let her gaze slide past him to a researcher, yawning loudly and staring dumbly at his computer screen. "I need you to contact a keyholder," she said.

He blinked, still not quite with it. "Who . . . ?"

She scribbled the address on a Post-it note. "This address." She stuck the note on the doorjamb. "Ivey, you're with me."

Ruth let the young constable drive so that she could call Carver. His phone was switched off, and she left a message. Steve Norris rented a dockside apartment built on what used to be Herculaneum Dock, the city's southernmost dock, now mostly infilled, a large development of four- and five-story-high apartment blocks.

The landlord was the keyholder. He met them at the entrance gates and they parked, following him into the complex on foot. He took them through a side gate, and Ruth caught a glimpse of water around the curve of the footpath. She made a detour to take a look.

"That's the back of the development," the landlord called. "You've gotta go round the front to get in."

Ruth stared at a wind-rippled body of water, stretching for a couple hundred yards and lined end to end by the apartment blocks in pinkish brick.

"Weird shape for a pond." It was straight along the sides and curved at the ends, like a drug capsule.

"One of the old gravings," the landlord said.

"A dry dock?" *Oh, boy . . .* That would be deep, and if Norris had gone into its greenish water, it would be a bastard to search. But the railings around the edge looked solid enough, so maybe it wouldn't come to that.

Ruth followed the landlord to the front of the building, with only a quick glance in DC Ivey's direction.

"It's on the top floor, I'm afraid," he said, peering ruefully up the stairwell. "And there's no lift in this building."

"We can manage a few stairs," Ruth said. "Lead the way."

He was in his late fifties, on the heavy side. He looked torn: hand the keys over and let them get on with it, or face a slog up the stairs? After a moment's hesitation, he took the second option; Ruth guessed he wanted a chance to find out what his tenant had been up to.

"He's not in any trouble, is he?" the landlord said, pausing, puffing slightly, at a turn in the stairs. They had taken the fire escape staircase, their footsteps echoing up the concrete well.

"Not that we know of," Ruth said. "Is he a good tenant?"

The landlord shrugged.

"Pays his rent on time. Never had any complaints from the people on his landing." He blocked the stairwell with his bulk. "So, if he's not in any bother, why are you looking for him?"

"Does he have friends staying over?"

"None of my business." The landlord turned his back and began trudging up the steps again. Apparently, he resented the lack of give-and-take in the conversation.

"You don't care what happens on your property?" Ruth asked.

"As long as he doesn't sublet, he can have who he likes to stay."

They hiked up ten flights in all, the landlord trying to wheedle information out of them, literally, at every turn.

At Norris's flat door, panting heavily, he pulled out a latchkey.

"Just a minute." Ruth examined the lock and door frame. There were no signs of forced entry, no telltale scratches around the key slot to indicate that it had been picked. She stepped back. "Okay." She held out her hand and the landlord handed over the key.

"If you wouldn't mind waiting outside, sir."

"Well, you could've told me that before we climbed this lot," he said.

But then she wouldn't have gotten a feel for the kind of relationship he had with his tenant.

She thanked him, closing the door after them, before producing a couple of pairs of nitrile gloves and handing a pair to DC Ivey.

She stood at the front door for a few moments.

"What's up, Sarge?" Ivey said, pulling on his gloves.

"Just getting a feel for the place," she said. "Notice any smells, any unusual noises?"

"No."

"Well, that's a good sign, isn't it?" Bad smells and buzzing insects were two things her years as a CSI had taught her to dread. Two doors across a narrow hallway; one, to the left, was closed. The other, directly ahead, stood wide, revealing an open plan kitchen/sitting room.

A hooded jacket lay on a sofa under the window. "Mr. Norris?" Ruth called. "It's the police."

No answer.

Ruth signaled Ivey to take the closed door, while she stepped into the living area. It was bright, with light coming in from the window above the sofa, and from a sliding door to the right, which gave onto a small balcony. What she glimpsed through them made the hairs stand up on the back of her neck.

"Bed's unmade, and there's a half-finished glass of beer growing mold on the nightstand," Ivey shouted.

A moment later, he appeared by her side. "Is something wrong, Sarge?"

She hadn't moved since he'd left the room.

"Did you check under the bed, and in the wardrobe?" Ruth asked.

"Yeah." He looked at her in question.

She nodded to the door onto the balcony. "What do you see?"

He followed her line of sight. "Is that—?"

"Yep."

She called CSM Hughes first and asked for a Scientific Support team.

"Are we looking at a crime scene?" he asked.

"Not sure," she said. "But if you can find anyone who hasn't dealt with the other scenes, that'd be good."

"Okay. Who's going to brief them?"

"I'll try to get hold of DCI Carver. If I can't—it'll be me." She ended the call and tried Carver's number again. This time, he answered.

"I got your voice mail," he said. "What did you find?"

She looked around her, without venturing farther into the apartment. "Signs of recent occupation, but none of the missing man, and no signs of struggle. It's a small apartment, but it's neat, and it looks undisturbed." The only mess she could see were the discarded jacket on the sofa and an empty bowl and spoon on the breakfast bar.

"So you've asked for forensics because . . . ?" Carver sounded puzzled.

"We're at the southern end of the riverside docks," she said. "By the Dingle."

She felt his close attention.

"I'm looking down at Dingle Railway Station—the CSIs are just packing up."

Carver swore softly.

"And there's a camera tripod on the balcony." She took a breath. "He was watching us, Greg."

27

Factions have begun to develop—pro and anti. Threats are being bandied back and forth like trading cards. Demands made that I explain myself. The notion is laughable—it's for others to *interpret* my art; I don't have to *explain* it.

Think Outside the Box captured their attention; they responded to the color and light of the first exhibit like babies drawn to a nursery mobile, excited by its three-dimensional appeal. And—like babies—they are tethered to the world by the concrete and tangible. Small wonder they couldn't cope with the abstract concepts inherent in *Catch the Gamma Wave* and *Life Passes*—after all, both require active brainwork. I had thought them capable of interpolating from the EEG readings back to the brain tissue of *Think Outside the Box*, building connections between the exhibits. Sadly, they don't have the maturity, the imagination, or the intellect. For such limited minds, a thing only exists if it is physically present.

If I'd had the option, I would have presented the trilogy in its true order, with the subjects' brain tissue preserved—symbolically *suspended*—as the end point, but priming followers with *Think Outside the Box* made it possible for them to see *Life Passes* as art, rather than butchery. There is no question in my mind that they would not have the wit to make that judgment unprompted. Reversing the natural order was the *only* choice available to me.

It's depressing, trawling through my Instagram feed. My supporters seem shamefully apologetic, trying to explain the works on my behalf—as if they ever could.

I should turn the damned phone off, but I feel compelled to check the screen once more. A new hashtag has appeared in my feed: #Triptych. It's trending, apparently; curiosity gets the better of me.

"#Triptych makes sense of @FerrymanArt."

"Look at this! #FerrymanFan #Triptych—now I get it!"

"Integrative #Triptych by #FerrymanFan @Kharon NAILS what @FerrymanArt is trying to do."

Trying to do . . . I wonder what this peasant has ever "tried" to achieve.

The pattern is repeated on Twitter and Facebook—and, it seems, Kharon is at the center of all this "buzz." News of his "Triptych" has been shared so many times that it takes a few minutes to drill down to the original post.

"Triptych is my homage to your mind-blowing artwork, @FerrymanArt—you inspire me."

He is respectful, I'll give him that.

He has hashtagged a few keywords to attract wider interest and attached a still from *Think Outside the Box*, adding a link to YouTube. Instagram doesn't allow clickable links, so I copy the address and paste it into a new Google tab. But watching the cursor blink, I can't seem to bring myself to click through.

Instead, I set the phone down on my workbench and walk away. It buzzes. I stare at it. It buzzes again, angry and insistent. I pick it up.

Two notifications—new followers. It buzzes again. And again. And again—until it's fizzing in my hand!

This has to be Kharon's doing, his *homage*, he calls it.

I click the link.

The screen is split three ways—one-third for each of the exhibits. In the first, the plexiglass disks displaying slices of brain tissue rotate in the wind, flashing blue and purple and green under the LEDs as they spin. The EEG traces of *Catch the Gamma Wave*, in the second segment, seem to pulse in rhythm with them; and in the third, the video of *Life Passes* adds energy and thrilling immediacy. The screen flickers, strobes, dies, reignites. The video of a beating heart retreats into the background and vanishes. A moment later, the panel housing *Think Outside the Box* jolts forward and seems to pop out of the screen. It slides right, as if on a carousel, over the heart, over the brain wave traces of *Catch the Gamma Wave* in the center panel, coming to rest on the far right of the screen. *Life Passes* emerges from the shadows and takes position as the left panel of the triptych. *Life Passes, Catch the Gamma Wave*, and finally, *Think Outside the Box*. Now the exhibits are in the order in which I created them. My God . . . he really does understand.

I feel a burning ache in the center of my chest, but I can't identify the emotion.

A burst of light, then the heart begins fibrillating in shock. A duplicate red ECG trace glides like a veil from the central panel, onto the first, tracing the heart's final death throes, and simultaneously, the blue peaks and troughs of brain wave activity ghost over the face of the disks in the last panel of the triptych.

The images begin to flicker: heart muscle; brain waves; heart trace; brain tissue, presented in briefer and briefer flashes, producing a strobe effect. Darkness for a second. A supernova of light explodes from the screen, and when the afterimage fades, I see a still of the crowd standing in front of *Think Outside the Box*. The cameras in their hands replicate the scene; dozens of tiny images, capturing the spectacle of brain tissue captured in plexiglass, suspended in the box, lit gorgeously with the LEDs at the point of transition from purple to green. The image doubles, quadruples, spiraling inward, in fractal of my original, on and on into infinity.

28

With so many detectives needed to check Norris's apartment building, DCI Carver had to call off the morning briefing. He read through the written actions and reports that had come in, then called Ruth Lake to his office.

"The killer hasn't used Matlock's debit card since shortly after the laptop purchases," he said.

They both knew that lowered their chances of catching the offender by a country mile.

"And the mysterious visitor to his flat was only seen a few times right after things went quiet on the block," Ruth added. "We're not going to catch him there."

"But Norris's is a different story," Carver said. "It's possible the offender isn't finished with the place. You've kept the CSI presence low-key?"

She nodded. "We're trying to do the same with house-to-house. But people are going to put two and two together—and this is big news—all it takes is one person to call the media or send a tweet."

"Let's hope we get lucky, then," Carver said. "This bastard has had things his own way for far too long."

"Steve Norris's parents have agreed to leave his credit card open," Ruth said. "And the card company will notify us of any activity as soon as they're aware of it."

Which reminded him: "Where is DC Ivey on the other credit cards?"

"Still working it," Ruth said. "He's identified several ATMs in small convenience stores that the killer used on multiple occasions."

"Anything Yi might use on his geographic profile?"

Ruth shook her head. "He used tills all over the city. But Ivey's gone to talk to the shop owners—see if they know any more—and he's taken photos of both Matlock and Norris."

Coming back to their new missing person, Carver said: "The partial footwear impression on Norris's balcony?"

"They're analyzing it now," Ruth said. "And they've already confirmed it's an Adidas trail running shoe."

"Same as the shoe impression we got above the railway arch," Carver said. "What does Norris wear?"

"The CSIs found two brand-new pairs of Asics shoes in the wardrobe: Metaruns and Gel-Blade 5s—both men's size nine."

"Brand-new, you say?" It was possible that Norris got rid of an old pair because it might incriminate him. "Do we know if he owns Adidas shoes?"

Ruth nodded—an indication that she followed his line of thought. "I've got a couple of volunteers checking till receipts from his flat," she said.

"Any sightings of him leaving his apartment the day he vanished?"

Ruth lifted one shoulder. "It's early days yet, but if I can show you on your PC—" He logged in, and she called up Google Maps, typed in the address, and clicked through a set of street-view photos.

Carver sneaked a look at her; she was her usual efficient and professional self, but he sensed a tension in her bearing. He knew that his resistance to talk to the psychologist had caused Ruth some trouble, but she didn't seem annoyed or resentful. Reading Ruth was never easy, but something was going on with her, and Carver was fairly sure it had nothing to do with him.

"There you go," she said.

The photograph showed a long, dead-end street, with parking bays and pools of tree plantings and bushes. The design of the buildings either side reminded Carver of the old tenements in London's East End—newer, cleaner versions, it had to be said, with neat parking bays and soft landscaping. He counted at least eight blocks on each side of the access road, each three or four stories high. There must be scores of windows overlooking the bays.

"There's a good chance Norris was seen," he said.

Ruth lifted her chin. "Yeah. But he was working early shifts before he disappeared, so there'd be fewer people about. And his car is still parked on the complex, so he may have gone out on foot."

Carver noticed a dazzle of light at the corner of the building, a hint of reflections on water. "Is there a pond at the back of the development?" he asked.

Ruth gave him a look that said, *Wait till you see it.*

She clicked to a photo of a brick-edged water feature large enough to have three sets of fountains along its length.

"It looks huge."

"It's about two hundred and fifty meters long," Ruth said. "Apparently, it's an old graving dock, used to dock cargo ships for repairs. In terms of depth, I'm thinking . . . ten meters?"

"Maybe more," Carver said, almost wincing as he asked, "Do we need to bring in divers?" Ruth would know the feasibility of such a move better than most.

"A search on that scale would cost."

"It would."

"And attract a lot of attention." Ruth tilted her head. "Anyway, drowning isn't really the Ferryman's MO."

"Okay. We can hold off for now," Carver said. "But when the CSIs have cleared out, I really want to have someone watch Norris's place. We know our guy went back to victims' properties, used them as drop-offs."

"D'you think Superintendent Wilshire would sanction it?"

"I doubt it," Carver said. "Last night's overtime alone is pushing us to the limits of our budget."

He felt a doomy sense of failure.

"D'you think he might cough up enough to monitor the flat electronically?" Ruth asked.

"Covert video?" Carver nodded. "That's a great idea."

"I could ask John Hughes to ask his lot to clear up any obvious evidence they've been there," Ruth said. "It'd cost next to nothing."

"I don't think Norris's family would have any objection," Carver said. "I'll give it a try."

His mobile rang.

The caller identified himself as Sergeant Bill Naylor, who was leading house-to-house inquiries at Norris's apartment block.

"Just a minute," Carver said. "I've got DS Lake with me, I'm putting you on speaker." He tapped the icon and held the phone on the palm of his hand. "Go ahead."

"I thought you'd want this ahead of the debrief, boss," the sergeant said. "Norris's next-door neighbor saw him leave for work at five thirty A.M. the day he went AWOL—that would've been in time for him to fit in a run before an early shift at St. Michael's Railway Station. On fine days, he always runs to work; it's a mile and a bit from his place, but he makes a detour through the Festival Gardens to boost it to two. This was four days ago."

"One day before *Catch the Gamma Wave*," Carver said. "The witness is sure about the day?"

"Yup. Says he remembers because they had a chat about Norris going to his parents' anniversary party," the sergeant said. "By coincidence, it was the neighbor's birthday, and he was heading out to catch an early train to London for a two-day minibreak."

"Was Norris wearing running gear when he set off?" Ruth asked.

There was a brief, muffled conversation, then the detective said, "Bright orange trainers, dark joggers, and T-shirt."

"The Metaruns in his wardrobe are black, and Gel-Blade 5s are bright green," Ruth said. "But Adidas and Nike both do orange running shoes." She fished her phone out of her jacket pocket and clicked through some webpages. "The soul plate patterns don't match the prints we found at Dingle Station."

"It's looking more and more like Norris never came home, isn't it?" Carver said.

"The neighbor hasn't seen him since," the sergeant said. "But there was someone in his flat."

"When?"

"Three days ago—the night of the light show at the old Dingle Station."

Carver felt a thrill of excitement.

"The neighbor's flat looks out onto the cliff and the station archway," Sergeant Naylor went on. "He'd just got back from his trip, heard the police sirens. He hasn't got a balcony, but he stuck his head out the window to get a better look, saw someone filming the goings-on from Norris's."

"Did he see who it was?" Ruth asked.

"Not well. Bloke was wearing a hoodie, and the angle isn't good—I took a squint at it myself—the window opens the wrong way for you to lean out and look toward Norris's. Witness says he assumed it was Steve Norris, but when he called across, he didn't get an answer."

Carver thanked him and ended the call. "Do we think the neighbor disturbed the Ferryman?"

"It would explain why he left the tripod behind," Ruth said. "Could be he cleared out fast after the neighbor called over to him."

"Is it possible that Norris was deliberately targeted so that the killer could use his apartment to film *Catch the Gamma Wave*?"

Ruth lifted one shoulder. "If he was, he must have been grabbed up on his run to work."

"Let's take a look at the route." Carver called up Google Maps and entered details of the start point, then switched to satellite view.

"The obvious way would be straight down to the river, hang a left along the roadway, then into the Festival Gardens," Ruth said.

"Agreed," Carver said. "But once inside the gardens, he could have taken half a dozen different paths."

"His family said he was training for a marathon—fitted in as much running as he could in a workday. If it was me, I'd go the longest circular route, keeping the river on my right . . ." Ruth traced a pathway that dipped down toward the river and ran almost along the length of the gardens. "This is where I'd turn my back to the river." She pointed to a place where the pathway met an access road. "Then I'd head up onto the roundabout and loop back via Riverside Drive, toward St. Michael's Station."

"I can't see him being ambushed on the first stretch of the route," Carver said, scouring the image. "It's too open. And anyway, there's so much CCTV in that area. The gardens don't allow cars, so if Norris was clobbered there, the abductor would have had to drag him to a vehicle to spirit him away."

Ruth peered at the monitor. "Can you zoom in on the gray patch to the bottom right?"

Carver obliged.

"That's a car park," Ruth said. "He wouldn't have had far to drag Norris if he parked the van there and ambushed him on his way out of the gardens."

"Let's get in touch with the council, see if they have CCTV," Carver said.

Ruth nodded. "Otherwise, it's got to be somewhere on Riverside Drive, before he heads in to the station."

"So what's his most likely route from Riverside Drive to the station?" Carver mused.

Most of Riverside Drive was wide open; a busy two-lane road with traffic lights and pedestrian crossings. To the north of it was a medium-sized housing development, bounded by the railway line. But the roads within the development were either crescents, curving back to the main road, or else dead ends.

"I don't see a way through to the station," he said.

"Zoom out a bit."

"There you are . . ." Carver murmured. A faint gray ribbon overlaid a patch of woodland on the map, beginning at the main road, and ending at St. Michael's Station.

A few hundred yards of wooded footpath seemed a perfect place to lie in wait. He switched to street view. At the far end, the pathway accessed the station frontage through a small gap in a sandstone wall. At Riverside Drive, the path started at a pedestrian crossing. Both sides of the road were signposted with heritage-style waymarkers to the Riverside Walkway in one direction and St. Michael's Station in the other.

A thin black line of shadow fell across the road at the crossing. Carver turned Google Maps's yellow Pegman full circle, then looked up. The shadow line was a CCTV camera pole, and the three domes perched at the top of it looked like high-end kit.

"Gotcha," he said. "If Norris was abducted nearby, we'll have it on camera."

"Mm," Ruth said. "But it's more likely he was attacked in the woods—which gives the abductor the same dilemma: where to park the abduction vehicle?"

They both knew that a car parked on a busy two-lane road with no laybys would be targeted by police in a matter of minutes.

As Ruth stared at the screen, he could swear he felt the intensity of her concentration coming off her like heat.

"Is there any access to the woods from the housing estate?" she asked.

Carver clicked to the east of the woods, and Pegman jumped to Moel Famau View, the last cluster of houses on the development.

"Could that be a cut-through just before the first house?" Ruth asked. About twenty yards along Moel Famau View, the grass edging seemed to dip down to a faint black line, heading left into the trees.

He marched Pegman up the slope of the road and swung him left.

Sure enough, a narrow footpath, shaded on both sides by trees, gave access into the woods along the boundary fence of the end house.

For a few seconds, neither spoke, simply enjoying the sheer exhilaration of the moment.

"I'm guessing you'll want a team down there," Ruth said, with a grin that lit up the room.

29

Ruth Lake was sorting out task allocations, ensuring that the special constables had adequate supervision from fully qualified officers, and wondering how long they could ask these volunteers to work full days at their paid jobs and then spend another eight hours unpaid on police work.

Parr came into the MIR with a set of car keys.

"Busy?" she said.

"Scut work." He hung the keys on the board and turned to face her. "What d'you need?"

"More scut work, I'm afraid."

He smiled. It was weary and knowing, but there was no resentment behind it. "What I'm here for, Sarge."

"I just sent a batch of questions to the printer. They're for the house-to-house teams at Moel Famau View. Can you get them to Sergeant Naylor for distribution?"

"Sure. No problem."

She watched him walk to the corner of the room and pick up the batches of collated and stapled questions. Parr was thirty or so, she estimated. Fit-looking, attractive, in an understated way. He wore his hair short, and he was always neatly turned out. He was focused, calm, and efficient—and he never complained. She made a mental note to have a word with the shift sergeant, try to get him on duties that would make better use of his talents.

Her thoughts were interrupted by a call from CSM Hughes.

"We've found Kharon," he said, without preamble.

"Wow. I thought the warrant application to trace his IP address was refused."

"It was, but he posted a new 'appreciation' of the Ferryman's exhibits on YouTube—have you seen it?"

"Not yet."

"You should take a look," he said.

She was already clicking through to Kharon's Instagram account on her laptop. "Got it." She watched the video for a few seconds. She had to admit it had a hypnotic quality—weird, and slightly nauseating, but there was certainly some skill at work.

"Scroll through the comments," Hughes said, with barely concealed glee.

"He seems to have quite the fan base." Ruth stopped at the third comment. "Aw, that's sweet—he's given a direct link to his website."

The link wasn't clickable, so she copied and pasted it into a new tab. It took her to a site called KharonMedia.

There wasn't much to see—a homepage, contacts, and a page of videos and images, mostly linked back to YouTube. "It's a bit light on content," she said.

"It's new—only went live last night," Hughes said. "He's been getting a lot of interest. I'm guessing he's hoping to start making money from his work, decided to set up in business."

Ruth checked out the contacts page, still trying to work out why Hughes sounded so pleased with himself. It had a contact form. "You traced the e-mail?" she speculated.

"That links to a Hotmail account," he said, his tone dismissive. "It's untraceable."

"Oh, now you're teasing me," Ruth said, smiling. She drummed her fingers on the desk. New website, set up in haste—there was only one way she could think to trace the owner without a warrant. Every website had to have a listing with a named owner and a physical address on the WHOIS database.

"You looked up the website URL on WHOIS?" she said.

"Yup," Hughes said. "*And* he left it set to default."

The default setting for WHOIS was "public"—if you didn't switch it to "private," anyone who cared to search the database could find your physical address.

Ruth laughed. "Could he *really* be that naive?"

"Don't be too hard on him," Hughes said, and she heard the smile in his voice. "He's been a busy boy these last few days."

"I suppose he has. So—what've you got?"

"Take your pick—we've got his real name, his e-mail, mobile phone number, and street address—also genuine."

"Just ping the lot to my phone," Ruth said, snapping her laptop closed and gathering her things. "We'd better go and scoop him up before somebody warns him."

An hour later, Ruth was sitting opposite Karl Obrazki, aka Kharon, in interview room 3. He was a dark-eyed, full-lipped kid, no older than nineteen or twenty, with a soft sweep of black hair that gleamed almost bluish under the cold light of the overhead fluorescents. His coffee-colored skin tone defied the sickening effect of the room's sage green walls and unforgiving lighting. He slouched, self-aware but not self-conscious, in his chair, his gray hoodie open, revealing a pristine white tee that gleamed under the lights.

"It's good of you to come in and talk to us, Mr. Obrazki." Ruth sat back from the table so that she could get a good look at him. This was not a formal interview, and Mr. Obrazki was not under caution, so for now it was just him and Ruth Lake; Carver was watching their "informal chat" via video link in a nearby room. Their aim was to find out how deeply involved Karl/Kharon was in the events of the last week.

Obrazki half closed his eyes in sleepy acknowledgment of her thanks, but under the table, his left foot was trapped behind his right ankle, and his right knee jittered, betraying his anxiety.

"I understand you're a student?"

"Film studies," he said, staring at the corner of the table.

"Fairfield Arts College, isn't it?" His eyes widened in a slight flare of anxiety—perhaps his tutors wouldn't approve of his extracurricular activities. "Well, what you're doing is impressive," she added, not wanting to rattle him into sullen silence.

She saw a slight shift in stance, a chin lift that might have been a shade on the defensive side, but the brief, dismissive eye contact he made suggested that he was thinking, *What would you know?*

"Seriously," she said. "A lot of people are saying you're really in tune with the Ferryman's art." It hurt her to call the crime scenes "art," but Ruth was expert at hiding her feelings.

"He's a genius," Karl said.

"Not everyone thought so, but you seem to've convinced a lot of people." By implication, that made him the greater genius. Karl nodded, slowly, just twice, and barely perceptibly, but Ruth saw it. "He was hemorrhaging followers before you broadcast *Triptych*."

Using the title of his work reinforced the positivity of her words, and he eased out of the "anchoring" position, placing both feet on the floor and widening his stance a little. They chatted for a few minutes about the montage, and he loosened up some more.

After he had explained the film origins of the split screen, Ruth asked, "How did you get that ghosting effect with the images?"

"Just video layers and shit," he said, with patent false modesty.

"Oh, I suppose there's programs for that kind of thing," she said, deliberately dismissive. "Just flick a switch and . . ."

"It's not that simple," he said, his pride pricked. "You've got to know how to use the programs. It takes practice and, you know, skill."

"And imagination," Ruth agreed, thinking, *This definitely is not the Ferryman.*

A slight shoulder lift said he'd accepted the compliment.

"So, d'you get paid to do this?"

"Paid?" He seemed offended by the suggestion. "This isn't about *money.*"

"No . . . sorry," Ruth said. "It's just, you seem to have a direct line to—whoever this is." She wouldn't ask him directly. Not yet. "It *was* you who sent out word about the display at the old railway station, wasn't it?"

"He messaged me," Karl said.

"Messaged?"

"On Instagram. Said he wanted me to put the word out about *Catch the Gamma Wave*, but he wanted to keep it under the radar."

"Did he say why?"

"No, just—you know—he didn't want it to go through the usual channels."

The Ferryman was furious that he'd been kept waiting by the Contact Center, yet he hadn't confided in Kharon. That was significant; Karl may be a hireling, or some kind of protégé—but it seemed unlikely that he was a conspirator in the killings.

"You didn't mind—him just telling you what to do?"

"Like I said—he's a genius."

"Fair enough."

"And I didn't really think there'd be any harm . . ."

Ruth wondered if Karl fully understood that three men had been murdered in the course of the "harmless" enterprise he so eagerly supported. But the best way to get information from a suspect is to keep him talking, so she gave a neutral nod and said, "This new video of yours—d'you think he minds you using his stuff?"

For a microsecond, he looked stricken, but he recovered quickly. "No . . . No."

That was one too many nos but she let it pass.

"*Triptych* is an integrative piece," he said. "It's a bit like 'sampling' in rap. You see something you like or admire, reshape it into something that is yours, but the original work is still—you know—*in* there."

"So you didn't help the Ferryman make the originals?"

At first, his face didn't register anything at all—it seemed the suggestion was simply too far from anything he'd ever considered before. Then his eyes widened.

With shock?

"Hah!" He stared past her, and Ruth realized that he was visualizing the possibilities—he wasn't shocked by the idea, he was excited. Which was bad, because although it looked like the Ferryman had been acting alone, Kharon would be a willing acolyte, and the possibility of persuading him to help the investigation was just about zero.

Ruth didn't show any of the thoughts that raced through her mind; her job was to keep Karl talking, give him time to let something slip. "Oh," she said, letting a hint of disappointment creep into her tone, "the way he trusts you, I got the feeling you knew him pretty well."

"You don't need to know the *person* to understand the art. He *trusts* me because I understand what drives him, artistically. *Nobody* knows who he really is. That's part of his charisma."

She thought it was a genuine response, but she pushed a little harder: "Seems weird, him not actually claiming his art, though?"

He scoffed. "You've heard of Banksy, right?"

"Yeah," she said. "But even Banksy has a few trusted friends who know his true identity."

"Not at the start. Not until he was a global name."

She tilted her head; maybe Obrazki hoped that, as the Ferryman became a global name, he would be one of the faithful allowed into his inner circle.

"You think the Ferryman will message you again?" She framed this in a dubious tone, and his eyes flashed defiantly.

"I *know* he will."

She wondered if he already had.

"Well, next time he does, you need to let me know," she said.

Obrazki slammed shut like a trapdoor—eyebrows lowered, shoulders hunched, legs twisted around each other like a pretzel. "No," he said. "I mean I don't know. I'm in a position of trust—I couldn't—"

"Karl, listen to me," Ruth said, thinking, *You moved too fast*. "This man is a killer. He enjoys killing. And he won't stop. If you help him, that's conspiracy to murder."

"No—that's not true—they were already dead."

"You might want to replay that last sentence in your head." Ruth stared at him for so long that he began to flush, but he looked more pissed off than ashamed. *He just isn't getting it.*

She gave him a few seconds longer to rethink, but he glared at her defiantly.

"Okay," she said. "I can see I'm going to have to spell it out: people are still going missing—young men—just like you. And the way it works is, if you know something that could help us to find the murderer, and you don't tell us, that's a crime. You could be charged with obstruction of justice, or impeding the police in the course of their duties."

His eyes widened.

"Let's say someone else goes missing—a young man." She watched for his reaction, saw no telltale signs that he knew about Steve Norris. "Say someone gets hurt—like they were hurt at the old railway station—you could be charged with aiding and abetting the man who murdered these people."

Kharon's composure was shot; he seemed upset that she had turned on him, when he thought she was a nice person.

"The thing about aiding and abetting, Karl," she said, "is the secondary party—that's you—is as guilty of the offense as the person who actually did the killing."

"But I *didn't*—"

"The law doesn't care," Ruth interrupted, keeping her gaze on him the whole time, speaking slowly and calmly, because the way his eyes were darting right and left, she'd say that his brain had switched to fight or flight, and he wasn't taking too much in.

"You see, the abettor's guilt *derives* from the guilt of the perpetrator—like your *Triptych* piece *derives* from the three 'exhibits' the Ferryman has already staged. The perpetrator—that's the Ferryman—and the abettor—that's you—are one and the same in the eyes of the law."

Karl Obrazki's coloring had taken on some of the sage green of the wall coverings. Now he was getting it. She slid a business card across the table to him.

"If he messages you, call me," she said. "If he rings you, call me. If he stops you on the street or—God forbid—turns up on your doorstep, call me. This is not a game. It's not art. It's murder."

30

On the drive home, Carver glanced across at Ruth Lake. The dying rays of a fabulous sunset lit the car interior in a blaze of red and orange, warming her skin, but during the day, he'd noticed an unusual pallor, and now the setting sun seemed to cast deeper shadows under her eyes.

"Have you been getting *any* sleep recently?" he asked.

"Says the man who's working twice the hours he's officially allowed," she shot back.

"Just concerned."

"Ditto."

He sucked his teeth, really not wanting to say anything about his late arrival that morning, but feeling he owed Ruth for all she'd done for him.

"I saw my therapist today," he said.

She didn't actually turn her head, but he caught her sideways glance. "On a weekday."

"Mm."

"Are you okay?"

"I'm dealing with it."

She opened her mouth, and for a second he thought she'd ask what, exactly, he was dealing with, but she changed her mind, nodded, said, "Good," and left it at that.

"So . . . are *you* okay?"

Her mouth twitched in a half smile. "I'm dealing with it."

He tugged his ear. "Well, I'm glad we've cleared that up."

Ruth laughed. "I'm *fine*. I just need a hot bath and bed."

A sudden gleam of light on a wall to their left drew his attention, and Carver focused on a stenciled image of the hooded figure that had come to represent the Ferryman. Dozens more of the graffiti stencils had appeared in the last two days, but this one glowed bright in their headlights.

"D'you see that?" he said.

She nodded. "They're using reflective paint now."

Ruth pulled up at a pedestrian crossing, and a male figure crossed slowly in front of them. He was wearing a gray hoodie, and he pulled the hood farther forward, casting his face in deep shadow. The lights changed and they drove on.

On the next street corner, another hoodie stood in the gathering gloom. Farther on, another, watching their approach, turning bodily as they passed.

"Am I being paranoid," Ruth said, "or . . . ?"

"Or," Carver said. "Definitely *or* . . ."

As they slowed for a turn the car headlights lit up one of the figures, reflecting, in a brilliant flash, a stylized *F* on the chest of his hoodie.

"Looks like the T-shirt entrepreneur has diversified his product lines," Ruth said.

The figure raised his right hand and tapped the logo with two fingers.

"Bloody hell . . ." Carver murmured.

After that, hooded figures seemed to show up every half mile or so along the route.

"It can't be coincidence that we interviewed the Ferryman's PR man, and a few hours later—this," Ruth said.

"I'm going to be bold and rule out coincidence," Carver agreed.

"That said, it's not what I would've expected from Kharon: he's a disciple, not a leader."

"My feeling exactly," Carver said. "He's totally transparent—exactly what he says he is, a fan."

"So what the hell is this?" Ruth jerked her chin toward the next apparition.

"I really don't know," Carver breathed.

Forty minutes later, Ruth had grabbed a sandwich and her first decent cup of coffee of the day. She took the coffee cup upstairs with her and turned on the shower, extra hot to purge the nasty feeling that had stayed with her all the way home. It was one thing knowing that the Ferryman had thousands of anonymous groupies online, but seeing them in the flesh was far more unsettling.

The crudely drawn tattoos forcibly inked on her forearm by a killer she and Carver had brought to book over the winter had faded to ghostly gray since her last laser treatment, but she saw them all too clearly. Felt them, too: the heat of a shower could set them off, or worry—even tiredness. Mostly, they were a gritty itch under her skin, but occasionally she would experience a sudden burn, which she knew was partly psychological. She dabbed the area dry and slathered on moisturizer before dressing in jeans, running shoes, and denim jacket for street anonymity.

But before she headed out again, she checked the street from her front bedroom window. It was empty and quiet. Even so, she would leave the car and flag a taxi—she couldn't risk her search for Adam Black being broadcast over social media.

She had tried every Adam Black on the electoral registry—he was not among them. Now her only option was to hit the streets, showing Adam's picture around, visiting places, talking to people she knew to be his associates or former associates.

Two hours on, Ruth had struck out at a drug rehab unit and three homeless shelters in the city center, stopped and talked to every sex worker who'd hung around long enough for her to reach them. She'd even rousted a couple of kids selling pills on street corners. She wasn't sure if she felt more relieved or frustrated that nobody recognized the guy with a topknot and a nose ring. She hadn't had time for proper exercise in a few days, so she ran the mile or so up the hill from the city center, aiming for Edge Lane, the southernmost boundary of Kensington.

Liverpool's Kensington district was the polar opposite of its London namesake. Some of the best acting talent of the city had emerged from its crumbling housing stock, but on a recent survey, 98 percent of "Kenny" residents were judged to be suffering the highest deprivation in the country. The area had recently undergone a bit of a spruce-up, but nearly a century of poverty and deprivation could not be purged by planting a few trees and installing Victorian-style streetlamps.

When he was in trouble, Adam used to lie low in a semiderelict squat facing Edge Lane, and that was where Ruth headed. She slowed as she approached the building; its windows and front door had been secured with perforated steel plates. She stopped, bracing her hands on her thighs while she caught her breath. Tellingly, there were no wheelie bins outside the property. She checked the shutters anyway, giving those within reach a tug; they were solid—nobody was getting into that house anytime soon. A quick recce around the back of the house revealed a narrow alley, barred by a security gate. These gated alleys had become commonplace around the city; intended as a deterrent to thieves and other criminals, they were usually only unlocked to allow access for rubbish collection. Ruth climbed over the gate, lowering herself carefully on the other side.

The alley was pitch dark and reeked of piss—and worse. She waited for a few seconds until her eyes acclimatized to the gloom, then counted three doors down to the target property. Another steel had been placed over the gate into the backyard, and she had to scramble over a six-foot wall to access the backyard. She needn't have bothered. The house was completely locked down.

Boosting herself over the wall again, she dropped nimbly into the alleyway at the back of the house and was immediately dazzled by a flashlight.

"What d'you think *you're* doin'?"

Ruth shielded her eyes with one hand, squinting past the light. Whoever was holding it wasn't particularly tall, and the voice sounded young. "It's all right, son," she said. "I'm leaving."

She heard a spattering of laughter; it echoed off the alley walls. There were at least two more of them.

A shadowy head appeared from around one of the back gates farther down the alley, just behind the flashlight-wielding kid. "What you got there, lad—a jigger rabbit?" This voice sounded deeper, older. "You looking for business, love?"

Alleyways were known locally as "jiggers." "Jigger rabbits" were alley cats; the implication was obvious.

"Like I said, I was just leaving," Ruth said.

"Nah." The deeper voice stepped out into the alley, behind the light, and another stocky form followed him. A clang on the other side of the gate warned her that someone else was guarding the gate that gave access to the street, cutting off her escape route.

"You wanna use this alley, you gotta pay the tax," Deep Voice said.

More sniggering. Insinuating and obscene, the echo magnified the sound, carrying with it the threat of violence.

"I understand," Ruth said, her voice low and controlled, though her heart beat hard against her rib cage. "You're protecting your properties, and your families." She was giving them a way out without losing face. "But I'm police."

The squirt with the flashlight cursed roundly, but Deep Voice wasn't ready to stand down.

"Prove it," he spat.

Ruth reached for her warrant card, held it up to the beam of light, simultaneously taking out her Casco baton.

More swearing.

Then the light went out.

Blinded, Ruth flicked the baton to full length and relied on her hearing to guide her. Someone rushed at her and she crouched. He missed her arm, but grabbed a handful of hair. She swung the baton low and hard, made contact with bone. He fell, screaming, dragging her with him.

As the green wash of afterimage faded from her retinas, she saw that her assailant was at least twice her bulk. He held on to her ponytail, cursing and howling in turns. This must be Deep Voice. Ruth whacked once, twice more, and he let go, gripping his leg, screaming so loudly that lights started to come on in houses up and down the alley. His trouser cuff was rucked up, and she saw that he was wearing an electronic ankle tag.

"Okay," she said, raising her voice above the curses and yells of her attacker. "I'm leaving now." Her breathing was ragged, and she fought to get it under control. "Anyone who tries to follow me will *not* get off as lightly as your friend."

She didn't wait for confirmation, but turned and ran to the end of the alley, lobbing her Casco baton over as she jumped. She got to two-thirds the height of the security gate, grabbed the top rail to hoist herself the last third, then tipped forward, allowing her body weight to carry her over. Grasping a bar halfway down the other side, she steadied herself, flipped sideways, and landed untidily on top of the lad who'd been standing guard, sending him sprawling.

Ruth disentangled herself while the youth took whooping breaths, winded by the impact. She sat him up and placed her hand flat on his back. "Okay?" she said.

After a few seconds, he nodded. Under the streetlights, she realized that he was barely in his teens, terrified, and that she recognized him.

She showed him her warrant card and checked up and down the street. "Am I going to have any more trouble from your mates?" she asked.

"Nah," the boy said. His voice hadn't broken yet, and he spoke with the piping trill of a boy soprano. But this was no choirboy.

She hauled him up and set him on his feet; he was such an underfed bag of bones, she was surprised he didn't rattle. "So it looks like it's just me and you, kid."

His face fell, his mouth turning down in an almost comic caricature of dismay. "I never done nothing," he whined.

"That remains to be seen," Ruth said. "Let's start with a name."

He opened his mouth and she lifted one finger to stay him. "Your *own* name—"

His features scrunched in a grimace that was half frustration and half tearful anxiety. "Kyle Nolan," he mumbled.

"You need to understand something, Kyle Nolan," Ruth said. "I never forget a face. Not ever. So, if you're lying to me, you'd better get ready to spend the rest of your life stuck indoors—because I'll be scanning the arrest records for every sorry little scall who's been picked up for antisocial behavior, or thieving, until I find you. And as soon as I've got your real name, you'll get a knock on the door."

She'd laid it on a bit thick, but it had the desired effect.

"I'm not lying. Honest, miss." He wiped his nose on his sleeve.

"Okay," she said. "Tell me—honestly, mind—why you were all the way down the Dingle three nights ago. I mean, it's not exactly your turf, is it?"

The boy's eyes widened, and she could see him trying to decide what he could own up to without earning himself a ride down to the cop shop.

He jutted his chin out. "Where'd you see me?" he demanded.

"That's not how it works, Kyle," Ruth said. "*You* tell me what you were doing, and *I* decide if I believe you."

He hung his head, swearing under his breath.

Ruth gave him a little shake. "Language," she said. Then: "I'm waiting."

"We seen the stuff about the bodies on telly, and our kid—" He stopped, knowing he'd made a gaff.

"Your brother is the big lad with the ankle tag?" He didn't answer, but she read in the boy's startled expression that she was right. "That's going to make it even easier to find you, if you've been lying to me. Remember that, Kyle."

Kyle's face screwed up into a tight ball. "He'll *kill* me . . ."

"Come on," she said. "You don't want to be seen blubbing in front of your mates. They *are* watching, aren't they?"

He nodded, miserably.

She glanced around, saw nothing, but these were kids who knew how to use the shadows.

"Okay," she said. "You're doing great. You say you saw the stuff on telly and . . ."

Kyle gave a groan of distress, but after a moment, he went on: "Our kid put in the hashtag—you know, for the Ferryman—on Twitter and that. Seen there was something going on down the Dingle, and . . ." Tears dripped mournfully from his chin, showing no sign of letup. "We just thought it'd be a laugh, miss."

"Kyle," she said. "Look at me."

He raised his eyes to her left shoulder, then to her face, but it seemed an effort.

"Is that the truth?"

"Yes, miss."

She searched his face, and he looked away, not because he was lying, she thought, but out of embarrassment.

"I'm going to trust you, Kyle."

He tensed, and she could tell he still wasn't sure how this would end. She suspected he'd been doing a bit of petty thieving with his brother at the *Catch the Gamma Wave* exhibit but had not a smidgen of evidence to support her gut feeling.

"Cheer up," she said. "If you've told me the truth, you'll be fine."

"You don't know our Neil." He froze. "Now he really *is* gonna kill me."

"It's okay," Ruth said. "I would've found out his name on the system anyway."

"Yeah, but—"

"Look, if it makes it any better, I'll even let you give me a bit of cheek when I let you go, okay?"

He stared at her, a fragile hope glittering through his tears. "You're gonna let me go?"

"Kyle, love, I wouldn't waste my time with a little tiddler like you," she said. "On the count of three. Ready?"

She felt him brace, ready to twist free of her when she eased her grip on his sweatshirt. Then he looked quickly into her face. "You won't tell me mam," he said.

"That you were giving cheek to the police?"

He looked at her like she must have lost her mind. "That I told you me *name*."

"Okay," she said. "On condition you haven't been lying to me."

"I haven't."

She kept her fist bunched around his collar, but he was free to run whenever he wanted. "I asked you a question!" she roared, and he startled, frightened all over again. "Just to make it look good," she whispered. "Off you go."

He made a big thing of the struggle to free himself, ran ten yards, then turned, arms spread wide, bent at the elbows.

"You wanna know who I am?" he yelled. "I'm Shifu the Kung Fu Panda, and I'll kick your friggin' ARSE, if you come bothering me and my mates again." He flicked her a two-fingered salute, one on each hand, to emphasize his defiance.

"Don't overdo it, kid," Ruth murmured, but she'd already dismissed the boy and had her eye on a shambling figure staggering up the side street toward the corner where she was standing. The kid would only complicate anything that went down—she needed him out of the way—so she made a feint toward Kyle, and finally, he turned and fled.

Now it was just her and the man. He was approaching fast, considering he took one step sideways for every two steps forward, and she distributed her weight more evenly, ready to act if he made a move.

He was carrying two plastic bags, one of them clinking musically with what she imagined was a couple bottles of extrastrength cider. He passed under a streetlight, twenty feet away, and she got a good look at his face. She could smell him at ten feet—the reek of filth forming a bubble around him.

He shifted the lighter of the two carrier bags to his wrist and held his hand out. "Spare some change for a cup of coffee, girl," he said.

"No, but I can tell you where you can get one free, and a sandwich to soak up some of the booze," she said.

He shoved his filthy hand at her again. "*G'waan*, love. Help an old man out."

"You're not so old," she said, thinking, *So why is he acting that way?*

He laughed, and a waft of bad breath hit her. "You're only as old as you feel, aren't you, girl?"

Still smiling, but with serious intent in his eyes, he murmured, "You wanna watch yourself."

"*What* did you say?" She took a step toward him and he backed off.

"Only trying to help."

"By *threatening* me?"

"No," he protested. "Not me . . . No, you got me all wrong . . . But look around you, girl. This is bandit territory, and you're a moving target." His eyes flicked right and left, and he lowered his voice to a whisper. "There's some bad men put the word out on you. You need to be careful."

31

DAY 7, EVENING

It was the end of another long day, and still no major progress in the case. Nothing, so far, from the Norris angle, although covert surveillance in his flat had caught his landlord sneaking into the property. The scene hadn't officially been released, but they'd let him off with a stern reprimand. Friends of the missing man had readily agreed to provide fingerprints for elimination purposes; it seemed that he was a regular, upstanding citizen, as were his friends. The forensics team had identified all but one set in the flat by the end of the day, and when Ruth suggested they do a comparison with the landlord's fingerprints—they were a match.

There were rumbles on the street—people were being terrorized by Ferryman fans wearing the *F*-logo hoodies. Wilshire wasn't happy; he was taking a lot of flak from higher-ups, added to which, the press were demanding a briefing on this new development—and if there was one thing Wilshire hated more than criminals, it was dealing with the press.

Ruth was driving Carver home, as usual, and they discussed all this on the journey. Ruth had varied the route for the last couple of days, but they still had a number of interactions with the Ferryman's ghouls, standing like waymarkers at road junctions. Ruth was feeling slightly spaced out from lack of sleep, and she found it hard to concentrate on what Carver was saying. She realized he was looking at her, waiting for a reply, and said, "Sorry, boss—I was distracted for a second." She nodded toward a gray, hooded figure, who seemed to be tapping something into his mobile phone as they passed.

Her phone rang, and Ruth took it, using hands-free.

"Ruth, John Hughes." He sounded tense. "Something weird is happening. Your location is being tweeted on social media."

Ruth exchanged a glance with Carver.

"We're being shadowed by our hooded stalkers again," she said. "I'll take a few evasive tactics, see if I can lose them."

She hung up and turned off the main road. For a few minutes they saw no sign of the hoodies, but as soon as they wound back on the arterial road again, Hughes was back on the line.

"What's your license plate number?" he asked.

Ruth reeled it off, with a sick sense of dread.

"They're sending it out on Twitter," he said.

Ruth checked her mirror. "I don't see anyone."

"Well, they see you," Hughes said. "They've tweeted a photo."

Ruth suppressed a tremor. This was more than weird; it was oppressive. Even so, she thanked Hughes with a steady voice and hung up.

"You're not concerned?" Carver said.

"They're a damned nuisance." She shrugged. "But there's nothing I can do about them."

"You might think about requesting a fleet car till we've got this case wrapped up."

"Maybe," she said, uncomfortable to have the focus of attention on her. "So what was it you were saying?"

"Just that Ivey's search of convenience store ATMs hasn't turned up anything yet."

"Ivey's a bit of a terrier," she said. "If there's anything to find, he'll dig it up."

Carver stared thoughtfully at the road ahead. "He does seem to have potential."

"No doubt in my mind."

"Mm."

The conversation was beginning to feel stilted, and Ruth suddenly became aware that Carver was tense. He was winding himself up to asking her a tricky question, and she wasn't sure she wanted to hear it. She tried distracting him with chat about the house-to-house inquiries around Norris's, and their good fortune that nobody had taken their story to the media yet, but he kept falling silent, and when he cleared his throat and said, "Ruth—" she knew there was no avoiding what was to come.

"I had a call from a pal on the Matrix team," he said.

"Oh?"

"He said you've been asking questions on the street."

Ruth's eyebrow twitched. "We've all been doing that, boss."

"About someone called Adam Black."

Oh, boy . . . "Yeah," she said, not giving anything away, although her mouth had dried when he said the name. He was looking straight at her, and there was no telling how much he could read in the freaky auras he saw around people.

"Would you like to clarify?" His tone was formal, implacable.

"Just routine," she said, wondering if the tip-off from his Matrix pal had anything to do with the homeless man's warning the previous night. He wasn't as old as he'd at first seemed, nor as drunk; could he have been an undercover cop?

Carver snuffed air through his nose and she realized she'd been silent for some time.

"Is this to do with the case?" he demanded.

"I don't think so."

That was an honest answer, but it certainly wasn't forthright, nor was it helpful.

"Who is he?"

She didn't answer.

"I've done some checking," Carver persisted. "So I know that Adam Black has a juvenile record. He was taken into care at age fourteen, ended up in secure accommodation for a few months at age fifteen, eventually released into foster care at sixteen, but he disappeared as soon as he was legally beyond the remit of the care system."

"Yeah," Ruth said, knowing he wouldn't allow her to leave it at that, and feeling a prickling itch in the joint of her elbow and forearm—the ghost tattoo playing up—reminding her that secrets and lies always came back to haunt you.

She turned off the main road, seeing another Ferryman hoodie watching them, intending to cut through a series of backstreets, but Carver was relentless.

"Ruth," he said. "I appreciate all you've done, and continue to do, to cover my back. But I won't tolerate you or anyone else withholding information from the case."

"That's fair," she said, trying to ignore the maddening itch of the ghost tattoo. "But I'm almost sure this has nothing to do with the case."

" 'Almost,' " he repeated.

"You know I'd tell you if it did."

After a tormenting silence that told her he wasn't convinced of that at all, Carver said, "What did Black do to end up in a secure unit?"

She wondered if she could hold him off long enough to find Adam and talk to him. On the other hand, if she held out, Carver would root the truth out for himself.

"Ruth?" he said, then, angrily: "Sergeant Lake?"

She took a breath, readying herself to confess, when Carver's mobile phone rang.

"Contact Center," he explained, adding: "This isn't finished."

He answered the phone and spoke in short, cryptic bursts: "When?" A pause. "Is that confirmed?" Then, "Give me the exact wording." After half a minute, he spoke again: "Best dispatch a Matrix team. I'm two minutes away—I'll head back. Make sure CSM Hughes gets a copy of the recording as soon as possible," he added.

"Where to?" Ruth said.

He closed the phone and gave her a terse instruction: "Turn around—head back toward Hope Street."

They were in a quiet side street that ran parallel to the arterial road, and she found a spot to turn.

"The Ferryman?" she asked.

"What's a sequela?" he said in answer.

The question threw her for a second, and she had to scramble for a definition. "It's um . . . a term used in pathology—it means a consequence of disease."

"It's sickness, then?"

"No, it's what *follows* from it."

He shifted irritably in his seat, clearly dissatisfied with her explanation, and Ruth reached for an example as she completed the maneuver.

"Think of it this way," she said. "Flu is viral; pneumonia is usually caused by bacteria—they're totally different pathogens—but catch the flu, and you're at much higher risk of pneumonia straight after. One is a consequence of the other."

"It doesn't make sense," he said, almost to himself. "They're already dead—how could there be a consequence?"

Ruth accelerated out into the flow of traffic on the main road, earning a honk from a following car driver. "It *is* the Ferryman, then?"

"Take the second right," Carver said.

"Why didn't the switchboard just put him through to you?" she said, as she made the turn.

"He didn't want to be put through. Gave instructions to have the message relayed."

"Well, what's pissed him off this time?" she wondered.

Carver didn't answer, and Ruth sensed that she would not be forgiven until she came clean about Adam Black. But that would have to wait. Right now, they were back in the Georgian Quarter, a mix of grand mansions, some complete with Doric columns, and rows of three-story town houses dating back to the early nineteenth century.

"There should be a narrow road on the left," Carver said, "immediately after this terrace."

Ruth drove slowly past the row of houses and found the place. Just wide enough for one vehicle, and laid with granite setts, it had No Through Road and No Parking signs, and a warning that cars left unattended would be towed. She squeezed the car into the roadway; a row of three tiny mews properties, converted from eighteenth-century stables, faced onto the street, butting onto an eight-foot wall topped with spikes, which ran to the end of the narrow lane.

"How far down is it?" Ruth asked. He didn't seem willing to share, so she went on, "Because if we roll right up to where he wants us, we could obliterate any tire tracks."

She saw a slight chin lift, which told her that Carver saw the sense in what she was saying. "Pull over here."

Since they were in the center of the roadway, and there was nowhere else for her to go, Ruth just stopped the car where it was and looked to Carver for instructions.

"The caller said to look for a gate about halfway down."

They grabbed a couple pairs of nitrile gloves and a flashlight from the boot of her car and walked the rest of the way, Ruth checking the gutter and curb for tire tread marks.

The gate was iron, black, recently painted—and it was secured with a chain and padlock.

She shone the flashlight through the bars of the gate and they peered into a garden laid out in a modern, minimalist design: a square of lawn, slate pathways, topiary specimen plants, and a feature water-wall. A white pillar, or plinth, stood at the center of the lawn, but it was impossible at that distance to make out what it was for.

Ruth crouched to get a better view of the lock and discovered that the shank was not fully engaged in the hasp. She looked up at Carver. "It's open."

He gave her the nod and she gloved up before unhooking the pad-lock from the chain. Having no better option to hand, she hung it loosely on her own key ring and held her keys by the fob to protect any evidence. Then she drew back the latch, and the gate swung open under its own weight.

"Have we got a crime scene, or not?" Carver said.

They stepped inside and Ruth played the beam over the white object at the center of the lawn; a clear box was attached to the top. "There's something in the box, but I can't make out what," she said.

For now, there was no sound of an emergency vehicle—unless there happened to be a team already deployed in the city center, it would take the Matrix team another ten minutes to make the journey from their new base on the outskirts of the city.

The garden was overlooked on two sides: backed onto by tall Georgian terraces in an inverted L-shape; the third wall was windowless, being the end of the mews terrace. Carver looked up at the windows, some lit, some not.

"He could be watching from any one of those," he said. "But on the other hand, that plinth could be a memorial to some famous person who lived here."

"There's one good way to find out," Ruth said.

He resisted. "I don't want to look a damned fool, and right now, this is looking like an elaborate hoax. I mean, if this is a new 'exhibit,' where are his followers?"

"Is there anything on Instagram?"

He checked. "Not a whisper."

"We need to take a look," Ruth said. She shone the flashlight low over the lawn. They'd had a couple of dry days, but the clay soil in the Merseyside basin held on to moisture, and if this *was* a crime scene, there was an outside chance that the CSIs might get a useful shoe print.

"I think the ground has been trodden along this line," she said, indicating with the light beam. "So if we take a diagonal line from the corner off to the right, we'd be less likely to track over any prints."

Ruth led the way, Carver treading as close as he could in her footsteps.

The plinth in the center of the lawn looked like marble, the clear box was probably plexiglass, and there was something inside it: a dark mass.

Ruth took another step, and spotlamps flared all around them, drenching them in light. Ruth ducked instinctively, reaching for her Casco baton. But Carver seemed transfixed, staring at what was inside the box.

"Jesus," he breathed. "It's a heart."

Ruth did a quick three-sixty, thinking the Ferryman must be watching—how else would he know the exact moment to flick the switch?

More windows lit up; a few opened as residents leaned out to see what was happening. It was only a matter of time before word got out to the Ferryman's followers—if he hadn't already sent it.

Ruth called for mobile unit backup and Scientific Support—they would need more than the Matrix team for this—then turned her attention to Carver.

He blinked and seemed to come out of some kind of trance. The heart was dripping red; the liquid oozed from under the plexiglass box. But even as she asked Carver if he was all right, she thought, *It doesn't look right for blood.*

Carver swallowed. "It's moving," he said.

Ruth was a scientist, a coolheaded logician, but she couldn't suppress a shudder of horror as she looked again at the heart and saw that it *did* seem to be moving. Tiny undulations of the muscle rippled through it, as if it was still alive. As they watched, the heart seemed to split in several places at once.

Incisions, Ruth thought. *He sliced through the tissue.*

The cuts opened and the source of rippling movement revealed itself, as a writhing mass of maggots burst out, and the heart disgorged handfuls of shiny gold coins onto the plinth.

Sound blasted suddenly from nearby, and Ruth jumped like a cat. Her heart rattling in her throat, she realized it was music—10cc, playing "Art for Art's Sake."

Simultaneously, an engine roared, and tires screeched on the roadway beyond the wall.

"Stay there," Ruth said, although she didn't think Carver was capable of moving at that moment.

She ran to the gate as five Ferryman groupies spilled out of a Vauxhall Corsa.

"Hell!" Sirens wailed nearby, but they would be too late to hold back the mob. *Sod it.* She slammed the gate and slipped the padlock through the chain, locking it.

32

An hour later, Carver stood at the edge of the garden, near the wall. The place had been floodlit for the CSIs who were processing the scene. The street's limited access was both a blessing and a curse: initial clearing of the area had been hairy as the crowd, disgruntled at being kept away from the exhibit, got aggressive. Ruth's car had been damaged by a few determined Ferryman fans who'd climbed onto it in an attempt to get shots of the garden, but the wall spikes had kept them out. The arrival of a double-crewed unit scattered a few of them, and the Matrix team had made some arrests when they showed up two minutes later, so the situation was quickly contained.

Carver watched DS Lake, who was talking on her phone a short distance away. At least he wouldn't have to nag her to switch to an unmarked car; insurance should cover a rental for the next week or two while she sorted repairs.

Detectives and uniform police were knocking on doors, canvassing the buildings that overlooked the scene. On Carver's order, the identity of anyone entering or leaving was being carefully checked and logged in the record.

Scientific Support had held back until the area was made safe, and even after they'd been given the okay, they'd had to park a couple hundred yards from the cordon and lug their equipment to the scene. Evidence boxes were stacked against the wall, next to their instrument cases and spare disposable suits, vinyl gloves, and overshoes. John Hughes had attended the Dingle crime scene, and protocol dictated that he could not go near this one, but he had pulled in two of his most experienced CSIs for the job and sent a tech with them to assess how this bit of "artistry" had been achieved.

The technician's first job was to check the area for high voltages: the SSU's high-powered floodlights had revealed cables radiating out like the spokes of a bicycle wheel to spotlamps placed in a circle around the plinth. He was small and stocky, but he worked fast, and the air around him glowed faintly with violet light. Having quickly established the area was safe, he turned off the sound system that was playing "Art for Art's Sake" at full blast in a continuous loop. Job done, he left the CSIs to get on with it, trotting over the aluminum stepping plates that marked their common approach path, light on his feet for a stocky man.

"The spotlights were rigged to a simple infrared sensor on the pedestal," he told Carver. "Ditto the music."

"Where's the sound coming from?" Carver asked.

The tech jerked a thumb over his shoulder. "A boombox on the far side of the plinth."

One of the CSIs, fully kitted out in oversuit, gloves, and overshoes, was shining a high-powered Crime-lite over the pedestal and plexiglass box, searching for prints.

Ruth ended her call and joined them. "Passive infrareds are mostly designed for wide-angle detection, aren't they?" she said.

The tech nodded.

"Those PIRs didn't trigger till we were within six to eight feet of it," she said.

"Are you sure he wasn't watching, turned this lot on remotely?" Carver asked.

"He could've," the tech said. "But I can't see why he'd go to the bother of wiring up the PIR in that case." He thought for a moment. "I can't take it apart till the CSIs have done their stuff, and I'll admit the maggots were a bit . . . distracting." He gave an involuntary shudder.

"But I'm pretty sure this is a model I've used myself. If I'm right—and I think I am—that PIR is fitted with a zoned Fresnel lens that is sensitive to slight movement, geared to detect human activity at around two meters away."

Carver took a breath, and the tech added: "Before you ask, you can pick one up online for around twenty quid."

"I didn't hear a generator."

"No—the power source is a car battery."

"Would it take technical know-how to rig something like this up?" Carver asked.

"Not much." The tech shrugged. "Let's face it, you can find a step-by-step video guide for just about anything on YouTube these days."

Which was exactly what he'd been afraid of. "Okay, but how the hell did he carry all that kit *and* a hunk of stone into the middle of a locked space without being seen?"

"Oh, that's not stone," the tech said, glancing toward the plinth. "That thing's made of a lightweight laminate, with a marble-effect vinyl wrap."

Carver gave a grunt of disgust.

"Sorry to pile on the misery, but the padlock is a brand-new Masterlock," Ruth said. "And I've just spoken to the building manager; he says the one he used to lock the gate this evening is a Chubb, and it's a good fifteen years old. So either the offender used bolt cutters, or he picked the original and replaced it with the new lock."

Across the lawn, the CSI shut off his Crime-lite and walked carefully across the stepping plates.

"No prints?" Ruth said.

"We got a couple of shoe prints from the grass—not good quality."

"No fingermarks on the plinth?"

He shook his head. "Not that I can see. We'll shift the lot to the chemical treatment lab, see if superglue pops anything for us, but . . ." He tilted his head, unwilling to say it outright: they had nothing.

33

It was nearly midnight by the time Ruth Lake got home. She went straight to the front bedroom of her small terraced house, opened up the wardrobe, and began lifting out shoeboxes, excavating down to where she'd stashed her family album.

The binding was padded blue leatherette, and the gold lettering on the front cover had mostly worn off. She turned the thick card pages: family groupings; Mum laughing at the camera as she opened a Christmas present; Ruth and her brother at a dojo in Everton, just before an Aikido competition; certificates of achievement. The self-adhesive backing and plastic overlay had kept the photographs firmly in place, their colors almost as vivid as when they had been set there. She wished her memories could be as happily preserved, but they had been altered—tainted by all she knew, and all she'd done.

She had to force herself to move on from the photographs because, complicated as her emotions were about the "make-believe" happy family snaps, they were simple, wholesome fare compared with what came next.

She couldn't stop thinking about her exchange with Carver in the car. She knew the man, and when he got that look in his eye, it meant he would not give up. Tonight's new developments in the case would buy her some time, but they wouldn't distract him for long—eventually he would come back to Adam Black. And if he decided to start his own inquiries, raked through the evidence, it might just uncover things she would want to keep buried.

Reluctance turned to determination, and she flipped to the newspaper cuttings, trying to fix in her mind what had been public knowledge at the time; she needed to have her story straight before Carver started coming to her with difficult questions. She moved quickly past the condolence cards, the notes of sympathy, and a pressed flower from a funeral wreath. Those were still too painful to read; even Dad's note—"I do love you. Never doubt that."—carried a burden of guilt.

Because she *had* doubted that he loved them and had hated their father for his hypocrisy for many years. But even that memory had altered with time, as new circumstances came to light. Her forensics training told her that context is everything. Context changes how you look at a scene, a statement, a person, a situation. It could not alter the facts, but it could change the way those facts were interpreted, and the weight placed on them as evidence. Context had the almost magical ability to transform a guilty person into innocent bystander—even hero.

Ruth sighed impatiently. She wasn't kneeling on this scratchy old carpet to indulge nostalgic feelings, or to philosophize on the fickle nature of human memory. This was a fact-checking mission. She took the album over to the bed and sat cross-legged while she made notes, created a timeline, listed the names of main players, descriptions of injuries, causes of deaths, as if the violence that had been visited on her own family were just another police investigation.

34

Ruth Lake was buzzed in at the hospital mortuary by Sam, a technician she'd worked with many times in her former role as a CSI. He beamed at her as he led her through to the gowning area.

"Haven't seen you in a bit," he said. "How're you getting on since that thing over Christmas?"

He was talking about the previous case. "Ancient history," she said, denying the faint burn she felt in the crook of her arm. He seemed ready to quibble, and to divert him, she asked after his wife and two kids. "Julie was training as a nurse, wasn't she?"

His smile broadened. "She's fully qualified now."

They chatted as Ruth locked her personal belongings away and slipped into green scrubs and overshoes before going through to the postmortem room.

The pathologist was a blue-eyed Irishman named Donnelly. Glancing up from the steel table, where the heart had been placed, still inside the plexiglass box, he recognized her and they exchanged greetings. Ruth gave a friendly nod to the CSI who would be taking photographs and assisting where necessary. She would also take the plexiglass away to the chemical treatment lab for fingerprint analysis.

The gold coins were still inside the box. Ruth now saw that they were newly minted pound coins, and that the heart muscle had been sliced through with a very sharp blade so that it had opened like a lotus flower under the force of the writhing mass of maggots.

A few larvae were in evidence, but the heart would have been kept in the dark, at just above freezing point, from the time it was delivered to the mortuary; she expected most of the nasty little things had retreated into the farthest recesses of the chambers and blood vessels. Those she could see were moving sluggishly. The translucent red liquid she'd seen dripping from the box at the crime scene had set to a semiopaque solid.

Wax, she thought. But she knew better than to say it—this pathologist was known to verbally lacerate anyone who dared to make a pronouncement of that kind during "his" postmortem examinations.

Donnelly went through the formal procedures, turning on the mic and giving the time, date, and purpose of the postmortem, asking everyone to name themselves for the record, before describing the heart: its appearance and condition, the amount of fatty tissue, as well as the number, position, depth, and angle of every incision, while the technician and CSI took photographs.

The maggots were removed and placed into specimen tubes. Samples of the waxy substance were scraped off into shallow tubs, and the coins were counted into a separate container, while the pathologist kept up a constant commentary for the record. About forty minutes in, he stopped, looked at the heart from various angles, then stood back from the table.

"Huh," he said, unhelpfully.

Ruth looked across the table to Sam and saw a twinkle of amusement in his eyes. They both knew that the Irishman liked audience participation, provided it was suitably deferential, but neither one of them was willing to play that game, so it fell to the CSI to fulfill the role.

"Something unexpected, Doctor?" she said.

"Well, now," he said, "there's a lot about this par-*ti*cular postmortem that isn't what you'd expect in the normal run of things. Like, for instance, not having an *actual* body. But since you ask—as I mentioned in my earlier observations, the entire heart has been coated in a thin film of the red, waxy substance you see on the base of the box." He paused to draw a magnifier down from overhead. "But in addition, all the major blood vessels—that's superior and inferior venae cavae, the vessels of the aortic arch, descending aorta . . . aaaand"—he continued his examination—"yup!—the pulmonary arteries and veins—have been blocked with the same."

He straightened up for a moment.

"Now, being partial to a wager as I am, I'd bet my next paycheck that your man plugged up the major arteries and veins with a very practical purpose in mind." He looked at each of them in turn. "Would anyone care to speculate what that might be?"

No one did.

"In my opinion, its function was to contain the maggots while he set up the scene. You see, young blowfly larvae usually crawl toward light. And these, ladies and gentlemen, are young blowfly larvae." He picked up one of the labeled containers and tapped them down to the cap, then held it horizontally and closed his hand around the bulk of the cylinder to demonstrate. The maggots obligingly crawled to the uncovered third, into the light.

"I'm thinking it would've spoiled the effect if they'd entered center stage ahead of cue, now wouldn't it?" He lifted the cylinder to eye height, addressing the rascally larvae as if he found them adorable.

"So they were trapped inside the chambers of the heart. But as soon as the lights turned on, they went wild, busting out all over—like springtime."

Ruth thought she could imagine few things that were less like springtime than what she had witnessed the previous night. She hated to spoil Donnelly's grandstanding moment, but she needed clarification. "It was four degrees Celsius at the scene yesterday— you'd expect the larvae to be sluggish at best—but those little buggers were pretty lively."

"Hm . . . Let's see if we can do some detective work on that, shall we?" The pathologist sounded positively jaunty. He turned to the CSI and asked if she'd gotten all the pictures she needed, then used a spatula to pry the heart, in its pool of set wax, out of the box. An orange gel pad lifted with it.

He gently turned the heart over and the CSI snapped off a few shots.

"Now, what is this?" Donnelly mused.

The CSI spoke up. "Looks like an instant 'hot pack.'"

"On what do you base this assumption?" Dr. Donnelly said, in the tone of a patrician rudely interrupted in the delivery of great oratory.

The CSI flushed, recognizing her blunder. But it seemed she was made of sterner stuff than Ruth had realized.

"I didn't *assume,*" she said. "I said 'it looks like,' because that's the exact shade of orange of the hot packs I use every weekend when I do agility training with my border collie. They're called Hot to Go. "

Donnelly seemed stunned, and Ruth wanted to applaud. Instead she gave Donnelly her most guileless look and said, "That'll save us both some detective work, won't it, Doctor?"

"Perhaps you'd like to share your 'special knowledge' with us and explain to us how they work," he said, ignoring Ruth and addressing the CSI with offensive sarcasm thinly disguised as icy civility.

"See the little metal doodad in the bottom of the pouch?" the CSI said, refusing to back down. "You just bend it, and the gel starts to crystallize, and it heats up. They're pretty warm once they get going." She gave a little shrug. "I suppose that could be why the maggots were so active."

"Well," Donnelly said, addressing Ruth and Sam in his favored snarky tone, but clearly tired of the exchange, "if you have any further questions, you may address them to my learned friend across the table."

Relating the story to Carver two hours later, Ruth even managed to coax a smile out of him. Carver had been on the receiving end of Donnelly's acid tongue on more than one occasion.

"I don't suppose we can expect his preliminary report before tomorrow, then?" he said.

"It's doubtful. And he was in too bad a mood to confirm much until lab investigations were complete, but if you want my *un*official version . . ."

"That's why I sent you, Ruth," he said. "You're my secret weapon."

"Let's see," she said, pleased that he had seemed to have called a truce over her stubborn refusal to talk about Adam Black. "The 'blood' dripping from the heart was, in fact, red wax—and it was used to hold the thing together until the Ferryman was ready for us. He used young larvae, because they crawl toward the light. Apparently, their behavior changes a few days before they pupate, and then they crawl *away* from it."

Carver nodded thoughtfully. "Suggesting either that our offender knew what he was doing, or he'd experimented and found the best option. Well, we know he hones his craft, so he'd need a quantity of maggots. We should check shops that sell fishing bait—there can't be that many around Liverpool these days, can there?"

"I'll get someone on it," she said. "But you can have them delivered by mail order, and they'll keep for about two weeks in the fridge."

He winced, and she wondered if it was frustration at the Ferryman's ability to stay ahead of them or disgust at the notion of keeping live maggots in a fridge.

"Were there any sightings of him setting up the scene?" she asked.

"The building manager locked up at dusk, as usual," Carver said. "A couple of residents noticed some activity in the garden—lights and a male figure carrying boxes through the gate from a white van. But they didn't take much notice—end of the day, getting dark, dinner to prepare, and so on."

"Even so, the man must have ice running through his veins," she said. "Anything from ANPR on the white van?"

"Not based on the number plate we've been running up to now. Which convinces me he's switched plates. I've got a couple of detectives checking CCTV in the area for something that meets the description of the van he used in London."

Ruth nodded. Carver definitely seemed more on top of things.

"Do we know if Kharon was there?" Locked inside the garden while the crowd was forced back, Ruth hadn't been able to check for herself.

Carver shook his head. "No one saw him. We'll just have to rely on the Matrix van's CCTV and assess the crowd. I've requested a copy. I know you're busy, but . . ."

"I'll find time," Ruth said.

"So—maggoty heart, gold—is this an obvious reference to money and corruption?" Carver asked.

"Beats me," Ruth said. "If we knew who the victim was—"

"I've put a rush on the DNA profile," Carver said. "As soon as that's done, we'll try to match it to our missing persons. Until then, all we've got is the PM results."

"There were ten coins . . . I'm not big on the Bible—and the New Testament definitely isn't my strong point—but . . ." Ruth frowned, trying to recall. "Wasn't there a parable about a merchant giving out gold to his servants?"

"The parable of the talents," Carver said. "A rich merchant goes away on a trip and gives each of his servants a talent to look after. I always assumed a talent was a gold coin." He dragged his laptop closer and typed in a search. "Yep." He scanned the screen. "There's a difference of opinion on its actual value, but several results talk about gold. Says here, one of the servants invested the money and returned ten talents to his boss."

"The thing about talent is it can be read two ways," Ruth said. "And our guy seems to be all about gaining recognition for his 'talent.'"

"If the ten gold coins are supposed to symbolize money *and* talent, the music makes more sense, too: 'Art for Art's Sake/Money for God's Sake.'"

"There's another meaning to 'art for art's sake,'" Ruth said. "I checked it out last night: it's based on Théophile Gautier's philosophy, '*L'art pour l'art*,' which means art, with a capital 'A,' doesn't have to justify itself, morally."

Carver scoffed. "Sounds like a psychopath's manifesto. Which reminds me—I've spoken to Dr. Yi. He urged, in the strongest terms, that we should leave our work phones at work when we're off duty. We're feeding into the Ferryman's narcissistic grandiosity, apparently."

"He's probably right," Ruth said. "But we've seen what happens when we deny him access—especially to you."

"I said the same thing," Carver said. "But I have agreed to step away from the mic, let Superintendent Wilshire be the public face of the investigation for a few days."

"Good idea." She might have added that it would give Carver more time to rest but decided that the comment would be unwelcome.

"I am worried, though," Carver said. "We denied the Ferryman his big reveal last night. Hughes tells me the techs haven't found any clear shots of the heart on the plinth. There've even been some disparaging comments suggesting that you'd see better art on a butcher's slab at your local supermarket."

"He really messed up, didn't he?" Ruth said.

"Yi thinks that he could be unraveling."

Ruth shook her head. "His timing was just off. Biology is harder to control than plastic disks and LED displays. But he's not going to like that we thwarted his latest presentation."

35

Nothing. Not a damned thing. I have two desktop computers, several tabs open on each: Instagram, Twitter, local news, and—zilch. Thousands of punters out there, and not *one* of them managed to get a decent still, never mind a few seconds of video.

I'd given the most active sharers and commenters a five-minute head start on the rest. They *had* the location, knew *exactly* where Carver and Lake would be—why the hell weren't they ready? Why the *hell* is the only shot of my exhibit blurred and botched by flare off the crime scene spotlamps?

"Shit!" I send a dissection tray, scalpels, spare blades crashing to the floor.

It doesn't make me feel any better.

I should have known—less than one in one thousand of my followers might have the initiative to do what was necessary for the success of the exhibit—and what tiny fraction of those would actually be in the area at the right time? At that level of uncertainty, I probably had a better chance of winning the damned lottery. If I *could* have been there, I would have been. And of course, I'd *considered* finding a quiet spot inside the building where I could watch Carver and Lake, perhaps do some filming of my own. But my close call at Norris's place gave me pause: his neighbor must have been five feet from me when he called across. I couldn't take that kind of risk again.

I had to rely on others, and they failed. Failed *me*. All the work that went into *Art for Art's Sake*, wasted. Finishing up as offal on a mortuary slab.

I am well aware that my art exhibits will all end up as exhibits of another kind; in fact, there's a kind of poetry in their dismemberment. They will be examined—weighed and tested; stored separate from one another in labeled boxes and tamper-evident bags; reduced to mere components—I can accept that because they have been *seen* and *appreciated*. But *Art for Art's Sake* is a central tenet of this series. Without it, all the rest lose coherence and integrity. It's impossible to understand the artistic narrative without having seen this one core artwork.

To hell with it. I may as well shut down and go and drink myself stupid.

I reach for the mouse.

There's a notification:

"#FerrymanFan is trending on Twitter."

I almost can't bear to look. He has attached an image to a tweet, linked it to his YouTube channel. The image looks sharp, but it's only a thumbnail—as soon as I click on it, I know it will make a mockery of my work.

I circle the YouTube image, hover the mouse pointer over the red play arrow, tell myself I won't do it. But I click anyway.

And it is *beautiful*.

36

Ruth Lake couldn't believe what she was seeing: a pin-sharp recording of her and Carver approaching the plinth in the center of the walled garden. Hughes had sent her the link a minute earlier.

A sudden blast of light and noise, Carver frozen in the spotlights.

"It's not possible," she said, watching herself turn at the screech of tires on the road beyond the wall.

"It was posted by @Kharon three minutes ago," Tom Ivey said.

Ruth checked the camera angles. "He must have been inside one of the apartment buildings." A quick glance around the incident room told her that everyone had seen the footage.

"Who was on door duty?" she demanded. "Who logged residents in and out of the building last night?" She barely raised her voice, but every man and woman in the room stopped what they were doing and looked at her.

A hand went up.

Parr.

"I handed the list off to the receiver last night, after the public areas of the building had been searched and cleared," he said.

So either Kharon/Karl had gained access to one of the apartments, or he'd walked straight past the police checkpoint.

Ruth called out to the receiver. This was the HOLMES 2 database specialist whose job it was to control the paper flow. Every document, statement, and report that came in went first to the receiver, who would pass it to the right person for logging into the computer system.

"Sarge?" He was partly hidden behind a cubicle panel, but he rolled his chair back to make eye contact.

"Can we get a copy of the log?" Ruth said.

"Got it here, Sarge." The receiver passed the handwritten list to her.

She skimmed the names. "He's right here. Left the building forty-five minutes after we'd shut the display down."

Parr flushed. "I'm sorry, Sarge, I didn't recognize him."

"Well, I'd sympathize with that, Jason. But since Karl gave you his real name, I'd say you did a bit more than not recognize him."

Carver took the news surprisingly well. "They're all exhausted, Ruth," he said. "Mistakes are bound to happen."

She shook her head, frustrated with herself as much as with Parr. "It's partly my fault—he's been doing stellar work around the office—I thought his talents were being wasted. I asked Bill Naylor to give him something more challenging," she said. "Five minutes out in the field, and *this* . . ."

"Well, now you know where his strengths lie," Carver said.

It was usually Ruth's job to be the voice of calm and reason in such circumstances; perhaps it was an indication of just how tired she was herself that Carver was fulfilling that role today.

"What did you do to him?" he asked.

"He's back on car monitor duties."

Carver nodded. "Probably for the best. And Kharon?"

"I've sent someone to bring him in."

"Let me know when he gets here."

Ruth opened the door, ready to get back into the fray, and almost bumped into Parr, standing outside.

"Parr, were you eavesdropping?"

"No! No, Sarge." He stepped back, avoiding her eye. "Tom Ivey said you'd be here. I thought you'd want to see this."

He showed her a clear plastic bag. It had a sheet of plain white paper inside it; written on it, in block capitals: "FERRYMAN—4, MER-SEYSIDE POLICE—0." He turned the sheet over. On the back, one word. "CLUELESS."

"What is this?" Ruth demanded.

"I found it in one of the unmarked job cars, Sarge. In the boot well."

"Which one?"

"Car seventeen."

"Did you touch it with your bare hands?" Parr was wearing pale blue vinyl gloves.

"Sorry, yes—I picked it up before I realized what it was. But I gloved up right away."

Two definite sources of contamination, then—the car boot well, and Parr himself. Plus a possible host of others between the car park and Carver's office, she reminded herself.

"What about the bag?"

He stared at her blankly.

"Did you bag it, too?"

"No—it was already in there."

"And did you open it?"

"No!" Clearly the idea horrified him.

"All right." She got on the line to CSM Hughes and asked him to send someone to collect it. In under ten minutes, it was bagged, tagged, and with forensics; Parr was back on car check duty; and the car was being given a going-over by CSIs.

Ruth Lake returned to Carver to catch him up on her initial checks.

"The car was driven to the crime scene last night. They parked it at the outer cordon."

"Locked, or unlocked?" Carver asked.

"They say locked, and in theory, it was under the watchful eye of uniform police, but you know how it got last night."

Carver nodded. "Any surveillance footage?"

"Matrix was focused on the area around the courtyard, but I've asked Rayburn to check," Ruth said. "And Doctor Yi says he'll phone you later this afternoon. Meanwhile, there's Karl Obrazki to deal with."

Ruth kept him waiting another twenty minutes, but sitting across the table from her, Kharon, aka Karl Obrazki, looked bright-eyed, untroubled, sure of himself.

"You didn't believe me when I told you this man is dangerous?" Ruth asked.

"I believed you." He slouched in his chair like a poor man's Brando in *On the Waterfront*. "I mean, it's obvious, because—you know—people died."

"They were murdered," Ruth corrected.

He shrugged, as if to say, *potayto/potahto*. "That wasn't personal—and anyway I don't think he's dangerous to me."

"You don't *think*?" She scratched the back of her neck. "If it was me, I'd want a hundred percent guarantee."

"Oh, you needn't worry—I don't think he's into the female form."

"Phew," she said. "But, wait a minute—doesn't that mean he *is* into the male form?" She widened her eyes as if she'd just realized that Karl fit the victim profile.

For a few seconds he stared at her as though she'd started speaking Maori; then she saw a flicker of alarm in his eyes. "No," he said. "You don't get it. I brought *Art for Art's Sake* to the public."

Ruth tilted her head. "*You* did, *he* didn't."

"But that's the way he wanted it. Did you *see* the feedback?" His eyes glittered with feverish intensity, and Ruth wondered if he was high on something. "I mean, people *love* what he did."

"They love that he murdered people?"

"No, not *that* . . ." He gazed around the room as if he might find the right words daubed on the walls. "I mean what he did with the coins and the maggots? All the shit ordinary working people have to take. Art is above that."

"You're not making sense," Ruth said. "Do you *really* believe that displaying the body parts of murdered people is art?"

"Maybe not the way *you* think of it—but it does what art is supposed to do. It challenges the way we see the world. Brings us face-to-face with death."

Ruth looked at the earnest half child, half man seated opposite her, his own features as yet unmarked by life, and thought that only someone who hadn't seen the ugly face of death could talk that way.

"So art isn't supposed to be uplifting, or consoling?" she said. "It can't be playful, or tender, or healing?"

"Well, *yeah* . . ." Even as he agreed, he dismissed her with a flip of a wrist and the slightest hint of a sneer. "But *Ferryman's* art is about shock and challenge and excitement."

"It's certainly shocking," she said, mildly.

He pushed his fingers through his hair—a self-conscious gesture of frustration. "You've got to see the artistry in it, the use of symbolism."

She was interested to hear his interpretation, so she tilted her head, inviting him to go on.

"Money ruins art," he said. "Art shouldn't be bought and sold—it belongs to everyone. It should come from the heart, and when it doesn't, it corrupts the best intentions of the artist."

You're so full of it, she thought. *The Ferryman wants fame and power—and if that doesn't corrupt, I don't know what does.* Even so, she sounded sincere when she said, "Wow, you really *do* understand him."

He dipped his head in a show of false modesty. "So people say."

"Does *he*?"

"Does he what?"

"Say you understand him?"

"He chose me to get the message out about *Catch the Gamma Wave*, so . . ."

"And last night?"

"No." A frown creased his smooth brow.

"He didn't message you?" she said, her tone coaxing, and with no hint of confrontation. "Ask you to record the scene, maybe?"

"I *wish*." The young fan sounded wistful. "I just—you know— did it."

"After he messaged you with the location."

"Me and a few others. But I got the jump on them, 'cos I was already tailing you."

"Were you indeed?"

"I just *knew* he was planning a new exhibit."

"And you were right."

He preened a little.

"How come you went inside the building—weren't you taking a chance you'd miss the whole thing?"

"As soon as I saw the place I could see it wasn't gonna work," he scoffed. "Your lot'd have us kettled in no time. At least inside the building, I stood a chance of finding a good spot."

"And you did."

Again, he quelled a triumphant smile, maybe thinking it wouldn't look cool.

Now he was feeling secure, she came back to something that had intrigued her. "Why are you so sure his choice of victims isn't personal?"

"Because . . . it's art, isn't it?"

He's still so sure of that. "Art is objective, then?"

"No . . . well, sometimes. But it's ways of seeing the world—we all see it different, but some artists have a gift of making other people see it their way."

"And if they don't see it your way?"

"Well, you can take it or leave it." He seemed to think it a stupid question.

"Like Professor Tennent?"

"I don't . . . ?"

"He didn't believe in the myth, and he ended up in what you so tactfully call an 'exhibit.' "

He flushed, uncomfortable at being challenged. "That was different—that was to prove the point."

"What point would that be?"

He gave an irritated shrug. "That the Ferryman isn't a myth."

"You mean, that there really is a killer snatching young men off the streets and murdering them."

"You're twisting my words."

"I don't believe I am," Ruth said. "But leaving that aside for now—you say you weren't in direct communication with the killer yesterday?"

"The Ferryman," he corrected. "No."

"Or since?"

"No."

"Would you be willing to prove that by letting us have your phone?"

A snort. "No."

"Why not, if you've nothing to hide?"

This time, he made no effort to hide his smile. "I got into that building through an open front door, found a good angle from a window in the public stairwell, took some video footage. Even gave my name to the nice PC plod when I left. Is any of that a criminal offense?"

"That depends if you're telling the truth."

"Be hard to prove any different, wouldn't it?" he said.

Of course, she thought. *He's been briefed.*

"Thought so," he said. Even had the cheek to wink at her as he left.

37

Kharon is standing outside Merseyside Police Headquarters. The press and media have been waiting for ninety minutes. A group of eighteen- to thirtysomethings form a guard of honor down the steps, every one of them wearing an *F*-logo hoodie.

Have they completely lost touch with reality? Honoring Kharon as if *he* created *Think Outside the Box*, as if *he* recorded the final, dying brain waves for *Catch the Gamma Wave*, the ECG readings for *Life Passes*. As if the imagination, skill, and technical resourcefulness that went into the execution of *Art for Art's Sake* were his.

The little bastard is pleased with himself, talking about "artistic integrity" and the "function" of art. Insect.

Don't test me, little flea . . .

There's no denying that he retrieved the situation—even turned it into a media triumph. But media triumph too often turns into media circus, and I cannot have the clowns running the circus.

Perhaps it's time I took control, brought him under my instructive wing. After all, Andy Warhol had an entire "factory" of artists working under his instruction. And Damien Hirst's self-described "pill mines" were little more than glorified sweatshops staffed by art graduates who ground their talent to dust, fashioning pills for reproductions of his "medicine cabinet" works. Imagine, a production line of apprentices disarticulating limbs ready for reassembly in an exhibit—piecework as a literal and metaphorical concept! While the notion appeals to my darker side, I think Kharon's talent for publicity is a far more valuable resource.

Often, it's hard to recall the exact instant that inspires a work—the emotion or image or feeling. But I feel a sudden, hot rush of excitement like fire in my veins, and I know I will always remember this is one. I shelve an idea I've been toying with for Steve Norris—an organic/ carbon fiber sculpture—using running blades. Because in this memorable instant, I know how I will induct Kharon into my series, and it will be *magnificent*.

38

DAY 8, EVENING

There was nothing of forensic use on the sheet of paper or inside the bag. The sheet itself was standard 80 gsm A4 printer paper, available from thousands of outlets across the city; the bag was a Tesco zip-seal. The only fingerprints on the outside of the bag were Parr's. Analysis of the ink would take longer, but it looked like cheap biro.

Dr. Yi had little to add. "There's not much to go on in the letter itself," he said. "It's unusual but not unheard of for serial killers to communicate with the investigators: the American serial killer Dennis Rader sent taunting messages to police and newspapers—and like your 'Ferryman' he gave himself a name—'BTK' in his case. There are other examples: in New York, George Metesky, aka 'The Mad Bomber,' sent letters and demands; the Beltway Snipers left messages scrawled on tarot cards at the scenes of some of their shootings. And of course, here in Britain—Jack the Ripper's infamous 'Dear Boss' letter ridiculed the police, taunting them with what he intended to do to his next victim."

"So we can expect more?"

"Almost certainly." He paused. "One thing worth considering: usually, killers send letters in the post, or leave them in public places. This man took a huge risk, planting this note. He must have ice running through his veins to leave it in a police vehicle under police surveillance."

Carver finished the call and considered calling Ruth in to his office, but he'd scheduled an appointment with the work-appointed psychologist for six o'clock, and it was already five forty-five. Anyway, Superintendent Wilshire had been sniffing around the MIR all day: he would have to leave it till the next morning to brief the team to be vigilant for anyone hanging around their cars. Carver packed up and headed out.

He arrived five minutes late and they got straight to it. Carver had been determined to try to tell the psychologist about the dreams that woke him every night, to admit to his fear that he was losing his mind. Instead, as usual, he ended up talking about the case. He lied to himself that he was opening up, admitting to Roman that he'd frozen when he saw the heart begin to move. But since the whole thing had been broadcast on social media as well as a few online news channels, he was only owning up to something the doctor would already have seen—telling him what was already blindingly obvious.

"I saw a brief clip," the doctor said. "You clearly found it deeply disturbing."

Dr. Roman seemed to swathe himself in a pale shimmer of calm.

They had been talking for a good thirty minutes by this point, and Dr. Roman asked the first question of the session: "Was there some particular aspect that disturbed you?"

Perhaps it was the fact that the psychologist had already seen his reaction to the Ferryman's latest outrage, or maybe it was something else, but whatever the reason, Carver began to explain: "The heart was cut in segments," he said. "When they began to fall outward, I saw . . ."

The therapist leaned closer, and although he couldn't look into the man's eyes, Carver felt his sympathetic attention.

Ruth's words echoed in his mind: *You need to open up to someone sometime.*

Here goes . . .

"I've had a recurring dream," he began again. "After I was shot. I call it a dream, but it feels so real . . ." He could feel his heart thudding against his rib cage and a wave of nausea made him stop.

He took a breath and let it go slowly. *Tell it from the beginning.*

"During my previous murder investigation, one of the victims looked very like Emma, my wife."

He saw a flash of Emma lying on a mortuary table and flinched.

"I'm sorry?" the doctor said.

Did I say that aloud?

Carver cleared his throat. "I said, Emma is fine."

The psychologist nodded, his expression saying, *That's a good thing, and it's safe to explore your fear.*

"In this vision, the victim—her name was Kara—she starts scream-ing." He saw the young student writhing on the mortuary table, the horror in her eyes. "I wuh . . ." His breath failed him, and he had to try again: "I want to help her, but she . . ." He swallowed. "It's like she's being sliced open, from—from the *inside*. And Emma . . . Emma is there. Suffocating. Fighting to get out."

The skin of the girl's face pares back and falls away and Carver sees Emma's, gory with Kara's blood, her eyes huge with horror.

"I can't . . ." He tried to catch his breath, but the pressure on his chest forced the air out of him. "I can't . . . I don't know how to h-help." He heard his voice rise in pitch and tone, and at last, he tore his eyes from the terrible vision unfolding in his mind.

The air in front of Dr. Roman's face darkened.

A sudden shaft of steel gray sliced through the distance between them. *Anxiety.*

Carver realized that he was seeing his own emotions in the psychol-ogist's aura. The therapist's body language and mind-set were holding a mirror up to Carver's own feelings.

He's empathizing.

Instantly, Carver felt himself pulled physically toward the darkness, into a vortex of emotion and terror that seemed to spark blue in the smoky haze that obscured the doctor's features.

Like a black hole, he thought. And like a black hole, there would be no return from it. He stood to leave.

"Open your eyes, Greg."

Carver didn't want to, but the voice was insistent.

"You're safe. You can open your eyes."

He did as he was told. Found himself lying on the floor in Dr. Roman's office.

"D'you think you can sit up?" The voice was Dr. Roman's.

Carver pushed up with both hands and struggled to a crouch. He tried to get to his feet and fell on his backside. His shoulders and chest ached as though he'd been lifting weights, and he felt weak.

"Just sit for a minute."

The therapist offered Carver a paper cup; he took a sip and handed it back but when he tried again to stand up, Roman pressed gently on his shoulders. "You need to catch your breath."

Carver shook him off. "What the hell just happened?"

"You stood to leave," Roman said, "and crumpled to the floor."

"I fainted?"

"You were conscious, but unresponsive."

Unresponsive—what does that mean? A rush of cold fear washed over Carver, flowing down his body and settling in his stomach.

"You're probably feeling some discomfort in your chest, perhaps tingling in your arms—"

Carver opened and closed his right fist. *How could he know this?*

"—and your mouth may be dry."

"Tell me what the *fuck* just happened," Carver said. "What do you mean, I was 'unresponsive'?"

"You collapsed to the floor, curled into a ball, and stayed that way for several minutes," Roman said in that same calm, annoying tone.

Carver couldn't make sense of it.

"I believe you experienced a dissociative episode."

Carver felt for the chair behind him and struggled into it.

Dr. Roman handed him the paper cup. "Your mind couldn't cope with the feelings and thoughts associated with the recurring dream; the emotion was too overwhelming. So it disconnected from reality, took you somewhere else." He paused. "It's a protective response."

"I know what it is—and I know why it happens. It's—" But Carver couldn't bring himself to say the words "post-traumatic stress." He looked at his hands. "It doesn't matter what you call it; I know what it means—I'm finished."

39

After a long night searching for Adam Black, Ruth Lake was tired and wired. She had scoured support services on the fringes of the system: drug counseling services, homeless charities, AA meetings, and got nothing.

More bad news had just arrived by e-mail, and rather than sit at her desk and grind her teeth, she zipped down to Carver's office.

He'd turned down her offer of a lift that morning and arrived into work an hour later than she had; he was freshly shaved and it looked like he'd even had his hair trimmed, but he still had that hollowed-out, gray look.

"Don't say it," he said.

"Say what?" She instinctively covered, thinking he was much easier to manage before he developed this newfound ability to read people.

He snuffed, shaking his head wearily. "What d'you want, Ruth?"

"A tiny bit of good luck would be very welcome—if that can be arranged."

"Not in my sphere of influence, I'm afraid," he said.

"Okay," she said. "There's bad news and there's worse news." Seeing the look on his face, she hurried on. "And I'm just going to launch in with the bad news: no progress on Steve Norris's place; I don't think our guy will go back there. No sightings of Steve Norris from around the Festival Gardens or the path through to St. Michael's Station on the morning he disappeared, either."

He nodded, seeming to accept it as a function of the way this murder inquiry rolled.

"It looked for a millisecond like DC Ivey might've made a breakthrough," Ruth added.

Carver perked up a little at that.

"He got hold of two images from CCTV cameras in corner grocery stores," she explained. "A man buying items with victims' credit or debit cards."

"But . . . ?" Carver said. "I feel there is a 'but' coming."

"Neither is much good: the angle is too high on one, and the image is blurred to buggery on the other."

"If we could find the bastard using an ATM, we'd stand a better chance of getting a useful image," Carver said.

"I wouldn't bet on it," she said. "Both of the CCTV screen-caps show the suspect wearing a scarf around the lower half of his face and a beanie hat pulled low over his brow."

Carver sighed. "Well, tell Ivey to keep trying—all we need is for this bastard to get careless once."

Ruth nodded. "I've suggested he should go back to every shop that we know victims' credit or debit cards were used, and leave copies of the CCTV images, in case our man comes back."

"Good idea," Carver said. "All right, I've heard bad news; I hesitate to ask about the worse news."

"The results have come through on the heart," Ruth said. "It doesn't match any of the missing persons on our list."

"Because this victim hasn't been reported missing yet, or because the killer's gone out of area again?" He was sharp today, despite his frail looks.

Carver rubbed his chin. "I hate to say it, Ruth, but we may need to widen our geographical area."

"I think you're right," she said. "But we're looking at a national pool of around thirty-four thousand males over the age of eighteen."

Carver's eyes widened. "That many go missing every year?"

"Mostly in the twenty-two to thirty-four age group." The stats were fresh in her mind from her searches for Adam Black. "Though only around three percent stay missing for more than a week."

"What about our victim? Do we know how long he'd been dead?"

"The pathologist says there was no sign that the heart had been frozen, and there were no signs of putrefaction—the maggots were stage dressing, rather than through natural causes."

"So this victim could have been killed within the last week or so?"

"I'm afraid so," Ruth said. "Longer, if he refrigerated the tissue."

"We can't search that many records, Ruth—we just don't have the resources to keep throwing more people at this. And even if I *could* find the personnel, we don't have the budget."

"I hear you," she said.

"If we could find a stronger link between them than age—"

"And Tennent doesn't exactly fit *that* criterion, either," Ruth said. "But we think he either pissed off the killer or was a vehicle to boost the Ferryman's visibility, so he doesn't fit with the other victims in any case. If we focus on the others—Eddings and Martin, and the other MisPers—they were all local to Merseyside. Say we limit our search area to a forty-five- to fifty-mile radius . . ."

Carver tapped a few instructions into his laptop, then swung it round for her to see. "This is what a forty-five-mile radius looks like," he said. The map he'd called up included five major towns and cities in northwest England, including Manchester, Warrington, and Preston; it even lassoed parts of North Wales in its noose.

"Right . . ." She thought for a few moments. "On the basis of the victims so far, we can exclude people suffering from depression or with known mental health problems—a sizable number of males who go missing do have mental health issues."

Carver nodded, the gleam in his eye telling her that he liked the idea.

"And ask the pathologist just how long heart tissue will keep if it's not frozen," he said. "See if he can give us a narrower time slot."

"While I'm at it, I'll ask if there's anything he can do to narrow the age range," Ruth said. "There might be some cytological tests he could try."

"Great." Carver checked his watch. "I have a meeting. Can you . . . ?"

"Sure," she said. "I've got it covered."

She saw him ghost past the MIR a few minutes later, his overcoat slung over one arm. He caught her watching and faltered for a second, seemed about to say something, but then changed his mind and walked on, heading for the stairs.

40

Fifteen minutes later, Carver was in Paul Halmead's office. Halmead was an eye movement and desensitization and reprocessing (EMDR) therapist who worked out of the same building as Dr. Roman; the office was similar—a few more paintings on the walls, a brighter rug in the reception area, perhaps—but essentially the same. It even looked out onto Rodney Street, as Roman's did.

His last session with Roman had ended in bewilderment and hope.

"I'm finished," Carver had said.

Dr. Roman had smiled. "No, Greg. This is the beginning. This is the moment you start to heal."

Carver had left Dr. Roman's office with a name, and an appointment for the next morning with Halmead.

The EMDR specialist was about Carver's age, a kind-eyed man, balding and perhaps a little soft around the middle, but Carver sensed a sharp intelligence behind his empathic exterior.

"You don't have to know . . . stuff, do you?" Carver asked. It wasn't the most auspicious opening to his first session, but he could not physically have coped with a second dissociative episode in the space of twenty-four hours.

"Stuff?" Halmead said.

"About me. About what happened to me."

"Let's start from the premise that *something* happened to you," Halmead said, his voice warm and unchallenging.

"So you *don't* need to know?"

The psychologist was silent for a few seconds. "It's quite normal for people to feel shame or guilt when they've been through trauma," he said. "But that's faulty thinking—it's caused by our natural human need to rationalize things that happen. The 'If I'd done *this*, then *that* would never have happened' type of scenario. Traumatic events don't happen to one person rather than another because they're bad, or because they deserve it."

"I know that," Carver said.

"Objectively, on an intellectual level, I don't doubt it," Halmead said. "But the part of the brain that responds to trauma is instinctual, prelinguistic, emotional—you might as well try to reason with your pet dog. The guilt you feel is at a visceral level."

"Look, Mr. Halmead, I know you're trying to help. But I went through all this with Dr. Roman. I really don't feel guilt, or shame. I'm just frustrated that I can't shake this thing. You see, I'm exposed to what you might call traumatic events on a regular basis in the work I do, and I keep having these flashbacks. Can you fix that?"

"The human brain isn't a machine," the therapist said mildly. "You can't tune it up like a lawnmower."

Carver braced his hands on his thighs, ready to stand.

"Look," the therapist said in the same quiet, unhurried tone. "Why don't you tell me what you want from these sessions."

Carver deliberated.

"I want to feel less afraid," he said at last. "I want to be able to deal with the everyday confrontations of my job without blacking out. I want to sleep at night."

"Doesn't seem much to ask, does it?" Halmead said quietly. "Can you tell me something about what happened to you—no details—just the bare outline of it. Was it a car crash, for instance? Or . . ."

"Someone tried to kill me," Carver blurted out. "They almost succeeded. I was conscious, but I couldn't—" He took a deep breath and let it go slowly. "I was trapped, paralyzed for a time."

He remembered the shadows, and the reek of whisky and gun-smoke.

"During the traumatic events, a primitive part of your brain called the amygdala is triggered," Halmead said. "The amygdala controls the 'fight or flight' response." He touched two points either side of his head, midway between his temples and ears. "Now, that's a good thing, *if* you're capable of fight or flight—but you were literally paralyzed—unable to do one or the other. You were powerless."

"That was then," Carver said. "Why can't I control it now?"

"The amygdala is nonverbal," Halmead said. "The message flashed direct from your sensory organs—your eyes, nose, and ears—to the amygdala, to this primitive 'lizard' brain that only *feels*. Your higher brain was cut out of the loop. The result: total communication break-down."

"That was then, this is now," Carver repeated.

"But the verbal and nonverbal parts of the brain are *still* not on speaking terms," Halmead said.

"What can I *do* about it?" Carver heard the note of desperation in his voice.

"We have to put them back in touch."

"I don't see how; I've tried everything."

"You haven't tried everything until you've tried EMDR," Halmead said.

"How does it work?"

Halmead smiled apologetically. "To be honest we don't really know how it does what it does. But we do know it works."

"But I don't have to talk about what happened, because I don't think I could—"

"No," Halmead reassured him. "But I won't lie to you—you *do* have to *think* about your experiences."

Carver took a breath and exhaled.

Halmead cocked his head. "I'd guess that you're having to clamp down so hard to control those feelings of helplessness that you're blocking even normal emotions."

Carver croaked a reply, cleared his throat, and said, "Yes."

The therapist watched him for a few moments. "There's a term in rehab: white-knuckle sobriety. You could be dry for years, but it's like being on a roller-coaster ride—you just grab the handrail and hang on, 'cos you know if you let go, it's a long way down."

"That's exactly what it feels like," Carver admitted.

"How would it be if you could think about those things as something unpleasant that happened in the past, but can't hurt you now, in the present—to be able to acknowledge the past, but let it go?"

Carver felt his face spasm, and he clenched his fists. *Get a grip, Carver.* "That would be bloody marvelous," he managed through gritted teeth.

"Well then," Halmead said. "It's time we made a start."

41

Almost five full days since she'd first seen Adam Black, Ruth Lake was running out of places to look; he'd vanished into the shadows—and Liverpool still had plenty of those, despite its little renaissance over the past decade.

Or maybe he isn't here at all. She stared, dispirited, at the tiled frontage of a pub across the road from her. She was in the seedier streets around Wavertree; they used to say there was a pub on every corner in this part of town. Ruth felt like she'd visited every one of them, but she wasn't even two-thirds of the way through.

She trotted across the street to the next corner pub and was about to open the door, when her work phone rang. She checked the screen; it was Carver, and her heart picked up a pace. Surely the Ferryman couldn't have come up with another exhibit so soon after the last?

"Ruth, I know it's late."

This was Carver's version of an apology. She reevaluated, mentally labeling the call "work-related, but not urgent."

A motorbike roared past and Carver said, "Are you out and about?" Then, "Anything I should know about?"

"No," she said. Sometimes keeping it simple was the best way to hide the truth.

"Okay," he said. "Look, I'm not going to hound you—"

Ruth gave a short laugh. It was rude, and unlike her—a measure, perhaps, of how tired and tense she was. "Sorry, boss," she said. "What d'you need?"

"To blow off steam, if I'm honest," he said. "It seems the only concrete evidence we've got is footwear marks."

"Not true," she said. "We've got sightings of the Ferryman using victims' credit cards; we've got the van; a possible sighting at Norris's place—and we've identified Kharon. The Ferryman is forensically savvy—he wears gloves. Maybe possibly overalls, too. But he's not infallible—he didn't wear overshoes—and since this isn't *Mission: Impossible*, he had to stand somewhere. That's something. And I'll take something over nothing, any day."

"It hasn't gotten us any closer to identifying the bastard, though," Carver said.

"Well, we do know for sure he's not a ghost," she said, "or Tom Cruise."

It was good to hear him laugh: it had been a while since Ruth had heard Greg Carver laugh.

"Well, if you think of anything—"

"You'll be the first to know," she said. She was about to end the call, when something did occur to her. "Greg, wait—there was one thing we haven't tried."

"I'm listening."

"How about sending the Hutton Institute a sample of the dirt the forensics team found on the balcony of Steve Norris's place?"

"I can't believe it—we're back to the footwear marks again!"

"Hey," she said. "You've gotta make the best of what you've got."

"Will it give us an ID?"

"You *know* it won't," she said, hearing sarcasm, but also a smile in his tone. "It might give us a location, however."

"How much are we talking?"

"Budget-wise? They don't come cheap, but . . ."

Ruth was distracted by a car. It drew up at the curb a few feet from her, right on a busy junction.

Audi 4x4, she registered—*high end*, the side and rear windows heavily tinted. A major Matrix police operation had seized a whole fleet of Audi 4x4s and sports cars from gangs running drugs a couple of years ago, and Audis were still the vehicle of choice for criminals in the city.

The homeless man's warning came to mind: *Bad men*, he'd said, *and you're a moving target.*

Ruth assessed the level of threat: three men, judging by the bulkiness of the shadows behind the tinted glass. She'd caught a glimpse of the driver as he'd skimmed past: bat-eared, youngish, with the narrow nose and pinched nostrils of a macaque monkey—enough for her to identify him again, if anything kicked off.

"Are you still there, Ruth?" asked Carver.

"Yeah," she said.

A man got out of the rear of the car. He was big across the shoulders and the bulk under his badly fitting suit jacket suggested long hours in the gym, plus a fair amount of testosterone boosting.

"Are you all right?" Carver said.

Ruth backed to the pub door. "I may have to get back to you on that," she said.

The pub door opened and, keeping her eye on the car, she turned sideways to slide past the drinker on his way out, but he filled the frame with his height and heft.

"Ruth," Carver said, "talk to me." His voice was tight with concern.

The driver stayed where he was, but another man got out of the Audi. This one, though skinny and small, frightened her most: the rage in his eyes and the twist of his mouth said he was capable of anything.

"What's she up to?" he said, looking over her head to the bouncer on the door.

The big man looked over her shoulder. "Talking to her boss."

"Hang up," the skinny man said, addressing Ruth.

"I'll call you back in thirty minutes," Ruth said into the phone. "If I don't, call the cavalry."

The big man plucked the phone from her fingers.

"You know I'm a police officer," Ruth said. "Don't do anything stupid."

The big man lobbed her phone over the top of the car to the gym bunny in the suit jacket. He caught it, cracked the back, dropped the battery into his palm, and pocketed the pieces like he could do it on a foggy night in a blackout.

Her left arm went dead from the shoulder to the elbow as the door-man's hand closed around her upper arm. He bent to whisper in her ear, his mouth so close to her skin that she could feel the heat of his breath.

"Only stupid people call me stupid," he said.

Ruth said nothing.

"Look at me," he said.

She looked into his face and recognized him with a sick lurch.

"You know me?" he said.

"I know who you work for."

"Well then."

The skinny thug held the rear passenger door open and the big man walked her to it.

Carver paced the floor of his apartment.

She's in trouble.

He ran a hand over his face. *Give it thirty minutes, then call the cavalry,* she had said. "Call the cavalry" was a phrase DS Lake had used once before, and that time, she had barely survived what followed.

He could ask for a trace on her phone, but he sensed that Ruth wanted time to see if she could manage the situation. *Yeah, and how did that turn out last time?*

Even so . . . he had a horrible feeling that this was all wrapped up in her search for Adam Black. If he'd been more on the ball, he'd have worked out exactly who Black was days ago—or forced the truth out of her.

Shit.

Ten minutes, he told himself. So, he waited, agonizing over every second. But when he called her, the phone went straight to voice mail.

"Ruth, call me as soon as you get this," he said.

You didn't agree to her terms—you don't have to wait thirty minutes. But even as the thought formed in his mind, he knew he would wait those long minutes for her call.

They didn't blindfold her or bind her hands—didn't even confiscate her Casco baton—but Ruth Lake did not underestimate the trouble she was in. They drove a mile or so west on Edge Lane, turning off the main road into the grounds of what had once been a wealthy merchant's house. Since the nineteenth century it had been an orphanage, a convent, a girl's college, and for the past twenty years, a hotel and family-friendly restaurant. At least, that was the front-of-house business. Dave Ryan, the man she was expecting to see, had many business interests—most of which were not family friendly at all.

Merseyside Police had targeted the place at various times, but neither covert surveillance nor raids had turned up any solid evidence of criminal behavior. Local folklorists spoke of the extensive tunnel network constructed by "the Mole of Edge Hill," a real-life philanthropist and eccentric of the eighteenth and nineteenth centuries, speculating that Ryan was using the tunnels to both transport and hide contraband.

The bat-eared driver pulled the car around to the back of the building, and the three passengers walked Ruth through the kitchens, where the staff were scrubbing down, ready to finish for the night. A few heads turned, but most avoided eye contact with the men, and they quickly got back to work.

Swing doors opened onto a tiled corridor lit by too-bright neon strip lighting. Ruth guessed that the door directly opposite probably gave onto the main restaurant. The walls were scuffed and scraped, and a few reddish stains splashed the walls. She hoped it was spaghetti sauce.

She considered stepping through into the restaurant, daring her captors to drag her away in front of witnesses, but the low hum of conversation beyond the door told her that the room was still relatively full, and she didn't want to risk civilian casualties in the fallout. She glanced quickly up and down the corridor. One door to her right, two more to the left, one of which was at the far end of the passage.

"Go left," the skinny man said—the first words he'd spoken since he'd told her to hang up on Carver. "All the way to the end."

Ruth felt a sinking dread at the finality of those words: the farther they went into the back-of-house areas, the worse her chances of getting out in one piece if things turned nasty. But with three men barring the way she'd come, she had no choice but to do as she was told.

The door was an extrawide, paneled affair in some rich wood, slightly warped with age, but surprisingly polished; it gleamed despite its dingy surroundings.

"Go 'ead, then," the skinny man said.

She turned the brass doorknob and let the door swing wide. The room was dimly lit after the glaring brightness of the corridor, and she took a moment to allow her eyes to adjust to the gloom. The skinny thug gave her a shove in the small of her back that sent her stumbling two steps forward, but she regained her balance fast, taking in a large square room, hung with what looked like original artwork. A door on the left, near the back of the room, stood closed. Two huge, moonlit windows to her right seemed a possible escape route, but on second glance, she realized that the garden borders, lawn, and ghost-white cherry blossom tree were in fact a series of paintings, skillfully applied to the wood shutter panels, which were closed and barred against the night.

No help there, then.

Dave Ryan sat at an antique desk at the far end of the room, drinking scotch from a tulip-shaped glass. He was a gray-haired man in his midfifties, with faded blue eyes that had a kindly look. Even so, when he fixed his gaze on her, Ruth's heart gave a little shudder.

"You've been making waves, Sergeant." He was soft-spoken, courteous.

"Have I?"

He smiled. Meet him in a city bar, you might mistake Ryan for an ordinary dad, out for a couple of pints and a trip down memory lane with the lads to revisit the glory days of his youth. But looks can deceive.

"Upsetting the street vendors, scaring off punters? Yeah, I'd say so," he said.

Cheeky sod had the nerve to call his drug peddlers and sex workers "street vendors." Ruth matched his smile, though her stomach roiled. "That's my *job*, making things difficult for criminals."

The smile didn't waver. "Just doing your job, then?" he said.

Ruth didn't see the need to answer the question twice, so she gazed guilelessly into his face, while her thoughts scurried. Had he brought her here to give her a literal or metaphorical slap? He must know she couldn't let that pass.

He tipped the glass in his hand and stared into it. "You're not being honest with me, Sergeant Lake," he said. "See, I know you're off duty."

You and half of Liverpool, what with the Ferryman's spies lurking on every corner, Ruth thought.

"So I'm wondering, why are you going around waving your warrant card, asking bizzie questions, like you're on actual, official police business?"

Ruth considered the question. Since she'd caused a stir among his "vendors," Ryan must know the "bizzie" questions she'd been asking. Her inner voice of reason whispered. *No harm in telling him, then.* But a second, stubborn voice countered: *No point in telling him, either—except to boost his fat ego.*

She lifted her chin and remained silent.

The next moment, she was on her knees, her head booming.

"Hey!"

At first Ruth thought Ryan was shouting at her, but he scowled at one of the men behind her. "Behave, will you? Show some manners."

She heard a shuffle of feet and the oppressive shadows of the men retreated a step.

"Get the sergeant a glass of water," Ryan ordered, all pretense at smiling pleasantry gone.

Born and raised Roman Catholic, Ryan had been rigorously educated and ruthlessly brutalized in equal measure by the Christian Brothers at a time when they still ruled their institutions of learning with the strap and holy terror. He'd always fancied himself a cut above the average Scouse villain, having stayed on at school to the age of eighteen and achieved good advanced-level grades. There were rumors he'd got an Open University degree in business studies during a stint in prison, too.

Ruth forced herself to her feet. Nausea rolled up from her stomach, and saliva flooded her mouth. She swallowed hard against the urge to vomit but refused the proffered glass.

"You know damn well I'm trying to find Adam Black."

Ryan rolled his eyes. "I do. I *do* know that. But here's the thing." He placed his whisky glass to one side and leaned across the desk. "You're treading on toes—I don't like that."

"You seem confused, Mr. Ryan," she said. "See, I don't answer to you."

The smile returned to his face, a complex mix of admiration and scorn. "Even so, it's got to stop."

Ryan was third-generation gangster. His great-grandfather had come over from Ireland during the potato famine and rose rapidly from petty thieving to smuggling contraband through the port of Liverpool. The family business had evolved in the years since, and cannabis and cocaine had largely replaced the tobacco and booze shipments that had been his great-grandfather's specialty, but the Ryan family had maintained their traditions of criminality, so when he said, "It's got to stop," the command was backed by the weight of nearly two hundred years of violence and intimidation.

Her heart raced and stuttered, but Ruth kept her hands still and her eyes on a spot on the wall behind Ryan.

"I can't promise that," she said.

A fluster of movement from the three thugs standing behind her told her she was pushing her luck. Ryan wasn't smiling anymore, but he was listening, so she forced herself to go on and was pleased to hear some power in her voice:

"I need to find Adam Black—on the quiet—or taking a more *official* route."

She thought Ryan's eyes widened—only a fraction, and hard to be certain—but either way, Ryan was sharp enough to know that the official route meant more police, and a hell of a lot more disruption to his activities on the street.

"So the sooner I find him, the better for both of us." It was hard to see what was going on behind those faded eyes; she gave him a moment, then asked, "Do you know where he is?"

He tilted his head. "I might."

"Don't mess with me, Ryan."

"Oh, I don't play games. Sergeant." The air chilled by ten degrees. "But we're both busy people, so let's get this over with. I know his precise location." Then, as if the thought had just occurred to him: "Question is, are you sure *you* want to know?"

Ruth's heart contracted. *Please, don't let him be in the life.* Thief, addict, "street vendor"—they all passed through her mind. She wished she had the option to turn her back, say, *You're right—I don't want to know.* But in truth, she had no choice in the matter: she *had* to know, because if she didn't trace Adam Black, Carver would, and Ruth owed it to Adam to hear his side of the story before her boss got anywhere near him.

Pride, and an instinct that Ryan would respond better to an ultimatum than to pleading, made her say, "If you've got information, let's hear it. If not, I've got better things to do."

He laughed softly. Still watching her, he made brief eye contact with one of his thugs. The skinny man took a few steps to the door to her left and opened it. A few seconds later, Adam was ushered in by a large, mono-browed man.

Adam was nearly six feet tall, but he looked small next to Ryan's goon.

His hair, so carefully styled into a man bun on the crime scene video, had come loose and hung in rattails over his right ear. His cheek was bruised, his eyes glistened with unshed tears, and he looked badly scared.

She saw a momentary relief at seeing her. He glanced, bewildered, to Ryan, and back to her. Then the shutters came down, as they always did, and he looked away, letting the big minder position him next to Ruth, his entire demeanor screaming defeat.

"He's all yours," Ryan said. "For what he's worth."

Her heart still tripping, Ruth straightened her back and waited for the quid pro quo.

But Ryan made a shooing gesture with one hand. "Go on then—piss off."

"That's it?" she said.

His eyes gleamed with mischief. "That's it."

There *had* to be more.

"You're just letting us walk away?"

"Let's call it the return of a favor."

Ruth sensed a sideways glance from Adam and felt a knot form just below her breastbone. "I don't know what you're talking about."

" 'Course you do." His eyes were all over her.

She blinked, raising one shoulder in a gesture of helpless confusion.

"Damien, my eldest," he said. "You seen to it justice was done."

Her heart suddenly slowed to a hard, painful thudding. *He's guess-*

ing, trying to get you to open up by bluffing that he knows more than he does. Even so, she had to summon up years of experience in facing down criminals and police senior ranks to keep her expression blank and her voice even.

"Damien Ryan," she said. "I remember the case. But that was a long time ago—I wasn't even police back then."

"I know." He blinked slowly. "But CSIs are the unsung heroes of the criminal justice system, aren't they?"

Jesus, he does know. She kept her stance relaxed, said firmly, "Mr. Ryan, you don't owe me a damn thing."

She felt Adam tense with alarm.

"Easy, tiger," Ryan said, laughing. "You're worrying the lad."

Ryan looked around at his minders, gathered in the background like vultures waiting for the kill. "Wait outside," he said.

No hesitation, they turned and left, pulling the office door shut behind them. Ruth had to hand it to him: he had a firm grip on his hired muscle.

After a second or two of silence, Ryan said, "Look . . . I don't want to embarrass you, and I'm not trying to trap you, all right?" Ruth thought she read the first genuine emotion in his facial expression since she'd first had sight of him. "I just reckon this"—he gestured to include Ruth and himself—"is long overdue."

Ruth was about to speak, but he raised a finger to stay her.

"I know you didn't have me in mind when you done the business, but we both got a result, didn't we? And one good turn deserves another, so this one's on me."

"I think we'll be going," Ruth said.

He looked at her for a long moment. Finally, he nodded, dismissing them. As Ruth turned to leave, he added, "But don't come poking around my manor again."

"From gratitude to threats," she said, "with barely a pause for breath."

He poured himself another whisky. "Nah," he said. "If it was a threat, he'd be leaving here in an ambulance." He jerked his chin toward Adam. "This, Sergeant, is a friendly warning."

He was watching her closely, but Ruth knew the real danger had passed; she wasn't about to let him see any signs of anxiety in her now.

"Careful with those friendly warnings, Mr. Ryan. Maybe I'll come back with a few hairy-arsed constables."

He laughed again. "Don't try to kid a kidder. We both know this little adventure of yours is completely off the books. And youse lot've got your hands full with this Ferryman character—you don't want to be bothered with a legitimate businessman, earning an honest bob."

This time Ruth laughed, but Ryan didn't seem to take it amiss. He grinned with her, hit a button on his desk, and when the door opened, he said, "Give Sergeant Lake her phone." His eyes flicked to Adam Black. "The lad can have his, too. Take her and Mr. Black wherever they want to go."

"Thanks," Ruth said, "but we'll hail a cab."

As soon as they were off the premises Adam tried to storm off. Ruth grabbed him by the collar and jerked him back.

"You can talk to me over a pint, or I can take you in and question you under caution," she said.

He shook free of her. "Think I'm stupid? You can't arrest me—I've done nothing."

"That has yet to be determined." She flagged a taxi and as it pulled up to the curb, she said, "Make up your mind. Which is it to be—a pint, or a prison cell?"

44

They ended up at Peter Kavanagh's pub, in a quiet street of modest Georgian houses near the Anglican Cathedral. Ruth knew the landlady from her days as a cop on the beat and gave her a nod as they entered. It was late, and the crowd was beginning to thin, so she sent Adam to the bar while she bagged a corner seat where she could keep an eye on both him and the door. They were safely out of Dave Ryan's area, but she was taking no chances.

She texted Carver with the brief message: "I'm fine. Call off the cavalry."

Within seconds, her phone pinged with the furious reply: "No. NO way. A text? After you just got shanghaied? Get on the phone NOW or I'll mount the damned charge myself!"

She rang him. "Boss, I'm fine," she said.

"How do I know you're not under duress?"

"I'm at Peter Kavanagh's. You know Rita, the landlady." She'd introduced him to Rita during the previous case when they went for a drink to discuss strategy. "I'll put her on."

Adam had returned with the drinks and Ruth gestured for him to sit, while she went to the bar.

"Rita, you got a minute? Greg Carver wants to say hi."

Rita looked at her like she'd gone soft, but Carver was a celebrity in the city, and she shrugged, held out her hand to accept the phone. "Hiya, lad. Heard you were doing better after—you know—what happened . . ." No bar owner worth her salt was going to mention a shooting in her pub, even if it did happen in a private house, a few miles down the road. She listened for a moment. "Well, you're welcome anytime. Come in and have one on the house." Carver must have said something, because she laughed.

"*Someone's* in trouble," she said, still chortling.

Ruth took the phone. "Don't I know it." She kept one eye on Adam, who was sipping his beer, sunk into a morose contemplation of his mobile phone. She didn't like that he still had access to it, and she wanted Carver off the phone as soon as possible so she could get back to him.

"What the bloody hell are you playing at?" Carver demanded.

"I'll explain, I promise," Ruth said.

"Now."

"As soon as I'm finished here."

"Finished with *what*?"

There was no way to get out of saying it: "Interviewing Adam Black."

She heard a muttered curse at the other end of the line, then, "I knew it."

Adam pocketed his phone and took a swallow of ale.

"Okay, I've gotta go before he drinks himself stupid." She hung up before Carver could say anything more.

Adam had supped half his pint in the few minutes it had taken Ruth to make the call.

"Slow down," she said, sliding onto the bench seat opposite him. "I need you to make sense."

His eyes on her, he took another good glug of beer. "What d'you want?"

She sighed. "All right, let's get this over with. You were caught on a crime scene video."

She saw a fleeting alarm in his eyes; then he tugged his neat goatee, said, "Could you vague that up a bit for me?"

He had straightened his disarranged hair, but the bruise on his cheek was darkening, and he'd probably have a good shiner by the morning. The bruise bothered her, but the nose ring was more off-putting: it seemed so at odds with her last image of Adam. *It's been nine years*, she told herself. *He's a grown man, a different person from the one you knew. A witness, and possible suspect in a murder investigation—get over the damn nose ring.*

"Six days ago," she said, watching for his reaction like she would any witness. "On the car park of the Nuffield Gym, by the old Dingle Railway Station."

Relief flooded his face, and she even saw a hint of amusement. "*Catch the Gamma Wave*," he said, giving it the Ferryman's chosen title. "What did you think of it?"

"Why were you there?"

The question seemed to perplex him. "I thought you'd approve of me going to an art exhibition."

She gave him a look she usually reserved for the slimiest bottom-feeders and scallies, and he rolled his eyes as if to say, *Fine, have it your way.*

"It's the biggest thing in art this century—why *wouldn't* I be there?"

"You call that art?"

He seemed to consider the question seriously. "Others do."

"That's not really an answer."

He shot her a hostile look that said, *You think I care?*

"What 'favor' did you do for Dave Ryan?" he demanded.

"None."

"Well, he seemed grateful."

"I told you, that was bullshit," she said. "He wanted to put me off balance."

"Because you're a bent cop?"

"Because I'm a pain in his arse." *What the hell are you doing, answering his questions? You need to take control of this interview.* She straightened her back and said, "Just before they brought you into the room, Ryan asked was I sure I wanted to know where you were—and, by implication, what you were up to. Why is that?"

No answer.

"He seemed to know you," she pressed. "It seemed to me that you'd met—maybe done business with him."

Adam wiped a hand over his mouth, covering a smile. "You could say that."

"Adam, I'm not messing about here. My boss has been on at me for days to bring you in. But I wanted to give you the chance to put your side of things, first."

He snuffed air through his nose. "Want the whole sob story—a blow-by-blow account of what happened to me after you fucked up my life? It's a bit late for that, Ruth."

That stung. "*You're* the one who slapped a noncontact order on me."

He shrugged. "Yeah, well, you were a pain in *my* arse, back then."

Okay, take a breath. "Why aren't you on any of the local registers I tried?"

"I don't use Adam Black much anymore."

"What *do* you use?"

"Got a notebook, Sergeant? I'd better write it down."

She decided to overlook the snide tone and handed over her notepad and pen, watched him write: "MadAdaM."

"Capital M, either end," he said. "What you call a palindrome—see?"

"And *are* you?" she said, unexpectedly touched by his defiant bravado.

"What?" he said. "A palindrome?"

"Mad," she said.

He looked her in the eye. "In all *kinds* of ways." He broke eye contact and drained his pint. "Fuck it, I'm getting pissed. D'you want another?"

She reached for the wallet she carried with her on duty, but he waved it away.

"My shout."

He peeled off the leather biker jacket and dumped it on the bench beside him as he stood. Under it, he wore a sleeveless T-shirt, and his right arm bore a tattoo of pistons overlaid by realistic-looking muscle and a few scraps of shredded skin. Ruth gasped, then tried to cover, but he had already turned away and was halfway to the bar.

She studied him as he ordered a fresh round of drinks, Rita smiling and joking with him. *He can turn on the charm, then. Just not for me.* His left arm was inked as gray metalware: bolts and pistons, cogs and conduits, some overlaid with armor. She could hardly bring herself to look at the tattoo that emerged from the neck of his tee: black lines, branching to nodes, suggesting a neural network.

A completely different person, she told herself, but as he set down the glasses, she couldn't help asking, "What's with the cyber tattoos?"

"Biomechanical," he corrected. "Cyber's more computer-oriented." He half turned and tapped the black lines on the back of his neck. "Like this." He sat next to her, more confident now, as if showing his tattoos gave him strength. "Anyway, I heard you got one of your own."

"*What* did you say?"

His eyebrow twitched. "Relax, Ruth—word gets around."

"Not about this, it doesn't." Even if he'd followed the case on TV, the tattoo inflicted on her by the Thorn Killer was not in the public domain.

"What?" he said again.

She stared him down. "You'd better explain yourself, right now, or I swear I'll kick your arse from here to the nearest nick."

"Just like old times, huh?" He tried a crooked grin, abandoned the effort. "It's no big deal," he said with a sigh. "You were seen, that's all."

"By who, and when?"

He sucked his teeth, and she half rose, ready to haul him in.

"All right—chill. Dude goes into the laser clinic to get a tattoo removed after it gets into an ugly mess. Which was his own fault because the stupid *wanker* did *not* follow simple aftercare instructions and . . ." He lifted a shoulder, let it fall. "Never mind. Upshot—he saw you."

She felt sick.

Adam must have misread what he saw in her face because he said, "Oh, come *on*. You're more recognizable than the *Kardashians* these days."

Ruth reflected that maybe she should have left it to others to interview Adam Black: he wasn't showing her any respect at all. But she dismissed the thought—she'd started this, and she would damn well finish it.

"So that's how you make a living," she asked. "As a tattoo artist?"

"Cop question, or d'you actually give a shit?"

"Both," she said.

"What makes you think—?"

"I'm guessing that the 'wanker' who had to have his tattoo removed was one of your clients."

He gave a short laugh, and, startled to hear something of the old Adam in it, she felt a sudden rush of dangerous emotion—was wildly, *unprofessionally* glad to see him happy.

"What've you been *doing* all these years, Adam?"

"Staying out of your way, mostly," he said, but he was still smiling.

She waited, and after half a minute he went on.

"After I got out—of care, not prison—all right?"

She said, "I assumed that's what you meant."

"Sure," he scoffed. He sipped his beer, which she read as him taking an opportunity to get himself back under control. "Anyway, after that, I got into the underground art scene."

She frowned, inviting an explanation.

"Street art," he said.

"Graffiti."

"Independent public art."

"The kind that gets spray-painted on walls and underpasses," she said.

He sucked his teeth. "But now I do trompe l'oeil, mostly. That's—"

"Pictures that fool the eye. I know." She assessed his clothing, haircut, and calculated that, urban casual though they were, they didn't come cheap. Her mind went back to Dave Ryan's office, and the false impression of a moonlit garden.

"So how do you get paid?"

He laughed again. "You always were the practical one."

"Yeah, well, I had to be."

She'd put some edge in her voice and he stared at her for a few moments. She thought maybe she saw a measure of acceptance in his brief nod before he went on. "Commissions," he said. "People like your art, they'll pay you to do it." For a second, she thought he was about to expand, but he bit down on his lower lip.

"People like Dave Ryan?" He hesitated, frowning in question, and she added, "The window shutters."

"Yeah, well . . ." he said. "And for info—I *am* a tattoo artist. A bloody good one."

She nodded. He was boastful and defensive, playful and resentful by turns. Classic ambivalence.

"So why the interest in the Ferryman?" she asked.

"The clue is in the job description." He gave her a hard look. "Or d'you think street art and tattooists don't qualify as 'real' artists?"

Defensive again. "That's not what I meant," Ruth said. "But let me ask you this: Do *you* think this 'Ferryman' is a real artist?"

"Why d'you ask?"

"It's a simple question."

"Without a simple answer."

"Come *on*. He's a cold-blooded killer."

"Oh, so that's the answer you wanted to hear—you should've said."

"It's what I'd hope to hear," she countered. "Surely, no right-thinking human being could call that 'art'?"

"Are you done asking me insulting questions? 'Cos I'd like to go home now."

"Not a chance," she said. "We're nowhere near finished yet."

They shared a taxi to his home. Adam's story was that he and two mates shared the upper floors of a disused pub near Clarence Dock at the north of the city. The lower half of the place was secured with steel roller shutters; a hand-painted sign, hung from the pub sign bracket, read DASH-ART above an image of a guerrilla-style figure with spray can in hand, finishing a graffito of a mermaid on a riverfront wall.

"All right," Adam said, "you've seen where I live. Now shove off."

Ruth paid the driver and stepped out of the cab.

"Oh, for f—" Adam raised his arms and let them drop.

"I want to see you let yourself in with your own latchkey," Ruth said. "Then you can show me a utility bill in your own name and make me a cup of coffee in your own kitchen." She also wanted an introduction to the rest of Team Dash-Art. Images floated into her mind of gray, hooded figures stenciled on walls and street furniture around the city.

Adam brought his hands to his sides and clenched them into fists.

"You want to get rid of me, that's the deal."

Through gritted teeth he said, "All right. Ten minutes."

The flat was accessed via a side door that gave directly onto a steep stairwell. Adam took her up and along the landing to the kitchen, passing two doors. Both stood open—she glimpsed a sofa in one and a bed in the other.

"No locks on the doors," she said. "You must trust your mates."

He didn't comment.

A second set of stairs at the far end of the landing led up to the top floor.

Ruth peered up the stairway while the kettle boiled. "What's up there?"

"Two more bedrooms, a bathroom," he said.

"Mind if I take a look around?"

"*Yes.*" He shoved a mug into her hand. "I mind. A *lot.*"

They carried their drinks through to the room with the sofa. It was battered brown leather. Adam flopped into one of two matching armchairs, balancing his coffee mug on the arm. The floor was bare boards, stained and varnished, but with paint spattered in places. There was no TV, but a desktop computer sat on a trestle table. The expanse of wall behind was covered in a mural in three parts. Ruth was no art expert, but she could see three distinct styles—graffiti art like the one of the shop sign, a middle panel that combined textiles and photographic elements with acrylic paint, and then there was Adam's contribution.

A man leaned out of a picture frame and angled his upper body, caught in the act of painting a pencil-sketched image of himself on the wall. The effect was three-dimensional, impressive, and disturbing.

Ruth felt his eyes on her, but when she glanced in his direction, he turned quickly away. She took a sip of coffee—it was foul—then paced to the window and looked down onto the street; there were no cars parked outside. "There doesn't seem to be anyone around."

"Wow," he said, "ace detective skills."

"Does anyone say 'ace' anymore?"

"Only when they're being sarcastic."

"You texted them, didn't you, from the pub?"

"Like I said—*ace*—"

"Okay. Find me a utility bill."

"Wouldn't do any good. Rogue pays the bills."

"Rogue," she said. "Does he have a real name?"

"That *is* his real name."

She cocked an eyebrow. "Take your time—I've got all night."

He sighed. "His *given* name is Roger Tickle."

"I can see why he'd go by Rogue."

"Piss off," he said, but the corner of his mouth twitched.

"Who's your other flatmate?" He didn't answer at first, and she said, "Come on, Adam, I can check with the landlord—or come back early tomorrow, wake them all up."

"Janus," he said. Then, "Jamie Havers."

She drifted to the end of the trestle table, where a few letters lay scattered next to a pile of flyers. The flyers advertised Dash-Art, the letters confirmed what Adam had just told her—there was even a letter addressed to "MadAdaM."

"You're not telling me your credit cards are made out to this name," she said.

"Nah, it's still plain Adam Black."

"But you're not on the electoral register."

"Never saw the point of voting."

She scanned the room. "I don't see a landline."

He snorted. "Who has a landline anymore?"

"You have cable."

His eyebrow twitched.

"In Roger's name, I suppose."

Adam shrugged, took a sip of coffee.

"Right. Mobile number, work number—and the address of the tattoo parlor where you work."

He almost choked on his drink. "Studio," he said. "It's a *studio*."

He pinged his mobile number to her, and when she checked the screen to list it in her contacts, she saw that she'd had a brace of texts from Carver. *Oh, he must be so pissed . . .*

"Work address, *and* number," she said. Adam gave her what she needed. The tattoo studio was on the other side of town; she dialed the number and got a voice-mail message. It was Adam's voice.

"Satisfied?" he said.

"Far from it." Ruth pinged her work and personal mobile numbers in return. She would have to bring him in for formal questioning in the next few days—maybe his housemates, too, but he didn't need to know that. Not yet, at least. She rang for a taxi, said, "I'll see myself out."

He smiled. "I wasn't born yesterday."

He walked her down the stairs a few minutes later, and as the taxi drew up, Ruth said, "You know where to find me."

The shock on his face looked like physical pain.

"It's your home, too, Adam."

45

Carver was brewing a third jug of coffee at 11:45. He jumped like a cat when he heard a soft tap at his flat door. Ruth Lake had a key to his place, and the odds were that it was her, but when he checked the street below, there was no sign of her car.

"Who is it?" he called, feeling both foolish and unreasonably anxious.

"Open up, Greg."

It was Ruth. Walking past him, she seemed agitated. He couldn't tell if it was excitement or anxiety, but it came off her like heat shimmer off a roadway.

"Is that proper coffee?" she said, shedding her jacket and walking past him to the kitchen.

Carver noticed the Casco baton attached to her trouser belt; strictly speaking, she should have checked it in at the end of her shift, but he was glad she'd at least had the sense to carry a defensive weapon. Slightly less pleased to think that she must have been expecting trouble.

She returned from his kitchen two minutes later with a mug for each of them, took a sip of her own, and swilled it around her mouth.

He crinkled his brow in question and she said: "Need to clear my palate of the pound-stretcher valu-bilge I've just been given by someone who should know better."

He took his coffee to an armchair and waited until she was seated on the sofa adjacent before saying, "So you found Black?"

"He found me. Or, more accurately, someone found him for me."

Carver shook his head. "No half-truths, no mysteries, Ruth."

She sipped her coffee for a half minute, clearly gathering her thoughts, and he suspected that even now she was working out how little she could get away with telling him.

"Let's start with what happened when we were cut off," he prompted.

"I was on the street, looking for Adam."

He noted the use of his given name—not "Adam Black," or "Black," but "Adam"—this was personal.

"I got scooped up by a carful of Dave Ryan's thugs."

"Bloody hell, Ruth . . ." Carver hadn't been with the Merseyside force for long, but he still knew Ryan by reputation.

"They took me to his place in Edge Hill. Apparently, my inquiries have been affecting business."

"Are you all right?" Carver asked. "Did he threaten you?"

"He's too smart to make an outright threat," Ruth said. "We had a chat, and a few minutes later, they brought Adam in."

"Was *he* hurt?"

"He'd been roughed up, but I don't think he'll be in a hurry to make a complaint."

"And he just . . . handed Black over to you. Why would he do that?"

"To get me off his back."

That was the truth. But something else shimmered behind her words; it wasn't the *whole* truth.

"He just opened the door and waved you on your way?"

"Even offered us a lift home." She paused. "I declined."

"So you've interviewed this Adam Black—what's your interest in him?"

"He was at *Catch the Gamma Wave*. He's an artist—claimed he was there out of professional interest."

"Do you believe him?"

"I don't know."

Carver scrutinized the air around her; no hint of lies or evasion in that answer, at least.

"You went to a lot of trouble to find him."

A hesitation.

"Ruth?"

She stared at him and he saw her struggle with a lifetime's habit of secrecy.

"You put yourself in danger trying to find this man."

"Yeah, well . . . there's a good reason for that."

He cocked his head to show he was listening, but she seemed to stall at the last moment.

This time, he asked outright: "Who *is* Adam Black to you?"

She took a breath, let it go slowly. "My kid brother."

Carver stared at her. He didn't even know she *had* a brother.

"Half brother?" he speculated.

"No, we had the same parents—I took my mother's maiden name."

"Your parents divorced?"

"They split up."

"And that's when you changed your name."

"Around then."

She's holding back. Carver let that pass for the moment. "Okay. But if Adam is mixed up in the Ferryman case, even on the periphery, I need to know."

She looked into his face—her own unreadable—and for one monumentally irritating moment, he thought she would try her usual evasive tactics on him, but her expression softened into a sad smile.

"I don't stand a cat in hell's chance of fooling you, these days, do I?" she said.

"It would be a mistake to try," he said. "Why was he in trouble as a juvenile? Why did he end up in secure accommodation?"

Ruth Lake usually brazened out questions she didn't care to answer with a calculatedly guileless look. But she couldn't answer his questions, and she couldn't meet his eye.

"Look," he said, "I understand you're trying to protect your brother—and I'll try to help you—but Ruth, I can only do that if you're honest with me."

"It wasn't anything so terrible," she said. "A bit of petty theft—he lived on the streets for a month, just after his fifteenth birthday. They took him back to his foster parents, but he just kept running away. A couple of months later, he was caught drug peddling—minor stuff—a bit of weed, a few tabs of Valium." She shook her head, remembering. "He was falling in with bad company; the judge sent him to a secure unit for his own protection."

Carver nodded, processing this. "But why was he taken into care in the first place? Couldn't your parents cope with him after the split?"

"It was me couldn't cope." She still couldn't look at him, and for a while she said nothing, but he didn't try to hurry her. She held her coffee mug in both hands, staring into it as if she could see the past in the cooling liquid. Finally, she placed it on the floor next to her and looked him in the eye.

"Mum and Dad were dead by the time Adam was fourteen."

"I'm sorry," he said, thinking, *How did I not know this?*

"It was kept out of my record."

She must have read his mind, as she so often did. They had worked together for over a year. Ruth had listened to him when his marriage began to fall apart, had supported him through his recovery after he was shot. Yet he didn't know more than the most superficial details of her life. He might make an excuse of Ruth's determined secrecy, her knack at deflecting questions, but he should have known—or at least tried to get to know—more. He replayed her last words. There were several reasons why her family circumstances might have been kept out of the record. Would she be honest with him this one time?

"What happened, Ruth?" he asked simply.

She began, slowly, as if testing her ability to keep her emotions in check at every step.

"Mum was murdered," she said. "They found her at my dad's business address. Witnesses saw him in a distressed state, leaving the scene twenty minutes before her b—" She balked at the word "body." "Before she was found." She clenched her hands tightly and drew them onto her lap. "He went on the run. Committed suicide a day later."

Her voice was empty of emotion, but Carver knew better than most the protective strategies we use to insulate us from a past trauma. He was certain that she was telling the truth, but he was just as sure that there was a lot more she wasn't telling him.

"When was this?"

"I was in my final year of university."

All true, he thought. But she was holding on to her emotions so tight the effort seemed to cling to her like a shadow. He searched for the question that would unlock her rigid control.

"Your father murdered your mother?"

She lifted her chin. "He confessed in a suicide note, admitted to the murder of his girlfriend, too."

"His *girlfriend*?"

"Mum and Dad had already separated when I was in my midteens."

Carver was exhausted. In any verbal sparring match, Ruth had all the moves, and she was infinitely lighter on her feet than Carver. She never gave up even minor personal details easily, and this was huge; she must have buried these secrets deep. But when he'd asked about her mother, there was a flare of emotion he couldn't identify.

He'd said, *Your father murdered your mother?* She'd said, *He confessed.* The lift of her chin, the words, were both ambiguous; they felt like a deflection. She was giving him facts, but not context. Suddenly, he had it.

"You don't believe he killed them?"

She closed her eyes for a second, and he realized she was every inch as weary as he was. "Doesn't matter what I believe," she said. "It won't bring them back."

That, coming from Ruth Lake, was blatant bullshit.

"Why would your father confess to something he didn't do?"

"I didn't say he did."

Carver raised an eyebrow. "You didn't say he didn't, either."

46

Ruth Lake addressed a packed Major Incident Room: "Based on cellular and physiological changes in the heart muscle of the latest victim, the pathologist has revised his age upward."

Dr. Donnelly had phoned her before sending his report by e-mail, clearly feeling the need to explain why he'd missed this in his first postmortem examination of the remains.

"Of course, the heart wasn't chemically preserved," he'd explained, "because *your man* wanted the maggots to stay lively for the big reveal." He went on. "And there'd already been some minor deterioration of the tissue, which made the changes harder to see."

Ruth felt some sympathy for Donnelly's bruised ego and had thanked him warmly for getting the results to her so fast.

"How old?" Carver asked. He was leaning against the wall at the side of the room. The dark circles under his eyes were testament to the late night she'd caused him, and she wondered if he needed the wall to prop him up.

"Collagen increases as we get older, along with a buildup of fatty deposits in the blood vessels," she said. "Dr. Donnelly said our victim's heart has unusually high levels of both—as a rough starting point, we should start looking at men aged forty-plus."

A rumble of appreciation from the gathering: this would make the search easier.

"And he says that the relatively low level of decomp suggests the heart was harvested less than two weeks ago."

"So we have a narrower demographic *and* narrower time frame." Carver looked energized; he stood up straight, although she noticed the fingertips of his right hand maintained contact with the wall.

"Here's what we'll do. For the next three days, we limit the search to males aged over forty who disappeared from home in the past two weeks. The families will already have supplied DNA samples for matching?" He addressed the question to Ruth.

"It's likely. But if Heart Guy had been reported missing, you would expect the relevant police force to've put a toothbrush sample on the DNA database, so we would've already had a hit against the heart."

"And since we *didn't* get a hit," Carver said, "either he's not been reported missing, or someone screwed up."

She nodded.

"All right," Carver said. "We've already extended the geographical area. If, after three days, we don't get a match to the heart, we'll gradually extend our search parameters, a little at a time, and just hope our victim gets entered into the system at some point."

Four hours later, Ruth was back in Carver's office, briefing him on the various house-to-house inquiries they had ongoing. They'd at last had a couple sightings of Steve Norris, the man who had vanished on his way to work: one witness placed him around the Festival Gardens the morning he'd disappeared, the second had seen him at the traffic lights at the edge of the gardens, close to St. Michael's Station, both shortly before he was expected to start work.

"So he almost certainly disappeared between the traffic lights and the footpath through to the railway station," Carver said, adding a note to the pad on his desk.

"Looks like," Ruth said.

"But no sign of the van . . ." He tapped the block of paper with the pen. "So maybe he's switched vehicles."

"It seems likely. D'you think it's time to stand down the canvass of that area, move people on to other duties?"

"Like interviewing Adam Black and his associates?"

She'd walked into that one.

"I'll follow up on that today."

He held her gaze. "We can keep your family relationship between the two of us, for now," he said. "But I want him brought in for formal questioning."

"Sure."

"*Today.*"

She took a breath. "Okay." Since telling Carver about Adam and what had happened to her parents, Ruth had felt lighter and more relaxed than she had in a long time. A tension she hadn't known was there had suddenly loosened in her chest, as if she'd been holding her breath underwater for too long, but now she'd broken the surface and could breathe again.

He nodded, apparently satisfied, but kept his eyes on her for a moment longer and she realized that the gold fleck that sometimes twinkled in his hazel eyes had returned, that Carver was sharper, more alert than he'd been in a while.

"What?" he said.

"You seem better," Ruth said.

"Better than what?"

"Better than you've been lately."

"Good to know."

She saw a faint smile at the corners of his mouth. His desk phone rang, and he picked up, a merry twinkle in his eyes, but all trace of humor vanished in a second. "Put him through."

He switched to speaker and said, "Get the door, would you?"

Ruth swung the door to. "Who is it?"

"Ferg Holst, from *Liverpool Daily*," Carver murmured.

A burst of background chatter told them the line was live and Carver introduced himself and Ruth. "I understand you've had a call, Mr. Holst."

"He claimed to be the Ferryman," Holst began. "He said, 'The police think they got the jump on me. They didn't. In fact, they couldn't find their collective arse with both hands and a wing mirror. They're holding back info about *Art for Art's Sake*—I'm telling you because people need to know. Are you writing this down?'"—Holst broke off—"I was: what I'm giving you now is verbatim. He said, 'The heart is from an older man.' He said he wanted me to print that, put it online."

Carver glanced up at Ruth. "We'd appreciate if you didn't do that, Mr. Holst."

"So it's true?"

"Did you ring for a confirmation quote," Carver said, "or—"

"—out of a sense of public duty?"

Carver waited.

"Look," Holst said, "I hate what's happening—believe me, I want this bastard caught as much as you do—but this could be *huge* for me."

"*If* it's true," Carver said. "*If* the call was genuine."

"How do I prove that?"

"What did he sound like?" Ruth asked.

"What—you mean his accent?"

They both held their breath.

"Brummy."

A Birmingham accent—like the Ferryman.

What Holst said next clinched it for Ruth.

"But it sounded put on. I think the caller was Scouse, through and through."

Exactly what the voice analyst had said about the Ferryman.

"I take it from your silence that's significant," Holst said.

"What do you want, Mr. Holst?" Carver said.

"I can hold off—like I said, I do want to help—but when the case breaks, I want my part in this acknowledged, and I want a direct quote from you, Chief Inspector—ahead of the press pack."

While Carver thought it over, Ruth said, "I don't suppose you recorded the conversation?"

She heard a chuckle at the other end of the line. "This came through the tip-off line. We wouldn't *get* any tips if callers thought their 'anonymous' calls were being recorded."

"But you'd recognize the voice again?"

"Oh, yeah."

"So you could record the *next* call—if he does call back?"

"I could certainly do that." Holst paused. "What d'you say?"

Carver looked at her in question and Ruth shrugged. What did they have to lose?

"Agreed," Carver said. "On condition that you pass on any and all recordings without delay, so our voice analysts can check them out."

"Done."

They exchanged mobile phone numbers and Carver closed the line.

"Do we have a leak?" he asked. "Is someone feeding privileged intel to the killer?"

Ruth shook her head slowly. "I don't know. It *could* be coincidence he released this information now . . ."

"D'you think it really is the Ferryman?"

She sighed, spread her hands. It was anyone's guess. "How d'you want to handle it?"

"We'll have to warn the team, of course—"

Ruth's phone buzzed like an angry wasp in her hand, and she checked the screen. "It's Kharon," she said.

"Put him on speaker."

Ruth told Kharon that he was on speakerphone, and that DCI Carver was listening. She didn't tell him that he was being recorded.

"You were right," he said. "He is dangerous." He spoke in a low voice, as if he was afraid of being overheard.

"When you say 'he'?" Ruth said.

"The Ferryman." His voice quavered. "I thought—I guess I hoped—that he was getting his . . . his . . . *materials* from an undertaker, but—" A loud clang in the background, a yelp of fear.

"Are you all right, Mr. Obrazki?" Ruth said.

"It's all good." He gave a nervous laugh. "I was passing a building site . . ."

"Where are you?" Ruth asked.

"I'm on my way into town," he said.

"Where exactly?" Carver said.

"I'm on Wood Street."

Carver looked in question to Ruth. "Back of Bold Street," Ruth said. Carver rolled his eyes; it was too secluded—and two of their victims had disappeared from that general area.

"It's not safe for you off the main drag," Ruth said. "You need to be somewhere more public."

"I don't know what to *do*." He sounded panicked.

"Get onto Bold Street, stay in the open, make sure you can be seen by plenty of people. Give me a call when you're there. We'll send a police car to pick you up."

"I've—I've really pissed him off."

"Who?" Ruth said. They needed him to say it.

"The Ferryman—he's really pissed off . . ."

"Then you should come in."

"I want to meet with you and Mr. Carver. But I can't be seen at police headquarters. I *can't*. If he—" He stopped, sounding choked.

Carver reached for his laptop with one hand, raising the other and tracing a small circle in the air with one finger. The message was clear: *Keep him talking.*

"All right," she said into the phone. "We can meet—but it's vital you get to safety."

No reply, just Kharon's anxious breathing, and the whip and crack of wind catching the mobile's microphone.

A moment later, Carver turned his laptop and pointed to a Google street scene.

"Meet us outside Bold Street Coffee," Ruth said. "It's near the top end of the street." It was a good choice; its plate glass window would give a clear view of the street, making it difficult for the Ferryman to snatch Kharon without being seen by scores of people, both in the café and on the street.

"No patrol cars." Kharon's voice faded in and out—he was running. "Just you and Mr. Carver. No one else."

"Just the two of us," she reassured him.

"Okay . . . Okay." He sounded calmer now. "I'll call you back."

"No, wait—"

But he'd already hung up.

He wasn't at the coffee bar.

Ruth had tried Kharon's phone three times on their way to pick up an unmarked car from the fleet; she tried it again now.

"Anything?" Carver asked.

"Straight to voice mail," Ruth said.

They split up, Ruth cutting through the square opposite to check out Wood Street, while Carver ducked into the café. They met outside five minutes later.

Ruth shook her head in answer to Carver's unspoken question.

"Well, we know where he lives," Carver said.

They had parked in a scruffy cul-de-sac on double-yellows, and Ruth saw a traffic warden sniffing around the car. She flashed her badge, asked if he'd seen an anxious dark-eyed, full-lipped kid with a soft sweep of black hair.

"In my job, it's not a good idea to go eyeballing people," he said.

"I take your point," Ruth said, "but this kid could be in serious trouble. You see anyone like that, call me, okay?" She handed him her card and he nodded.

Carver had been on his mobile. He closed the phone. "I had the techs ping his mobile," he said. "He was actually in Fairfield when he made the call."

"His flat is in the Fairfield district," Ruth said.

Carver nodded grimly. "The little shit set us up."

Ruth unlocked the car. "Where is he now?"

"Phone's switched off."

47

Kharon, aka Karl Obrazki, rented a studio flat in a converted Victorian house on Sheil Road—not far from the last known location of his mobile phone. Four purple wheelie bins cluttered the narrow strip of concrete below the ground-floor window, and haunting country music blasted out from an open window of one of the upstairs flats.

Carver leaned on Kharon's doorbell, while Ruth checked the upper floors for signs of movement. When that failed, he punched every door-bell on the panel. Finally, an upper window next to the music lover's was thrown open, and an angry face appeared.

"What the fuck d'you want?" he yelled.

Ruth showed her warrant card. "Police," she said. "Can you open up? We need to speak to Mr. Obrazki."

The window slammed shut, and for a moment it looked like they were being left out in the cold. Seconds later, the front door was flung open and they were confronted by a man in shorts and a T-shirt. The angry face from the upstairs window.

"You can tell him to turn that shit off, while you're at it," he said. "*I* can't get no joy out of him."

Ruth glanced at Carver. "Another setup?"

He shrugged. There was only one way to find out.

Carver hammered on the door of the flat, and for a few seconds there was silence. Then the music started up again, a mix of banjo and guitar, maybe even a fiddle.

"Police, Mr. Obrazki," Carver yelled. "Open up."

No response.

"What are those lyrics?" Carver asked.

"Something about rowing," Ruth said, with a prickle of uncertainty. She listened more closely. "Oh, God—I think it's about the Ferryman."

Carver hammered louder, and suddenly, the music cut out.

Ruth saw Carver's eyes widen. "Did you hear that?"

She began to shake her head, but then she heard it, too. A low, choking sound.

"Jesus," Carver said. "Call for paramedics—and we'll need backup." His hands braced for balance on the banister behind him, he kicked the door, hard. It gave with a creak and crack of splintering wood.

Ruth finished the call and followed him through the door.

It gave onto an inner hall. Straight ahead, a blank wall. One door was visible to their left across the hallway, about fifteen feet from the entrance. The choking, stuttering breathing seemed to be coming from somewhere closer.

It's amplified, Ruth thought.

They moved left and found an open door at the end of the blank wall—a tiny galley kitchen. Empty.

Tucked in a recess at right angles to the kitchen was a second door. The choking sound was coming from behind it. Carver locked gazes with her and Ruth nodded, sliding her Casco baton from her belt and deploying it with a sharp flick of her wrist. He turned the handle and the door swung open smoothly.

And they looked on a scene from hell.

Three six-foot-by-six picture frames had been rigged in the center of the room. In the first, a montage of photographs—the four crime scenes to date. In the third, one large, hi-res photograph of a bench. It was laid out with trays containing the tools of the Ferryman's trade: scalpels, knives, scissors, chisels, forceps, retractors, a rotary autopsy saw.

The centerpiece of the triptych was Karl Obrazki. He was bound with zip ties to an armchair set behind the empty center frame, but his left leg and right arm extended beyond it. The arm, palm up, was strapped to the wooden armrest of the chair. A large-gauge hypodermic syringe had been inserted into a vein, and the clear plastic tube attached to it drained blood into a gallon demijohn, set on the floor in front of the frame. The jar had overflowed, and some of the dark red liquid oozed down the sides, already congealing on the filthy vinyl floor covering. Obrazki's throat had been slashed straight across; Ruth could see the white cartilage of his trachea. The larynx had been severed.

His sunglasses were jammed on his nose, the lenses overpainted with brown eyes—good facsimiles of Karl/Kharon's, Ruth realized with dull horror. The awful choking breaths went on, relentlessly, and Carver made a move.

"No." Ruth caught his arm. Carver tried to shake her off. "The choking is not him, Greg. Karl is dead—see the neck wound?" It was a wonder the head was still attached to the torso.

Carver stopped struggling. "There's hardly any blood," he murmured.

"The poor kid exsanguinated before the bastard ever cut his throat." Ruth jerked her chin toward a Sonos speaker by the window. "Probably recorded him as he died." She stood where she was and looked carefully around the room. It was sparsely furnished, just the chair in which Karl's body was posed; a sofa and coffee table had been stood on their end against the wall to make room for the gory triptych. The two end panels were big enough to hide someone small, but she could see clear through the centerpiece frame, and when she angled her body and stooped to a crouch, she had a good line of sight behind both.

Words printed in gold around the edge of the center frame read, "What dust do I raise! *L. Abstemius.*"

"What the hell does that mean?" Carver asked.

"I don't know." Ruth tore her gaze from the dead man. "Look, it's just Obrazki in here. We need to back off, let the CSIs do their stuff."

Carver took a step back into the little recess by the kitchen.

A quiet *flump* a little farther down the hallway sent a shock wave through Ruth. They both turned. This time, she took point. Two doors, either side of the corridor. The door to the left stood wide.

Bathroom, Ruth registered.

Carver swung left. "Clear," he murmured. "But there's blood."

The door to the right—bedroom, must be—opened a half inch, then bumped shut against the jamb. It swung open a hairbreadth and bumped against the jamb again.

Ruth and Carver exchanged a look—they had to go in. Carver eased close behind her. A furtive movement just inside the room made the hairs on Ruth's arms and neck prickle.

She raised her baton over her right shoulder, keeping it tight to her body.

"Police," she called out. "We're coming in." With her left hand, she shoved the door wide.

A wild howl, then a ball of shrieking, spitting fury hurled itself at her from the bed. Ruth swung the baton low and hard, missed, realizing at the same moment that her assailant was a cat. It streaked past her and out through the open flat door.

The window was open a crack, allowing a slight breeze. Ruth checked under the bed, and inside the tiny melamine wardrobe, before taking a peek out the window. It was a forty-foot drop to the street below; nobody had left that way. Sirens blared abruptly, as police and paramedics negotiated a sharp bend in the road. They braked to a halt on the street below. Backup had arrived.

Simultaneously, Ruth's phone rang. "CSM Hughes," she said, sliding the bar to answer.

"You're being video-streamed, live, online," Hughes said, as the police and paramedics' footsteps pounded up the stairs.

Ruth's eyes snapped to Carver's. "We need to get out of here," she said. "*Now.*"

48

Two hours later, Carver assembled a small team in the Major Incident Room. The crime scene had been turned over to the forensics specialists as soon as they'd jammed Wi-Fi signals around Karl Obrazki's flat, effectively taking down the spy cameras the Ferryman must have installed inside. Tracing the livestream URL had taken longer, but Carver had called in a computer forensics expert to help Hughes's techs and he'd just received word that the job was done.

Ruth Lake came into the room alongside CSM Hughes. Dr. Yi had arrived early; he sat at a desk to Carver's left, watching the others as they came through the door. DC Ivey, pale and even leaner after his many days of pounding the streets in search of an elusive ATM image of the killer, had taken a seat near the front. Sergeant Naylor, the thirty-year police veteran managing house-to-house, sat next to a detective who was organizing interviews of the scores of people who'd attended the Ferryman's "exhibits." A few volunteers made up the rest of the gathering; Carver recognized Parr, the special who'd messed up at the *Art for Art's Sake* scene. He'd doggedly turned up for duty every day since, and from all accounts was working hard to atone for his lapse.

Superintendent Wilshire was absent but had sent a text to say he'd try to make an appearance at some point. Carver didn't envy him, fielding press queries after this latest outrage.

He opened the meeting by asking Ruth to brief them on the pathologist's preliminary comments.

"The CSIs need the body in situ while they search for trace," she began. "So all we have for now is Dr. Donnelly's external examination."

She looked around the room, her calm brown eyes taking in far more than most of her colleagues would ever suspect.

"Karl's throat was cut from left to right by a wide and extremely sharp-bladed knife, possibly a butcher's knife, with a long flat section and a curved tip. It sliced through the lower end of the larynx and the upper part of the trachea. The carotid veins, esophagus, carotid arteries, and major nerves were all severed, and C7 and C8 vertebrae were damaged."

"He was almost decapitated," someone murmured.

Ruth nodded. "Yet there was very little blood loss at the site of the wound or blood spatter around the chair, suggesting he bled out before his throat was cut."

Carver glanced around the room, seeing a mud-brown mix of confused emotions, shot through with orange flashes of hot anger.

"The head was held in place by heavy-gauge wire, which was stitched into the skin at the back of the head, then pushed through the fabric of the armchair and twisted into a knot behind the chair back."

A few winces at that.

"And he took the eyes."

Carver blinked against a sudden confused explosion of light and color around the room.

Naylor muttered, "Jesus, Mary, and Joseph."

Hughes had seen the crime scene video, but even he frowned and gave a minute shake of his head, as if his mind refused to accept the cruelty he had seen inflicted on Karl.

Ruth continued without comment, her delivery cool—some might say distant—but Carver knew that her distance and her coolness were her armor, as essential to her as Kevlar to a firearms officer. He wondered, momentarily, if she was thinking of her own brother as she spoke of Karl's terrible death.

"A coin had been placed in his mouth," she was saying. "A penny, dated 1978—the date might be significant."

"Liverpool won the European Cup."

A few laughed, and DC Ivey seemed appalled that he'd said that aloud.

"We'll keep that in mind," Ruth said, deadpan, and the young detective blushed brick red.

"Any signs of struggle?" Carver asked, remembering the blood he'd seen in the bathroom.

"Donnelly thinks he was heavily drugged—he's put a rush on the basic tox screen, but even so, it looks like Karl struggled against his bonds for at least part of the time."

"All that staging must've taken hours," Carver said. "And we spoke to Karl, what—thirty, forty minutes before we found him? How the hell did he have time?"

John Hughes spoke up: "I had a sound engineer look at the call you took from Karl." He glanced around the room before adding, "All calls to both DCI Carver's and DS Lake's work phones are being recorded, in case a call from the killer comes in. When the engineer focused on specific components of the background noise, he saw anomalies—traffic noise that seems to vanish from one response to the next, for instance. I asked the language analyst to have a listen, and he said there are some linguistic and tonal anomalies as well." He dug a flash drive from his pocket. "Can I . . . ?"

Ruth stood to one side, giving him access to the demo laptop at the front of the room.

He played the recording from the loud clang at Karl's end of the line. It ran on:

RUTH: "Are you all right, Mr. Obrazki?"

KARL: "It's all good." A nervous laugh. "I was passing a building site . . ."

RUTH: "Where are you?"
KARL: "I'm on my way into town."
CARVER: "Where exactly?"
KARL: "I'm on Wood Street."

Hughes stopped the tape, and Carver glanced at Ruth. Her head tilted slightly, she seemed to be running through the questions and answers again in her head.

"Oh, hell . . ." she breathed.

Carver was stumped—it sounded like a straightforward question and answer to him. "What?" he said.

Ruth looked pained. "He's reading a script."

Hughes nodded. "DS Lake says, 'Where are you?' You would expect Karl to say, 'On my way into town.' He uses the *same* sentence structure a moment later. When DCI Carver says, 'Where exactly?' You would've expected the reply to be a sentence fragment—'Wood Street,' for example, but Karl answers in a *full* sentence."

Hughes glanced at Ruth again. "And when you told him to go to Bold Street, that you'd send a patrol car to pick him up—"

"*He* said, 'I've really pissed him off.'" Ruth raked her fingers through her hair. "He didn't respond to what I'd said *at all*."

Hughes shook his head. "The whole thing was prerecorded. We found the audio file on his mobile phone."

"Coerced?" Carver asked.

"It's hard to be sure, but the linguist thinks not—the way Karl laughs after the building site noise seems spontaneous, he said. And he sounds too relaxed at other points in the recording."

"So, prerecorded, *not* coerced, which means he was in collusion with the Ferryman for at least part of this."

"And the audio file was date-stamped yesterday, at two thirty P.M." Hughes frowned, his weathered face settling in lines of regret. "My guess is the kid was long dead before you even got the call."

Carver allowed himself a few moments to process the information.

"The website hosting the livestream from Karl Obrazki's flat has been taken down," he said, feeling that time had in some way been fractured by this new evidence, needing to speak his thoughts to reason through the sequence of events.

Hughes nodded. "Even so, images have been circulated. It had two thousand hits within five minutes of it being posted."

"If the web host closed it down, that means it's traceable, using, what was it—WHOIS?"

"I'm afraid not. Unlike Karl, this guy covered his tracks. He didn't even register a domain."

"I didn't know that was possible."

"You can set up a website without registering a domain using one of a dozen blogger domains—WordPress, Weebly, Tumblr—whatever," Hughes said. "So we tried tracing him through his IP address—that's the unique number which identifies every computer on a network, *and* its location. But he used a virtual private network, a VPN."

"You can't trace his computer *or* his location."

"Precisely."

Carver blew out air. "Okay. The site went live as we entered the property, yes?"

"Yes."

"So he must've had eyes on the place."

Hughes nodded. "We've found five granny cams secreted around the sitting room, bathroom, and bedroom; there may be others. We've got a specialist coming in to sweep the place later tonight, but in the meantime, we'll just keep jamming the Wi-Fi till we're sure we've got them all."

"The website was brand-new," Carver said. "How did his followers know about it?"

"He posted a short video and a link on Instagram."

DC Ivey spoke up. "Hang on—Instagram doesn't allow links to outside sites."

"Not in individual posts," Hughes said. "But you can paste a link into your profile. The Ferryman changed his bio and included the link to his livestream content as soon as Ruth and Greg were inside Kharon's flat. The blogsite organized the takedown ten minutes after our request went in."

"Even so, @FerrymanArt is getting hundreds of comments," Ivey said, tapping through windows on his smartphone.

Hughes must have seen the concern on Carver's face because he said, "You want them to close the Instagram account, they said they'll do it."

"No," Carver said. "I don't want this to disappear onto the Dark Web; at least we can monitor traffic while he stays visible."

Hughes nodded. "I think you're right."

"Let's see the Instagram video."

Hughes closed the audio file and clicked to a new folder.

An instant of blurring, then the camera focused on Karl Obrazki, alias Kharon, in the armchair in his flat. Straps around his arms, feet, and chest held him immobile. He was gagged, and his head drooped forward onto his chest. Half-conscious, groaning, as his blood drained into the glass demijohn. The jar looked one-third full.

A murmur of exclamations.

Someone muttered, "Jesus wept."

He wasn't wearing sunglasses, and as he fought to open his eyes, it was clear that they were intact.

"Good work, containing this so fast," Carver said.

"The web works faster," Hughes said. "A few ghouls got screencaps and video GIFs before we could take it down."

"Video of Karl?" Carver said.

"And of the two of you searching the place." He avoided Carver's gaze. "There's stuff popping up all over the Web."

How much had the cameras seen? Carver wondered.

Hughes moved on: "He's calling this one *Fly on a Chariot Wheel*."

"*Fly on a Chariot Wheel*," Carver said. "What is that?"

"It's linked to the words 'What dust do I raise!' on the center frame of the triptych," DC Ivey said.

Hughes's phone buzzed and he excused himself, stepping out into the corridor. Carver kept his focus on the young detective, and Ivey went on.

"In the fable, a fly lands on a chariot wheel during a race and boasts about how much dust he's kicking up."

"Claiming credit, when he's just along for the ride," Carver said.

"The Ferryman does like his symbolism, doesn't he?" Yi commented, seemingly to himself, making a note.

"There's more," Ivey said. "Wiki says the story first appeared in the fourteen nineties. It was part of a collection by a scholar called Laurentius Abstemius, but *most* people think it's one of Aesop's fables, partly 'cos someone got the source wrong in the *sixteen* hundreds."

"Bloody hell, Ivey lad," the house-to-house organizer grumbled, "you've gotta stop googling or you'll go blind."

Ivey blushed to the roots of his ginger hair.

Dr. Yi looked up from his notes. "Wrong attribution?" he said. "And an inflated sense of self . . ."

"You think it's significant?" Carver asked.

Yi stared at a point above Carver's head for a few seconds. "As I said, the Ferryman likes his symbolism. The vainglory of the fly, imagining himself the agent of power and action—and the fact that Aesop was wrongly credited as the author of the fable—could well refer to Karl/Kharon's unearned celebrity and recognition, which is, after all, based entirely on the Ferryman's work."

Naylor turned down the corners of his mouth, considering. "Well, when you put it that way . . ." He turned to Ivey—"Fair dues, lad; you spotted it and I didn't."

Bill Naylor might be a dinosaur, but he wasn't mean-spirited.

The young detective blushed even more violently, and Carver shifted attention away from him by asking about the song track that was playing when they'd arrived at the victim's house. "Has that been identified yet?"

DC Ivey surprised him by speaking up again. "The Ferryman's

followers nailed it in less than half an hour, boss." His color remained hectic, but he sounded calm and confident as he continued: "The song title is 'The Ferryman.' It's by an Aussie band called Graveyard Train—they play a type of country music called 'horror country' or 'psychobilly.'"

Layers upon layers of meaning, Carver thought, watching Dr. Yi add to his notes.

"Could you send me the song lyrics?" Yi said, glancing up at Ivey for a second.

Ivey's thumbs flew over his mobile phone screen. "I texted you a link," he said.

Hughes returned from the hallway at that moment. "That was the senior CSI at the scene. They haven't found a weapon. Looks like the killer took the knife and any other tools he used with him."

But there was *some* good news—Carver saw it in the gleam in his eye.

"ESLA got us a few good lifts," Hughes said. The electrostatic lifting apparatus was often the first line of approach in identifying latent footwear impressions.

"And?"

"Preliminary checks of footwear marks on the lino in the sitting room show the killer walking backward and forward as he sets up the scene," Hughes said. "Then he stands back to admire his work. And leaves a couple of *beautiful* marks—Adidas Terrex CMTK GTX trail runners—there's some lovely unique features on them."

"Unique." A word to make any detective glow with happiness.

"Did they match the trail runners from previous scenes?" Carver asked.

Hughes nodded. "The partial footwear mark at Steve Norris's apartment over at Herculaneum Dock, *and* the partial we got off the cliff at *Catch the Gamma Wave.*"

"Did we ever establish if Steve Norris owned a pair of Adidas trainers?" Carver asked.

"There's nothing in his credit card history," Hughes said.

"He had two brand-new pairs of trainers in his flat," Ruth said. "Where'd he get them? Were they a gift?" She turned to DC Ivey. "Tom, did you find any sports shoe purchases on the victims' stolen credit cards?"

Carver saw where she was going with this: if the trainers showed up on a victim's credit card, Norris could be their man.

Ivey shook his head. "Electronic goods, cash withdrawals, and food—that's pretty much it."

"Anyway, Steve Norris wears a size nine," Hughes chipped in. "And the shoe imprints we found at Kharon's place are somewhere between eleven and twelve."

"Norris is looking more and more like a victim," Ivey said.

"There could be other victims, other credit cards out there," Carver cautioned. "To be on the safe side, let's talk to the family—see where those trainers came from."

"I think I might know, boss." Naylor was thumbing through his notebook. "When I asked Norris's neighbor what he was wearing the morning he disappeared, he said Norris changes trainers quicker than most of us change toothbrushes.

"I said it must cost him a bomb, and *he* said . . ." He leafed through a few more pages. "Here we are . . . 'I think he had a sponsor.'"

"We need to know who that was," Carver said. Ruth made a note, and he turned again to Hughes. "Any other trace of the killer?"

"We're still looking. A tiny amount of residue from the shoes—high-quality analysis might give us a steer toward his location."

His tone implied a request, and Carver said, "You have a suggestion?"

"I'd like to have a sample couriered to the soil scientists at the Hutton Institute in Aberdeen," Hughes said, as though he expected a refusal.

Carver recalled his conversation with Ruth Lake about the very same thing, cut short by Dave Ryan's thugs. He did a quick mental calculation: secure transport and analysis would not come cheap.

"Do it."

The man who'd given the okay was Detective Superintendent Wilshire. He stood just inside the doorway, in full uniform, looking tense and somber. *Probably straight from the press conference*, Carver thought.

"Carry on, DCI Carver," he said.

"Thank you, sir," Carver said, matching the superintendent's own formality; the press must have given Wilshire hell. He switched his attention back to Hughes and gave him the nod to continue.

"The computer techs are scouring Karl's laptop for DMs, notes, images, and whatnot to see if there's anything useful," Hughes finished.

"In the meantime," Carver said, "we have house-to-house interviews to conduct and we need to talk to Kharon's associates and friends." He turned to Ruth Lake. "He is—or was—an art student, wasn't he?"

"Film studies," Ruth corrected. "At Fairfield Art College."

"Okay—talk to his peers, pals, and tutors. Did anyone know he was Kharon, and did he share anything about his special relationship with the Ferryman. Other suggestions?"

"Are we assuming there wasn't a break-in at Karl's place?" Naylor asked.

"You mean apart from DCI Carver kicking the door down?" Hughes said.

That raised a few smiles.

"So it's possible Karl invited the killer in," Carver said. "But was he expecting the visit—did he tell his friends he was meeting up with the Ferryman? Or was it an unexpected knock at the door?"

"Either way, there's got to be a good chance the killer was seen," Ruth said.

"He must've had to carry his materials into the house from the vehicle," she went on. "There was a lot of kit in there, so it probably took a few journeys to and from the flat to shift it, and that's a busy road. We should check with traffic patrols: Did they have to move a vehicle on? Were there complaints from the public? Did anyone in the area notice the comings and goings?"

"Looks like we'll have to open another box of bobbies," Naylor said, with heavy sarcasm.

Carver sympathized. "We could stand down the canvass around St. Michael's Station," he said.

"It'll take a hell of a lot more than *that* to do the job," Naylor complained.

Superintendent Wilshire spoke: "I'll make some calls. See if Cheshire Police can help out." He left the room with a nod to Carver and a stilted, "Keep up the good work," to the rest of the team.

Now Carver asked Dr. Yi for his thoughts. Yi had looked at a recorded version of the livestreaming from Kharon's flat and Ruth Lake had briefed him before the meeting.

"There are notable differences between this and other scenes," Yi began. "It's indoors, for one thing, and the Ferryman made no public announcement beforehand. It seems that he wanted you and DS Lake to be first on the scene—which mirrors the *Art for Art's Sake* scenario, but this time, he ensured that he had full control of it, and that his followers would have broader access—but only when he was ready for them to see it."

He paused, and Carver knew what was coming next.

"I know you don't want to hear this," Yi said, "but you have to accept that there is a real risk of physical harm to you, and possibly Sergeant Lake."

"Risk of physical harm is part of the job," Carver said.

Yi looked inclined to argue the point, but Carver said firmly, "Should we be reading any particular message into the fact that he took the eyes?"

For a moment, it seemed he wouldn't answer; then Yi seemed to give a mental shrug.

"Symbolically," he said, "it could suggest that Karl appropriated the Ferryman's artistic 'vision' by assimilating his work into his own presentations—which, significantly, were very successful in their own right. The trompe l'oeil eyes painted on the lenses of Kharon's sunglasses could also reference the imitative, or 'fake' nature of Kharon's work."

"Is that why he set the scene up as a triptych?" Ruth asked.

"To mock Karl's triptych?" Yi replied. "It seems likely. And the penny in Karl's mouth carries its own message: in ancient tradition, the dead were buried with a copper coin called an 'obol' in the mouth so that they would have money to pay the ferryman for his efforts in carrying them across the river Styx to Hades." He paused. "It was often called 'Kharon's obol.'"

"I bloody hate this smartarse," Naylor muttered.

"He does seem to want us to know he's inventive, smart, well read," Yi said. "It really isn't enough that *he* knows—he wants others to acknowledge his cleverness. He needs to be *told* how brilliant he is."

"He's a narcissist," Carver said, thinking, *We already know this.*

"He's a narcissist with a fragile ego," Yi countered. "This type seems confident, boastful, even, but underlying that is a rather pathetic need for approval. Which is why he responds with rage if he feels challenged or slighted—or if his ego is threatened or injured in any way."

A spike of orange light flashed to the left of Carver, followed by a wash of gray. He couldn't locate the source, but he'd felt a powerful burst of sullen rage in that flash of emotional energy.

"I don't know where you're going with this," Carver said, feeling he'd missed part of the argument.

"I am saying that Karl Obrazki *wasn't* snatched randomly—he had a strong personal connection with the killer."

"He felt threatened by the recognition Karl was gaining?" Carver asked.

"It seems likely."

"All right." Carver folded his arms and thought for a few seconds. "We need to focus all our attention on Karl's last few hours. He *hasn't* been missing for months—we found him just hours after his death; he didn't turn up at some impersonal public location, he was in his own home. The Ferryman had to gain access to the flat, and since Karl cooperated in making the recording yesterday, it's also possible that he gave the Ferryman that access. The exhibit used a lot of materials, as Ruth pointed out: the frames, the jar, the photographs for the montage, the canvas backing for the two end panels. So—did someone see the Ferryman bringing the stuff in? Maybe Karl helped him? Did the neighbors hear anything of what went on? Talk to local PCSOs and special constables. Someone must have seen something."

Naylor made notes—these questions would shape their strategy in the house-to-house inquiries—and Carver went on.

"There was blood in the bathroom sink. Let's find out if any of it belonged to the killer."

A nod from Hughes. "Already in hand."

"Oh, Jesus."

All eyes turned to Ivey. He was staring at his mobile phone, his skin so pale it was almost translucent.

"What?"

"A new website just got shared by the Ferryman's followers." Ivey swallowed, still staring at the screen.

Ruth stepped over to him and rapped his desk. "Talk to us, Ivey."

The younger detective's hand went to his mouth and he shoved his chair back, putting distance between himself and the image on-screen.

Ruth reached to pick up his phone. "Dear God," she murmured. "It's a recording of Karl Obrazki. He was alive when the Ferryman took his eyes."

49

Karl was almost delirious with excitement when I contacted him.

Meeting him, I had a taste of what fame is like. He was breathless, thrilled, daunted—almost manic in his gabbled attempts to tell me just how much he admired and respected me.

His dark eyes shining, he tells me that my work "totally taps into the zeitgeist."

"Really?" I say. "And how would you define the 'spirit of our age'?"

He knows his history: quotes Hegel and Goethe, but he lets himself down referencing Peter Joseph's film, with its tedious mishmash of conspiracy theories.

"I don't want to know what you've been *told*," I say. "I want to know what you *think*."

"The human race is programmed to self-destruct," he says. "We're a zombie race cannibalizing our planet—destroying nature, laying waste so we can build—then laying waste to what we've built."

"That being the case," I say, "we're well and truly screwed. But what about society, the common good?"

"Society is a failed experiment."

"Oh? Why is that?"

"'Society' as a big melting pot is a filthy lie," he says. "We're divided by gender, class, age, race, religion, nationality—" He rakes his hair from his face, and it immediately flops forward over one eye. "By its very nature, it creates in-groups and out-groups—those who are *in* possession, and the *dis*possessed. Ultimately, it's destructive."

Communism, anarchism, a whiff of nihilism—he seems to've covered all the bases.

"And what part does art play in all this?"

"It reflects society—challenges us to examine our actions, analyze our motivations. But if you want to know about my art—"

I don't. But I nod encouragement, anyway—I need a cooperative little drone for what I have planned.

He bites his lower lip, thinking. He must know that this is it—his big sales pitch.

"I want to draw attention to the dissonance between *having* and *being*. To shine a spotlight on the hypocrisy of a world that talks about individual freedom, when only the richest ten percent have any freedom at all."

I'm tempted to slit his throat there and then, just to shut him up. Instead, I say:

"You're talking about money, when I asked about art. And what do *you* hope to gain from this collaboration, Kharon? Hmm?" He opens his mouth, but I raise one finger, and he stops, his lips twitching.

"Is it F . . . A . . . M . . . E? Surely you know that money always follows fame?"

He is mortified. Stammers an apology—he only wants the chance to work with "Genius." Genius, I note, with a capital *G*.

"I'll tell you what *I* think. The world is afraid of change. Paralyzed by misanthropy. Risk averse. The result? Beige art."

"Yes! Yes!" His eyes burn with passion, but he's as blind as all the rest.

"The only people who challenge that view are the outliers," he says. "Those on the fringes."

"You see me as a *fringe* artist, Kharon?"

"Noooo!" He launches into a new, fawning appreciation of my work.

This is why I don't usually allow subjects the opportunity to speak. They're chosen, gathered, harvested, and reconstructed, without the grinding boredom of having to listen to them. I made an exception for Kharon because he professed an understanding—and to give him his due, he did have an inkling of the force behind my art.

I wait for him to run out of apologies and explanations.

"You understand the concept of catharsis?"

He nods, stupidly.

"Tell me."

"It's the purging of emotions through art."

"Do you know its Greek origins?"

His eyes dart left. He licks his lips again, doesn't want to admit he doesn't have a clue.

"It's a purification," I say.

He smiles, nervous. "Of the emotions, yes?"

"Specifically of pity and fear—two emotions, Aristotle says, that make us weak."

"Pity makes us weak?"

"New worlds are not conquered with pity."

I see him scrolling through his filmography of my work; he's troubled but trying to adjust.

"The word comes from the Greek 'cathartic'—a medicinal remedy that speeds defecation."

"You mean, like, a laxative?"

"No. A laxative *eases* the process. Catharsis is a painful cleansing."

He nods but doesn't really understand.

He assembled most of the triptych himself: the end panels and the center frame, following my instructions with the joy of an acolyte who feels chosen for greater things. I'd told him that this would be the grand reveal—that I would be the centerpiece, seated, at ease, in his armchair. He would record the exhibit and send it out to the world.

Of course, I made him leave the room while I made the final adjustments, called him in when I had the hypodermic ready. Asked him to pose for me, so that I could be sure I'd got the angles right. He couldn't have been happier to oblige. I think he truly understood catharsis at the moment the hypo went into his arm.

Fly on a Chariot Wheel is my most spontaneous piece of the series— two days from conception to inception—and my greatest success, judging by the clamor on social media. And I'm the lead feature on the national news.

I should do this again.

Whoever said power corrupts was wrong. Power enables. Absolute power transforms.

50

Ruth Lake stood outside her brother's place of work. It had the look of a Victorian emporium, and possibly it had been: this was an old quarter of the city. Two tinted windows either side of the door were divided into plate glass below, and eight equal glazed squares above, all painted black. Soul Art Tattoo Studio was listed on Yelp as one of the top ten in the city, and gold gothic-style lettering confirmed its status as "Liverpool's finest." It was just a short walk from police headquarters—admittedly through a maze of backstreets—but Ruth was still astonished they'd never chanced to meet in the years since Adam had slipped out of her life.

She pushed open the door. The wood floors were clean swept and waxed; glass cabinets displayed sample art; more mounted and framed examples hung on the walls. A set of open steel steps, also black, led up to a mezzanine, while the ground floor was divided into the shop front, with a reception desk built in rough-cut wood, and behind that, the tattoo area. Two men and a woman in her twenties sat in a row of red club chairs to the right of the door, waiting their turn. The men seemed absorbed with their mobile phones, but the woman shot Ruth a curious glance.

Ruth checked out two more customers, seated stoically in leather recliners as tattooists, perched on ergonomic stools, worked with intense concentration on their ink. Some form of grunge rock was playing at moderate volume, more or less covering the rattle of the inking machines. She didn't see Adam.

She turned her attention to the reception desk. The girl at the counter had jet black hair, multiple ear and brow piercings, and the tattoo of a gnarled tree, decked with pink cherry blossoms, and delicately rendered, twisting sinuously from her left arm to her neck. She eyed Ruth with kindly amusement.

"First time?" she asked.

"Actually, no," Ruth said, feeling a phantom itch from the erased tattoo in the crook of her left arm.

"Want to book a session?"

Ruth glanced up to the mezzanine. "Is Adam about?"

The girl's untroubled brow creased for a microsecond. "Oh, *Mad-AdaM*," she said, as if Ruth had made an embarrassing error, but she was too polite to point it out. "He's just finishing with a client."

At that moment, Adam himself appeared at the top of the mezzanine stairs. His eyes widened, then shot a warning glare, aimed like a bullet at Ruth. Adam waved his client ahead, and followed a short distance behind, his eyes fixed on Ruth as though she might start overturning the furniture.

The customer seemed oblivious, but that might have been because he was in a delirium of pain. He seemed to be in the process of having a complicated tattoo in the form of a metal zipper, which, unzipped, revealed the inner workings of his arm. The blood and sinews were only sketched out as yet, but his skin was an angry shade of red, and where the zip teeth had been inked in bold black, his flesh was raised and sore-looking.

Ruth made way at the counter, and Adam left his client safely with the receptionist, asking her to advise on aftercare and skin-calming products.

"Back in ten," he said, reinforcing the time limitation with a forceful glance in Ruth's direction.

We'll see, Ruth thought. *We'll see*.

He stepped out onto the street and began walking, didn't turn back until they had rounded a corner into a quieter backstreet.

"What the hell are you playing at?" he demanded.

She was surprised to note that he had covered the bruise on his cheek with some kind of makeup.

"Aren't you even going to grab a jacket?" she said. After a few mild springlike days, the wind direction had changed, sweeping in cold polar air, and the temperature had dropped from twelve to around four Celsius.

"What were you even *thinking*?" he said. "And don't do that."

"Do what?"

"The mother-hen thing. It didn't suit you when I was fourteen—it definitely doesn't suit you now." Every muscle in his shoulders and neck was tense, and the gray metalware inked on his left arm had taken on a definite blue tint, but she could see that he would rather freeze into a solid block of faux machinery than admit he was cold.

"Okay," she said.

"Okay, *what*? Why are you here, Ruth?"

The truth was she couldn't cleanse her mind of trompe l'oeil eyes painted on Kharon's sunglasses, the hollowed eye sockets beneath them. And she kept flashing to the painting on her brother's sitting room wall: the painter painting himself. That was the reason for her unannounced visit to her brother's workplace.

"There's been another killing," she said.

"Kharon, I know. What's that got to do with me?"

"Nothing, I hope."

There was something in the way he said Karl Obrazki's Instagram name that made Ruth think maybe Adam knew the victim personally. She would come back to that.

"So?" He bugged his eyes and gave an irritable shrug.

She thought, *I need to be sure you aren't mixed up in the horror show playing out in the city. I need to talk to your friends to be sure they aren't, either.*

But she settled for: "I need you to come in and give a statement." It was the safest opener she could think of.

"Oh, *what*? Look—I told you—I went to that damn exhibit out of curiosity."

"My boss needs to hear that for himself."

"Fuck." He half turned from her, then swung back. "Why d'you even have to tell him I was *there*?"

"I'm a cop," she said evenly. "It's my job."

His sneer said everything she needed to know about what he thought of her job.

"I'm trying to find a killer, Adam. Give me a break."

"So why're you wasting time hassling me?"

"He's an artist—or calls himself one. You're an artist. So are your friends." She dipped her head. "I'm thinking maybe you'd have insights." Flattery was often far more effective than threats, and she waited, head cocked on one side, giving him time to think about what she'd said.

He folded his arms and she watched him wage an inward battle with himself.

"How did you find me?" he said at last.

"I didn't," she said dryly. "Your gangster friend, Ryan, did."

"It was you he did the favor for," Adam shot back.

"Come on, Adam," she said. "He knew exactly where to find you— he'd already commissioned your art."

"He didn't *always* know. He saw my work on the street, decided he wanted it, did what art collectors do."

"He checked out the galleries," Ruth said, wondering how graffiti artists got their work into galleries. "But unless you signed your name, he'd have to identify your gallery work by—what, your *style*?"

Adam twitched an eyebrow. "It might've helped that I won the UK Street Art Award for Young Talent."

"You won a prize?"

He frowned. "That's surprising?"

"I didn't say that."

"You kinda did."

"No . . ." Why did he always manage to put her on the defensive? "Your work is—"

"Is what?"

"Clever . . . I suppose," she said, with a roll of her eyes, and a slight shrug. She saw him physically loosen up. He let his arms drop to his sides and in spite of the cold, his shoulders relaxed. He even smiled a little. For that small moment Ruth saw her brother as he was before their parents died and their relationship got irretrievably messed up.

She wondered if the time had come to ask him how he knew the latest victim—she was sure he did know Kharon, but she didn't want to alienate him just as they were beginning to connect. In the end, she came at the problem crabwise.

"D'you think your friends might be able to help?"

He frowned. "How?"

"Maybe some of them know Karl—or were in touch with him as 'Kharon.'"

She saw again the tightening around the eyes, which said that Karl Obrazki meant more to her brother than a name on social media. But people didn't like to be read, so she said, "What?"

He took a breath, and she waited, a calculated look of naive curiosity on her face.

He tugged at his goatee, scratched the short hair over his left ear. "I knew Kharon," he said.

She kept quiet, and he went on. "We weren't close, or anything, but . . . yeah, I knew him."

"So you'll help?"

He sucked his teeth, and she waited. Finally, with a decisive nod, he said, "Let me talk to a few people, see if they'd be willing to chat."

51

Back at the office, Ruth pulled together all the new information she could find before going to DCI Carver—she wanted a few distractions to hand, in case she needed to deflect attention from herself.

She found him frowning at his laptop.

"Something up?" she said.

"I don't think so," he said, his eyes still focused on the screen. After a few seconds, he snapped the lid closed and looked at her. "I couldn't find you earlier."

Time to deflect.

"I've done a quick roundup of 'breaking news' on house-to-house," she said, sidestepping the implied question. "The team canvassing at Karl Obrazki's place have found a shop owner who saw a man heading out of the house in coveralls—a painter and decorator, he believes. There were paint splashes on the coveralls."

"Paint splashes," Carver echoed.

"Some red, apparently."

"When was this?" he asked.

"Around lunchtime."

"Which puts it around the time we took the fake call from Karl Obrazki. Did the witness give a description?"

Ruth shook her head. "The suit hood was pulled up and he was wearing a protective mask."

"Of *course* he was," Carver said, with a bitter smile.

"The witness described him as tall, medium build, white. Couldn't guess at age—but not old. He was driving a white van, so with a bit of luck, he's still using the same one. Witness didn't get the number plate. We're still waiting on CCTV in the area."

She had a sudden thought. "He didn't leave the van on the main road all morning—I checked and there were no complaints to traffic control—and I can't imagine him driving the thing all the way back to wherever it is he hides it, because he'd have to go and fetch it later. He must've parked in a side street nearby."

Carver seemed to catch some of her excitement. "And he'd have to take his mask off if he was a distance away."

She nodded. "I'll ask Bill Naylor to extend the canvass."

"Do that. Do we know when the van arrived at Karl's house?"

"The first sighting so far is at around seven A.M.—and Karl was seen going in and out of the house with materials. No signs he was coerced. Witnesses say he seemed cheery—excited, even."

"Poor, stupid kid," Carver said.

"It gets worse," Ruth said. "The SSU found Karl's fingerprints on one of the triptych panels. It looks like Karl helped to build the apparatus."

"What kind of sadist does that and calls it art?"

"Beats me," Ruth said. "But Doctor Yi says, 'For him, sadism and art are inextricable.'"

A sudden pounding of footsteps in the corridor was followed by an excited knock at Carver's door. Ruth opened it and DC Ivey almost fell into the office. His face was flushed and he was out of breath.

"Tom?" Ruth said.

"We've had a call about the police canvass around St. Michael's Station," he panted.

"They were stood down hours ago," Carver said.

"Yeah—I mean, yes, sir. But this guy—one of the residents at Moel Famau View—he's just got back from holiday, and his neighbors told him about all the excitement in the close. He phoned the hotline, and—"

"And the upshot is . . . ?" Ruth said.

"Sorry, Sarge. The day Steve Norris disappeared, he saw two guys—one was helping the other into a white van parked near the end of the road."

"We need to bring him in." Carver was on his feet.

"He's on his way over, right now," Ivey said.

Another knock, this time at the open door. Jason Parr. He seemed daunted to find all three of them in the room together.

"We just got a buzz from reception. There's a man waiting—says you're expecting him, sir. It's about Steve Norris—the lad who went missing," he added, as if they would need a reminder.

"Put him in an interview room," Carver said. "I'll be down shortly."

There was no sign of Parr when they took the lift down to the interview rooms, and Carver was annoyed to have to ask where the witness had been placed.

Frank Hollis was a sprightly man in his midseventies. He waved away Carver's apology for keeping him waiting.

"Not like I've got a full schedule," he said. "When you've been retired ten years, you're looking for things to occupy your time." He looked about him. "Never been in a police station before. Is this where you—you know—give 'em the third degree?"

"It's not really like that anymore, Mr. Hollis," Carver said.

"Oh? 'Cos my missus is a big fan of crime on telly and she—"

Carver cut him off, anticipating a long ramble about *CSI* or *Luther*. "So—you think you saw Steve Norris?"

The man squared his shoulders, collecting his thoughts before launching in. "I was walking my dogs in Priory Wood," he said. "Saw a man on the footpath, half carrying his friend."

"Did you speak to them?" Carver asked.

"I asked what'd happened. The older one said his mate had tripped and banged his head."

"Did the injured man say anything?"

"No. The younger lad seemed a bit out of it—I was worried about that. He mumbled something, but I couldn't make any sense of it. I told his mate, that kind of thing can be serious—you know, concussion and that. I offered to call for an ambulance, but the other feller said he was taking the lad straight to the hospital."

"Can you describe the men?"

Mr. Hollis dug in his jacket pocket and dragged out a flyer the canvassing team had been handing out to the public, pointed to the image of Steve Norris. "That's the lad that was hurt."

"You're sure of this?"

"Not a shadow of doubt."

"And the other man?"

Hollis clasped his hand to the back of his neck. "Now you're asking . . . I was paying more attention to the boy who was injured, you see. He was in running gear, same as this lad. Dark, I think."

"Running shoes?"

He shook his head slowly. "I suppose . . . Didn't really notice, I'm afraid—"

"What time of day was this?" Carver asked.

"Must have been between five thirty and five forty-five in the morning," he said promptly, clearly happy to be on firmer ground. "I always walk the dogs at the same time, summer or winter."

Carver glanced quickly at Ruth. It was the right time frame. "Do you remember the day?"

"Certainly—look." He pulled out his mobile phone and called up the calendar. "The wife warned me to get back before ten to six—we were catching a bus at seven o' clock—coach trip to Llandudno. We were there two weeks, for the walking, you know." He turned the screen so that they could read it. "See?"

It was the date Steve Norris failed to show up at work. The day before *Catch the Gamma Wave*.

"You said that the other man was older," Ruth said.

"Yes." He frowned, concentrating. "Late thirties, maybe—hard to say, these days. It's true what they say: 'You know you're getting old when the police start looking younger.'" He dropped Ruth a cheeky wink.

"Hair color?" Carver said.

Hollis gave a slight shake of his head. "He wore one of those hooded things all the young lads are wearing these days." He tapped the photo of the van on the flyer. "But I'm pretty sure he was in the van your lot were asking about. Rainbow reflections off the window, bit of a dent in the offside front wing."

Ruth asked the next question. "Did you happen to notice the number plate?"

"Oh, yes. It had one of those vanity plates—personalized like."

Hollis closed his eyes and Carver held his breath.

"A33 VAN," he said. "Not that hard to remember, even when you get to my age . . ."

Ruth was out of the door before Hollis could finish.

52

Ruth Lake drove at the speed limit along an empty stretch of motorway heading northeast out of Liverpool. She'd just arrived home from work when Adam called to arrange a meeting at the motorway services at Burtonwood, a thirty-minute drive east.

Only a few vehicles were parked on the service station car park, and the only people in the café were a middle-aged couple, pale with exhaustion, a group of five Newcastle United supporters, huddled around one table, and a blond woman who sat with Adam in the center of the room, with a view of the entrance. This must be Tia Lowe, Karl Obrazki's on-off girlfriend.

The air temperature had dropped to freezing around ten, and the cold-white downlights seemed to add an extra chill. A server was sleepwalking from table to table, scooping used coffee cups into a bag attached to a trolley, swiping the surfaces halfheartedly with a dingy-looking cloth.

Tia stood to greet her; she was taller than Ruth by a couple of inches. Dressed in khaki shorts and a gray wide-lapel mac with unfinished seams and slashes cut to reveal its yellow floral lining, she was hardly dressed to blend in, but Ruth had to admit she carried off the look with some style.

Ms. Lowe offered her hand. It was stacked with rings in silver and gold, including the thumb, which made for an uncomfortable handshake.

They sat at the table, Tia sipping black coffee from a paper cup,

Adam with his legs sprawled out to the side and half turned away from them. He kept his eyes on a pool of spilled coffee on the table-top and began tracing a finger through it, sketching shapes, bringing the liquid into an amorphous puddle every few seconds and starting again.

"Karl was ecstatic." Tia's soft Yorkshire accent belied the sharpness of her appearance. "He was sure this was going to make him famous."

"He didn't tell you what he was planning to do?" Ruth asked.

A brief shake of her head. Her makeup was so perfectly done that it gave her skin a masklike perfection, and it was impossible to search for lies in subtle changes of skin coloring.

"Well, did he say it was a job, or a commission?"

"He called it a 'collaboration,'" Tia said. "Said it was going to make him a lot of money."

She hid her eyes behind lowered eyelids that must have been weighted by two or maybe three sets of false eyelashes.

"That didn't ring any warning bells?" Ruth said, deliberately harsh.

Adam glanced up, his focus on Tia, how she would react.

Tia set her coffee cup down, and when she raised her eyes, Ruth saw anger in them. "You're asking if I knew he'd pitched in with the Ferryman."

Ruth jerked her chin.

Tia's face remained as smooth as a Botoxed film star's, but the muscles of her shoulders popped with suppressed emotion. "If I knew, I'd've warned him off. I would never have—" She stopped suddenly and glanced away.

"Take your time," Ruth murmured.

Tia sniffed and lifted her chin, squaring her shoulders before she went on. "He thought this—whatever it was—would give him an 'in' with one of the TV or film studios. Said he'd help me get my company recognized when he had more clout."

"Is that what Karl was like?" Ruth said. "The sort who would help people out?"

"He was with *me*." The last word sounded like a plea.

"He must have spoken to you about the Ferryman before—while he was compiling his bits of video and so on?" Ruth asked.

Tia eyed her with contempt.

"He told me about his *compilations*, if that's what you mean. Asked for my opinion."

"But not this time."

"You need trust in collaborative works—if you think your creative partner's going to blab about the concept—" Tia spread her slim, beringed hands. "I think Karl was scared someone would break the story before he was ready to go public. He told me not to come near the flat—he would call me when he was finished." She winced, realizing what she'd just said, and she looked into the distance, her mouth working as she fought back emotion.

After a few moments, she thumbed tears from her eyes and tutted when they came away blacked. She dug in her bag, pulling out first a tissue, then a mirror compact.

"God, I need to fix this mess." She stood, oriented herself, then stalked off toward the restrooms.

Adam watched her go from the corner of his eye.

"So," Ruth said. "You knew Karl Obrazki."

He returned to his coffee doodle.

"Adam?"

Her brother's shoulder barely twitched, but the thought behind the gesture was plain: *So what?*

"Did you speak to him about the Ferryman?"

"It's weird," Adam said, "you calling him 'Ferryman'—I thought police didn't like giving names to serial killers."

"We didn't name him," Ruth said. "His followers did."

Another tiny twitch of his shoulder, but still no eye contact.

Push him.

"People like you."

That hit the mark.

Adam's dark eyes flared briefly; then he reached for a napkin and wiped up the coffee spill. "I don't 'follow,' " he said.

"Really?" She let her gaze track from the tattoos on his neck to his carefully styled hair and beard.

Adam tugged self-consciously at his Vandyke goatee.

"When did you last speak to Karl?"

"Let's see . . ." Adam gazed at the ceiling. "We did a module together for a term, must be a year, maybe a year and a half ago."

"Where?"

"Fairfield."

"You were at art college?"

He shrugged. "Fairfield *is* an art college, so . . ."

"Did you talk to him about the Ferryman?"

"I'm not clairvoyant, Ruth. Like I said, I haven't seen him in over a year."

"Why d'you think he was so obsessed with the Ferryman?" She could tell by the eye roll that he was going to repeat his last answer, so she added, "I mean in general terms—what is it that draws artistic types to this man?"

He didn't look up. "He creates art that makes you think about life."

"Do you think it's *okay*, what this man is doing?"

"We're back to that again?"

"Yeah, sorry to be boring, but I'm investigating the deaths of five men—they're just the ones we know about—and the murderer is creating *art* from their dead bodies."

Adam stared at her, his eyes hard and calculating. "You want to talk ethics?"

"I do."

"Fine. There's this Canadian artist—Rick Gibson—made a pair of earrings out of freeze-dried fetuses, hung them on a mannequin. Is that okay? In nineteen eighty-nine, he buys a rat from a pet shop, sticks it in a plexiglass cylinder between two canvases on a street in downtown Vancouver, hangs a twenty-five-kilogram block over it. Puts a sign under the rat, says, 'This rat is going to die.' Is *that* 'okay'?"

He was watching for her reaction; she gave him nothing. "I want to know what *you* think," she countered.

A frown creased Adam's brow for a microsecond and was gone. "The pet shop sold the rat as live food for snakes and lizards—and they also sold snakes and lizards. Whichever way you look at it, the rat *was* going to die. You have to decide—which is the more humane death—trapping a live rat in a glass tank with a python with no escape, letting the python slowly crush the life out of it? Or dying like that?" He clapped his hands in a fast, explosive instant, startling the server and drawing the attention of the Newcastle United fans.

A movement to her right and a whiff of perfume signaled that Tia had returned.

"Oh," she said. "This looks intense. Should I give you two a few more minutes?"

Adam broke eye contact and Ruth placed a notepad and pen on the table. "Karl's friends," she said. "All of them."

Adam stared at them for a long time without moving, but finally he dragged the pad and pencil across the table.

53

Unable to sleep, Greg Carver sat in an armchair next to the bay window in his flat, sipping tea and gazing down onto the empty street. He tried to focus on the investigation, but his thoughts kept circling to Karl Obrazki, his throat slashed, the lenses of his sunglasses overpainted with disturbingly realistic eyes, the surreal cruelty of his death.

When they'd first looked on that hellish scene, Carver had flashed back to his own apartment the night he was shot. Was it the smell of blood, congealing on the floor at his feet, or the way Karl was sprawled in his chair that had triggered it? He couldn't say, but he knew for sure that he'd lost touch with reality for a few seconds.

That was then, this is now. Take a breath, keep your mind on the job.

They'd traced the owner of A33 VAN only minutes after their witness had given his statement. An armed team sent to arrest the owner had scooped up a startled painter and decorator as he arrived home, still in his white overalls. The personalized number plates, A33 VAN, were on the vehicle, but it was steel gray, rather than white, a Renault Kangoo, rather than a Ford Transit—and there was no damage anywhere on the bodywork.

The tradesman had been working on interior decorations at a house at the south end of the city from 8:30 A.M. till 5:30 P.M., according to the house owner, and he hadn't left the premises, apart from a thirty-minute lunch break—which he'd taken in his van, sitting in the drive of the house.

Ruth Lake had conducted the interview. "The man's a grafter," she'd said. "I might just ask him for his business card." The plates had been stolen off his van the night before Steve Norris was snatched, but he hadn't reported the theft because it was the second set to have been stolen in six months. The last time, he'd lost a few hours' work and gained nothing, so on this occasion he'd simply replaced the plates and got on with his life. With a little luck, the killer had kept hold of the plates and was still using them on the suspect van.

As for Norris's new running shoes—it turned out that he'd run record times as an amateur in a couple marathons and was aiming to qualify for the Commonwealth Games. A local sports retailer had seen him on the front page of the *Liverpool Echo* and approached him with a sponsorship offer. One mystery solved, one more victim added to the Ferryman's list.

Headlight beams tracked across the wall at the end of the street as a car turned the corner. It pulled up outside his place, and Ruth Lake got out. She glanced up to his window but didn't wave. A few seconds later, he heard her trotting lightly up the stairs.

Ruth had been to Carver's apartment many times since he was shot, but she'd almost always restricted her visits to pickup and drop-off at the roadside. So why was she troubling to come inside? It couldn't be a break in the case—she would have called ahead. Carver felt a cold chill in the pit of his stomach; had she noticed his episode at Karl's flat? Was that why Ruth Lake was at his door at eleven thirty at night?

As she reached the top of the stairs, he opened the door, not waiting for the knock.

"Coffee?" he said.

She walked past him, crackling with energy, and apparently not in the mood for banter.

"Maybe chamomile tea would be a better option," he added, quirking his brow.

"Adam phoned," Ruth said, unsmiling. "He hasn't had much luck trying to get Karl Obrazki's friends to talk."

"Worried about their street cred?" Carver said, wondering why this couldn't wait till morning.

"Paranoid that they'll be arrested, more likely," she said. "I gather a few of them were involved in the Ferryman graffiti we've been seeing around the city. That, and they're terrified that the Ferryman could be watching."

Carver saw Karl, his throat slashed, exposing the white cartilage of his windpipe. He banished the vision, and focused on Ruth. "Even so, he *will* have to give us their names."

She handed him a folded sheet of paper from her pocket and he tilted his head in question.

"Karl's friends," she said. "Adam doesn't have addresses for all of them, only hangouts."

He skimmed the list; there must have been twenty names on the sheet. "You got all this over the phone?"

"Not exactly," Ruth said.

"That's not an answer." Carver searched her face, but she was at her most unreadable. "Ruth?"

"He rang from Burtonwood services on the M62."

About a fifteen-mile drive from the city, by Carver's estimate.

"He said he'd persuaded Karl's girlfriend to talk to me," she went on. "But she wouldn't come to the station."

"You *met* them?" He felt a stab of horror. "Ruth, tell me you didn't go alone."

"Why wouldn't I? He's my brother."

"You barely know him."

"Of course I do."

"You *knew* him—past tense—what, eight? Ten years ago? He was a teenager back then, Ruth. Now he's mixed up with Dave Ryan. People change."

She tilted her head. "Maybe."

"For God's sake, wake up. Have you forgotten what happened today? Karl Obrazki was murdered and mutilated in his *own flat*, with his neighbor sitting behind paper-thin walls just a few *feet* from him, and you're telling me you went *alone* to an empty motorway café to meet with a *complete stranger*? Have you lost your mind?"

"Come on, Greg . . ." she said, and for once her tone was placatory. "She didn't want anyone else there—I couldn't just let her quietly disappear, now, could I?"

"Protocol, Ruth. You should've called: I could've arranged a covert follow."

"There wasn't time," she said. "And anyway, I was careful."

"Careful *how*, exactly? Young, fit men have vanished without trace—" He faltered, realizing that wasn't true—traces of them had turned up—and in the vilest of circumstances. He tasted bile at the back of his throat and swallowed hard.

She started to say something, but he cut her off: "You're not thinking straight, Ruth. First the unsanctioned inquiries to find Adam. Now this." He shook his head. "You're a bloody danger to yourself—I should suspend you from duty."

He saw an anxious flare of blue around her face, but the emotion was gone before it took hold.

"Okay," she said. "I'm sorry, I should have let you know where I was going." After a barely decent pause, she went on: "So, the girlfriend—Tia Lowe . . . ?"

He stared at her, unable to find words.

"What?" she said.

"You're *un*believable."

"I know . . . But the thing is, I've already been and gone and done it. And I'm back in one piece, so we might as well use the intel."

He sighed. "Okay," he said, too tired to argue. "All right—let's hear it."

It took her just five minutes to give a concise and efficient summary of her interview of Obrazki's girlfriend, as well as her conversation with Adam about a rat in a box under a concrete weight. How Ruth could think that Adam was "okay," listening to his cold ethical arguments about snakes and lizards and live food and art was a mystery to Carver.

"We'll make a start on this in the morning—you can put a couple of teams on it."

"Um . . . I was thinking I'd start on the list tonight," Ruth said.

Carver checked his watch. "It's almost midnight," he said. "What's the rush?"

She smiled. "No rush—it's just these aren't really morning people."

It was dark and cold. A fine rain misted the streets as they left the house, and easing into the passenger seat, Carver's thoughts turned again to the risks Ruth had taken, first in hunting down her brother, then in meeting Adam and Tia Lowe on her own.

Ruth slotted the key into the lock and started the engine.

"This can't go on," Carver said. "You do know that?"

"I don't follow." She pulled away from the curb.

He saw bile-green light shimmer at the edges of his vision—she was lying—she knew *exactly* what he was talking about. But what the hell—if she wanted him to state the obvious . . . "Adam is a person of interest in a murder investigation."

"A *person of interest*," she repeated, "Meaning a *suspect*."

"I didn't say that."

She shot him a look that said he didn't need to.

"But I *do* think he's been dishonest."

"Okay, I'll give you that."

"At the very least, he should be treated as a hostile witness," Carver went on.

She glanced across sharply. "Because?"

"He knew Karl yet he said nothing."

"And now he's opened up—given us *twenty-three* people who knew Karl. He's helping, Greg."

"You have to ask yourself why."

"Why he's helping, or why he withheld information in the first place?"

"Both," Carver said, firmly. "Come on, Ruth—you know how this works."

"I've been around the block a few times," Ruth said. "Yeah, I know."

"I'm not questioning your experience," Carver said, hearing the resentment in her tone. "But you could use a bit more objectivity."

She gripped the wheel a little tighter but didn't respond.

He wasn't getting through.

So try again.

"I know this is hard," he began. "We do all we can to separate our personal lives from our work, to leave our bad experiences in our past, but—"

She turned to him, and he saw a complicated mix of colors around her.

"Who are you trying to convince," she said, "me, or yourself?"

He supposed he deserved that. They drove in silence for the next few miles.

Waiting at a set of traffic lights with the wipers ticking intermittently and cars sweeping past at a rate of one every ten seconds, he took a different tack: "You lost your brother for a while; it's understandable that you'd want to protect him now you're back in touch. But, Ruth, you need to find some perspective."

"That's rich, coming from you," she scoffed.

"I don't think I—" *She saw you flip out at Karl's flat. She knows.*

"Of course you do. Come *on*, Greg!"

A clammy sweat gathered on his forehead, and he stared ahead, his hands fisted in his lap, waiting for her to say it.

"I found you virtually collapsed in the toilets a few days ago," she said, "but I so much as ask if you're all right, you shut me down."

He felt a surge of relief. *She doesn't know. So tell her—you owe her that much.*

Instead, Carver heard himself say, "I want Adam's whereabouts checked out for every 'exhibit' the Ferryman has staged since this thing started."

"Goes without saying," Ruth said.

He cleared his throat. "I want you to task someone else with the job."

She took a breath, then clamped her mouth shut and gave a curt nod. "You're the boss."

The next few minutes, the only sound inside the car was the occasional swish of the wipers.

"You're angry," he said at last. "I suppose you've a right to be—as a sister. But you're *police*, Ruth. You can't be partisan about this."

She didn't say a word, but the cool look she gave him carried so much meaning: Hadn't she saved his career last winter by being partisan—protecting his sorry, drunken arse for no better reason than friendship and misplaced loyalty?

54

Ruth sat at her kitchen table, weary from the unproductive interviews she and Carver had managed to conduct with a couple of Karl's acquaintances before calling it a night. The blue leatherette photo album was open in front of her. Next to it, the timeline she'd sketched out just three days earlier. Judging by her conversation with Greg Carver, she'd need to have every detail clear, every response rehearsed.

From her late teens, Ruth had developed the knack of separating her personal life from her work. Creating a firewall between the two had kept her safe—and able to function—through the traumatic years following her mother's murder. Sometimes, it felt as if home and career existed in different domains, with no bridge between them. As a young CSI, her focus was so absolute that she had worked on a domestic murder scene and not made the connection with her mother until she stood preparing dinner for Adam and herself that evening. A therapist had warned her that blocking her feelings was not healthy, but for Ruth back then it meant the difference between survival and mental collapse, and after a while, it had become as much a part of her makeup as her extraordinary ability to recognize faces.

So she'd shut off her personal anxieties and sorrows from her studies and her work. Only one person had ever been able to penetrate her armor shielding: Adam. When he was still living in the family home, and even after he'd cut himself off from her, worries about Adam would intrude on her thoughts, and sometimes, out of nowhere, she would feel a wave of terrible sorrow for his loss. In some ways it was greater than hers, because for Adam, the security of home and family had been snatched away from him just as he'd begun the transition from boy to man and had needed parental guidance most. If he had known all he should know about what Dad had done, perhaps it might have been easier for him, but Ruth could never tell him all she knew.

Maybe Carver was right, maybe she was partisan, but guilt, too, had played a role in her feelings for her brother, her tolerance for his transgressions. Because she had lied to Adam, kept secrets, withheld the truth. If it had been to protect Adam she might have felt less tormented, but the ugly truth was that her lies and omissions were all to protect herself. And now Adam was back in her life, crowding her thoughts and breaking in on her daily activities just like old times—and as if the situation wasn't complicated enough, he'd forged links with Dave Ryan.

Ruth went through the album, the pages crackling as she broke the static attraction between them, and her nostrils were filled with the musty almonds-and-dust smell of old paper. She went quickly through the family snapshots, her eyes unfocused, in the hope that what followed would cause her less pain.

"Woman Found Dead in Deeside." This was Ffion, Dad's girlfriend. The report said she had "serious head injuries" and was pronounced dead at the scene.

That was the night Dad came to the family home; it was also the last time Ruth saw him alive.

Over the twenty-four hours that followed, news media had reported on the head injuries Ffion had sustained, attaching helpful images to their reports of the kind of clawhammer that was thought to have been used in the "frenzied attack."

The detectives knew that Dad had turned up on their doorstep the night Ffion's body was found, and all three of them had been questioned. Ruth remembered the fear in Adam's eyes as he'd retold the circumstances, describing the blood on Dad's clothing, the crazed look in his eyes, his threat, "You're next!"

A watch had been placed on the house, in case he came back, but he never did.

Neither did Mum, after that day.

Ruth flipped quickly past the headline: "Liverpool Mum of Two Slain"; she could recite the text verbatim. Like Ffion, Mum had been murdered with a clawhammer, her body discovered inside Dad's business premises in Deeside.

All the headlines after that were variations on "Liverpool Man Sought in Brutal Double Murder." She'd avoided the news then, but years later, Ruth had been given urgent cause to go looking for those reports. The media had trotted out all the usual clichés: "Mum Slain," "Frenzied Attack," "Neighbors Shocked." Mum was always "Mum of two"; the media didn't seem able to cope with the concept that a woman can carry many roles. Sara Black, née Lake, had been a carer and nursery school assistant; she'd been secretary, receptionist, and bookkeeper to Dad's firm before the banking crisis put them out of business. She'd retrained as a nurse after Dad left, and she would have hated to be defined in such narrow terms as "Mum of two." Even so, for Adam and Ruth that's who she was, and the way Mum had been torn from them felt like a physical wound. Those scars remained, under the armor plating, just as the ghost of the Thorn Killer's tattoos lay under Ruth's skin.

The media had an opportunity to file a few more stock phrases when Dad turned up dead. It was just two days after Ffion's murder, and headlines summed up the stories, saving busy people the time and effort of reading the details: "Double-Murder Suspect Dead in Suicide Leap."

Ruth had kept no cuttings of the Ryan case, although she carried the details in her head. A double murder—Damien Ryan, eldest son of gangland boss Dave Ryan, and Naomi, his bride of three months. The couple had been discovered battered about the head; the murder weapon—a clawhammer—found nearby. Naomi was two months pregnant when she died.

Ruth had been a CSI at the time; it was during a spate of gangland killings across Merseyside: shootings, stabbings, firebombings—a grenade had even been used in one attack. Ruth had worked on one of the stabbings, and while the others were of interest, they were not part of her brief, and the curious focus that had saved her from mental breakdown after the traumatic events of her late teens had also caused her to block the Ryan murders from her thoughts.

Dave Ryan had said, *You saw to it justice was done*, and in a sense she had, though some years later. By then, Ruth had been promoted from CSI to crime scene coordinator and was also a part-time police trainer. Ruth had been tasked with supervising evidence collection and analysis on the murders of John and Millie Garrod, an elderly couple, bludgeoned to death in their home. The probable weapon: a clawhammer. Initially, investigators took the approach that the killings were most likely a burglary gone wrong. Then it emerged that the couple were key witnesses scheduled to testify in the high-profile drug trial of Alan Jones, North Wales cannabis grower, brothel owner, and drug racketeer. Although the drug trial foundered, Jones was eventually convicted of the Garrod murders.

Damien and Naomi Ryan's deaths were not mentioned, even in passing, before, during, or after Jones's conviction. Yet last night, Ryan had praised CSIs as the unsung heroes of the criminal justice system. She recalled his slow blink, then: *We both got a result, didn't we?*

Of course, Ryan could have been making an innocent reference to the double murder of the elderly couple. But she doubted if Ryan had made an innocent remark in thirty years.

Ruth had read the report on the murders of Dave Ryan's son, his daughter-in-law, and their unborn child. Jones's business interests extended across the Welsh border into Deeside and Wirral, and there was a known rivalry between Ryan and Alan Jones in their criminal endeavors. The police investigation had considered Jones a suspect, but there was very little physical evidence to work on, and nothing to tie Jones directly to the killings. The evidence against Jones in the Garrods' deaths, on the other hand, was irrefutable; the case had been solved, Jones sentenced to life, justice served.

If it had ended there, perhaps Ruth would not have been burdened with so much guilt. But Alan Jones was murdered two weeks after he'd landed in prison—battered about the head and left in a corner of his cell to choke to death on his own blood.

Men like Alan Jones led brutal lives and made deadly enemies. His imprisonment had left a void in the drug supply network on the Welsh border, and his murder might be seen as inevitable—there were plenty of ambitious Welsh hard men who might have put a contract out on him. But Ryan's slow blink when he'd said *We got a result* spoke of an understanding between Ruth and the gangster—it said he knew what she'd done to place Jones with his back to the wall in a prison cell. Ryan's thugs had no doubt carried out the execution, but Ruth's actions had put him there in the first place.

The puzzle was, why had Ryan brought it up now, after all these years?

She closed the album and set it square in the center of the table, a solid, sickening realization settling in the pit of her stomach. Ryan was a strategist: Adam hadn't forged links with Ryan, Dave Ryan had sought him out.

A firm believer in the maxim "knowledge is power," Ryan gathered information and filed it away until he found a use for it. He'd formed an association with Adam because it gave him power over Ruth. Yet he hadn't exercised that power until Ruth had rippled the waters of his toxic pond.

Ruth had made sure that none of the physical evidence from Jones's trial could lead back to her—but even a guess in that direction could give Ryan a slight advantage. He could hurt Ruth with what he knew—or thought he knew—and in a man of Ryan's type, that kind of power was extremely dangerous.

55

Ruth Lake stared up at the ugly 1950s building that housed Fairfield Arts College. Originally a technical college, it had been hastily constructed postwar, one of many such buildings that had grown—or been thrown—up to repopulate the bomb-devastated landscape of Liverpool. The gray concrete structure squatted in the center of a large car park, evoking Stalinist Russia rather than twenty-first-century Britain. Recent attempts had been made to soften the brutal look of the place with small birch trees and a few clumps of forsythia. The birch was still dormant, but the sulfur-yellow flowers of forsythia lit up a border at the edge of a grassy mound—all that was left of what used to be a sports field.

Her visit was a follow-up to the information Adam had reluctantly given them the day before. She had spoken to Karl Obrazki's personal tutor earlier that morning, and he arranged for her to stop by one of his seminars.

As Ruth passed through the glass doorway, she noted a gray shadow on the foyer wall: a stenciled image of the Ferryman. She stopped at the reception desk and was buzzed through the barrier.

Heads turned as she strode down the corridor; some of the students were wearing hoodies etched with the *F* logo.

The tutor was already in the room waiting for his class of ten to arrive. He was chatting quietly with a student while zipping through a PowerPoint presentation on his laptop. He offered to step out of the room while Ruth spoke to the students.

"That's okay, Mr. Milner." She thought it might be useful to see who squirmed the most as she asked her questions, and the presence of someone who knew them would make it harder for them to get away with putting on an act. She asked Milner to stand out of their direct line of sight, though—she didn't want them looking to him for approval, or to gauge his reaction. Milner was in his late thirties, she estimated. Fair-haired, tall, but not exceptionally so. He had gray-blue eyes with pale, almost translucent eyebrows, and he kept his hair short, trimmed close to his broad, smooth forehead.

The two who knew Karl were a badly frightened girl and a monstrously hungover lad. Both denied any knowledge that Kharon was Karl's alter ego. The girl in particular seemed terrified that the Ferryman might think she had any inside knowledge, while the boy seemed resentful that Karl had won the attention of the media. Presumably he felt that in Karl's place, he would have managed things differently—emerging as the triumphant hero instead of winding up dead.

Milner followed her into the corridor afterward. "I'm afraid that wasn't much help," he said.

"Do you believe they had no idea that Karl was Kharon?" she asked.

"Karl kept to himself," he said. "He was apt to go off and do his own thing, so, yes . . . it's entirely possible they didn't know."

"You've been following the case?"

"The exhibits—yes, of course. Hasn't everyone?"

With the Ferryman's followers rising by the hour, she couldn't disagree. "This obsession with death," she said. "Is it big in art right now?" She was thinking of Adam and his nasty story about the artist and the rat.

Milner didn't answer immediately. He stood in silent thought for a few seconds, then said, "Death has preoccupied artists since the beginning of time. When you have a moment, you should take a stroll around the Walker Art Gallery—death is represented in its many forms on just about every wall in the building. From religious art to Roman mythology."

"Do you have an opinion on what this killer is doing?"

"Given the constraints and the difficulty of the settings, the quality of the work is exceptional," he said.

"I meant, do you think it is immoral?"

"Ah, now that's a different question entirely," he said. "He's driven, inventive—cruel, certainly."

"Do you condemn him—as an artist yourself?"

He considered. "I try not to condemn disturbing and challenging works: they often have the most to say to us. But context is so important in art. A lot of people have a problem with Tracey Emin's work *My Bed*. But place it in the context of autobiographical art—the fact that she stayed in that bed—or a version of it—for several days contemplating suicide, and you begin to understand it."

"Contemplating suicide is very different from actually committing murder," Ruth said.

"And yet suicide was a criminal offense here in the UK until nineteen sixty-one." Milner smiled. "I can see you're not convinced. But you have to acknowledge his work has impact."

"If we're talking about impact, the Yorkshire Ripper had that—and nobody called him an artist."

He nodded. "Fair point. Is there anything else I can do for you, Sergeant?"

"It'd be helpful if more of Karl's friends came forward." She handed him her card. "We need to track his movements in the days before he died."

"I'll speak to my classes," he said.

Ruth called in to Carver's office as soon as she got back and gave him the bad news.

"John Hughes called while you were out," he said. "The SSU found a partial print on one of the hinges of the triptych."

Metal, Ruth thought—it should give them a good-quality lift. "Fingerprint?" she said.

Carver shook his head. "The *edge* of a hand. But there's nothing in the database."

They only kept the edge prints of people arrested for suspected terrorist offenses, so that was no surprise.

"We also got some hits from ANPR on the stolen number plates. A vehicle matching the suspect van's description was spotted near St. Michael's Station and at various points through the city on the day Steve Norris was abducted. It's possible he's still using the A33 VAN number plates."

"Well, it's about time we had some good luck," she said.

Carver dipped his head. "It's not all good. They lost him at the north end of the city, after he turned off the Dock Road into a housing estate."

Ruth felt her shoulders sag, but Carver seemed to take the disappointment in his stride; he looked rested and focused, and it occurred to her that his new therapist must be working wonders.

"We just keep plowing away like we always do, Ruth," Carver added. "Something will turn up. Which reminds me—any news on the soil samples?"

"Early days," Ruth said.

His desk phone rang, and Ruth gave Carver a nod and left him to it, closing the door after her.

As she reached the Major Incident Room, Carver appeared in the corridor.

"Something just turned up," he said.

56

Ruth reserved a briefing room on the next floor for the meeting, well out of sight and hearing of the MIR. As Carver walked in, the buzz of conversation stilled, though the nervous tension felt like a breath held.

"Doctor Yi?" he asked.

"He's away at a conference," Ruth said, "but he was able to access a secure line. He's on speaker now."

Carver greeted him, thanking the psychologist for breaking into his schedule.

"Happy to assist," Dr. Yi said.

"I'm going to address the team," Carver said. "DS Lake is standing by—let her know if you need anything repeated."

"Will do," Yi said.

Carver called the room to order. "DNA samples from the heart have been identified as belonging to Marcus Fenst," he began. "Mr. Fenst was a banker at Alderson Bank."

Ruth felt the excitement in the room as a hum in her veins. But they'd identified other victims, and in truth, she couldn't really see how this one would be any different from Professor Tennent, or Steve Norris—or Karl Obrazki, for that matter. The Ferryman was clever, he was careful, and he'd left little trace of himself.

What about the edge print at Karl's flat? her inner optimist whispered. *Maybe he's getting careless—maybe this victim will be the one that helps us to nail the bastard.*

Ruth watched every face in the room. The sharper, more ambitious detectives were already working through possibilities, thinking of avenues to explore. DC Gorman looked bored, as usual; Tom Ivey was typing something into his laptop, glancing up every few seconds as though he was afraid he'd miss something.

"Alderson is a private bank based in Manchester."

Frowns and murmurs.

"That's right. This victim wasn't from Liverpool—the Ferryman has strayed out of his usual hunting grounds again. Mr. Fenst doesn't fit the pattern of the other missing men, either: he's older, for one thing—aged forty-five. He's also wealthy, while the others, with the exception of Professor Tennent, were not."

"When did he go missing?" Naylor asked.

"Thirteen days ago," Carver said.

"And we're only hearing about it now? Why wasn't his DNA in the national database?"

"The investigating officer was seriously injured in a road accident," Ruth supplied. "The sample went AWOL. It happens."

Carver spoke again: "We need to know *everything* there is to know about this man—his family, his friends, his enemies. His disappearance was reported by his wife. He also has two kids—but let's dig deep. Was he having an affair? Did he have sexual preferences he kept from his wife? Did his banking partners have any concerns over financial misdeeds? To all appearances, Mr. Fenst was Establishment with a capital *E*—but *something* made him vulnerable. We need to know what that was."

Ruth took stock, matching the strengths of the personnel present with the tasks to be allocated.

"Look around you," Carver said. "Memorize the people in this room. They are the *only* people you can discuss this with."

Ruth saw confusion and doubt as the team exchanged glances.

"I know it won't be easy," Carver went on. "I'm asking you to hold back information from your coworkers—but there's a good reason." He paused. "We may have a leak from within the team."

That caused a ripple of exclamations.

"Yesterday, a local press reporter got a phone call from someone claiming to be the Ferryman. He spoke with a fake Midlands accent, and he knew that we'd reevaluated the age of the heart victim, who we now know is Mr. Fenst."

"Doesn't mean it was leaked by one of our lot, boss," Gorman said. "Could be the Ferryman just guessed we'd've worked that out by now."

"It's possible," Carver said. "But we can't take any chances. This killer has been ahead of us every step of the way. For once, we're ahead of him. We need to play that advantage—if we can establish a link to Mr. Fenst, it might lead us right to his door."

Carver turned toward the conference phone. "Doctor Yi. We know that Mr. Fenst's heart had been stuffed with coins and maggots. Now, I can see the rather obvious allusion to bankers, money, and corruption, but Fenst was not an obvious target for this offender."

Yi agreed. "But I would prefer to wait until you've gathered more information about Mr. Fenst before I comment—anything I say now would be purely speculative."

It wasn't particularly helpful, but Yi was taking a properly scientific approach, and Ruth could identify with that.

"Could he have knocked the killer back on a loan, or something?" Sergeant Naylor suggested.

"Uh, he's not that kind of banker, Sarge," Ivey said, looking up from his laptop. "I'm looking at Alderson Bank's website; they provide services for—and I'm quoting—'ultra-high-net-worth individuals.'"

Someone at the back said, "Ooh, get them!"

Ivey colored slightly. "Fenst's LinkedIn profile says he's an investment banker specializing in 'resurgence.'"

"What the hell's that?" Naylor demanded, apparently still ruffled by the fact that Fenst's DNA wasn't on the missing persons database.

Ivey's eyes darted from the keyboard to the screen as he typed in a search term. "According to Google, it means they buy shares and equity in undervalued and failing firms and make money on them."

"Asset strippers?" Carver said. "That'd make him a lot of enemies."

Ivey seemed to be swapping screens every few seconds. "The *Financial Times* reckons a good number of companies this bank has taken on have returned to profit."

"Okay," Carver said, "so we look for the ones that didn't get turned around."

"I don't suppose any of them's art galleries?" The smirk on Gorman's face said he was joking, but Carver seemed to take the question seriously.

"That's a good question," Carver said. "Let's find out."

As people gathered their belongings, Carver called them to order one last time. "Remember what I said: this does not go beyond the people gathered in this room." He waited for a "Yes, boss" from every one of them before he dismissed them.

57

Three hours later, tasks allocated and liaison established with Greater Manchester Police, Ruth got a call from Carver.

"I've spoken to Mr. Fenst's widow," he said. "The DCI at Manchester Police who's coordinating with us broke the news to her a couple of hours ago. She's agreed to speak to us. Can we get to Hale Barns by four if we leave now?"

Ruth checked her watch; it was 2:25. "That's South Manchester?"

"Not far from the airport, apparently."

"We should have plenty of time," she said. "I'll grab a car, see you down below."

As she left the MIR, she saw Superintendent Wilshire about to enter Carver's office, and she ducked into the stairwell to avoid him.

Voices echoed up from a couple of flights down.

". . . I don't know what you're on about, mate."

Tom Ivey.

"Sure you do. Eight members of the team disappear for half an hour, come back looking like constipated ferrets."

Ruth recognized the second voice; it was Parr.

"What does a constipated ferret look like, then?"

"Like they're keeping something in that's paining them. Come on, Tommy. Something's up."

"It's Tom," Ivey said. "And yeah, something's up—a serial killer's on the loose. You need to read your memos, mate."

Ivey was toughening up. Good for him.

"Very funny," Parr said. "Bloody hilarious."

Ruth heard a shuffle, then Tom raised his voice. "Get out of my way."

"Keeping secrets is bad for you—d'you know that?" Parr hissed. "I guess you would."

"What does that mean?" Ivey said.

"Secrets, Tommy. Things locked in closets." He affected an offensive lisp.

"Piss off, Parr," Tom said.

She heard a brief scuffle, then a harsh, unpleasant laugh from Parr. Ruth opened the door to the stairwell again, slamming it wide, and began trotting down the stairs. Parr waited at the turn in the stairs for her to pass. She looked in his eyes and saw no hint of the nastiness in his exchange with Ivey. He gave her a respectful nod and carried on.

Ruth caught Ivey as he was about to exit the stairwell on the next floor down.

"Okay, Tom?" He looked at her in question, and she added, "I couldn't help hearing."

He was pale but seemed more angry than shaken. "Nothing I can't handle," he said.

"Okay. In that case, I need a favor."

Carver was shrugging into his jacket and shutting down his computer when Detective Superintendent Wilshire poked his head around the door.

"Good work on the identification," he said.

"Team effort, sir," Carver said. "But thank you—I'll pass it on."

"You're heading home—good. You've been looking washed out recently."

"It took a few days to settle in, but I'm finding my stride now, sir."

Wilshire eyed Carver suspiciously as he stuffed his personal phone in one jacket pocket and his work phone in the other. "You *are* heading home?"

"Just on my way out now," Carver said, avoiding a direct lie.

Wilshire looked unconvinced.

"Ruth and I are taking our work phones home with us for the duration," Carver explained. "It's all been cleared."

He heard footsteps in the corridor, then DC Ivey's voice. "Sorry, sir," he said, peering around Wilshire's impressive bulk. "The chief inspector's taxi's waiting at the gate."

"Tell them I'm on my way," Carver said.

Wilshire left a moment later, and Ivey caught Carver as he passed the Major Incident Room.

"Ruth said she'd meet you just inside the gates of the Albert Dock," the young detective murmured.

"Good lad," Carver said, suppressing a smile.

Traffic was heavy along each of the three motorways they had to navigate to get to south Manchester, and it took thirty minutes longer than it should have, but they made it in time. Hale Barns was an affluent suburb and the Fenst family home was one of the larger Edwardian properties in the area, comfortably settled on a tree-lined street. The iron gates securing the driveway were closed, but Ruth buzzed the call button on a pole at the entrance and they slid open.

Mrs. Fenst met them at the front door. She was dressed immaculately in a skirt suit, her brown hair cut close to the nape of her neck; she looked as if she'd stepped out of a business meeting.

They presented their warrant cards, and Mrs. Fenst studied both with a keen eye before stepping back to let them in. The hall floor was honey-colored parquet, polished to a liquid gleam.

Mrs. Fenst insisted on taking their coats, and as Carver shucked out of his, he glanced up the wide staircase to the half landing on which someone stood, stone-white, poised with one foot forward. Carver broke out in a sweat: the legs were shapely, well-rounded, but the body was twisted horribly at the waist.

Not now, he thought. *I can't do this now.*

"It's a striking piece, isn't it," Mrs. Fenst said, following his line of sight.

Carver blinked. The figure resolved into a marble sculpture.

"It's called *Body Dysmorphia*," she said. "The artist had just come out of a long period of anorexia and bulimia."

Carver slowed his breathing, and the feeling of scrabbling panic abated. Mrs. Fenst showed them through to a sitting room twice the size of Carver's entire flat. It was done out in Edwardian style, in pale blue and lemon, and thankfully, the paintings hung on the walls were more tranquil than the sculpture on the landing. A MacBook Air lay on a glass coffee table, next to an iPhone and a tray of coffee makings.

"Do sit," she said. "I hope coffee's all right?"

They murmured their thanks and as she poured from a cafetière into fine china mugs, Ruth made brief eye contact, a question on her face. She would have seen his reaction to the sculpture and would know that he found it more than just *striking*.

He gave a quick nod in answer: *I'm fine.*

"Help yourself to milk and sugar," Mrs. Fenst said, acting the perfect host, despite the turmoil she must be in.

It is *an act*, Carver thought, focusing on the widow to distract himself. Watching her, he was reminded of his therapist's description of "white-knuckle sobriety"; it seemed that behind her composure Mrs. Fenst was keeping just as tight a grip on her emotions.

When she was seated, Carver said, "We're very sorry to intrude at such a difficult time."

She gave a minute shake of her head. "I've known Marcus was dead since the day he disappeared." Her voice was strong. "He would never have voluntarily put us through this . . . hell."

She paused, and her eyes flicked to the large bay window to her left. "Before you ask your questions, I must ask—do I need to keep the children away from the TV, their tablets? They're at an inquisitive age, Chief Inspector—I don't want them to see—"

Carver saw deep emotional pain gather at her brow, and he spoke before her feelings could overwhelm her. "We won't release this to the press, Mrs. Fenst," he said. "And—again, I'm sorry—I know this must be hard, but if you could limit who you tell for now, it would give us a better chance of catching the person responsible."

She clicked smartly into business mode. "I've already informed the chairman of the board; he will have told the director; our immediate family know, of course." Her eyes darted to the laptop. "It should be possible to contain it."

"Complete containment is often difficult in such circumstances, despite everyone's best efforts," Carver said, gently. "And once it *is* in the public domain, you will want to shield your children. Manchester Police will arrange for a family liaison officer to advise—"

"I've told them I'm quite capable of dealing with this without outside interference," she said firmly.

"I'm sure," he said. "But they can also keep you informed about the progress of the investigation."

"Oh, I didn't realize . . ." Her face crumpled for a second, and she stood and took two quick steps away from them, seemingly appalled at her sudden loss of control.

"Do you collect art?" Ruth asked, looking at the artwork around the room.

It seemed exactly the right question. Mrs. Fenst cleared her throat and smoothed her skirt before sitting down again; just as a police officer might fall back on their training in a dangerous situation, Mrs. Fenst's social training kicked in. Required to make polite conversation, she was able to regain her composure.

"I dabble," she said. "But my purchases are mostly for my shop, or for clients." She must have seen a question on Ruth's face, because she added, "I have an interior design business based in Wilmslow. Marcus is the serious collector—I mean, he *was*. His bank even sponsors a prize for new talent."

"*Artistic* talent?" Ruth said.

"Well, yes . . ." Mrs. Fenst seemed to understand that she'd said something significant, but wasn't sure what that might be.

"So there's a competition?" Ruth said. Her tone was perfectly neutral, and Carver was happy to let her take the lead.

"The Alderson Bank Art Awards, yes. As well as grant applications—small one-off payments for a specific project—you know the sort of thing. Marcus has chaired the judging panel for the award for the past five or six years."

Carver glanced across to Ruth. This could add another layer of meaning to *Art for Art's Sake*.

"Who manages the entries?" Ruth asked.

Mrs. Fenst looked stricken. "Do you think that had something to do with Marcus's—with what happened to Marcus?"

"We're simply running down every possible line of inquiry," Ruth said smoothly. Her calm, unreadable expression seemed to mollify Mrs. Fenst. She took a sip of coffee before asking, "Does it attract many entries?"

"Hundreds," the widow said.

"Who else was on the judging panel with your husband?" Carver asked.

"I'm not sure—they tend to rotate. Jim Barrow would know—he owns a gallery in Manchester. Marcus drafted him in to help with the grant applications initially, but now he helps with the judging process, too. I can give you his contact details."

"It would be helpful to see him today," Carver said, "if you could set that up."

"Oh, of course—I should have thought . . ." Her self-possession slipped; she clattered her coffee mug onto the glass tabletop, reached for her phone, and began frantically searching her contacts list.

"It's really good of you to do this," Ruth murmured in that same warm and reassuring tone, and the widow became calmer, scrolling through her contacts with more purpose.

A moment later, she tapped her phone screen; her head came up, and she tucked a curl of hair behind her left ear as she put the phone to it. "Jim?" she said. "It's Anna. I have two Merseyside Police detectives here with me." She paused. "I'm afraid so. Look, I know you're busy, but might you have time to speak to them, if they come over now?" She glanced at Carver and gave him a nod. "That's awfully good of you." She hesitated. "Jim—they want to keep this under wraps for now."

She listened to his reply. "Yes . . . Yes, thank you, I will."

Carver avoided looking at the sculpture on the landing as they collected their coats: he'd seen enough torment for one day.

"What was that?" Ruth asked.

They were in the car again, winding their way through the tree-lined streets, some of them in soft green leaf.

"What was what?"

"When you saw the sculpture on the stairs," she reminded him. "That."

"I don't know what you mean."

"You freaked out."

Shit.

He forced a laugh. "I *really* don't know what you mean."

She swung the car in to the curb and yanked the handbrake on so hard the back end dipped. "You're such a liar."

"Ruth, what the hell is this?"

"This is me not being partisan," she said. "This is 'objectivity.' You looked at that sculpture like you'd seen a ghost."

He scoffed, though he felt sick. "Rubbish."

She turned to face him and he saw red-hot anger.

Tell her the truth, for God's sake. He opened his mouth, but the words stuck in his throat.

"All right," she said. "Let me give you my *perspective*: I've been your unofficial driver since you came back to work—which is fine, except you've asked me again and again to take you on ride-alongs when I should've dropped you at home, *per protocol*—this afternoon, *this journey* being one example of many. You've blanked in meetings, and I've covered your arse. You've forgotten names and dates and times, and like a partisan idiot, I've supplied them for you."

"And I'm grateful," he said. "But—"

"No buts, Greg—you can't have it both ways," she said. "You can't tell me to be nonpartisan and objective, but only where it doesn't concern you. You can't tell me to ask difficult questions—but not of you. You looked like you'd pass out when you saw that sculpture—and now I want an honest answer: What did you see?"

He took a breath, let it go slowly. "A person," he said simply. "I thought it was real and . . ."

"So you're hallucinating again?"

"No."

She slammed her palms against the steering wheel. "*Jeez*, don't *lie* to me."

"I'm not," he said. "I wasn't hallucinating, but I am having distortions of perception."

"Isn't that the same thing?" The question seemed genuine.

"I'm told not."

He saw her log that one away.

"I *am* experiencing hallucinations—but that wasn't one of them. I'm having flashbacks, too."

She faced the front and her hands slid from the wheel into her lap like they'd suddenly become boneless. "Then we really are screwed," she said.

He laughed, and she said, "You think this is funny?"

"No." He turned to her. "It's just that those are almost exactly the words I used to my therapist."

"It was the therapist who told you the difference between hallucinations and distortions of perception?"

He nodded. "You told me I needed to open up to someone, and you were right."

It felt so good to be honest with her, he felt foolishly, humiliatingly close to tears.

"You were right," he repeated, just to hear the sound of it, "and I was wrong."

She blinked.

"I've been such a damn hypocrite, lecturing you on balance and perspective, while putting you in this impossible situation."

"Okay . . ." For once, it seemed, Ruth Lake did not know how to respond.

"I have to tell you something," he said.

"Greg, it's okay." She seemed suddenly appalled.

"No, listen," he said. "I *have* to tell you. And if you decide you can't do all those things you've been doing to make it possible for me to work—well, then I'll understand. I'll step away from the investigation and take time out—even resign, if I have to."

Her eyes widened. "Jesus, Greg, don't—"

"I froze," he said, before he could argue himself out of it.

"What?" She frowned; apparently this was not what she'd expected to hear. "When?"

"Yesterday, at Karl's flat. I froze."

Ruth shook her head. "No."

"Yes." He took a breath and exhaled slowly. "I had a full-blown dissociative episode."

"*No*," she said again. "You were with me all the way." She looked into his face as if she expected him to crack a smile, tell her it was all a bad joke.

"I didn't know where the hell I was, Ruth. I thought I was—*Shit* . . ." He wiped a hand over his face. "I don't know what I thought."

"I . . . Greg, I'm sorry. I didn't even . . ." She faltered.

"You shouldn't be apologizing," Carver said. "I'm the one who put us both at risk. All because I convinced myself that if you want to get through PTSD, all you need to do is grit your teeth and keep going."

"PTSD?" she echoed.

"Yeah." He stared at his hands. "That."

"I never thought I'd hear you say those words."

"Technically, those are letters," he said. "Not words."

She huffed a laugh, but her eyes shone with tears. "Even so," she said.

"I want you to know I'm dealing with it," he said. "I mean, properly dealing with it—with a therapist."

"*A* therapist?" she said, sharp as knives. "Not *the* therapist—as in the job-appointed shrink?"

He smiled; this was one of the reasons he loved working with Ruth. "*A* therapist," he confirmed. "A specialist in . . ."

"PTSD," she said. "It's okay, you can say it."

"So what d'you say?"

She shifted into first gear and pulled out. "You *do* realize you've put me in an impossible situation—again?"

"Oh, God . . . Ruth, I'm—"

He shot her a guilty look, and realized she was smiling.

"You're okay with it, then?"

"Oh, I didn't say that," she said.

"Whatever you want, I'll do it."

She tapped the steering wheel with one finger, working out her list of demands. "You go to the sessions and you do the tasks they set you—that's both therapists."

"Of course," he said.

"And you're completely honest with me," she said. "If you need a break. If you start seeing hobgoblins or 'distortions' or whatever—you tell me. And if I tell you it's time to go home—you go home."

"Wait a minute," he protested. "Who's the boss here?"

"That's the deal," she said. "Take it or leave it."

Ruth Lake had a way of disconnecting her emotions that went far beyond normal cop distancing—but Carver could see that she was covering extreme emotion just now. If he refused, their partnership was over.

"It's a deal," he said. "All terms accepted."

She slid him a sideways glance that said she would not be taking his promise at face value.

58

By the time they arrived at the swanky shop front of Barrow Fine Art, the gallery was closed for the night and perforated black metal screens covered the windows. The lights were on, but it was impossible to see inside. Ruth pressed the doorbell at the side entrance and Jim Barrow appeared a minute later. He was younger than Carver had expected, with a shock of red hair he gelled into an impossible quiff.

"Come through," he said. "I've been setting up a new display in the main gallery."

He led them through to the front of the shop, past metal and stone sculptures, plinths highlighting smaller works, glass cabinets ranged with pottery and glasswork. A young woman and a skinny youth were hanging a painting on the wall; they gave Carver and Lake no more than a cursory glance before continuing.

"Remember—spirit level," Barrow said in passing.

A painting half a meter high and three meters wide had been hung on one wall, with nothing to obstruct the sight line. It was thickly daubed with acrylic paint that looked like it had been applied with a palette knife rather than a brush; silver and dove grays darkened to blue grays and black.

Carver couldn't take his eyes off it, and the gallery owner said, "Oh, that. It's called—"

"*Depression*," Carver said.

"You know the artist?"

Carver blinked. *Did I say that aloud?* "No, I—"

"Oh, wow . . ." Barrow walked around Carver, eyeing him up and down as if he were a new exhibit. "You're a synesthete. That is *very* cool. So is the artist—this piece was *made* for you."

"I don't think so."

"Nonsense—you're attuned."

"Thanks, but even if I had a wall big enough, I don't think I'd survive it," Carver said.

"Point taken." Barrow stood for a moment, one arm across his chest, his chin resting on the fist of his free hand. "You know—he does happy work, too. Lemme show you."

Light on his feet, Barrow bounced to a panel off to the right of the big painting and set at forty-five degrees to it. He raised a hand in a dramatic gesture, indicating a picture in the same dot-and-daub style, but in this one the color palette was an explosion of gold, buttery yellows, lemon, and white; it looked like sunshine and happiness.

"I mean, isn't it?" Barrow said, as though Carver had said something. "The technique is called impasto—the paint is practically buttered onto the canvas—that's what gives it these rich, sexy, sumptuous tones. It *is* sexy, hm?"

Dashes of green flecked the work, and Carver couldn't help but respond to the uncompromising exuberance of both the picture and the gallery owner. "If we could speak in private, Mr. Barrow—this is rather urgent . . ."

"Oh, God, sorry, yes—I get a bit manic before a big exhibition. *Note to self*: take a lithium pill. This way." He headed off to the far side of the room and disappeared behind another panel.

Carver exchanged a look with Ruth, and she covered a smile.

The panel concealed a door into a passageway that gave access to the gallery owner's office. As they arrived, Carver was surprised to see Barrow taking a pill with a sip of water. It seemed he wasn't joking about the medication.

Barrow's office was modern and minimal, the walls of the room bare but painted in a two-tone design with black lines forming a kind of artwork. A glass table served as his desk; a laptop and a notepad were the sum total of clutter, the built-in cupboards hiding the rest, Carver supposed.

Barrow set the water glass on the table and offered them a seat in two '50s-style retro armchairs. He took a third, facing them, his hands trapped between his knees.

"So," he said. "You wanted to know about the Alderson Award?"

"That'll do for a start," Carver said.

"It focuses on art in public spaces, including monumental sculpture, installations, and friezes for public buildings. Art submitted may be permanent, or ephemeral."

Carver frowned. "Art that doesn't last?"

"Street art, graffiti, displays designed to decay—we had a lot of exhibits based around entropy this year. A reflection of the times we live in, I fear."

"Did Mr. Fenst fall out with applicants over the award?"

Barrow rolled his eyes. "These are *artists*, Chief Inspector. You may have noticed that I don't have artwork in my office. Why? Because the *minute* a possible exhibitor sees another person's art on the walls, their hackles are up. You can see their little brains working: 'Why that artist and not me?' Or they think you couldn't *possibly* understand or appreciate their work if you have *that* artist on your walls. It just gets so bloody, it's simpler to have none at all."

"When you say 'bloody' . . ."

"We do have a strict rule for the award—judges' decision final; no correspondence, no appeal, et cetera, but you know how it is—some people don't think the rules apply to them."

"Any names come to mind?" Ruth asked.

"I'm not good with names."

"Did Mr. Fenst mention any worries, anyone hassling him?"

Barrow took a breath and looked to the top-right corner of the room as if something was written there. But after ten seconds his shoulders sagged and he exhaled in a rush. "Sorry," he said.

"You haven't announced the winner yet?" Carver asked.

"We're still on the long list—or were. They'll have to appoint someone else from the board to chair."

Carver could see he was itching to pick up his phone and make the call.

"I'd wait for them to contact you, sir," he said.

"Oh, shit, yes, of course—discretion and all that."

"Do you keep records of applications?" Ruth again.

"We do. At least, the *bank* does—I just sit with Marcus and zip through the submissions as they come in—decide which of them are worth a second look." He looked suddenly stunned, and Carver wondered if he'd remembered something important.

"Mr. Barrow?" he said.

"I've just realized," Barrow said. "He's really gone."

Carver gave him a moment, and he leaned forward and picked up the water glass. His hand trembled as he held it to his lips to take another swallow.

"How does the submissions process work?" Carver asked.

Barrow turned his head in Carver's direction but seemed to have trouble focusing on his face. "What?"

"The submissions process," Carver repeated.

"For the award?"

"Grants, too."

"The artists write a page or so, explaining why their project should be awarded a grant, or considered for the award," he began. As he spoke, gradually he became less dazed, and his pace picked up. "Most artists send images or video electronically. Once they've been sifted to ensure eligibility, Marcus and I decide the long list. We send for the real thing if they're short-listed—if that's even possible—given that some submissions are street art. We arrange a face-to-face meeting so that the judges can quiz the short-listed entries."

"Can we see the applications for the last two years?"

He looked uncertain again. "It's possible, but are you sure you'd want to? There must be over two thousand in our archives."

"Are they listed on a database?"

He nodded. "Excel, I think."

"Who is eligible?" Carver asked.

"Anyone who hasn't had a major exhibition of their work can apply. Oh, and there's a residential requirement—they must have been born in the northwest of England, or be living here now."

That didn't really help.

"Any age requirement?" Ruth put in.

"Twenty-five to forty."

"What are you looking for in art projects you sponsor?"

"Originality, innovation. Works that excite, challenge, and provoke." Barrow chewed the inside of his lip as he thought through the rest. "Art that invites interaction, or even better, participation."

"So you would reject art that is . . . what?"

"Dull, lacking originality, fails to excite or challenge."

"And the judges send written comments?" Ruth said. Carver began to ask why, but she preempted his question: "So we can word search them."

"All the judges have to send a written summary for the long list and the short list," Barrow said. "I could e-mail those over—I have copies."

"Okay, we'd need to see all submissions, rejections, and if possible, reasons for rejection, too."

"I *could* get them, but I'd have to talk to Marcus's PA," Barrow said. "I only saw the eligible subs."

"Probably best if I sort that with the bank myself," Ruth said.

"And if you could send what you have over to me in the meantime . . ." Carver handed Barrow a business card. "My direct e-mail is on the back."

He saw them out in a much more somber mood than when they had arrived, but as Carver was stepping out onto the street, Barrow tapped him on the shoulder.

"I could probably get you a deal on that painting," he said. "The artist is Gordon Jakes—he'd be thrilled to see his work go to a fellow synesthete. Think about it overnight—the title of the happy painting is—"

"*Joy*," Carver said.

"Now, *that* is just spooky," Barrow said.

59

Ruth arrived home at eight thirty.

Even before she stepped inside, something felt off. Down the hall, she saw that the kitchen door was open a crack; she always shut it before she left the house. She froze, the key still in the lock. A bass rumble, like heavy artillery—she experienced it deep in her chest. With it, an icy trickle of fear in her gut. Then the unmistakable sound of a fist striking flesh, a choked cry, the crack of bones. Under it, a bass beat; counterpoint to the drone of cellos and bassoons—insistent unsettling, bringing to mind war and rumor, and present danger.

Someone was playing one of her Xbox games.

Ruth was still using a fleet car, but the Ferryman could have had his ghost army of hoodies trail her home before she was even aware of them.

Well, screw 'em.

She left the front door open, treading softly to the sitting room door, paused to flick open her Casco baton, and, heart thudding, turned the handle and swung the door wide. A quick glance left, then she stepped inside. The curtains were drawn, the only light from the flickering scenes on the TV screen in the back half of the room. Two long legs sprawled out across her rug. A tall male. The top half of his body was hidden behind the recess in the wall. The room reeked of beer.

Baton over her right shoulder, tight to her body, she stepped forward.

Adam.

She exhaled in a rush.

He was so focused on the screen, he didn't see her, and she was tempted to whack him once in the knee, for the scare he'd given her. Instead, she moved in front of him, blocking his view of the TV.

He almost dropped the control. "Holy shit! Jesus, Ruth—don't creep up on a guy like that."

"I don't think I was in any danger," she said. "It's not like you could shoot me with your imaginary gun."

He tried to peer around her, but she plucked the console from his hands and turned off the TV. "Game over, sunshine," she said. "Now, what are you doing here?"

"Like you said, it's my home, too."

"It is, but it's not nice to steal other people's toys, now is it?" She set the control down and surveyed the litter around his feet: six empty beer bottles and two takeaway cartons. "And I'm guessing you didn't bring that beer with you."

"They were just sitting there in the fridge, so . . ." He flashed her a crooked smile.

She telescoped the Casco baton and slid it back into the holder on her belt. "How did you get in, Adam?"

"MadAdaM." He was slurring a little and seemed to be having trouble keeping the soppy smile on his face.

She waited, still standing over him, and after a moment or two, he dug in his jeans pocket and came out with a Yale front door key on a ring hooked around his middle finger.

"You can always rely on ol' Peggy to have a spare," he said.

"You should have rung."

"When did you get all middle class?"

Ruth went to close the front door and carried on through to the kitchen to brew coffee.

A minute or two later, the clink of glass on glass warned her that Adam was coming down the hall.

"See," he said, stacking the empties on the work surface. "Tidying up after myself."

She handed him a mug and he added milk. "Got any sugar?" he asked, opening and closing doors at random. Ruth opened one of the lower cupboards and he dived in, coming out with a jar and casting about for a spoon. She handed him one from the cutlery drawer and he heaped in three spoonfuls.

"You've done the place up nice," he said.

She nodded, watching him, wondering what the hell he wanted from her.

"D'you still do the garden?"

"Yeah," she said. "I garden."

"Granddad always loved that garden." He nodded: two big, loose jerks of his head.

"He did." She softened toward him a little, remembering how Adam had idolized his grandfather: Grandma called them Heckle and Jeckle; to Mum, they were Grandpa and Eddie Munster. Granddad had more or less lived with them after Dad moved out—he was a widower by then. He'd died two months before Mum was murdered, and Ruth wondered how different things might have been if Adam had had his "partner in crime" to turn to.

Adam dutifully replaced the lid on the sugar and crouched to replace it in the cupboard.

"Oh-ho," he murmured. "Now, what's this?" and she knew he'd found the bottle of vodka that had been sitting in there unopened since last Easter.

He reached in to the back of the cupboard, scattering packets and jars as he clumsily withdrew his prize.

"Come on," Ruth said, holding out her hand. "You've already had more than enough."

He held the vodka close to his chest and struggled to his feet. "Well, you know the old saying—you don't know you've had enough till you've had too much."

"Adam, I'm not joking," she said. "You need to eat something or drink some coffee—sober up."

He leaned back against the counter and cracked the seal.

"You sanctimonious hypocrite," he said. "Criticizing *my* morals when you do deals with criminals."

He was talking about Dave Ryan.

"I told you, Ryan is full of it."

"Yeah?" He took a swallow of vodka, grimacing against the burn. "I looked up 'his eldest'—yeah, you're not the only one around here with detective skills. Damien Ryan, a chip off the old block, slated to inherit a criminal empire. Naomi Ryan, his wife. Both murdered months after they were married, her pregnant, too. Know what the weapon was?"

"A hammer." She couldn't look him in the eye.

"And Ryan thinks you saw justice done. What does that mean?"

"I told you, I don't know."

"'Cos they never found the hammer attacker."

"Which is why I said Ryan is full of it."

"What's the murder of Dave Ryan's son got to do with Mum?"

She almost told him. She was so heartsick of carrying this burden around, she almost blurted out the whole terrible story, but Adam was never any good at waiting—he always thought he knew all the answers already.

"What did you do—talk Dad into topping himself?"

The idea was so outrageous—so wide of the mark—that she almost laughed. "Where the hell did that come from? Didn't you check the dates when you were doing your brilliant detective work?"

She could see from his confusion that he hadn't.

"No, of course not. You just got tanked up, googled a few news items, and came up with a half-arsed conspiracy theory. Well done, little brother." She was losing her cool. She never lost her cool. *Except around Adam*, her inner voice murmured.

She took a breath. "To set the record straight, Ryan's son and daughter-in-law were murdered *years* after Mum died."

He snorted. "Yeah, right."

"Go ahead, google it."

"Fuck off," he said. "I *know* you did something. And by the way—why would you keep a framed photograph of Dad with the two of us?"

It was a tactic—she knew it of old—finding himself in the wrong, he'd go on the attack. Even so, he was right. "I know it might seem weird—"

"Pride of place on the bookcase in your homely little reading corner—you're damn right it seems weird. D'you *like* being reminded he bashed Mum's head in?"

"Adam, stop," she said.

"I can't even stand to *look* at that evil, murdering bastard."

"I know," she said. "I felt the same, for a long time."

"And now, what—you're *okay* with it?" He took another mouthful of vodka. "Why are you still living in this place, with its tainted memories? Just thinking about him, standing where you're standing now, arguing with Mum—makes me want to throw up."

"You were too young to fully understand what was happening at that time."

"I was fourteen years old. I knew *exactly* what was happening. He screwed his secretary, screwed up his marriage, screwed up his business, and as always he expected Mum to bail him out."

"I know. He did all that. But that night—I think if maybe we'd just listened—"

Adam flung his arms wide, laughing wildly. "He turned up on our doorstep, covered in *blood*. Said his girlfriend—his *girlfriend*—was dead, and Mum *had* to help him. Fucking psychopath."

"He also said he didn't do it," Ruth reminded him.

"Yeah, well, he said a lot of things, over the years." His skin was grayish and sheened in a light sweat; he looked close to collapse, and Ruth realized he must have been half drunk even before he'd started in on the beers. "Annnnnyway—you're the one who tried to call the cops."

"Like I said, if we'd listened . . ."

It was pointless antagonizing him like this; she couldn't back it up with anything concrete, anything that might make sense. *Just shut up and let him go and sleep it off.*

"Look, Adam, why don't I—"

"MadAdaM."

"Oh, come *on* . . ."

"What—you can change your name, but I can't?" He rubbed his nose furiously. "Oh, now that's a good point." He banged the base of the bottle twice, hard, on the work surface. "If you thought Dad was so *misunderstood*, why did you change your name? Hm? I'll tell you why. Because you didn't want to be allied to that murdering *scum*. 'He said he didn't do it.' *You* didn't believe him any more than *I* did."

"You're right," she said. "I didn't believe him. Not then, but things change."

"*Nothing* has changed, Ruth." He was yelling now. "Mum is still dead. You and me—we're still fucked up." He began to cry, but Ruth knew better than to go to him. He was raging at her because he was angry with himself, at what he would regard as weakness. Since Mum died, Ruth had seen him cry only once: that was on the day of Mum's funeral; she'd tried to comfort him then, and it hadn't ended well.

"I can't believe you're defending him," he said, wiping tears from his face with his shirtsleeve. "He doesn't deserve to be buried in the same *earth* as Mum, let alone in the same cemetery."

Mum and Dad were buried within three days of each other at opposite ends of Springwood Cemetery, Mum in her family grave, Dad in a new plot. Ruth and Adam did not attend their father's burial, and since there was no trial, they'd never had the opportunity to achieve what their therapists glibly called "closure."

"It comforted Grandma and Granddad Black," she said.

"Oh, well, so long as *they're* okay." He was swinging the vodka bottle dangerously wide in the small kitchen. "If I had my way, I'd dig the bastard up and chuck what's left of him in the landfill. He murdered our mother, tore our family apart, and didn't even have the balls to face up to the consequences."

He glared at the door into the hallway as though he expected their father to come through it at any second. Finally, he slammed the bottle down onto the kitchen table, ripped the door open, and stormed into the living room. Ruth followed him.

He seized the photo frame and struggled with the hardboard backing, but he was too drunk to make his fingers do the task. So he dropped it onto the boards and ground it under his heel. Then he extracted the photo and, shaking shards of glass onto the floor, he tore it into pieces.

Ruth did nothing to stop him. For four years after Mum died, she had hated and despised their father with the same intensity. She let Adam make his defiant stand, his fists bunched, and waited for the anger to leave him. He was shaking, still, but at least the crying had stopped.

"You're bleeding," she said.

He looked at his hands as though they didn't belong to him. "Fuck," he said dully, "I gotta work tomorrow."

He allowed her to lead him through to the kitchen and sit him at the table. He made a feeble play for the vodka, but she swiped it out of reach and poured what was left down the sink, then took down a first aid kit from one of the wall cupboards.

He sat still while she cleaned the cuts to his fingers and smeared them with Savlon, before wrapping them in gauze and bandaging them. He didn't flinch once, and she wondered if he'd gone through the pain of all those tattoos to help numb his emotional suffering.

Her eyes blurred with tears and she blinked them away.

Adam seemed to come to, as if he'd been floating some distance away and had returned to himself. He ducked his head and looked into her face; she read surprise and concern in his expression.

She looked back at him in question, and he said, "Crying over a stupid snapshot?"

"No, Adam . . ." She felt unspeakably tired. "Not the snapshot."

"Us, then." It wasn't a question, and she didn't feel the need to answer. "I didn't come here to have a go at you," he began. "But I just don't get it . . . You deal with psychopaths and predators every day, but you can't see it in your own father."

"He was selfish and feckless, a manipulator and a womanizer—a *monumental* screwup as a businessman," she said. "I see that. But what happened to Mum . . ." She shook her head. "I just don't think he would do such a terrible thing."

"You don't *think* . . . ?" Adam seemed to catch himself, and when he went on, his tone was intense, but rational. "It took *three* of us to get him out of the house that night. He only left because he heard the police sirens."

"I know it looked bad—"

He cut her off with a harsh laugh. "He confessed, Ruth—or did you forget?"

"I know, but—"

He interrupted again. "He murdered his girlfriend, he murdered Mum, and then he did what he always did when things got hard for him. He took the easy way out."

Ruth stared at him, thinking, *No, he didn't Adam. He really didn't.* But she couldn't explain—could never explain what her father did to protect them, and what Ruth herself did to try to restore their lives to some sort of balance.

60

Ruth was awakened by the wet smack of a hammer on human flesh. She sat up, staring, trembling, heart beating so hard it hurt.

She pressed her left hand to her chest, used her right to lift her alarm clock. It was 4:15—pointless trying to get back to sleep. She jammed her feet into a pair of trainers, picked up her laptop, and headed down to the kitchen in jogging bottoms and a T-shirt, thinking to check on any reports that had come in during the night.

The central heating had kicked in, and the house felt overwarm. Ruth went through to the TV room to turn the radiators down and check on her brother. Adam was passed out on the sofa, the family photograph he'd destroyed still in pieces on the floor.

Ruth picked up the debris and tried not to think about how horribly their lives had gone wrong.

Even in the dark, she could see a slick of unhealthy sweat on Adam's skin. She touched his forehead, surprised to find it was cold. His arms, ornamented as half man, half machine, were pimpled with gooseflesh. Ruth fetched a glass of water and a bowl from the kitchen, then took a throw from the sofa in her reading room and gently placed it over him.

At 4:50, she gave in to the temptation of a vape and opened the back door. Ruth had made a promise to her mother she would stay away from the cigs. She'd broken that promise, but she had never smoked in the house—a minor penance for having let Mum down.

The light was on in Peggy's kitchen next door, and Ruth guessed she would have heard her argument with Adam. Sometimes Ruth ducked old Peggy, but to do so now would be unkind, so she sucked on her vape and blew clouds into the night air, contemplating the spring daffodils that had broken through in the soggy borders, trying to remember which varieties she had placed where, and waiting for the sound of a bolt being drawn on her neighbor's back door.

It came five minutes later.

"All right, Ruthie, love?" The old woman's greeting sounded half apologetic, and Ruth wondered if she'd sat up, worrying over the row next door.

"Fine, Peggy," she said. "D'you want to come round? I've got a pot of coffee on."

"I'll get me coat."

Ruth unfastened the bolt on the back gate and Peggy Connolly appeared a couple of minutes later, slightly out of breath. Winter or summer, the old woman wore a mac buttoned tight across her middle. She was four foot ten and almost the same in circumference, she walked with a roll. Already an institution when Ruth's parents came to live in the street, it was impossible to guess Peggy's age, and no one dared ask, but she claimed to have vivid memories of the Second World War, and Ruth had no reason to disbelieve her.

Ruth turned off her vape and helped her neighbor over the high step into her kitchen. Seated in the warmth with a milky coffee cupped in her hands, Peggy unbuttoned her coat and began talking. Small talk, at first: the unseasonable weather; her children and their children—as a child, Ruth had played on the street with some of Peggy's grandchildren. Eventually, she worked around to Adam's sudden appearance yesterday.

"I went out to do some messages before the shops shut. Got back around sixish, 'cos Mrs. H in number seventeen asked me in for a cup of tea and a chinwag. Adam was sitting on your wall."

"I hope he didn't frighten you."

"Nah . . ." Peggy laughed heartily, clacking her overlarge false teeth. "I knew him soon's I clapped eyes on him. He's got the Black family good looks," she said.

They heard loud coughing from the room adjoining the kitchen, and both stopped to listen. Adam cleared his throat, stumbled out into the hall, and padded upstairs. A few moments later, the bathroom toilet flushed, then the central heating boiler fired up; the shower was running.

"I *am* sorry, about the key, girl." Peggy screwed up her face in a grimace of remorse. "I thought it'd be all right."

"I was—it is," Ruth reassured her. "It's been a while—we had some air to clear, that's all."

The boiler cut off abruptly and they heard the thud of Adam's footsteps as he padded about the bathroom.

"Well," Peggy said, shoving back her chair and offering Ruth a hand to haul her up, "I'd better leave youse two to get reacquainted."

Ruth saw her safely back to her own house. On her back step, the old woman reached out and grasped Ruth's arm, her grip surprisingly strong.

"Don't be too hard on him," she said. "He's a good lad at heart—helped me put me shopping away, listened to an old woman's ramblings for a good hour before he made a move to go." She nodded to herself. "That's kindness, that is." She pulled Ruth closer and leaned in, lowering her voice. "Not sure about them tattoos, though." She shuddered. "Still, they've all got them now, haven't they—the girls as well as the lads—even my Betty's grandson . . ." She shook her grizzled head, for once lost for words, and turning, she disappeared inside.

Ruth had just settled down to work on her laptop in the kitchen when Adam came in. His beard unwaxed and his hair pulled roughly into a ponytail, he looked more like her brother than he had on any of the other occasions she'd seen him these last few days. Even fresh from the shower, he looked horribly hungover and a little sheepish.

He edged past the table and turned on the cold water, drinking straight from the tap.

She arched an eyebrow. "We do have glasses, you know."

She stood and took one out of the cupboard for him.

"That the best they could do?" he asked, taking the glass without looking at it.

She glanced down and saw he was staring at the faint remains of the tattoos on the inner aspect of her left arm, just in the crease of her elbow.

Ruth poured him a coffee and went back to her laptop.

"You know, laser removal's got its own problems—and it looks like you had a lot of blowout from the original," he went on, apparently undaunted by her lack of communication. "It's horrible work."

"It isn't 'work' at all," she snapped.

"No, sorry," he said. "My bad." It seemed he could empathize with her on this point because he cared about the terrible "art" inflicted on her. "I could do a cover-up," he suggested. "Something nice. No one would ever know that other shit was ever there."

"*I* would," Ruth said, her voice tight, even to her own ears.

He shrugged. "Well, if you change your mind . . ."

After an uncomfortable silence, he wandered back into the living room. As he closed the door, Ruth cursed herself. This was supposed to be the day she started mending bridges with her brother. Instead, she'd refused his sympathy, his help, and alienated him further. *Way to go, Ruth.*

She sighed, turning again to her laptop screen, but couldn't focus her attention, and minutes later, she caught herself scratching her arm as if tormented by a maddening itch. But it wasn't an itch she felt. What she experienced was an *absence* of feeling—a numbness—nerve damage caused by the toxins the killer used on her. She snapped her laptop closed and headed upstairs to shower.

Adam had gone by the time she came downstairs. He'd left the borrowed front door key on the kitchen table.

61

After the morning briefing, Carver took time out to see his therapist, not begrudging the break in his working day. He was feeling so much better, sleeping well, feeling less anxious and tense.

In the taxi heading back to headquarters, he got a call from Ruth.

"John Hughes rang," she said. "When can you get back?"

He noticed two things: she didn't ask where he was—which meant she already had a good idea—and she sounded excited.

"Five minutes."

Ruth, John Hughes, and DC Ivey were clustered around the digital projector screen when he got to the Major Incident Room; a few other detectives were working the phones.

Hughes acknowledged Carver with a nod and started straight in. The first slide was an image of one of the disks used in *Think Outside the Box*. It was labeled with an evidence number and identified as Professor Tennent's remains. Photographed from above, the image had been taken prior to the pathologist's postmortem examination of the remains, so it was intact: a pale pink disk, containing a complete section across Tennent's brain. The disk measured twenty centimeters across, according to the ruler the forensic photographer had laid next to it.

"As you know, we didn't find any fingermarks on the three disks," Hughes said, "so we focused on other aspects of analysis—DNA, tox screens, and so on. But when we found the palm-edge print on the triptych, I thought it might be worth taking a second look."

Carver felt a stirring of optimism.

"The first two sections yielded nothing," Hughes said. "Then we examined Professor Tennent's." He clicked to a slide showing the same disk of brain tissue, photographed edge-on; the ruler indicated that the disk was three centimeters thick. "See that line?" Hughes pointed to the image. It was just possible to make out a faint line about two and a half centimeters from the bottom of the disk.

"When you embed stuff in plexiglass, you have to do it in layers," Hughes said. "Plexiglass, then the sample—brain tissue in this instance—then another, or sometimes several more, leaving each layer to almost set before adding the next.

"Our man had to put a rush on the professor's section to have it ready in time. And he must have gotten impatient—because at some point, he tested the set by touching the acrylic with an ungloved finger."

Carver smiled. "He left a fingerprint on the set layer?"

"On the *partially* set layer," Hughes corrected. "He must have realized it was tacky, left it to prove a little longer, then overlaid it with another layer of liquid acrylic, not realizing that he'd trapped the print in there like a fly in amber."

He moved to another slide, but Carver couldn't see an imprint. He looked at Ruth, and she jerked her chin toward the screen. Her smile said, *Give him his moment.*

"So we tried shining a focused beam of light at an oblique angle and . . ." He moved to the next slide.

"Oh, wow," DC Ivey said.

The oblique light had lit up the ridges of the print, deepening the shadows of the troughs just as a lowering autumn sun will show the bumps and depressions in a lawn.

"That's a good fingerprint with great ridge detail," Hughes said. "We're searching IDENT1 now, to see if it's in the system."

"Great work," Carver said.

Ivey's phone buzzed, and he excused himself. A moment later, he was back in the incident room, his pale skin flushed with excitement.

"That was the owner of one of the shops I've been canvassing," he said. "A guy just used Steve Norris's Mastercard."

Heads came up around the room, and Ruth was already on her feet.

"Where?" Carver said.

Ivey gave a location in Aigburth. "He's gone, boss. The shopkeeper's wife tried to delay him, but he wasn't having it."

Carver was itching to send a team over, but he saw that Ivey wasn't finished.

"The good news is, she had the presence of mind to offer the guy a scratch card. Shoved it straight into his hand, but he refused it . . . his prints must be all over it."

There were a few cries of "Yes!"

Grinning, Carver said, "We need CCTV from the shop, a two-car crew to scout the area, see if they can't scoop him up, and—" He glanced at John Hughes.

"I'll get a CSI over there, and as soon as we have the IDENT1 results, I'll let you know."

Two hours later, they had him in custody.

Carver watched via video link as Ruth Lake led the interview with DC Ivey sitting next to her. This was his arrest, and Carver could see in the fizzing energy around the young detective that he was itching to have a go at the suspect. But this needed a more experienced hand, and Ivey had agreed that Ruth should take the lead. Even so, he was literally gripping the seat of his chair in his effort to contain himself.

Drew Scanlon was what Carver, a London incomer, now recognized as a through-and-through Scouse scally. The type that could boast five generations of forebears who were also Scouse scallies, Liverpool born-and-dragged-up going back over a century. To qualify as a true scally, it was necessary to forswear aspiration as poncey and soft. Education was for snobs, steady jobs for knobheads. The trick was to never aspire to anything, do the minimum, and have enough street savvy to stay out of reach of the law. Admittedly, Scanlon had occasionally gotten into trouble—which was why his fingerprints were in the system, but only for minor infractions: antisocial behavior, a car theft at the age of sixteen, getting involved in a public brawl after a derby match that didn't go Everton FC's way.

At first, he said he found the cards.

"When was that?" Ruth asked.

"Yesterday."

"What time?" Her tone was pleasant.

"About four o'clock."

She made a note. "Where?"

"On the street."

"Which street would that be, Drew?"

"I dunno—"

"You don't know." Ruth gazed at him, her eyes wide and unjudging. Some mistook that look for innocence, but Carver had been under its scrutiny often enough to know how unsettling Ruth Lake's dark eyes could be.

Scanlon clearly felt the same way. He shuffled in his seat and mumbled the name of a street near his home in Anfield.

Ruth continued to gaze at him while she appeared to be considering his answer. "That's a main road," she said. "I wonder if there's CCTV around there." She glanced at DC Ivey. "We could probably get Drew actually picking it up."

"I'll go and check, shall I?" Ivey said, following her lead, his relaxed tone implying that all he had to do was go to a magical room somewhere in the building and tap in the street name and time of day.

Scanlon scratched the back of his neck. "It might have been later. Or somewhere else."

"Oh." Ruth sounded disappointed on his behalf. She didn't say anything more, and in the silence, Carver could almost *hear* the sweat popping out on Scanlon's brow.

Despite his newly minted ability to "see" mood as color, Carver still wasn't the best at reading body language, but Ruth must have seen some signal in Scanlon, because she sat back and began speaking in a low tone. "Without video footage, the magistrate is going to assume you stole it, you see, Drew. That's theft and fraud in one neat little package."

"Someone give me it," he said.

"Someone?" Ruth said.

"This feller. I thought it was his—he said he'd had a bit of argybargy with the shop owner, wanted me to get the stuff for him—I was gonna give it back."

"This fellow," Ruth said. "What did he call himself?"

Scanlon's eyes practically rolled back into his head. He knew he'd goofed. "The feller on the card. Norris."

"I'm having trouble believing you, Drew," Ruth said, her tone regretful. "I think you knew the card was stolen. Which means we could add handling stolen goods to the list of charges." She tilted her head on one side as if thinking through every charge that could be laid at his door—all in the interests of clarity. "And then there's conspiracy to pervert the course of justice."

He blanched.

"Because he knew the card was stolen?" Ivey said helpfully.

"Wait—no . . ."

"Mm," Ruth said, "and conspiracy carries a heavier tariff."

"A *what*?"

"Longer sentence," she translated, in that same helpful tone.

"You can't do that—I'm a victim."

Ruth blinked. "A victim?" she repeated. "Of . . . ?"

"I was threatened. He said if I didn't do as I was told, I'd be next."

Ruth watched him for a few moments, then nodded, thoughtfully.

"You believe me?"

"No," she said, gently.

Drew wiped a hand over his face.

"The thing about lies, Drew, is you need to be convincing."

"I'm telling the *truth*."

She shook her head. "Lies, end to end. The giveaway there was you said, 'I was threatened.' That's what we call vague and unspecific phrasing. Which suggests a lie. You got a bit more specific when you said, '*He* said if . . .' and so on."

"Well, he did."

"Who?"

"The *Ferryman*."

Carver smiled. He'd spoken without thinking—now Ruth had him.

"You spoke to the Ferryman."

He licked his lips, realizing he'd been caught in another lie. "No . . . ?"

"Now, that came out as a question—you're asking me what I'd *like* to hear. What I'd like to hear is the truth. But go on, Drew," Ruth encouraged. "Keep telling your lies for as long as you like. This is entertaining."

Scanlon folded his arms, closed his eyes, and snuffed air through his nose. "Fuck." After a few moments, he let his arms fall and opened his eyes. "All right," he said. "He promised me hard cash. Plus, he said I could use the card as long as I wanted—or till someone sussed me."

This sounded more like the truth.

Carver could have watched Ruth all day, but just before Drew Scanlon was brought in, he'd received an e-mail from Alderson Bank about their art competition. Attached to it, a spreadsheet with a full list of applicants, including people whose entries were turned down or who didn't make the long list. Carver flicked the video link off and made his way to his office.

62

Ruth Lake made a quick dash to Cow & Co to grab a sandwich and coffee. The fresh spring air blowing in from the river was welcome after the sweaty stuffiness of the interview room, even though she had to sprint back through a sudden rain shower.

Carver was busy, so she carried her sandwich and coffee through to the MIR. Ivey was eating a bagel and swigging Coke from a bottle; a few detectives staffing the phones drifted out to find their own lunches, while one or two came in, dripping, cursing the change in the weather. Five minutes later, Ruth's desk phone rang.

"Are you ready to catch me up on the Scanlon interview?" Carver asked.

"Sure—I'll come to your office." She ditched the rest of the sandwich, taking the coffee with her.

Carver was alone, and in a somber mood.

"Trouble?" she said.

"Fill me in on Scanlon."

That was terse.

"Okay." She began to summarize the interview, but Carver interrupted.

"I watched the first part—take it from his admission that he helped the Ferryman for the money."

She paused, mentally running through the interview, taking her time. Whatever was going on with Carver, she wasn't going to let it rattle her.

"He swears he can't describe the Ferryman because they never met," she said. "They communicated via messaging on Drew's Instagram account. Drew was sent a key to a bedsit in a slum house in Aigburth. The clothing was left on a chair in the room, the card was in an envelope, together with instructions, in one of the kitchen drawers."

"Is he *suicidal*?" Carver demanded. "Did he see what the Ferryman did to Karl Obrazki?"

"He thinks he's immune because Karl/Kharon was stealing the Ferryman's ideas, taking credit for his work—all Drew was interested in was the wodge of fivers he left in the envelope along with Steve Norris's credit card." She saw a question form in Carver's mind and added, "He binned the envelope, says he spent the cash."

"And the clothing?"

If the Ferryman had given Drew the clothing he'd worn, there was an outside chance they would get DNA evidence from it.

Ruth dipped her head. "He said he ditched it after the woman in the shop gave him aggro—his words."

Carver seemed distracted. "Ask John Hughes to send a team of CSIs to the bedsit, will you?"

"Sure," she said. "I'll get on it."

She turned to leave, and Carver spoke again.

"I had the first batch of names from Fenst's bank today."

"Yeah, you told me."

"Just a list of names and addresses—they've promised to send the adjudicators' correspondence separately; Mr. Fenst had apparently archived them under a separate password—their tech specialists are working on it."

Ruth regarded Carver coolly. He'd flipped from terse and uncommunicative to overexplaining in an instant. *There's something he doesn't want to tell me.*

"Boss," she said. "What's wrong?"

"The entrants who didn't make it to the final round are marked off," he said.

"That's . . . helpful." Frustrated, she looked into his hazel eyes and saw sadness.

For me?

"Oh, God . . . Adam's name is on the list, isn't it?"

"Yes."

"But wait," she said, recovering fast, though she still felt sick. "He's getting commissions, started his own business. And he's already won an award," she suddenly remembered. "I don't see why he'd go psycho over a minor knockback."

"What's that award?" Carver asked.

"I'll check," she said, embarrassed to have shot her mouth off without having the facts to hand.

He gave her a look that fell somewhere between exasperation and sympathy.

"You want me to go and pick him up?"

"He's already on his way in. He'll be questioned under caution."

"Of course, I'll get the CSIs sorted, then—"

"I'll task someone else with the interview, Ruth."

"Boss," she said, "I need to do it."

"There's no way I can let you," Carver said.

"Don't you trust me to be impartial?"

"Come on, Ruth," he said. "You know you can't be, where Adam is concerned."

Ruth took a moment to compose herself. Carver was working according to protocol, but they both knew he didn't always—his flagrant manipulation of his working hours was evidence of that.

"Adam is angry. Questioned by a stranger, he'll clam up, refuse to cooperate. At least let me *try*."

Carver began to shake his head. Ruth hated talking about her private life. But she supposed Carver already had more inside knowledge than most, so she took the only option she had left: a plea to his compassion.

"Look, Greg, Adam turned up at our house last night. He was drunk; things got a bit heated. So—"

"So tensions will be high—all the more reason to leave this to someone else." She began to argue, but he cut her short. "That's my final word on the matter, DS Lake."

The use of her rank settled it—Carver was not going to budge.

In the event, Carver conducted Adam's interview himself—another break with protocol.

Two hours later, he called Ruth out of the incident room and they stood outside.

"He's given the names of friends who will vouch for him on at least three occasions when Ferryman exhibits appeared." Carver kept his voice down, clearly wanting to apprise her of the situation before he let the rest know. "I've got someone checking now."

"Okay," she said.

"But you know as well as I do that an alibi provided by friends is dodgy at the very least."

That stung. "I suppose that depends on who your friends are."

"What the hell does that mean?"

"Nothing." She took a breath. "I'm sorry. It's just—this is hard, you know?"

"I know, Ruth," he said. "Why d'you think *I* interviewed him? It's actually a bit below my pay grade, you know."

She did know, of course, and she saw in the set of his brow that he was genuinely trying to do what was best for her—as her senior officer, and as a friend.

"Yeah," she said. "Thanks."

He grunted.

"I mean it."

This time he nodded.

"I asked about the artwork that was turned down by the competition judges," Carver said. "He wasn't forthcoming. When I pushed him, he said, 'You've seen the submission.' But as we both know, the actual submissions aren't kept on digital file, and because Adam didn't make it past the submission stage, that wasn't much help."

"He shares a flat above an art shop front with two friends out toward Clarence Dock," she reminded him. "He might have it stashed there."

"He claims he destroyed the piece—said it was no good."

"And you think he's lying."

"Not a doubt in my mind."

"Was there a description of the work? Submission notes?"

Carver hesitated and she got the impression it was out of consideration for her feelings.

"What?" she said.

"The submission notes describe the work as an exploration of gendered violence. The title was *Battered Wife*."

Ruth swore softly.

Carver's phone buzzed in his pocket and he checked the screen. "The DC I sent to check on Adam's whereabouts on the nights of the 'exhibits,'" he said.

He answered the phone, but didn't switch it to speaker, said a few words, then hung up, asking the constable to keep him informed.

"Two of Adam's alibis check out," he said. "And the people he was with on the night of *Catch the Gamma Wave* say he worked through the afternoon at the tattoo studio with them, and when Adam received a DM from Kharon on Instagram, they locked up the shop and went straight to the old railway arch in Dingle."

"So maybe Adam *is* telling the truth," Ruth said.

"And maybe his friends are just loyal."

She bit back a sharp answer; it was a fair assessment, and in his position, she would have said the same thing. "So what's the plan?"

"We can't arrest him on the basis that he seems to have a chip on his shoulder," Carver said. "And a solicitor turned up partway through the interview—she's demanding that we charge or release him."

Ruth thought about it, trying to remain objective. "The options are to arrest him and start the PACE clock ticking, or turn him loose and haul him back in if we need to. Option two would give us more time to check him out."

He sighed, letting go of the tension in his shoulders. "You're right—I'll talk to the custody sergeant."

Ruth said, "Okay." But she couldn't let it go at that. "Boss?"

"What?"

The corridor was empty, so she asked straight out: "What did you see?"

They both knew that she meant Carver's synesthesia, his auras.

"Rage," he said simply. "I'm sorry, Ruth, he *really* resents you."

"He ended up in care because I couldn't deal with our messed-up home life," she said. "I think he's entitled to a certain amount of resentment."

"You were a kid yourself."

She saw sympathy in his eyes. Ruth could face down aggression, hate, sarcasm, and mistrust; it was easy—she just donned the psychological armor she'd worn since young adulthood. But sympathy? She couldn't put a guard up against that, and she didn't want Carver to see just how deeply this was affecting her. She needed to stay on this case. So she did the only thing she could think of; she changed the subject.

"Why did Adam ask for a solicitor?"

Carver looked thrown by the question.

"He didn't—she just showed up." He paused, clearly weighing the fact with greater significance now.

"So who sent her?" As soon as she said it, she wished she hadn't, because a name popped into her head.

"Honestly, I thought maybe you had." He offered an apologetic smile.

"Honestly, I might have, if I'd thought of it," she admitted. "So who . . . ?"

"An associate at Felix Welsh and Co. Do you know the firm?"

"I know of them," she said, deliberately vague, wishing she'd thought of a different distraction. "Fairly high end."

In fact, Felix Welsh & Co. represented the guilty-as-sin rich; they wouldn't pick up the phone for a tattooist and jobbing artist like Adam. But if someone like Dave Ryan were to make the call . . . And Ruth happened to know that Felix himself was Dave Ryan's go-to man in legal matters.

63

Forty minutes later, Ruth Lake was waiting for Adam outside the custody suite.

He cursed under his breath. "You escorting me out now?"

"I thought you might like to leave through the main entrance, instead of sneaking out like a scally. But . . ." She turned her hands palms up, leaving it up to him, knowing he'd take the more dignified option. In truth, she wanted to show Adam out through the front of the building because it would give them more time to talk.

The way things went, she might have saved herself the trouble. Her brother was not in a chatty mood. He glared straight ahead, walking at a brisk pace, ignoring her questions about his friends, the interview, the artwork Fenst had rejected for the prize.

To hell with it, just ask him.

"What's in the picture, Adam?"

He looked askance. "The *painting*, d'you mean?" He carried on walking. "Do you even care?"

"It's called *Battered Wife*—yes, I care."

"You want me to explain it to you?"

"I'd prefer to see it."

"Nuh-uh."

She stepped in front of him and turned, barring his way. His eyes blazed for a second; then she read only contempt in them. Staring into her brother's face, she thought she really didn't know Adam at all. *Okay, then, treat him like the stranger he is.*

"DCI Carver said a solicitor turned up during your interview."

"Got a problem with me having legal representation, Sergeant?"

"Everyone's entitled," Ruth said. "But here's the thing—most people we bring in for questioning would have to ask for a phone book to look one up."

He shrugged. "I guess I was lucky."

"Or prepared."

"Oh, so you assume I'm guilty."

"That's not what I meant."

"Really? 'Cos that's how it sounds."

"You know what I do have a problem with?" she said, feeling her anger rise. "Who's paying."

"What d'you mean? She said this is pro bono." His other responses had felt like an act, but this felt genuine. Adam was confused.

"Dave Ryan is Felix Welsh's biggest client," she said. "*He* organized your legal counsel."

Adam sidestepped her and began walking again. "So *what* if Ryan is with the same company? Like I said, this is pro bono."

"Yeah, well, money isn't the only way to pay."

"Fuck off, *Sergeant*."

They had reached the foyer and he turned briskly toward the door, then stopped dead, staring at a man who was talking to Tom Ivey. Tall, fair-haired, his crew cut bedewed with raindrops, it was Graham Milner.

Milner was carrying a large black artist's portfolio.

"What's *he* doing here?"

Ruth looked at Adam. "You know him?"

"You could say that."

More hostility. "What's he to you?"

He didn't answer.

Milner glanced away from Ivey for a moment and smiled in recognition at Ruth; she lifted her chin in acknowledgment.

Adam looked from Ruth to Milner, an expression of pure hate on his face. Tom Ivey gestured to Ruth, and Milner approached, portfolio case in his left hand, his right out, ready to shake hers, but he slowed as he noticed her brother.

"Adam?" In the slightly pained look on his face, Ruth saw embarrassment and perhaps regret.

Adam sucked his teeth. "Fuck this." He strode out the door without looking back.

Milner watched him leave.

"Mr. Milner asked to speak to a member of the team," Ivey said.

"Thanks, Tom," she said, dismissing him with a polite nod. "How can I help you, Mr. Milner?"

"That *was* Adam Black, wasn't it?" he said.

"How do you know him?"

"I tutored him—only for a half semester—about . . . eighteen months ago? He was in his second year at Fairfield," he said, staring pensively at the empty doorway Adam had disappeared through. "Attended a couple of my modules. Talented student."

Milner dragged his gaze from the doorway. "Sorry," he said. "I know you're busy. I brought . . . That is . . . I thought . . ." He lifted the A3-sized carrier. "Some of Karl's work. I thought it might . . ." He stopped, seeming suddenly abashed. "I don't know what I thought, really. It's just—I can't seem to get his peers to open up, and I wanted to do *something* . . ."

"I'll take a look," she said, holding her hand out.

He seemed suddenly reluctant to pass it to her; perhaps he thought he was wasting her time.

"Sometimes it helps to understand the victim as a person," she said.

He seemed relieved—grateful, almost. When she took it, the grip was warm and slightly slick. She guessed that the exchange with Adam was partly to blame for his discomfort. Interesting that Milner recognized her brother.

"You must see hundreds of students," she said. "Yet you recognized Mr. Black after a short teaching interaction, eighteen months ago—he must have made an impression." Ruth herself could never imagine forgetting a face, but she knew that most people could be thrown off even by seeing a person out of their usual context—and Milner had remembered Adam's name, too.

"Oh, I'm usually terrible with students," he said with an embarrassed smile. "I have to keep a crib sheet in my desk drawer—but Adam was exceptional. And when one of your students wins an award, it tends to stick."

"He won an award?" Ruth feigned ignorance, thinking, *He wasn't lying about that, then.*

"UK Street Art 'Young Talent' category—for the under twenty-fives." He added with a rueful smile, "Oh, to be young and cocksure again."

It wasn't a characterization Ruth would have made, but it seemed Adam had changed in more ways than she'd realized.

"I wonder what he's working on now?"

"Trompe l'oeil, mostly," she said, without thinking.

He glanced quickly at her, and she saw surprise in the quirk of his eyebrows, then embarrassment that he'd assumed a level of ignorance in her. Odd, how different he was outside of the classroom. He'd seemed so at ease among his students.

"He didn't complete the course?" she said.

"What made you think . . . ?"

"You seemed disappointed."

He sighed. "I think I let him down. If I'd handled things better . . ."

Ruth cocked her head and waited. It was a technique that worked well in the interview room. Silences made people uneasy, and if you doubled the strain by showing an interest, they felt obliged to say something interesting.

"We had a . . . difference of opinion over an ethical question," Milner said. "It resulted in Adam dropping out."

Ruth remembered what Adam had said about ethics not being his strong point, and curiosity piqued, she said, "What happened?"

Milner shook his head, apparently still angry with himself.

She kept her eyes wide, her posture receptive, sending the message that it was okay, that she was listening, that he could tell her anything—that she wouldn't be shocked.

"Imitation, modification, experimenting with form—it's all part of an artist's evolution and Adam was—I'm sure still is—very mature, in that respect. At that time, he was dabbling in bioart. It's a niche group who create art from living tissues."

The base of Ruth's scalp began to prickle. "For instance?"

"On the microscale, it could be bacteria, or nerve cells, or genetically engineered skin tissue—a three-dimensional landscape composed entirely of different bacteria with a range of colors and forms—for instance. But Adam became interested in macrolevel art, and because that deals with whole organisms, it can raise controversy."

"I can imagine," she murmured.

"Certainly, it's challenging. When you draw attention to the grotesque and bizarre in nature, you can get knee-jerk responses from those who prefer their art to be soothing and lovely, and to complement the color scheme of their family room."

He smiled, and she saw the merest hint of mischief in it.

Ruth was thinking of Adam talking about the prospect of a live rat being smashed under a weight, its remains spattered across two canvases, the sharp thunderclap of noise as Adam had brought his hands together, startling the late-night travelers.

"He mentioned Rick Gibson," she said.

"*Did* he?" Milner grimaced. "Fetus earrings, cannibalism, squashed rats—shock art," he said, "without much artistry. There are better examples—Suzanne Anker, for example, has produced a truly remarkable range of work."

"You described this bioart movement as 'niche,'" Ruth said, hoping it might narrow the focus of their inquiry. "Would you call it marginal?"

He laughed. "A select group, but far from marginal—Suzanne Anker's work has been exhibited at the Smithsonian in Washington and the Getty Museum; she's lectured all over the world—including the Royal Society in London."

"I don't get it," Ruth said. "If bioart is a valid art form, how did Mr. Black get into trouble?"

"Adam was strongly focused on the integration of humans into artwork," he said, and Ruth's stomach did a slow roll. "He had been experimenting with an installation based around Joseph Wright's painting of the infamous *Experiment on a Bird in the Air Pump*."

"I know it," Ruth said. "It was in at least three of my chemistry textbooks at school."

"So you will know that in the painting, a cockatoo is trapped in a bell jar, and all the air is being gradually removed by a pump."

Ruth nodded. "It's a classic experiment of the eighteenth century. Wright's painting was a reflection on Lavoisier's new 'oxygen theory.'"

Milner's delight was apparent. "Have you seen the original?"

"No," Ruth said.

"Oh, you *must*—it's at the National Gallery. Wright was an asthmatic; can you imagine painting that poor animal's suffering, knowing what it felt like to suffocate?"

"Terrible, I should think."

"Indeed. As you say, little was known about the air we breathe at that time, so for Wright, Lavoisier's new theory must have been particularly compelling."

Ruth could see vividly in her mind's eye the avid expression on a little boy's face in the left of the painting, two girls on the right, clearly sisters, one with her eyes covered as the white cockatoo fluttered desperately in the bell jar. The younger girl looked anxiously at her older sister. Next to the girls, an older man—Ruth always thought of him as their father—urging them to engage fully with the experiment.

"The people watching all respond differently to the experiment," she said, half to herself.

"For me, that's one of the most remarkable things about the painting," Milner said. "The response of the observers is portrayed as an integral part of the experience."

Hadn't Jim Barrow said Alderson Bank's Art Awards favored submissions that invited audience interaction?

Interaction, participation, she thought. That was exactly what the Ferryman was doing in his exhibits—inviting engagement.

How did that fit with Adam's spat with the college? What had he done that would alienate his open-minded lecturers to the point that he couldn't go back? She thought she knew, and if given the choice, she would rather not hear the details. But Adam was a person of interest, if not a suspect. She needed to keep in mind that he was a stranger; she could not assume he was, in essence, the fourteen-year-old she had shared home and family with all those years ago.

"I take it Mr. Black's 'installation' was a kind of performance?" she said.

Milner nodded. "His original presentation plan used a 3-D print of a cockatoo. He incorporated some clever light effects to create the effect of chiaroscuro—light and dark—in the demonstration, which made it look like the bird was moving. As the air was extracted, the bird's movements became more frantic, then feebler, until the jar faded into darkness."

Ruth experienced a queasy certainty as to where Milner was going with this.

"It was powerful," Milner said. "Everyone who saw it had a visceral reaction to the installation. He got people *talking*."

"About what?"

"Piety and hypocrisy; fascination versus voyeurism—about the *function* of art in society. It was easily good enough to guarantee him a first." He took a breath and exhaled. "But 'good enough' is *never* enough for a perfectionist like Adam. So . . ."

Ruth knew what he was going to say before he even opened his mouth.

"In the finals, he substituted the 3-D print with a live cockatoo."

She kept emotion out of her voice. "Was he expelled?"

Milner shook his head. "I caught the substitution in time, stopped the demonstration, but Adam couldn't accept it. It was terrible. Terrible," he said with bitter self-reproach. "I should have given him more time to reflect; he was just overenthusiastic. He'd allowed himself to be seduced by the idea without thinking of the consequences. With guidance, I'm sure he could have experimented without transgressing ethical boundaries."

"Did you tell him that?" Ruth asked, all the time wondering how many birds Adam had experimented on as he perfected his technique.

"Of course," Milner said. "But I couldn't persuade him to see it that way. In the end, it was taken out of my hands."

"How so?"

"Since I couldn't persuade him to modify his installation design, I was forced to take it to the college ethics committee. They had recently appointed a new chairman, and he was keen to make his mark. He called us to a meeting and asked Adam to account for his work. He was defiant—adamant he wouldn't change a thing."

That sounded like Adam, all right.

"He was given an ultimatum," Milner went on: "Modify the design or face suspension. He walked out of the meeting, never came back."

64

Ruth sat at her desk, googling the UK Street Art Awards. It was after hours, and Carver and most of the other members of the team had gone home. Drew Scanlon had been charged with fraudulent use of Steve Norris's credit card and released on police bail. Carver had placed a watch on him, sanctioned reluctantly by Superintendent Wilshire; Karl Obrazki's murder had given Carver enough leverage to win that argument. True to form, DC Ivey had volunteered for the first shift. Overspending on the case was reaching spectacular levels, so he was working alone, with instructions to follow at a discreet distance and radio for assistance immediately if he felt uneasy.

She clicked through the Street Art Awards gallery of prizewinners, and moments later she was staring at a photograph of Adam with a "screw you" look on his face. He was standing in front of a giant image of an antique bird cage, painted on a brick wall. Inside the cage, a white cockatoo lay dead. The cage door had been forced open from the inside, the bars around it pried apart, and a ghostly image of the bird seemed to rise, bursting triumphant from its cage.

Adam had painted the graffito artwork on a side wall of Fairfield College shortly after he quit, it seemed. A year later, it had won him the Young Talent award.

Cocky bastard. Now Ruth understood Milner's cryptic remark, and his rueful smile.

She rang Adam's mobile. It went straight to voice mail. After three attempts, she gave up.

The phantom itch of the ghost tattoo burned in the crease of her left arm, and she caught herself tearing at it as she brooded over Adam.

Time to go home, Ruth.

She looked up and saw Jason Parr watching her from across the room. He quickly glanced away and busied himself with some paperwork. She hadn't seen him come in. But that was just like Parr: always creeping around, just out of eyeline, listening at doorways, earwigging canteen gossip. He'd kept his head down since the scuffle on the stairwell with Tom Ivey the day before, but the man was beginning to seriously bug her.

She kept her gaze on him till he finally got the hint and headed out of the office, with a murmured, "G'night, Sarge."

When she was sure he was out of earshot, she rang Mick Driscoll, the shift sergeant responsible for the special volunteers. He picked up straightaway. Ruth heard a gabble of voices and laughter in the background.

"Hold on," he said. "Can't hear meself think with this row." A second later he spoke again. "That's better."

"Sorry, Mick," she said. "I hope I haven't dragged you away from a family do."

"Grandson's ninth birthday party," he said. "The wife volunteered our place 'cos we've got the room, *apparently*. We've already had two rope burns from the tug-of-war, one major strop over the Lego treasure hunt, and a falling-out over 'Pass the Parcel.' I was about to be roped in for a highly inappropriate game of 'Murder in the Dark'—you might just have saved me from a fate worse than death."

Ruth laughed. Driscoll wasn't usually so expansive, and she guessed that he was secretly having rollicking good fun.

"So," he said, "what can I do for you?"

Ruth checked she was alone. "I'm getting some bad vibes from one of the specials. I wanted to get your take on him."

"Let me guess," he said. "Parr."

"He's got a reputation?"

"Let's say he doesn't play well with others," Driscoll said.

"I heard he'd applied to be regular police, but needed more experience."

Driscoll snuffed. "He's been a special for five years," he said. "More likely they told him he needed a better attitude."

"Meaning?"

"He's a bighead. Likes to boss the others about. Bit shifty, too."

"Yeah," she said. "He's keen, though."

"There's keen," Driscoll said, "and then there's officious. Take that hoo-ha over the scene log the other day—you know, when he let that poor lad Karl slip past him with all those photos."

"I'd call that incompetent, not officious," Ruth said.

"Except he wasn't supposed to be doing that job. In fact—till it came up at the debrief, I didn't know he was there at all."

Ruth's scalp prickled.

"I'd put one of the younger volunteers on the door," Driscoll explained. "Good lad. Studying for a degree, he is, wants to be a cop when he graduates—he'll be a good one an' all, if he ever learns to stand up for himself. But Parr shows up, and the silly bugger let himself get bullied into handing over the scene log. So what's he been up to now?"

"I caught him trying to lean on a detective constable yesterday," she said. "And he's always in places he shouldn't be, always with a glib excuse—"

Driscoll chuckled. "I tell you—that lad can get in places olive oil can't."

A few moments later, the party spilled into the hallway. Driscoll apologized—he was wanted.

Stiff from a day of office work and interview rooms, Ruth decided to run. It was only three miles, and she'd brought her running gear in a backpack that morning and stowed it in her locker. She logged out of her account and trotted down the stairs to the changing room.

The bag clunked against the metal of the cabinet as she lifted it out, and she set it down on the bench seat while she made up her mind what to do next.

After a minute, she took a steadying breath, then removed the sports gear and running jacket from the bag. Packed neatly under them was an evidence box, tape-sealed and further protected inside a ziplock bag. There was no evidence label on the bag or the box—because inside was one of the beer bottles Adam had been drinking from the night before—and it would not be admissible as evidence.

She placed the box on the bench, changed into her sweats, and began her warm-up routine, still undecided. The bottle would certainly have Adam's DNA around the rim, but even if she could sneak it by John Hughes, an undocumented DNA check would raise questions. There were latent fingerprints on the bottle. She was sure John would've had the Ferryman's fingermark scanned into the system by now, but even fingerprint checks required paperwork.

As she finished tying her shoelaces, Ruth realized that she really didn't need to go through IDENT1, or the DNA database. She scrolled through her contacts to John Hughes.

"Hey, John. I know it's late, but those slides you showed us earlier of the fingermark—"

"From the disk," he said. "What about it?"

"You couldn't just zap them across to me, could you?"

"I *could* do, but . . ."

"I think it'd be good to show the rest of the team—give them a bit of a boost. I might give 'em the pep talk about small details . . ."

He huffed a laugh. Ruth had delivered the same spiel as a CSM and an instructor, guest lecturing at Liverpool JMU, when Hughes was a late-entry student, studying forensic science.

"I'm at home right now," he said. "But I'll send it over first thing."

"Thanks," she said, as if it was nothing.

The outer door of the changing room thumped open, and Ruth swiped the box up and pushed it out of sight inside her locker.

Whoever it was disappeared into one of the toilet cubicles, and Ruth stuffed her work clothes into the backpack, locked up, and left. She would take lifts of the latent prints from the bottle tomorrow and do a physical comparison with the print John Hughes had found in the plexiglass.

Just one more task to complete, and then she could go home.

There weren't many pay phones left in Liverpool, but Ruth knew where there was a bank of them. She jogged to the city's mainline railway station on Lime Street, avoiding the main drag, dodging into a late-opening shop to use their changing rooms, where she took off her running top and replaced it with the suit jacket. You couldn't sneeze in this part of the city without it being recorded on CCTV, so as an extra precaution, she donned a baseball cap for the last leg, tucking her hair under it and keeping her head down, mingling with the crowds. It was dark by now, and that would help, but in the station, she would be visible to a dozen cameras.

Thankfully, the concourse was busy, and she allowed herself to be caught up with a gang of tourists being shepherded from one end to the other. Ruth peeled off at the phone bank and fed coins into the slot.

She was put straight through to Dave Ryan.

"I thought we were quits," she said.

"I'm not with you," he said, his tone inviting further explanation.

"A solicitor from Felix Welsh's firm turned up at work today."

"Busy legal practice, that," he said. "Keeping the law fair and equitable in this city's a full-time job."

"The solicitor in question was sent to provide legal representation to my brother."

"Sorry to hear he's in trouble," he said, sounding bored now. "But what's this got to do with me?"

"Ryan, I'm warning you," she said. "Lay off."

"I take it he's out now?"

She didn't answer.

"You're welcome," he said. "Like I said, one good turn deserves another."

The Tannoy loudspeaker boomed and the crowds around her seemed to slow; for one full second, her heart stopped. Then it began a rapid, jittery beat. *Stay cool. All he has is suspicions.* But suspicion was more than enough to finish a policing career.

When the announcement was finished, she said, "Are you there?"

But the line was dead.

65

Drew Scanlon gave me the slip in the city center, shortly after the police let him go. Never trust a scall to do a job right: he was supposed to give the cops the runaround. I'd assumed he'd know how to use a stolen card without getting himself arrested. And the thing is, the little shit saw me. Arrived early to the bedsit, eager to stick his nose in the trough. We passed on the stairs; he looked away—presumably not wanting to be identifiable. But that cuts both ways—and *he* saw *me*.

It crossed my mind that I might use my network of hoodie fans to locate him but I didn't want to take the chance that they'd decide to stick around. I do *not* need any more witnesses.

As it turned out, it wasn't hard to track down his address. So here I am, three hours later, freezing my balls off, waiting for him to show up.

And here he is. Finally. He's drifting a little, which is a good sign. No doubt he's been the toast of the alehouse, impressing his cronies with tales of his brush with the Ferryman.

Here we go . . .

I slip out of the shadows and fall in step behind him. He's fumbling in his pocket for his keys as I reach the perimeter wall. Staggers two steps backward, pulls his pocket lining inside out, and steps forward again, all his limited brainpower concentrated on finding the key slot.

I have the knife ready, swing it out and up in an arc.

A yell. Footsteps pounding down the street.

Drew turns. He shouts, bringing his arm up to protect himself.

SEARING PAIN. My elbow!

The knife clatters to the concrete.

I turn, grabbing the assailant with my good arm, dragging him to the ground.

Drew is sprawled nearby, swearing, his heels scraping the ground as he tries to get up. The other man is stronger than he looks. He wrestles one arm free and tries to take another swing at me. Police baton. DC Ivey. *Bastard.*

I hit him in the face, scramble for the knife.

I have it! I slash wildly, but the cop rolls out of reach, boosts himself to his feet just as Drew scrambles to his knees. Drew's coordination is off and he pitches forward, knocking the cop sideways. I try one more swing, make contact, hear the cop grunt in pain.

Drew is staring stupidly at the cop as he bleeds. A police car screams around the corner, lights blazing. He hits the siren, accelerating toward me, and I'm off, running.

66

"What do we know?" Carver said.

He was in a fleet car; Ruth Lake was driving—at slightly over the limit—toward Canning Place. Ruth had roused Carver from an exhausted sleep, but now he was buzzing with energy and eager for the chase.

"The flats where Drew Scanlon lives have security cameras in the public areas," Ruth said. "They've given us full access."

"Tell me they got the bastard on camera."

Ruth scooted around a cab dropping off a fare on Princes Boulevard, maneuvering smoothly back into the inside lane, ready for the turn left toward the riverside.

"They got him," she said. "But he was wearing a balaclava as well as a coat and scarf."

"Anything we can use?" he asked.

"Scientific Support have someone working on the drive now, we'll see when we get to the office."

"What about Scanlon—did he recognize the attacker?"

"He's drunk as a skunk—says it was all a blur—and he still swears he doesn't know the Ferryman's identity."

"D'you believe him?"

"He's terrified. I think if he knew, he'd say."

Carver thought through the sequence, as he understood it: a knife attack; external factors the Ferryman could not control; no social media links; no "exhibit."

"Has Instagram picked up on this yet?" he asked.

"Not a whisper." Ruth sped along Upper Parliament Street, lighting up hoodie graffiti on walls and street cabinets.

"This seems way off-whack for the Ferryman," Carver said. "Impulsive, badly planned."

"Yeah," Ruth agreed. "There's signs all around the building: 'Smile, you're entering a CCTV area'—he usually knows his locations literally inside and out before he makes a move."

"We could do with Dr. Yi's opinion on that."

"I left a message on his phone."

"Good. What's the status of the search?"

Marked cars and a couple of Matrix vans had descended on the area within minutes of Tom Ivey's emergency call.

"He's gone to ground," Ruth said.

"And the crime scene?"

"CSIs are working on them as we speak."

"There's more than one scene?"

"Our man laid in wait in the garden of an empty house."

Carver nodded; when offenders got bored waiting, they did stupid things—like leaving trace of themselves at a crime scene. "Where's Scanlon now?"

"Waiting in one of the interview rooms, working through a takeaway meal and a can of Coke." Ruth paused. "It's already on the Web. And someone named him."

"One of his drinking pals looking for his fifteen minutes of fame, or another leak?" Carver asked.

"Impossible to say."

"We'll need to sort out a place of safety for him."

"Sure. I'll get that organized."

She drove the rest of the way in silence, mulling over what Mick Driscoll had told her about Jason Parr. Was he the source of the leak? Was it possible he got himself the job of logging people in and out at *Art for Art's Sake* because he *knew* Karl Obrazki was inside filming? Did he deliberately let Karl leave unchallenged? It seemed far-fetched, unless he had a line of communication with the Ferryman—and she didn't even want to think about that. But the question remained: Why was he even there when his name wasn't on the rota? Not out of a sense of duty, that was for sure. Of course, it was possible he'd picked up on the social media buzz and headed out like the Ferryman's followers, looking for *glory*. And why let Karl go? *For power*? . . . Possibly. *Control?* She didn't need a diagnosis from Yi to tell her that Parr was a narcissist as well as a bully—the row she'd overheard between Parr and Tom Ivey was proof of that. He was also arrogant and intrusive, constantly lurking at the edges, digging for information, stowing it away for later use. She could tell Greg Carver—but what would be the point? Dealing with difficult work colleagues was part of the job, and all she had now was a bad feeling about Parr. If she wanted to take this to the boss, she needed evidence that he had stepped over the line.

At headquarters, they headed straight to the incident room, where a skeleton crew was waiting, called back in from their beds or a rare night in front of the TV. They'd had more offers, as word got out that one of their own had been injured, but Carver had limited the number—they would be needed, rested and keen, when the investigation really got going in the morning.

"Anything further on Tom Ivey?" he asked.

Ruth shook her head.

Carver knew Ruth had been mentoring the detective, and as she walked through the doorway ahead of him, he saw a troubled shimmer of blue around her, which she quelled in a moment.

"Call the hospital when you have a minute, will you?" Carver said, just to give her the excuse.

Ruth opened her mouth to speak, then stopped. "I don't think that'll be necessary." She nodded toward the interior of the room.

Ivey was sitting in front of the projector screen, larger than life, his back to them, watching CCTV footage of the attack.

"Ivey," Carver said, "what the hell are you doing here?"

Ivey turned stiffly in his seat. His right eye was bruised, his left arm bulked up by a dressing under his shirtsleeve. "I'm fine, boss," he said.

"Well, you *look* terrible. How's the arm?"

Ivey dismissed his injury with a shrug. "It only took a few stitches."

"You shouldn't be here," Carver said. "You should be resting."

"I'm a bit vague on the details, sir," Ivey said. "I wanted to see if the security footage jogged my memory—before it goes right out of my mind."

Carver shook his head, and Ivey seemed to misinterpret his exasperation for disappointment.

"I know," he said. "I messed up." Behind him, his violent tussle with the would-be killer played out on the projector screen.

"Tom," Carver said, "you came within an inch of catching the Ferryman. And if you hadn't acted so fast, we'd be looking at another murder victim—you saved Drew Scanlon's life."

DC Ivey shook his head. "I let the bastard get away."

"You did what you're supposed to do: you protected the witness. Now—"

Ruth Lake cleared her throat; her eyebrows raised, a smile quirking the corner of her mouth, she was challenging him.

He glared at her, and she bugged her eyes. He began to wish he hadn't become so adept at reading people, but he knew exactly what she meant with that look: Hadn't he hauled himself to work and stayed long hours when he was supposed to be on limited duties? Hadn't he dragged Ruth into the deception with his "ride-alongs" in her car, when he was supposed to be at home?

He looked away for a moment. "Okay," he said. "All right . . ."

By then, ten members of the team had gathered. They sat on chairs or perched on desks close to the screen. Parr hurried through the door looking slightly disheveled, and Carver read surprise in Parr's face as he noticed Tom Ivey, followed by a snarl of dislike.

A vivid flash of orange surged around Ruth as she watched the late arrival take his seat.

Carver decided to ask her what was going on between her and the special constable after the meeting, but for now he turned to the tech and said, "Play the recording from the start, will you?"

"It'll take a minute to set up," the CSI said, looking pressured by the attention. "I've had to grab footage off two different cameras."

"That's all right," Carver said. "DC Ivey can talk us through events up to the attack."

Ivey had his notebook on the desk in front of him; he glanced at it before making a start. "Scanlon got home from police HQ at nineteen thirty-seven hours," he said. "He was a bit twitchy—almost gave me the slip a couple of times. Didn't stay home long, though. At twenty thirteen, he walked half a mile to the Arkles pub, corner of Arkles Lane and Anfield Road."

"Any suspicious activity?"

"No, but Scanlon was expecting trouble, checked over his shoulder every five seconds, so I hung back. I didn't see anyone following."

Carver nodded.

"I found a spot where I could keep an eye on him, he stayed till twenty-two fifty, then walked—I should say *staggered*—home. I kept my distance—again, didn't notice anything suspect on the way.

"I didn't want to spook him, so I waited till he'd turned the corner into his street before following him round. Must've been—I dunno—twenty meters back, when I saw someone coming out of the garden of a derelict house ahead of me. I called it in; they said they had a unit on the way . . ." He frowned, as if he was having trouble remembering. "I saw a glint of light on metal, yelled to warn Scanlon—I was sure it was a knife."

Ivey shook his head. "It gets fuzzy after that."

The technician caught his eye, and Carver gave him the nod to run the security video.

The footage showed Drew Scanlon taking a key out of his pocket and squinting at the door frame. A few seconds later, he turned, bring-

.ing his hand up defensively, eyes widening, mouth open in a yell. A blur of movement, then Scanlon lying on the ground, a knife close by. The image was blurred and kept breaking up into clusters of blocky pixels, but in the clearer images between, they could see the attacker was wearing a balaclava, a dark coat, and gloves.

"Yeah," Ivey said, his eyes fixed on the screen, following the action. "I remember now. I whacked the attacker a good one on the elbow, and he dropped the knife. He punched me in the face, then . . ."

He seemed confused, and Carver wondered if the hospital had checked him for concussion.

Ruth spoke up: "The other recording looked better quality."

"It is." The technician stopped the recording and switched to the second camera. "This machine is newer, better in low light."

The struggle between Ivey and the attacker continued. The offender had recovered the knife and began swinging it at Ivey, on the ground. Ivey rolled and was on his feet in a second. Then Scanlon half rose and abruptly pitched face forward, knocking Ivey off-balance.

"Ah . . ." Ivey said. "I thought the attacker had punched me again, but that was Scanlon. Then I felt the knife go in. Knew what it was—it was so cold. I was too slow . . ."

"No," Carver said, "you were fast. You'd just had the wind knocked out of you, but you bounced to your feet like it was nothing at all. You didn't see his face because you *couldn't* have. It was covered. You did everything you could."

On-screen, the attacker froze for a second and light flared off the camera. This was the moment the first responders had arrived. He turned and ran.

Ruth was staring at the screen; it was her stillness that Carver responded to: "Did you see something?"

"Not sure. Can you go back and freeze the screen when he starts swinging the knife at Tom?"

The tech obliged.

"Now advance it frame by frame."

The attacker's coat sleeve had ridden up in the struggle. The tattoos on them were clearly visible.

"Ruth?" Carver said.

"There's a second as he turns to run," she said. "You get a glimpse of the back of his neck." Her voice gave nothing away.

The attacker's neck had been tattooed with parallel lines ending in nodes. They seemed familiar. Carver leaned in for a closer look.

"Now, where have I seen those before?"

"It's Adam," Ruth said, and Carver thought he heard a small *click* as she swallowed. "Adam Black."

67

DAY 13

Armed police raided Adam's shared house at two A.M. He wasn't there, nor was there any sign of the white van. They searched every inch of the place, including the loft space, got nothing. Carver asked the police search adviser to keep a look out for the picture Adam submitted to Alderson Bank's Art Awards.

"We can do that," the PolSA said. "What do I tell them to look for?"

Carver hardly knew. All he had to work with was the title, so he went with that. But if it was ever there, it wasn't now—in fact, very few of Adam's paintings were in the flat, and there was nothing in his room to indicate where he might have gone. His flatmates claimed they hadn't heard from him since the previous morning.

Meanwhile, Drew Scanlon was still waiting for his escort to a safe house. They showed him a still of the attacker's tattoos; he didn't recognize them. Didn't pick Adam out of an array of photos, either, but he was still in shock, not really thinking straight—he might see things differently when they had him tucked away safe.

Carver went home at three thirty A.M. and slept like he'd been felled by a sledgehammer but woke at six feeling alert and ready for work. With the morning briefing scheduled for eight A.M., he wanted to be on top of any reports that had come through overnight, so he phoned for a cab and was at his desk before seven.

Blood found at the scene of the attack was still being analyzed, he discovered. There had been no reported sightings of Adam Black overnight, and the Ferryman's Instagram account remained ominously silent. Carver would have to decide soon if they should go public on Adam's arrest warrant.

Scanning down the list of e-mails in his inbox, his eye snagged on one from Alderson Bank. It was Marcus Fenst's PA, apologizing for the delay, but they'd had an unusually large number of entries last year, and the archived submissions had been housed in another part of the country. He would have them sent by courier to Merseyside Police HQ; Carver should expect them by the end of the day.

Dismayed by the thought of hundreds of forms arriving in the middle of the chaos he was already dealing with, Carver skipped to the bottom of the e-mail and found a direct landline contact. He dialed through, expecting to be connected to voice mail, but the phone was picked up immediately, and Mr. Concannon seemed pretty chipper, given the early hour.

Carver introduced himself and explained that he was really only interested in grant applications or competition entries Fenst had knocked back.

"Oh," Concannon said. "I'm afraid we don't separate the wheat from the chaff when it comes to the paper trail—we find it's easier to keep everything for a particular year together."

"How many entries are we looking at?" Carver asked.

"Over seven hundred forms—and then there's quite a stack of correspondence, too."

Concannon broke Carver's appalled silence: "The judges felt the same way," he said. "The burden of dealing with so many entries took its toll—in fact, that was the impetus for changing the entry requirements."

"You changed the rules? When was that?"

"Last year," Concannon said. "That is—for this round of submissions."

"What was the change?"

"The age range. Previously it was twenty-five and up, but Marcus petitioned the board for an upper age limit of forty years."

"Did it help?"

"We got slightly *more* entries, if anything," Concannon said, with a chuckle. "The press made a few 'ageist' headlines out of it. But almost half were disqualified on the age criterion, so it meant a lot less work for Marcus and Jim in the long run."

"There must have been fallout?"

"Some did find it hard to accept."

"Any who were particularly vocal?"

"Not that I recall."

"Could you give it some thought, let me know?"

"Well, I'll do my *best* . . ." For the first time in the conversation, Concannon sounded flustered. "But we're just coming up to our annual general meeting and I have a heavy workload—and since Marcus . . ." Mentioning his boss's name seemed to give him pause, and for a moment, he was silent. "I could send you a spreadsheet of names—like the one Jim sent you. We had an intern weed out the ineligible entries—he and Marcus worked out a code for rejection criteria—that might help you to select those for whom you would want further details."

Carver called up the spreadsheet he'd had from Jim Barrow. "Okay—how does the code work?"

"If you see 'R/A,' in the rejection column, you know that they failed to meet the age criterion," Concannon said.

"Just a minute." Carver scanned across the columns. "I don't see that code on Jim Barrow's spreadsheet. In fact, I can't find a rejection column at all."

A moment's silence, then, "Oh, lord . . . Sorry—no—you wouldn't," Concannon said. "My mistake—Marcus and Jim only saw the entries that fit the criteria. They created their long list from the vetted entries."

"Can you send me the spreadsheets for this year and last?" Carver said.

"Yes, of course," Concannon said. "I'm so sorry for the mix-up."

At the morning briefing, Ruth herself handed out photos of Adam—screen captures from his interview under caution the previous day. The search for him had continued overnight, and Ruth would go with DC Ivey to the tattoo studio and interview the staff as soon as it opened.

"Adam Black, aka 'MadAdaM,' has sleeve tattoos on both arms, similar to these," she said, clicking to example photos she must have downloaded from the Web. "He'll probably hide those. You're more likely to see his neck tattoos." She clicked to a still from the CCTV recording outside Drew Scanlon's apartment block. A few people sketched the image into their notebooks.

She looked around the room, her gaze cool, her face expressionless. "You should also know"—she paused as heads came up—"that Adam Black is my brother."

Among the exclamations and comments, no one seemed more shocked than John Hughes.

Carver saw Ruth retreat into herself, shut down, as if she'd thrown up a physical barrier, and he called on the crime scene manager to talk through his report. Like the pro he was, Hughes clicked straight into presentation mode.

"Hutton sent their analysis of the soil sample trace from the shoe print we found at Steve Norris's apartment," Hughes said. "It's a unique mix of alluvial clay-size particles and Shirdley Hill sand, plus a combination of pollens, spores, and organic matter that is a match to Priory Wood, where we believe Norris was abducted."

"So the Ferryman grabbed Norris in the woods as he ran to work, then came back to the victim's flat to record *Catch the Gamma Wave* at the old railway station across the way?" Carver said.

"It looks like it."

"Are you seriously suggesting Norris was killed for the view from his *flat*?" This was DC Gorman, the paunchy detective with a bad attitude.

"Why not?"

Heads turned. It seemed that Dr. Yi had rearranged his schedule to be at the briefing. He stood at the back of the room, unruffled by the dozens of pairs of eyes on him. "Serial killers choose victims because they *look* like someone the killer hates or is fixated on. Or because they're wearing a particular style of *shoe*. I once treated a patient who stabbed a waiter to death because he didn't like the man's line in table patter."

Carver heard his team take a collective breath.

"Even so—does it matter *why*?" Sergeant Naylor said. "He picks them for whatever reason and uses their apartments as a base. Maybe he snatched Norris, took him back to where he does what he does, then nipped over to Norris's flat to pick up his credit cards and anything else worth lifting. He looks out the window and sees the cliff and thinks, 'That'll do for the next show.'"

A few nods from the rest. Carver was ready to speak up on the need to find links between the victims, but Yi wasn't finished.

"You say his motivation is of no interest," he said. "But if you knew how the killer was choosing his victims, it would help you to identify the *actual* victims out of the twelve or more you have on your list of missing persons. Which would free up more personnel to ask the *right* people questions and give you a better chance of creating real meaningful leads."

This was the most passionate he'd ever heard the psychologist.

"The 'why' is often tightly bound to the 'how,' in the way that serial killers operate," Yi concluded.

Carver let the lesson sink in for a moment before saying. "Are we clear on that?" He waited for the dissenters to chime in with "Yes, boss," before adding, "If anyone has any bright ideas about what our victims *do* have in common, let me or Ruth Lake know."

He was about to move on, when Hughes spoke up again. "A couple more things: the Hutton scientists also found rust particles—presumably from the van interior, as well as sump oil—and a puzzling one: tea powder."

Carver had thought Ruth too preoccupied with her own concerns to be paying much attention to the briefing, but at the mention of tea powder, she unfolded her arms and turned to Hughes.

"Didn't you find a brown particulate in the plexiglass disks used in *Think Outside the Box*?" she asked.

"We did," the scientist said.

"Could that be tea powder?"

"Impossible to be definitive," he said. "We didn't find any pollen grains . . ." He glanced at the nonscientists, regarding him with different levels of bafflement. "The tea plant's a close cousin to the camellia—you know, the pink roselike blossoms you see in early spring?" A few nods from the gardeners on the team. "Anyway, no pollen, but to answer your question, yes—it could be tea dust."

Ruth said, "The Ford Transit with the A33 VAN plates was tracked to the north end of the docks the day Norris went missing. Great Howard Street, around the Vauxhall district, wasn't it?"

A rumble of agreement from the rest.

"What're you thinking?" Carver asked.

Ruth pulled up Google Maps on the demo screen and tapped in the street name. "That end of the docks has a lot of derelict warehouses," she said, flicking straight to street view and scooting Google's Pegman along the roadway, pausing every hundred yards or so, ending at Stone Street, the location of *Think Outside the Box*.

"There you go."

On the corner of the street opposite, an ancient redbrick building with barred windows—the storage warehouse they'd approached for CCTV footage the day after *Think Outside the Box* had appeared. Carver couldn't see what had arrested her attention until Ruth panned upward to a sign—white lettering on a gray background—painted onto the brickwork high up the building. It was faded by time, and some of the lettering was almost erased, but still legible 140 years on: BONDED TEA WAREHOUSE, and below that, LIVERPOOL WAREHOUSING.

"We know that building is currently in use, and there's CCTV all over it, so it's not likely our guy is using it as his base," Ruth said. "But what if there are smaller warehouses nearby? Facilities like that would be built in clusters, wouldn't they?"

"Let's find out," Carver said.

68

Task allocations organized, Ruth Lake stopped at DC Ivey's desk.

"You ready?"

"Sure."

He suppressed a groan as he got to his feet, and Ruth said, "I can take someone else if—"

"Let's go," he said, in a tone that brooked no argument.

"Well, okay . . ." She followed after him, smiling at his back—Tom Ivey had come a long way in the few months since their first case.

Her phone buzzed as she got to the door; it was Hughes.

"A word in private," he said.

Whatever this was about, it sounded like trouble.

"Sure," she said.

"Not here. West stairwell, between the third and fourth floors."

"Okay." Ruth saw Ivey waiting for her at the lifts. "Grab us a set of keys off the board," she said. "We'll take a fleet car—I'll meet you in the car park in ten minutes."

She jogged to the other end of the building, where CSM Hughes was waiting, looking mightily pissed off.

"The print we found in the plexiglass," he said. "Why did you want it?"

"Like I said, it's a good teaching tool," she lied.

"Come off it, Ruth. You think it's Adam's." The disappointment on his craggy face made her feel ashamed.

"I didn't know what to think, John," she said. "But I needed to find out."

"And now you think your suspicions were justified?"

She tilted her head, but didn't speak, unwilling to condemn her brother, even now.

"My guess is you've got his prints on something?" he said.

She gave a single, brief nod.

"Where?"

"In my locker."

"Go and get it. I'll wait."

She was there and back in under six minutes and handed over the evidence box inside an innocuous-looking M&S carrier bag.

He dangled the bag from one bony finger. "If it's a match, I have to take this to Wilshire and Carver—you know that?"

"Of course. B-b—" She stopped, astonished by her own sudden, stammering uncertainty. "Just . . . let me know first, okay?" she finished.

He hesitated.

"We'll have Adam's prints, anyway, when the CSIs have finished processing his house," she said. "I just need to be . . . ready."

Ruth had known John since that guest lecture she'd given at the university all those years ago. When he'd passed his master's degree, she was his first boss. As he'd risen to become a senior member of the team, they became friends. They had continued to work together even after she'd switched careers to policing. Hughes knew her better than most, and she hoped he trusted her, too.

Hughes sighed. "All right."

69

Soul Art Tattoo Studio was empty when Ruth Lake and Tom Ivey walked in.

The place was as neat and gleaming as the last time Ruth had visited, and the same pierced and tattooed receptionist sat behind the desk. She was flicking through a magazine when they arrived, but seeing Ruth, she sat up.

"Guys!" she called over her shoulder.

"Is he in?" Ruth said.

"MadAd?" the girl said.

Ruth caught Ivey's quick glance from the corner of her eye but didn't return the look.

"What's up?" a male voice said.

The girl looked from Ruth Lake to Tom Ivey. "It's the police."

A man appeared from the back of the shop.

Ruth showed her warrant card. "We're looking for Adam Black," she said.

"He's canceled his bookings." This man hadn't been among the others during her first visit, but he seemed to be in charge. He was dressed in jeans and a black shirt topped by a fancy waistcoat in blue jacquard material. He would have looked conservative but for the steampunk tattoo of a half hunter watch etched onto the back of his right hand.

"Canceled," Ruth said, "for the day?"

"Today, tomorrow—and for the foreseeable future."

"Can you reach him, Mr. . . . ?"

"Nope. His mobile's switched off."

They knew this, having tried to ping Adam's phone to establish his location.

"And you've no idea where he might be?"

A slight shrug. "Home, probably."

Ruth nodded, watching for any hint of uneasiness, and concluded that he was irritated, but not anxious. "I'll need your name and contact details," she said. At first, she thought he would refuse, but after a few seconds, he said, "Hugo Watson." He jerked his chin toward the desk. "Annie will give you anything else you need."

It sounded like an invented name, but it seemed that was the way they played it here. Ruth might have insisted on getting his details there and then, but she needed his cooperation, so she let the small rebellion pass and took a couple of cleaned-up stills from her pocket—images from the attack on Drew, including close-ups of the neck tattoos.

"I know tattoo artists don't usually do their own tattoos," she said, handing him the first printout. "Was this work done by someone here?"

Hugo took the picture and seemed vaguely amused. After a moment he glanced up at Ruth. "Let's find out." He called over his shoulder: "Cap—can you take a look at this?"

A second man appeared out of the break room.

The receptionist came around to the front of the store as two more tattooists Ruth had spoken to the previous day came from different parts of the shop. They were smiling as "Cap" took the stills from Hugo.

Cap was small and pale-skinned, which made the black circuitry tattoos on his arms seem all the more vivid.

"I don't get it," he said. "Is this a joke?" The skin around his eyes grew pink and his jaw tightened as two of the observers covered their mouths, hiding smiles.

"If it is, I'm not getting it, either," Ruth said.

Cap shoved the picture at his steampunk rival. "Fuck off."

"Come on, man, this is serious," Hugo said. "They're looking for MadAdaM."

Cap turned his face to Ruth. "And you assumed this—this *piece of shit* was my work?"

"I don't assume anything," Ruth said. "I'm asking a question."

He took a couple of breaths, exhaling hard through flared nostrils. The receptionist and one of the other tattooists exchanged an uneasy glance, but Ruth kept an open posture, her gaze fixed on Cap. She sensed that Ivey had tensed, but she was sure enough of him that he would follow her lead. She could see that Cap was genuinely insulted, but the "angry man" posturing was an act.

"Is it yours?" she asked, implacable, calm.

"Like I said—piece of shit. Look at it—there's no depth or shading," the tattooist said.

Ruth wasn't sure how you could achieve depth from a series of unshaded lines, but then she wasn't an artist, and from the malicious gleam in Hugo's eyes, she suspected that Cap was often the butt of this sort of windup.

So, she apologized—fully, and without reservation. "I really don't know much about tattoos," she went on, "but this was filmed at the scene of an assault last night, and it looked like—"

"MadAd," he finished for her.

"Yeah . . ." She glanced at his colleagues but addressed Cap directly. "Could we have a chat in private?" She wanted him to take another look at the tattoos, but she also wanted to take a peek inside the break room, and they had no search warrant for the premises.

Cap eyeballed her, his natural suspicion keeping him undecided, but finally he turned and stamped toward the back of the shop, head forward, shoulders back.

Ruth decided to interpret that as an invitation; she followed him, and he waited outside the door and waved her through in an unexpected show of gallantry.

The room was small, but well kitted out with a microwave, kettle, toaster, and sink. They sat at a small oak table, and Cap picked up the mug of coffee he'd apparently abandoned a few minutes earlier.

"Sorry," he said. "D'you want—?"

"I'm fine," she said. "Thanks."

On the other side of the shop, Ruth heard DC Ivey begin to take names and contact details, and satisfied that she could focus all her attention on Cap, she said, "Don't take this the wrong way—I'm asking because I need to explain it to my boss—why are you so sure this isn't your work?"

He took the pictures with his free hand and set them side by side on the table. "See the lines?" he said. "Gray—my inking's *never* gray unless it's *supposed* to be."

"But camera quality—poor lighting—couldn't they affect how the ink looks?"

He slid an enlarged shot center of the table. "Look at the color of the jacket. The hat. Black—see? MadAd's ink is as black as that. 'Cos that's the way I made it—right? And it's not gonna look *less* black than a woolly hat on the same photo, just 'cos the camera's a bit shit, now is it?"

"Makes sense," Ruth said.

He picked up one of the offending images and held it to the light. "Hang on." He disappeared into the shop and returned a few moments later with a handheld magnifier. He examined the images, then hissed.

"I'm not even sure that's a genuine tattoo—look." He shoved one of the shots into Ruth's hand, along with the magnifier.

"What am I looking for?"

"See a slight gap between that bit of ink and that?" he said, indicating with a pencil point.

Ruth saw a tiny gap in a line that had looked continuous. "He's missed a bit."

"Right," Cap said. "And you don't get that with proper inking."

"So what d'you think it is?" Ruth asked.

He frowned at the remaining images on the table. "Ink drawing . . . a transfer, maybe?" He shrugged. "Whatever. It's not real. And it's not mine."

Ruth felt a burst of optimism. *It isn't Adam.* But she had to ask the next question, to be certain: "Just so we're clear," she said. "You did do Adam's neck tattoo?"

"You're bloody right I did," he said. "And *that* is nothing like it."

Greg Carver was in his office when Lake and Ivey returned, but Ruth didn't go straight to him. To convince him that the man in the CCTV stills wasn't Adam, she needed to know her facts—*and* she needed a plausible theory as to who the tattooed knifeman really was. She had a theory, and she made a few calls to gather further intel.

Carver was working through printed spreadsheets at his desk, highlighting comments, when she finally went to see him. The list of submissions for the Alderson Bank's Art Awards, she guessed. He set his pen aside and gave her his full attention as she explained what Cap had told her.

After a few moments, he said, "Where's the evidence, Ruth? All you have is this tattooist's word for it that the attacker wasn't Adam."

"He wasn't lying, Greg."

Carver folded his arms, frowning. "Even if Cap *believes* he's telling the truth, it's still a matter of opinion whether the tattoo is genuine or not."

"So show the photos to a few more tattooists—see what they think."

She could see he was about to refuse and added, "We've done it before."

Her phone buzzed and she checked the screen. "It's a text from John Hughes."

Carver lifted his chin. "What's he got?"

She looked into Carver's expectant face and realized she had some explaining to do. "When I recognized the tattoo on the assailant's neck, I asked John for a favor," she said.

Carver's frown deepened to a scowl, and she pressed on: "I gave him a bottle with Adam's latent fingermarks on it. Asked him to do a physical comparison with the print inside the plexiglass disk."

Carver sucked his teeth. "And?"

"It's not Adam." Ruth smiled, feeling a rush of relief like cool air on her face.

But Carver wasn't smiling.

"Greg, if it had been a match, I'd've filled out the warrant form myself."

He gave a tacit nod of acceptance. "But you're not thinking straight, Ruth," he said. "The print in the plexiglass block suggests that Adam didn't make the brain sections, but that doesn't mean he's not involved. He wouldn't be the first susceptible individual the Ferryman has roped in as a stooge."

"I agree. But it wasn't Adam who leaked the info to the press about the heart being older than we'd first thought, was it?"

"Maybe, maybe not—but anyway, that's a separate issue."

"Not necessarily," Ruth countered. "You said yourself, the Ferryman has been one step ahead of us all the way . . ." She faltered, then said the rest in a rush: "What if he's police?"

Carver sat back in his chair. "*What?*"

"Why not? You know how it is—once you've been through all the vetting and background checks and passed your training, you're in. Trusted."

Carver shook his head. "You heard Doctor Yi—he would need flexibility—time off, or at least some freedom to work to his own schedule—maybe not in employment at all—"

"Like a volunteer, for instance?"

"A special?"

She watched his face and saw him think through the idea and discount it a second later.

"No, it won't wash. Volunteers work full-time jobs—many of them, anyway. Then they spend their evenings and weekends shoring up staffing shortages among the regulars."

"*Many* of them," she said, working hard to contain her excitement, trying to present this as the logical analysis it was, but knowing that her brother's future depended on it. "But not all are full-time workers. You've got retirees and part-timers; carers who take a day or two out of the week to do something to keep them connected to the world; students wanting to build their CV—"

He raised a hand, cutting off the litany. "All right. I'm assuming you've narrowed the field: no females, no retirees—we know this guy isn't old."

"The man I have in mind is over twenty-five—which is another of Dr. Yi's criteria," she said. "He's taking a year out. Worked in an abattoir as a student."

She saw Carver focus more intently on what she was saying.

"He dropped out in the middle of the second year."

"Like your brother," Carver pointed out.

"Yeah, but Adam didn't enlist in the army, then buy himself out after eight months. This guy couldn't hack it. He's applied to be regular police three times—got knocked back. *He* says because he didn't have enough experience, but the truth is, he can't get on with his peers. He's high-handed and officious; a braggart and a bully; and he doesn't take criticism well."

"You're talking about Parr."

It was a statement, not a question.

"How'd you know?"

"Never mind," he said.

No doubt one of Carver's weird synesthetic insights.

"The night of *Art for Art's Sake* he wasn't even supposed to be working. He suddenly appears after we missed the Ferryman by minutes, elbows another volunteer off the door, then coolly lets Karl Obrazki walk past him with a recording of the crime scene," Ruth said.

"You say coolly, I'd say incompetently."

"He's also the one who conveniently found the taunting note in the job car."

Carver shook his head. "Why would he bring the note to me if he'd written it—why not let someone else find it?"

"Because he wanted the glory? Or maybe he just wanted to see your face as you read the word 'CLUELESS.'"

"It makes a good story," Carver conceded.

He's not convinced. *Convince him.* "After the closed session to brief the core team on Mr. Fenst, he was desperate to know what was said." She hesitated, chose her words carefully, not wanting to "out" Tom Ivey: "I even heard him trying to coerce one of the team."

A sharp scowl. "Who?"

"Tom Ivey, and believe me, he was having *none* of it. But hours later, Tom is attacked by someone in disguise."

"Coincidence," Carver said. "We already had concerns that Scanlon might be targeted—Tom just got in the way." He stared at her. "Ruth, are you saying that Parr is the leak *and* that he's the Ferryman?"

Every fiber of her unreasoning, lizard brain screamed, *Yes!*, but the rational scientist in her argued that she didn't have enough on Parr to be certain. "I don't know," she admitted at last. "But this guy ticks every narcissistic psychopath box on the form."

"That's one percent of the population, isn't it?" Carver said, with a twitch of his eyebrows. "He may be an unpleasant dick, but that doesn't make him a killer."

Ruth placed her ace card on the table. "Remember Mr. Hollis?"

"I have a brain injury, Ruth," Carver said, calmly, "not Alzheimer's."

"Sorry," she said.

He sighed. "What's your point?"

"Hollis recognized Steve Norris from the photo. So maybe he'd recognize the abductor, too."

Carver nodded slowly, and she thought he was beginning to get it. "It was Parr who brought the message that Hollis had arrived," he said, remembering.

"And you told him to take the old man to an interview room."

"But he wasn't there when we got downstairs," Carver added.

"I checked," Ruth said. "Apparently, he palmed the job off onto another volunteer."

After the longest moment, Carver said, "All right. I'll concede he has questions to answer. Bring him in."

"He's already here," she said. "I've got him doing some busywork."

Parr was printing questionnaires when they got to the MIR; when he saw them, he blanched. His eyes darted to the door, but he quickly recovered.

"Almost done with the scut work," he said, smiling. "Am I forgiven now? Can I get out and do some real policing?"

"We need to ask you some questions," Ruth said.

He looked her up and down, and Carver saw an instantaneous hot glow around Parr's eyes, extinguished in a second, and Carver had the strangest sensation. It seemed that a liquid ghost of the man duplicated and shone for a brief moment just outside the contours of his face, then vanished, leaving a flat gray light.

At that moment, Carver knew that Parr was guilty. "Get your jacket," he said. "You might not be coming back."

Heads turned, and a hush fell over the room as they walked the special constable out.

They talked over interview strategy while Parr sweated it out in one of the smaller interview rooms. When they began the interview, he was stone-cold emotionless.

Carver began by asking about the note Parr had supposedly found in the fleet car.

"Are you suggesting *I* put it there?"

"Did you?"

"Did you find any evidence of me on the note? Inside the bag?"

Carver didn't answer.

He saw the tiniest gleam of satisfaction in the constable's eye. "That's what I thought."

"The crew who used the car say they locked it at the scene," Carver said.

"Well, they *would*, wouldn't they?"

"Surveillance recordings taken at the scene do not suggest that the car was interfered with in any way."

Parr shrugged. "The keys are on the board. Anyone could've—"

"The car in question remained in the secure car park overnight," Carver said. "CCTV shows nobody went near the car. Except you."

Ruth had been thorough, as usual—she'd had answers to most of the objections Parr might raise, even before she voiced her suspicions to Carver.

"Those cars are in and out all day," Parr said. "It's impossible to say when the note was put there."

"It's a coincidence that *you* found it," Carver said.

"You got me," Parr said. "I'm guilty. Of doing my job."

Ruth placed a printout in front of him. "This is a copy of a mobile phone log. It was used at exactly the time, and for the same duration, as a call to a crime reporter at *Liverpool Daily*, three days ago. The caller claimed to be the Ferryman, and he had inside information on the case."

"That's not my mobile," Parr said.

"No," Ruth said. "It's a police mobile. Logged out to you on that day."

"I left it on my desk for a bit—it's not like they're password locked, is it?"

He didn't miss a beat. And the lies kept on coming.

"In fact, I thought I'd lost it at one point—finally unearthed it from a pile of paperwork, right where I'd left it." He smiled, but the attempt at self-deprecating humor did not reach the eyes.

There's nothing behind the eyes, Carver thought.

Carver nodded to Ruth, and she opened a buff document folder, slid out a thick wad of papers: duplicates of documents and memos; crime scene photos obviously snapped in the MIR—a couple from PowerPoint presentations at briefings.

"These were in your locker," he said. "Can you explain why you had sensitive and confidential documents and images?"

"Helps me to think about the case," Parr said.

"If we search your home, will we find more of these?" Carver asked.

"Maybe. But where's the harm in that? The rumor mill says you had half the reports on your last case tacked up on your bedroom wall."

He's trying to rattle you. Carver deliberately relaxed the tension in his shoulders and smiled.

He saw a flare of anger as a marmalade glow off the man, then he faded to gray again.

"Is that what you do, Jason? Dig the dirt on your coworkers?"

"Nah," Parr said. "I'm just curious about people. Goes with the job, curiosity. It's a strength in a good cop, isn't it?"

"Not when you try to coerce information out of your colleagues," Carver said.

He thought he saw a slight check there.

"I don't know what you mean."

"You were asking questions about a closed meeting. A meeting you weren't invited to, and which was none of your business. You threatened a colleague when they refused to talk to you about it."

"Well, I can guess who that would be. Is that what he said—that I threatened him?"

"No," Ruth said. "That's what *I* say." She held his gaze, and Carver felt an almost physical push of willpower between Ruth Lake and their suspect.

Parr looked away with a sneer. "I know he's your pet project, Sarge, but Tom Ivey's hiding *way* more than I am—I can promise you that."

"Where were you yesterday evening at eleven thirty P.M.?" Carver asked.

"Is that when he was attacked?"

"Answer the question, Jason," Ruth said.

"Let's see . . ." Parr leaned back in his chair and clasped his fingers behind his head. "Went for a swim in the HQ gym at nine thirty. Finished around ten forty. Had a pint at the Baltic Fleet. They stop serving at eleven, weekdays, but I met a couple of mates, so we went down to the Albert Dock for another at chucking-out time. You'll be wanting to check that. We're probably on CCTV half a dozen times, but I can give you their names and numbers, if you like."

71

Parr's alibi held good, but he was now subject to a disciplinary hearing, and he was sent home on suspension and told to stay there until he was called. Carver hadn't said anything, but Ruth knew he was thinking they were back at square one, and dead center of that square was Adam.

He's right. Wishful thinking does not prove innocence.

In the months after their parents died, Adam had tantrums, destructive rages—he'd slammed the kitchen door in her face after one major row, shattering the glass panes and cascading her in shards. His look of horror and remorse was instant and genuine. He'd wept in her arms, begging for forgiveness. What had he said? *I've got all this hate in me and I don't know what to do with it.*

Could the kid brother who'd wept in her arms seek relief from the rage he carried around with him by hurting other people? The trompe l'oeil in his flat of the artist painting himself was unsettling, but it was clever and witty, too. The scene painted on the window shutters of Dave Ryan's lair was realistic and beautiful. But then there was Adam's failed attempt to reconstruct *Experiment on a Bird in the Air Pump*—and what about the missing painting, *Battered Wife*?

Ruth reached across the desk for her mobile and rang John Hughes. "Thanks for the info on the fingerprint," she said.

"How did Carver take it?"

"Well." She immediately changed the subject: "Is the search of Adam's place finished?"

"Not yet. Was there something in particular you were interested in?"

"His paintings. You didn't find any more?"

"Just three in the shop front, and the one painted directly onto the wall," Hughes said.

"Okay, thanks, John."

Adam's housemates had been displaced by the police search, but she had temporary addresses for them. She grabbed her jacket and headed out, wanting to ask her questions face-to-face, but an hour later, she was no closer to finding her brother. His two business partners were loyal to Adam, and in no mood to help her. They couldn't—or wouldn't—say where he might be, claiming that Adam did most of his work on-site at the homes or businesses of his clients. They were lying through their teeth.

Frustrated, she pulled her phone out of her jacket pocket on the way back to her car and scrolled down her contacts to Milner's number.

She composed herself and hit the dial icon.

He greeted her cordially and asked how he might help.

"Would you happen to know if Adam Black has a studio?" Ruth asked, taking care to keep her tone neutral.

"Is he missing?" he asked, then immediately apologized. "Sorry—none of my business. Let me see now . . . Yes—*yes*, he *did* have a studio when he was at Fairfield. A room in an old Board School building in Kensington; I visited it a couple of times."

"D'you have an address?"

"Not an exact one, I'm afraid, but it was on the corner of Low Hill and West Derby Street—it should be easy to find."

She drove north and then east, avoiding the worst of the city center traffic by skimming past the University of Liverpool along Brownlow Hill. At the top of the hill, taking a left turn past the cool, gleaming, glass-and-tile structures of the new biosciences buildings, she began to have misgivings. Fifty yards on, she knew she'd made a wasted journey:

ahead of her, the roadworks that had disrupted traffic flow for nearly three years. She could see the hoardings that marked the outer edge of the new, and some said jinxed, Royal Liverpool Hospital. The old school, along with every building along half a mile of roadway, had been demolished to make way for the hospital.

72

DC Ivey knocked at Greg Carver's door at around eleven A.M.

"Looks like we caught a break, boss," he said.

Carver waved him into the office.

"House-to-house near the North Docks turned up a witness," Ivey said. "A white van pulled up outside a house on one of the new estates in Vauxhall. Householder sees a man fiddling with the rear number plate, goes out to ask what's going on. Van driver says his number plate's come loose; he's just tightening it up. Registration: A33 VAN."

"When was this?" Carver reached for his phone, ready to call in the Matrix team. "Is it possible he's still in the area?"

Ivey shook his head. "Sorry, boss—he didn't hang about. But he had to do a three-point turn to get out of the street—that estate is all linked closes—one way in, one way out. The witness noticed that he had different plates front and rear."

"Did he get the rear plate?"

"He did better than that: he snapped a sneaky photo from inside the house." Ivey grinned, placing a printout of the photo on Carver's desk.

Carver felt a surge of optimism. "We need to get a description of the driver from the witness."

"Someone's bringing him in as we speak."

Carver arranged to have the rear plate number circulated and given as a priority to staff checking ANPR for the stolen vehicle.

Then he rang Ruth.

"D'you need me there?" she asked.

"Depends," he said. "What are you doing?"

"It seemed odd we haven't found more of Adam's artwork, and I was thinking maybe he rents a studio," she said. "His flatmates were no help, but Mr. Milner gave me a lead on a place he used in college."

"Don't approach him alone, Ruth," Carver warned. "I know he's your brother, but I don't want you taking any chances."

"The place he used isn't there anymore," she said. "Demolished to make way for the new hospital, but I'm thinking if it was compulsory-purchased, the tenants might have been offered alternative accommodation."

"What's your plan?"

"I'll head over to the council offices, see if I can find out any more."

"All right," he said. "But if you get an address, call it in and we'll send an armed team out. Okay?"

"Sure."

He knew that tone. Tell them whatever they want to hear, then do as you see fit.

"Ruth, I mean it."

"Yeah," she said. "Me too."

Then she was gone. His phone rang and he forgot about her for a spell, turning his attention instead to coordinating the search for the white van. ANPR checks on the new plate number quickly paid off. Sightings took the search to a tiny quadrant of the North Docks. From there, they worked back through CCTV recordings of that stretch of road for the last five days.

Every sighting added to a pattern; the pattern, as it emerged, narrowed the search perimeter. Carver sent out a message to concentrate on older buildings—if the Ferryman *was* using a tea warehouse, it would not have been built any later than 1910.

73

Until recently, the council offices had been housed in municipal buildings, a huge block in the city center: Town Hall, Education Department, Housing and Benefits, all side by side in a stone-faced building that would not have looked out of place in the center of Paris. But the bulk of it had been sold off to a hotel chain in 2016 and departments relocated all over the city. Ruth found what she was looking for in the Cunard Building at the Pier Head. Previously home to one of the great shipping lines, it was designated one of the "Three Graces" of Liverpool; clad in Portland stone, it gleamed like pristine snow in the spring sunshine.

From the grand marble hallway, DS Lake was directed to the Planning Department and found her way through an oak door into a large open-plan office. For a couple of minutes, she was studiously ignored. Then she knocked on the countertop and called, "Service!"

A woman glanced up from a desk on the far side of the counter. "Help you, love?" She was middle-aged, unshowy, but neatly turned out—the kind who carried herself with quiet confidence and brooked no nonsense.

Ruth showed her warrant card and was allowed through to the office. Around fifteen people were working at computers or taking calls; the office hummed with understated industriousness.

"Sorry about the wait," the woman said. "We're a bit short-staffed."

"Norovirus?" Ruth asked.

"No doubt there was some projectile vomiting involved, but all self-inflicted."

Ruth cocked an eyebrow.

"A syndicate of three lads from the office hit the jackpot on the Pools." She meant the Football Pools—top prize, a million pounds. "They haven't been in all week."

"Partying too hard?" Ruth asked.

"In the Caribbean, no less. One of the silly sods stuck a photo on Facebook. Talk about rubbing salt in the wound—I could murder them, honestly, I could."

She seemed to reflect on the folly of youth for a second, then shrugged. "Now, what can I do for you?"

Ruth gave the location and name of the old Board School where Adam had rented a studio. "Problem is, it's now part of the new Royal building site," Ruth said.

The admin officer rolled her eyes—delays, cracks in the structure, and later the sudden and catastrophic collapse of Carillion, the multi-national company tasked with building it, had put the hospital's completion, as well as hundreds of jobs on Merseyside, in doubt.

Ruth twitched an eyebrow. "What can you say?"

"If you're asking, I'd say give the women the top jobs, something might actually get done right," the woman answered with some passion.

Ruth smiled. "Wouldn't that be something?"

Rapport established, the woman said, "So what d'you want to know about the old school?"

"I was thinking there must have been compulsory-purchase order on it," Ruth said. "I'm looking for one of the previous tenants: Adam Black."

"And you'll be wanting to know if we offered alternative premises to the displaced tenants."

"Yes."

"Well, we don't rehouse private tenants, and my guess is the school's buildings would've been privately owned after it was decommissioned by the council," the administrator explained. "But we might've advised on relocation."

She shook the mouse on her desk to wake up her computer and tapped in commands, clicking through screens. "Adam Black . . ." she murmured. "Adam Black . . . No. Sorry, Sergeant. He's not there."

"He might be registered under a street name," Ruth suggested. "MadAdaM."

The woman's eyebrows twitched, but she didn't comment.

Ruth dictated the spelling and capitalization, and the admin officer typed it in and resumed her search.

"Oh." She stopped, clicked through some more tabs, and a new screen came up. "There he is—MadAdaM. Apparently, we suggested several possible properties. I'll print the list."

She clicked through the printing instructions, logged out, and stood. "I need to go to the printer room to pick it up," she said, adding dryly, "Efficiency measures devised by a man." She squinted to a glass-fronted office at the end of the room. "Looks like there's a queue at the machines, but I'll be as fast as I can."

Ruth sat in the waiting area, thinking about the Pools syndicate and what it must be like to just walk away from your old life, start a new one with none of the baggage attached to it. The idea had its attractions, and the Ferryman's known victims—and many of those who were still missing—had expressed a hankering for travel and adventure.

The fact was, in the end they had stayed put. Sure, Eddings had *talked* about using his lottery win to travel the world, but he'd ended up buying a property instead. Martin, too, had dug in and worked hard, even postponing his engagement to keep his focus.

An idea was beginning to form in her head. It didn't have substance, yet, but her blood fizzed. The connection was there—she just had to find it.

She took out her phone and searched for the *Echo* article on Eddings, found a beaming photo of him accepting his check. Norris was in the local paper, too, photographed streaking through the finish line at the London Marathon the previous year. A "ballot" entry, he'd nevertheless completed the course in just two hours twenty—only eleven minutes behind the leaders on one of the hottest marathon days on record. Scrolling down the page, she found a link to a second article; Norris was pictured shaking hands with a sports retailer who'd stepped in to sponsor his Commonwealth Games ambitions. Norris's sponsorship, Eddings's lottery win—and then there was Karl Obrazki, beaming out of the front pages of the nationals.

Could the Ferryman be choosing his victims because he happened to see them online, or in the local press? Karl had been on BBC local news, too, after they'd brought him in for questioning.

Her heart thrumming, she typed in a new search for Dillon Martin but found nothing. And what about Tyler Matlock? The council would hardly have publicized the fact that they'd made a payout to him—they'd have been inundated with claims from anyone who'd skidded on ice during the winter they ran out of road salt.

Even so, she sent a text to Carver—it'd be worth talking to Martin's relatives, see if there was any publicity around his bursary.

Then the administrator called her name, and for a time, she forgot all about her tentative theory.

74

The sun has a rare clarity and warmth for the time of year, and I'm driving with the window down. Traffic is heavy; I don't enjoy the fumes, but the sonic vibrations of the heavy goods lorries that pound up and down this stretch of the docks are as good as any hard-rock riff.

I left the van at the usual place. I've been driving the Toyota hatchback for the last hour, trying to clear my head. The incident in Vauxhall was hairy; I'm fairly sure the old tosser didn't get a good look at me, but he saw the vehicle all right, and he might have spotted the plate.

Time to find new transport. I should've dumped the damn thing on the next patch of scrubland and torched it, but I'll admit the old guy rattled me. Problem is I can't risk leaving the van where it is—it's too close to my gallery. Which means I'll have to pick it up, do what I should have done after the old bastard challenged me: torch it.

It's well hidden off the main road, along a side street of disused warehouses and empty lots, under a railway bridge, left, then right. Abandoned commercial properties, on isolated, empty streets, unlit at night.

Almost there; at the end of the next street is the entrance to a disused junkyard. Anything salable is long gone, leaving only a few bits of rusted scrap and black oil stains on the poisoned earth. The van is parked out of sight, around the back of a tilting wooden shack that used to serve as an office.

I slow for the turn and catch a flash of blue-and-lemon-yellow checkerboard livery.

Police.

Shit. I ease past. Three cars, at least five police in uniform.

They've found the van!

How the hell . . . ?

A helicopter clatters overhead.

Oh, Jesus, no. This *cannot* be happening.

I carry on, at a slow pace, driving around potholes, taking my time. Perhaps they'll think I'm just another idiot who put too much trust in the SatNav.

75

Greg Carver was at his desk, working through the list of art competition entrants. He'd passed Ruth's query on to the liaison officers dealing with the victims' families and apparently, Dillon Martin had been interviewed on BBC Radio Merseyside when his firm won a regional business award. Matlock's cronies said he'd boasted about his compensation payment in just about every pub and bar in the city. As Carver sat highlighting the names of the bank's Art Awards rejects, a team was sifting through the list of missing men, searching for anyone who'd been featured on local media after a stroke of good fortune. Meanwhile, three disused tea warehouses had been identified in the North Docks; a team of three was in the process of contacting landlords and checking them out.

His desk phone rang. The call had been patched through from a patrol unit at the North Docks.

"We've got the van," the cop said.

"Where?"

"Parked in an abandoned junkyard in the middle of no-man's-land at the north end of the Dock Road."

Carver remembered the sump-oil residue the scientists had identified from the trace at Norris's flat. It seemed Ruth was right to put her faith in the shoe print analysis. "How did you find it?"

"Eye in the sky caught the heat of the engine on thermal imaging," the cop said. "The vanity plates are still inside."

"And it's still warm? He could be around then."

"It isn't exactly *hot*," the cop said. "Could've been parked awhile. We've got a two-crewed unit cruising the area—but in all honesty, he could be long gone."

"It's still a win," Carver said. "*If* the van is intact?"

"All in one piece," the cop said.

Carver punched the air. "You've secured the scene?"

"Setting up the perimeter as we—" The cop broke off. "Is he lost, or what?"

"Talk to me," Carver said.

"A steel-gray Toyota Yaris just cruised past the end of the street. Gimme a minute."

The line went quiet for a short while.

"I put a call through to the mobile unit," the cop said, when he came back. "They're only a couple of blocks away—they'll see what's what."

"Tell them to approach with extreme caution," Carver said.

"Will do."

"Give me your coordinates," he added, thinking of the Ferryman's army of followers descending on the *Art for Art's Sake* exhibit, besieging the garden, throwing missiles. "I'll get Scientific Support and a Matrix unit out to you just as soon as possible. And keep me informed."

76

How did they find the van? There's no CCTV for half a mile around, no bystanders, no witnesses—even a gutter-crawling smackhead would turn its nose up at this crumbling quarter of the city.

Jesus—how long have they been there? What have they found?

Nothing. A few fingerprints, maybe—but since they're not on record . . . And I've been careful—haven't even driven the van onto a petrol station forecourt since I got back from London.

Shit. I stopped for diesel a couple of nights ago. Filled a couple of cans, stuck them in the boot of the Toyota. What did I do with the receipt?

I drag my wallet out of my back pocket, keep one eye on the road as I check.

It's not there.

Oh, God. I threw it on the passenger seat when I got in the van. Paid by credit card. *Fuck!*

For a full five seconds I'm driving blind. I literally *cannot see* past the black fog clouding my vision.

Look. It's *fine.* Just a receipt, right? The van is clean—you gloved up whenever you used it. Ditch the card, tell them you didn't notice it was missing.

A fresh kick of fear. *The gallery*—there's *plenty* of evidence in the gallery.

"Fuck. Fuck. FUCK!"

Calm down. You paid cash for the gallery—it's untraceable.

Sure, until my face is all over the media—that should jog the memory of the guys who brought the meat locker across town from the delivery address. And what about the electrician who wired it into the mains?

Stop panicking and think. There's time to sort the gallery; they're not going to find it straightaway. I just need to get to it before they do, get rid of paperwork, the laptops.

A police car appears in my rearview mirror.

Take it slow and easy.

It accelerates down the cobbled road, gaining on me. They turn on the light bar. If they pick me up now, I might not get to the gallery in time. If they find that, I'm finished.

I hit the gas, my chest constricting, a throbbing pulse blocking my throat.

The police siren blasts behind me; they flash their headlights. I throw the car right, feel it fishtail. I fight with the wheel, hear a crunch, feel an impact—the rear panel on the passenger side scrapes along the corner of a building and sparks fly. I brake, hit the accelerator again. If I can get onto the Dock Road, head for the city center, I'll dump the car and disappear into the crowds.

Turn the car around. Drive it straight at the bastards. I twitch the wheel, but the tire bumps the curb and the car leaps a foot in the air then crashes, nose down, into a pothole.

I jink left, squeezing the Toyota down a narrow alleyway. The police car slews around the bend after me, hits the walls on both sides. Metal groans—both front panels of the cop car crumple like tinfoil; the impact seems to rush past me as a judder of air and sound.

"Yes!"

Keep a cool head, you can still beat this. You just have to get to the gallery before they find it.

All I need is a few minutes—and a little strategic distraction.

77

Carver's work mobile rang.

"Bill Naylor, boss. I'm at one of the old tea warehouses off the Dock Road. Landlord's with me. We can't gain access—he says the locks've been changed."

Carver felt a prickling in the back of his skull. "I'm going to request an ARV." He reached for the desk phone and keyed through to the switchboard as he spoke: "Be advised, a patrol unit has located the van, and they had a suspicious vehicle near the scene—a gray Toyota Yaris. If it's him, there's no telling what he'll do—so be careful."

"I was born careful," Naylor said, with a chuckle.

Request for backup made, Carver hung up the landline.

"They're on their way—ETA eight minutes." The phone buzzed in his hand. "Stand by, Bill."

He tapped the swap icon to take the second call. It was from the patrol unit guarding the van.

"The lads in the other unit intercepted the Toyota, but he made a run for it. Pursuit vehicle crashed."

"Casualties?"

"Not unless you count the car—that's a write-off."

"They lost him?" Carver said. The main set in the patrol vehicle blared out, but he couldn't make out the words. "What's happening?"

"That was our eye in the sky—they've got eyeballs on him. He's going nowhere," the cop said with grim satisfaction.

"Have we got the registered keeper's ID?"

"A seventy-five-year-old man from Kirkby who *actually* drives a Volvo."

"Stolen plates again," Carver said.

"That'd be my guess."

"The Matrix unit is dispatched. Hang tight." He switched back to Naylor's call. "Bill, are you still there?"

"Like patience on a monument," Naylor said.

Carver updated him on the situation as he made his way down the corridor to the incident room.

"I can hear the chopper," Naylor said. "Can't see it yet, though. The landlord said there's another way in round the back—a roller door for vehicle access—but he didn't have the remote with him. He's gone to fetch it."

Carver briefed the few detectives in the MIR and gave orders for the house-to-house teams to stand by; they might be needed elsewhere.

Tom Ivey listened with one eye on his computer; his shiner was turning black as the hours passed.

Carver considered sending him home, but he decided that would be hypocritical, under the circumstances.

Ivey suddenly snapped upright. "Boss. The Ferryman just sent out a public message. He's mobilizing his fans—sending them to the scrapyard, looks like. Says there's a new exhibit."

"Great—half the scallies in the north end'll be out looking for a bit of aggro," DC Gorman grumbled.

"Well, you'd better get out there and sort them, hadn't you?" Carver said.

The rest of the crew were already reaching for jackets, patting pockets for car keys.

"You know where to go," Carver said, as they made their way to the door. "I want everyone in body armor. No exceptions. You'll take your lead from the Matrix team, clear?"

Nods, a few ragged shouts of "Sir" and "Boss!"

Carver saw DC Ivey limping toward the door. "Not you, Tom," he said.

Ivey began to argue and Carver said, "That's an order."

"What am I supposed to do, stuck here?" Ivey protested.

"Keep an eye on Instagram traffic—let me know if anything new crops up, take any calls that come in." It wasn't much to offer by way of compensation, but Ivey was in no fit state to tackle an ugly crowd, and it was the best he could do.

Moments later, he was talking to Sergeant Farrow at the Contact Center.

"We'll set up a couple of roadblocks, see if we can hold them back," the Contact Center manager said. "But there's a lot of wasteland in the area—they could just drive over it if they don't mind risking their tires."

"What's the word on the Toyota?" Carver asked.

"It stopped for about a minute, then drove off again. We've got it heading south on the backstreets."

Carver checked the map on his laptop screen.

"He's heading toward the warehouse, using his fans to draw police away. We need that ARV at Naylor's location." He heard someone shout in the background.

"Stand by," Farrow said.

Carver heard a muffled exchange, then:

"We just lost the chopper—a couple of clowns shining laser lights into the cockpit. They've had to return to base."

Carver muttered a curse. "Bill Naylor's at the warehouse with no backup—do we know when that ARV will arrive?"

"It's en route. Stand by—we've just had a shout from Naylor."

"Put me on speaker," Carver said.

The hum of voices from the Contact Center got louder, and Carver heard Naylor's voice. "—steel gray Toyota Yaris." He reeled off the registration.

"That's him," Carver said.

"Charlie Tango; this is Lima Mike four-two. He's just sitting there, over."

"Do *not* approach," Carver said.

"That you, boss?" Naylor said. "Like I said, born careful, over."

A second later, he spoke again, all informality gone: "Charlie Tango; Lima Mike four-two. Urgent call."

The Contact Center chatter dropped to almost nothing, call handlers and police officers citywide clearing the airwaves for Naylor's message. As a career bobby, Naylor had seen just about everything there was to see in the job—he wouldn't request radio silence unless something serious was brewing.

"Toyota is approaching." A pause. *"What the hell—?"*

A second later, the roar of an engine, a shout of dismay. A thud. Then silence.

The police were waiting. I don't know how they could've . . . But there's no time for that. Deal with the situation, there'll be time for analysis later.

I've gathered my laptops. I know better than to leave them for the police techs to play with. The rest can burn, pile incriminating items on the dissection table: paperwork; credit cards; letters sent to my work address.

I open the cold store as I hear the sirens. They won't get in through the front door. I made sure of that. But I still need a way out. I've sent DMs to a few local supporters—offered a cash reward for what I need. Well, I am asking them to enter a burning building, when all's said—I had to offer a greater incentive than thwarting the police and earning a place in art history—

I pour petrol over everything, lay a trail to the door, step into the corridor, pluck a match from the book, light the rest with it, and toss the lot inside. A blast of hot air knocks me sideways. I leave the door open, feel cool air rush past me, sucked in by the fire. The other flammables in the workshop will feed the blaze.

Carver had only just reached his office when his mobile rang. It was Sergeant Farrow with an update.

"The Toyota mounted the pavement and crashed," he said, without preamble. "The ARV is on-site. Blood at the entrance to the building; no sign of Bill Naylor. His PR's still working, but he's not responding. Matrix team arrival is imminent, and an ambulance is on its way."

If his personal radio wasn't damaged by the impact, there could be hope for Bill—having an ambulance on-site was a good move.

"What about the team at the scrapyard—are they managing?"

"Only one carful turned up. The occupants are watching from a distance, but they've been no trouble. Stand by." He spoke to one of the call handlers, and a second later, came back with, "They just left."

Carver rang through to Tom Ivey's desk. "Anything happening on the Ferryman's Instagram?" he said.

"I was about to buzz you, boss," Ivey said. "He's redirecting them—'Change of venue,' he says. 'Wanna visit my bricks-and-mortar gallery? It's Open Day.' *Bloody hell*—he's sending them to the warehouse."

Carver relayed the information and Farrow rung off. Immediately, his mobile buzzed again.

It was Sergeant Rayburn. "The warehouse is burning," he said. "Fire Service has been alerted and I've requested all patrols able to assist."

"Bill Naylor could be in there, Rob," Carver said. "The suspect, too."

"The rear of the building's been breached," Rayburn said. "And we've got rubberneckers and troublemakers turning up at the scene. We'll have to clear them before firefighters can move in. I think the suspect's legged it, though."

"Because?"

"When we rolled up, four cars suddenly sped off, heading in different directions."

Carver closed his eyes. "Diversionary tactic," he said. "The Ferryman is in one of those cars."

"That's what I'm thinking," Rayburn said. "But we don't have the personnel to give chase."

Carver heard someone call Rayburn's name.

"Okay—gotta go."

"Be safe, Ray," he said.

"Where's the fun in that?" He heard the smile in Rayburn's voice.

80

Ruth Lake stood on Simpson Street, in the heart of what was known as Liverpool's "Baltic Triangle." The area was still under development, so it had an interesting mix of high-end apartment conversions of Victorian properties alongside low-end unit rentals with leaking rainwater pipes and buddleia bushes growing from cracks in the walls.

Carver wasn't picking up, so she'd left a voice mail on his mobile, giving him a quick rundown of her inquiries. The council had suggested three suitable places where Adam might relocate after the compulsory purchase of his old studio. And here she was, less than a mile away from the police HQ, in a four-story redbrick building that must have provided both warehouse and office space back in the day, but now housed a furniture warehouse, upholstery service, and a range of small businesses dealing in bespoke art and craft work. The lower windows were protected by steel rollers—open at this time of day; the windows of the first and second floors with grilles. Cars lined either side of the street.

Ruth stepped inside. The listings at the bottom of the damp and drafty stairwell said that MadAdaM's studio was on the third floor. She returned to the pavement to try to work out which of the latticed windows would be his, and noticed that the upper two floors, though begrimed by salt river-spume and fifty years of neglect, were free of bars, shutters, or grilles.

She caught a glint of something bright at a third-floor window. An almighty crash, then glass cascaded from above. Ruth ducked and turned away, instinctively shielding her eyes. Immediately after it, a large object; it hit the ground, exploding on the pavement only yards from her. She heard the *punk, thock* of punctured metal as the shattered object sent shards of pottery in all directions. Car alarms blared; someone screamed.

Ruth rose from a crouch and saw the frightened face of a woman behind the wheel of a Ford Focus. A section of white display plinth was embedded in the roof of her car. Ruth beckoned her out, and she obeyed, but began walking toward her.

"Get to the other side of the road," Ruth yelled, glancing up to check the window above. Its frame was twisted and broken, and glass bejeweled the street. A man came out of nowhere and dragged the woman out of the way. Two teenaged boys emerged from a café opposite and began recording on their mobile phones.

"POLICE," she bellowed. "Get *back* inside."

By now, Ruth had her work phone in her hand. She hit the emergency button.

Ducking behind a car on the far side of the street, she kept her eyes on the window as she called in her location and shouted a request for backup. She couldn't hear the reply, nor could she hear any further signs of struggle above the constant blast of car horns and the screech of alarms. A man appeared in the doorway of the warehouse block, hands in his pockets. Looking perplexed, but not particularly worried, he called over to her:

"What's to do, love?"

"How many people are on the premises?" Ruth shouted.

"Can't say about the rest, but on the ground floor—three staff, six customers," he said.

"Can you secure the doors from inside?"

"Yeah."

"Do it," she yelled. "Don't open it for anyone but police in uniform."

A car had stalled at the corner of the street, the driver's side pockmarked by debris from the shattered plinth. The driver scrambled across to the passenger side and climbed out. Ruth waved him over and tugged him to a crouch next to her.

With cars blocking traffic in both directions, it should prevent people driving into danger.

Ruth heard the distant wail of sirens.

The car alarms were silenced, one by one, until there was nothing but the ghosts of blaring horns in her ears.

A chair tumbled out of the studio window, and Ruth heard a scream from above.

The man next to her swore, then crossed himself, and Ruth made a decision.

"I'm going in," she said into the phone. With her mobile clipped to her belt, and still in a crouch, she deployed her Casco baton, then ran across the street and ducked inside the entrance.

A crash echoed from above—wood against wood. Then nothing. She took the concrete stairs two at a time, peeking around the corner at each turn, but nobody showed their face. On the third floor, she saw that the studio door was open. An eerie quiet had descended.

A man poked his head out from the next-door premises; he looked terrified. Ruth shooed him back inside, mouthing *"Police."* Then mimed, *Lock it*.

Flattening herself against the wall next to the open door, she heard a soft *flump* and recalled the awful spectacle she'd seen at Karl Obrazki's flat.

Bracing herself, she announced herself as police.

"Show yourself!" she shouted.

Silence.

"If you are able to speak, make yourself known."

Nothing.

Finally, she inhaled shakily, steadying herself on the outbreath.

"Adam?" She waited but heard no sound. "It's me, Ruth." She kept her tone calm, conversational. "Look, I know things have been tough for you, and I'm truly sorry for that. Whatever you've done, I'll try to help, but you have to stop now."

Still no answer.

She eased the door wider with her fingertips and saw the art teacher, Graham Milner, lying facedown on the floor. Blood pooled around his head, and there were cuts to his neck. He was ominously still.

Ruth positioned the baton over her right shoulder, adjusting her grip, tightening her fingers around it.

Standing in the doorway, she did a rapid check of the area: side to side, ceiling.

Smashed glass, artwork, and photographs littered the floor. She recognized some of the sketches as outline plans of the Ferryman's exhibits, and her heart contracted.

Adam . . . Oh, Adam . . .

On the wall opposite, next to the gaping window, a large canvas. It depicted a woman, one eye as big as a dinner plate. Ruth recognized the subject as her mother. Inside the pupil of the eye, a reflection—a boy child—Adam at the age of six or seven. In the foreground, her back to the viewer, a younger female. Ruth could tell by the slope of the figure's shoulders that she felt sad and helpless, gazing on the woman and child.

It's me, she thought. Adam had painted her as she had been at nineteen, and she knew with complete certainty that this was the missing painting, *Battered Wife.*

Her throat closed.

81

Carver heard the sound of running footsteps in the corridor.

Tom Ivey burst through the door without knocking; he was gripping his injured arm with one hand, and the bruising around his eye was livid against the ghastly pallor of his skin.

"Ruth hit the red button," he said.

The room tilted suddenly. "Where is she?"

"Simpson Street in the Baltic Triangle."

Carver snatched up his mobile, remembering Ruth's call. "What's the situation?"

As Ivey filled him in on the details, Carver found Ruth's voice mail and listened for a few seconds. "It's Adam Black's studio," he said.

"An armed response unit is on its way," Ivey said. "But she went inside."

"Oh, jeez . . ." Carver rang through to Farrow at the Contact Center. "Sitrep on the Baltic incident," he said.

"We've got units on the way," Farrow said.

"We need to evacuate that building." He finished the call and spoke to Ivey. "Can you drive?"

Ivey looked confused.

"With that." Carver jerked his chin, indicating the injured arm. "I'm not cleared to drive—can you drive?"

"Yes. Certainly. Absolutely I can," Ivey said.

"Let's go then." Carver grabbed his jacket from the back of his chair, and his eye snagged on the list of art competition rejects, still only halfway checked, on his desk. "Oh, hell."

He snatched up the stapled sheets and the document seemed to scintillate color. *You're reading your own aura—calm the hell down.* He steadied himself and told Ivey to sort out transport. "I need to make a couple more calls," he said.

Ruth eased carefully into the room. At the base of the wall to her right, a tarpaulin sheet. Her brother was slumped next to it. He had a knife in his hand.

"Two males, Graham Milner and Adam Black," she said for the mic. "Both unresponsive, Adam Black is in possession of a knife."

Keeping her eyes on Adam, Ruth crouched to check Mr. Milner: he was alive. She relayed the information, then went to her brother and gently took away the knife before checking his pulse: it was thin and thready. "Black is disarmed," she said. "Need paramedic unit urgently."

A coil of orange nylon cord lay nearby—it was a good bet this was the cord found near Professor Tennent's abduction site. A groan from Milner; he was coming to.

Seeing Ruth, his eyes widened.

"Mr. Milner, it's all right," Ruth said. "I'm Sergeant Lake—do you remember me?"

She bent to him, but he whimpered, tried to fend her off.

"Try to lie still," she said. "You've had a head injury, you could have a fracture."

He didn't seem to understand her, seemed to be unable to articulate.

The sirens of the first responders were drawing close, so she set the knife down out of reach and tried again to reassure him. "It's all right," she said. "You're safe. D'you hear the sirens? That's police and ambulance." He sobbed, clutching at the cuts on his neck.

"We'll get those seen to," she said. "Don't worry, the paramedics will be here any second."

Milner's eyes were wild with fear. He tried to peer around her, to get a view of Adam.

"He can't hurt you," she said.

He shook his head, tears welling in his eyes.

Ruth heard the thud of boots on the stairwell; Matrix team, or Rapid Response Unit. They would be armed. She called out to them, identifying herself, and the sound of boots on concrete halted.

"I have two seriously injured males in the room," she said. "They are not armed. I repeat—they are *not* armed."

She stood and moved toward the door.

Three things happened at once: her personal phone buzzed, Adam cried out, and she tripped headlong onto the glass and debris on the floor.

She got to her knees, feeling glass pierce the fabric of her trousers.

Milner was standing over her. He kicked her Casco baton away and slammed the door shut. His foot came back a second time. Ruth dodged that one, but he landed the next, and she felt a rib crack. Milner hauled her backward by the scruff of her neck across broken glass and splintered wood. She couldn't find enough traction to fight him. He slammed her hard against the wall at the back of the room and, winded, she slumped to the floor.

Carver arrived at Adam Black's studio as Matrix team officers were guiding frightened tenants out of the building. The area was gridlocked, and they'd been forced to abandon Ivey's car a couple of streets away. At the police tape, an officer in uniform was in a quiet but clearly heated argument with a bystander.

"Listen to me," the man was saying. "It won't take a minute. I need to—"

"I'm sorry, sir," the cop said. "You're not going back in there. Now get behind the line."

"You *people* bundled me out of my own premises without even a please, thank you, or kiss my arse. I've got projects near completion in there. Sensitive information." The business owner was thin and rangy, with protruding eyes and a nervy manner that suggested hyperthyroidism—or a serious amphetamine habit.

"The place has been cleared," Carver said, flashing his warrant card. "Am I right, Constable?"

"All except the premises on the third floor—"

"Right next door to *my office*." The man was shouting now. "What if this madman decides to poke around?"

"What makes you think he'd *want* to?" Carver said.

"What are you getting at?" The man's colors flashed off a high-alert warning.

"Our priority is public safety," the Matrix cop said.

The man snorted.

"Sir," Carver said. "Mr. . . . ?"

"What's it to you?"

This guy is paranoid, Carver thought.

"It's not safe in there," Carver said. "You won't be allowed back in until it is. So please move behind the tape."

The Matrix cop touched the man on the elbow and he jerked away, but he turned, allowing himself to be guided to the scene tape, where he shifted from one foot to the other, glaring angrily at the cops, and periodically glancing up at the shattered window on the third floor.

"Who's in charge?" Carver asked. He saw Sergeant Rayburn talking to four of his team over by one of the two Matrix vans in attendance and said, "Never mind. I see him."

Carver walked to the van and waited for Rayburn to finish giving instructions. "Operations said you were pinned down at the warehouse fire."

"As soon as word got out about the hostage situation, the Ferryman's fans blew away like smoke," the Matrix team leader said.

"Well, I'm glad you're here. You got my message?"

"I got it." Rayburn fixed him with a look. "How sure are you?"

"Milner was one of the earliest applicants to submit work to the

Alderson Bank art competition," Carver said. "He was rejected with no right to appeal because he was over the newly imposed age limit by *one day*."

"Ouch."

"This was eight months ago. For five solid weeks he bombarded the competition website with complaints—sometimes twenty a day. He spammed the bank's Twitter account and even made threats. Mr. Fenst was subjected to some of the worst abuse. Milner only stopped after his department head received a letter of complaint from the bank and he was brought before the dean of the college for a disciplinary hearing—his second in two years."

"The disappearances started when?"

"Six months ago."

"When all this stuff kicked off. That's a hell of a coincidence," Rayburn said.

An image of Karl Obrazki came into Carver's head, and he felt a sudden chill.

"What?" Rayburn asked.

"He placed a penny in Karl Obrazki's mouth—it was dated 1978—the year Milner was born."

Rayburn shook his head. "Can't expect to follow the weird logic of a crazy bastard like that."

"I don't think he *is* crazy," Carver said. "He's calculating and heartless, but . . ." He remembered Dr. Yi's words on narcissists' fragile egos.

Rayburn shifted restlessly. "Can we reason with him?"

"For now, maybe, but the forensic psych warned us that he's likely to respond with blind rage if he feels slighted or threatened."

Rayburn laughed mirthlessly. "He's got half of Merseyside Police waiting to lay hands on him. I'd say he's already having a lousy day, mate." He glanced around the crowd as if calculating the risk to their safety. "Just how unstable is he?"

"I've put a call in to Dr. Yi," Carver said. "He's in session at Ashworth—I've made an urgent request for someone to go and dig him out. But if you want a layman's assessment, Milner has already torched one warehouse—it's only a matter of time till he gets it into his head to make that double."

Rayburn nodded, a deep groove appearing between his eyebrows as he absorbed the information.

"So," Carver said. "What's the plan?"

"We tested the strength of the door—it's solid," Rayburn said. "The only other option is to rappel in from the rooftop, and to do that, we need eyes in there."

82

Ruth tried to fight, but her ribs burned and she felt sick; in a moment, Milner had her hands tied. He worked on Adam next. Ruth tried to pull him away from her brother, but he backhanded her, smacking her head against the wall a second time. She slid sideways, the room tilting alarmingly.

Just breathe, Ruth . . .

She eased herself up, assessing the situation.

The door was barred. The hall outside quiet, but she knew Rayburn and his team would be busy. Adam was fading in and out of consciousness.

Milner picked up a three-foot length of wood from one of the smashed artworks and hefted it, testing its weight, watching her, his head cocked in an attitude of listening, a small, self-satisfied smile on his face. But his eyes betrayed him: his gaze darted nervously from the door to the window. Even in bright sunlight Ruth could see the flicker of emergency service lights reflecting off the high brick walls and ceiling of the room. Milner must know that the police would not walk away from this. Careful planner though he was, his luck had turned, and he had no escape plan.

Adam roused with a sudden shout and stared wildly about him.

"It's okay, Mr. Black," she said. It would not be good for Milner to know they were related.

Milner laughed. "This situation is a lot of things, but one thing it most certainly *isn't* is 'okay,'" he said.

Adam struggled stupidly with his bonds.

Shock, Ruth thought.

"Why are you doing this?" He looked at Ruth, his eyes glittering, feverish. "Why is he doing this?"

"Mr. Milner thought he'd be able to convince the world that *you* are the Ferryman," Ruth said. This was for the tactical squad, as much as it was for Adam: if her phone was still working, they would be listening in. She couldn't see it, and she could only hope that it had survived her tussle with Milner.

"What? That's mad," Adam slurred.

"You think so? I told Sergeant Lake it was *you* who set up *Experiment on a Bird in the Bell Jar*." Milner smiled. "*She* accepted it without even blinking."

Adam turned to her, his eyes unfocused. The hurt on his face was almost unbearable.

"Like déjà vu all over again, isn't it, Adam?" Milner turned his attention to Ruth. "He came to the ethics committee meeting, eighteen months ago, expecting to expose me. Found himself in the hot seat instead."

Ruth felt a wave of sorrow for her brother. "Milner convinced the committee that it was *your* design."

"The truth is, he didn't put up much of a fight," Milner said. "When they asked him for evidence against me, he reverted to the inarticulate, moody child he really is."

Adam made to boost himself up off the floor, but Milner sent him sprawling with a shove from the tip of the hunk of wood. "Stormed off with barely a word."

"They didn't believe me, Ruth," Adam mumbled.

"Milner is a psychopath," Ruth said, shifting her position to face Adam. "Lying is easy for him." She felt a subtle shift in Adam's posture. "*That* is why Milner managed to keep his job, while you dropped out. Not because you're not good enough—but because he has an overinflated idea of who he is."

"Yet you're the one tied up on the floor," Milner said.

"Look out the window," Ruth shot back. "Tell me your hands aren't tied."

Milner ran his tongue over his teeth, considering.

"Adam will kill you, but he'll die in the struggle," he said. "I'll barely get away with my life."

Ruth controlled the panicky flutter of her heart with a few slow breaths. "You can't implicate Adam in the murders. See, we already had you."

"Not a chance," Milner said. "I've been careful."

She held up her hands, bound at the wrists with orange cord. "This rope was used to garrote Professor Tennent." She saw surprise in the killer's face. "Yep, you dropped it when you abducted him. What—you didn't even notice it was missing?" She clicked her tongue. "Sloppy."

He raised his gloved hands. "My DNA isn't on there."

"You're sure about that?" she said. "And you left a fingerprint in the plexiglass disk you made for Tennent's 'exhibit' . . ."

He smiled, shrugged. "I've never been fingerprinted, so . . ."

"Oh, you will be."

Milner froze.

"Do you *really* think you can play the victim and the police'll just take your word for it?" She held his gaze. "That's the trouble with narcissists—they always think the opposition is too stupid to see through them."

Ruth glanced toward the window. *Where are you, guys?*

Were they waiting for her to convince Milner the best out was to surrender? *Okay, then—hit him with the evidence.*

"The detective you stabbed last night thinks he caught you a good one in the fight," she went on, satisfied to see sweat break out on Milner's upper lip. "You bled and fled, Milner. Bet you left DNA at *that* scene."

Milner shook his head, but it looked like he was denying the horror of his situation, rather than the truth of what she said.

"You messed up. Your type always does."

"My *type*?"

"Psychopaths, narcissists. Killers."

"Well then, it wasn't very bright of you, putting *him* in harm's way, now was it?" He jerked his chin toward Adam. "You even asked for my help to find him."

"Let's face it, you would've gotten around to him eventually," Ruth said, giving no ground, though she wanted to weep at her own gullibility. "You convinced the ethics committee that *Bird in a Bell Jar* was Black's work, for what? Don't get me wrong—I love this city—but a job at a former Liverpool technical college? Really? It's not exactly the Royal College of Art, now, is it?"

He stared at her, his fingers twitching.

"Must've rankled when Black won that prize just months after he left. Nice touch, that, painting it on the college wall." She faked a wince. "And you thinking, 'That should've been me!'"

"He should've been prosecuted."

"Didn't you say that challenging works have the most to say to us?"

He chewed the inside of his lip.

"You must have twenty years on Black—how many competitions have *you* won?"

Milner's head jerked. An involuntary action that told her the answer as clearly as if he'd said it.

"I'm guessing you sent something in to the Alderson Bank Art Awards."

She saw a shiver of pain pass across his irises.

"You didn't even make it past the first round, did you? Poor Marcus Fenst—murdered for good taste."

Milner stooped suddenly, grabbed her by her jacket lapels, and twisted, raising her a foot off the floor.

Ruth snatched at him, gasping with pain, but her bindings prevented her from gaining a grip. She made herself relax, even dropped her hands, forcing him to take her full weight. He pitched forward and she caught a whiff of something on his hands or clothing.

Oh, dear God—he reeks of accelerant.

"New cologne?" she said. "Or is that turpentine I smell on you?" Another one for the tactical squad. Telling them to get a bloody *wiggle* on.

"Did you firebomb your own *studio*?"

Milner bared his teeth, and she smelled the hot stink of his breath in her nostrils, on her skin, but she saw strain on his face; his jaw worked, popping the muscles in his cheeks, and he looked ready to cry.

Abruptly, he dropped her, and Ruth banged her tailbone painfully.

She whooped in air, willed away the pain. "All so you can go back to your old life, watching younger, more talented artists do better than you."

He booted her in the side and she grayed out for a second. When she came to, Milner had Adam by the ponytail, the block of wood raised in his other hand, ready to strike.

"No!" Ruth screamed.

Her phone rang out.

Milner slammed Adam against the wall and rummaged under the scattered art, finally picking up the mobile and sliding the bar to answer. He placed it to his ear, but recoiled as if he'd been stung.

Ruth guessed it was the police negotiator, and he'd used Milner's name.

"Smile . . ." Ruth hissed, sucking in air, every breath agony. "You're on Candid Camera."

He stared at her. "What? What is this?" He held out the phone as if expecting her to explain its workings.

"I hit the red button," she gasped. "You hit the red button, the line stays open, no matter what."

He dropped the phone.

"They heard every word . . ." Ruth said, her voice gaining strength as the pain subsided.

He crunched the phone under his heel, staring at Ruth with such hatred that she steeled herself for another attack. Then he scooped up the twisted remains and flung them out onto the street.

"There's no . . . way out, Milner. Give yourself up."

Milner stared down at her. "And go to prison?"

She wondered, for a moment, if it was a genuine question.

Then his face twisted in rage and he reached out for her again.

Adam launched himself at Milner with a roar. And crumpled, a look of astonishment on his face. Blood shone on the back of his leather jacket.

"Ruthie . . . I don't feel so good," he muttered.

Ruth reached for his collar and dragged him closer. "You've been stabbed." She tried to put pressure on the wound, but he twisted away from her. "Stay still—don't *fight* me, Adam."

Looking from Ruth to her brother, Milner smiled. "I've been puzzling over you two, but now I have it: yin-yang, the Taoist philosophy of opposites."

Adam was still at last, slumped against her, his weight adding to the strain on her damaged ribs.

"Ruth is yin, the coolness of heaven, and you, Adam, are yang, the heat of earth. The yin is the darker swirl, the female side, but with a dot or seed of yang at the heart of it. Yang, the white, represents fire. It can be destructive, yet it contains the seed of yin at its center. In balance, the two complement and unify each other."

"Save it for your followers, shithead," Adam said. "You're not in the lecture room now."

Milner blinked like a cat. "Brother and sister, reunited, completed in death. It has a certain beauty."

He must have seen something in Adam's reaction because he said, "Of *course* I knew you were siblings—the second I saw you in the foyer of the police headquarters, I saw it. I see more than you could *possibly* imagine."

He turned and paced across the room and, clearing glass and debris, picked up a laptop and flipped it open.

"Still working. How *about* that?" He thrust it under Adam's nose. "I'll be needing the password."

Ruth swallowed and heard a click at the back of her throat. She knew exactly what he planned: Milner intended to go out with his biggest exhibit yet.

83

Greg Carver stared up at the shattered window Ruth Lake's phone had come sailing out of exactly three minutes ago. Sergeant Rayburn had sent two men into the building opposite to scout out a vantage point. A sniper would be the obvious solution to the situation, but they would have to clear the area for at least a block in all directions and even then, they'd have to wait for permission from the brass: this was a hostage situation, not a terrorist threat. Listening in one of the Matrix vans, Carver had heard Ruth calmly describe the stink of turpentine on Milner's clothing and saw again the nightmare image that had haunted his dreams: Ruth drowning in a lake of fire.

"Boss."

Carver dragged his gaze from the broken lattice of the window and gave his attention to DC Ivey. The young detective's expression turned his guts to iced water.

"He's livestreaming them." Ivey handed over his phone.

Ruth seemed to have her hands at her brother's back. "Black is hurt," Carver said.

Ivey nodded. "He's bleeding."

Carver stared at the screen; the layout was unfamiliar. "This isn't Instagram."

"Milner is migrating his fans over to Facebook."

"He's . . . what?"

"He posted a message on his Ferryman Instagram page, told his followers where to find him," Ivey explained. "This is Milner's Facebook page, in his own name." He hesitated. "Boss, Facebook Live lets people post comments and questions—they're goading him, telling him to finish it."

"Jesus." Carver sought out Rayburn. "Sergeant, you need to see this."

Rayburn strode over to them, tension and subdued excitement sparking off him.

Carver tilted the mobile screen and Rayburn cupped his hands around it to reduce the glare.

"Okay . . ." His expression didn't change, but Carver knew he would be shifting gear, moving mentally from a containment situation toward active intervention.

"We need to move in," Carver said.

"I'll brief the negotiator," Rayburn said. "See if he can establish contact."

"You did." Carver glanced toward the smashed phone, still lying inside the police cordon. "The result is lying in the street over there. We lost audio contact."

"Yeah, well, now we've got audio *and* visual." Rayburn winced as soon as the words were out of his mouth. "Sorry. Look, have a word with your forensic psych. I'd bet my next payslip Milner won't do anything till he's got a good audience."

"You'd bet? That's classy, Rayburn."

"It's just a turn of phrase. Come on, man—I'm on your side."

"Then get them out of there."

"I will."

Carver assessed the crowd: residents and workers displaced from the buildings around them; rubberneckers and tourists and Ferryman fans, all jostling for a view. Many of them were recording the unfolding events on their mobile phones. One by one, their expressions changed, people switched from recording to staring at their screens. Word was spreading.

"Look around you. They think this is reality TV." He wanted to slap the phones out of every ghoulish hand and grind them into dust.

"I know," Rayburn said. "And I'll stop the bastard. But, Greg—mate—you need to step back, let me do my job."

He turned on his heel, and Carver watched him walk away with a sense of helplessness.

"Um, boss," Ivey murmured, "I've got an idea—but it's a bit of a long shot."

"Right now, I'll take anything, Tom," Carver said, feeling more drained now than he had in three months.

I think I've chosen the right hashtag for *Yin-Yang*—#FerrymanFinale has a nice ring to it. It's satisfying—no, let's not be coy—it's *exciting* to be able to declare my identity, to be recognized at last. Immediately after I post the first few pictures of Ruth and Adam, the images start trending.

A short video of the two on Instagram, followed up by the yin-yang symbol was all it took: my Facebook page has had a solid, but uninspiring, five hundred followers for a couple of years. But now . . . It's exhilarating to see those numbers rise and rise.

Carver put a call through to John Hughes.

"John—"

"Ruth," Hughes interrupted, "I know—it's all over the Web. What can I do?"

"Ask your tech-savvy guys to grab their mobile phones, tablets, whatever," Carver said. "I've got Tom Ivey with me—he thinks he can run interference on Milner's livestreaming."

"Put him on," Hughes said.

Carver passed his phone to Ivey. He needed to get inside the building. Ideally, he'd like a plan of the place—but the Matrix team had precedence and Rayburn had already made it clear he was not about to share. Carver left Ivey to talk his plan through with CSM Hughes and went in search of Adam's paranoid neighbor.

The crowd, held back at the police cordon, was growing by the minute, and Carver was beginning to lose hope when he heard raised voices, and the man came around the corner of the building, just beyond the cordon. He was struggling with an officer in uniform, trying to pull free.

"Get your *bloody* hands off me!" he shouted.

Carver ducked under the tape and strode to them.

"Calm down." The cop had a good grip; he was a foot taller and must have a good four-stone advantage over the skinny man. "Now get off home, or I'll find you a bed for the night down the nick," the constable warned.

"Last time I checked, this was still a free country." The man was red in the face, furious and clearly humiliated at being held against his will.

"Problem, five-three-one-nine?" Carver said.

Using the cop's "collar number" would prime him that Carver was police, but the constable eyed him with suspicion. "And you are?"

Carver presented his warrant card.

"Sorry, sir."

"It's fine. What's the problem?"

The cop held on to the unnamed man, who for now had stopped wriggling.

"He was trying to gain access to the building next door."

"Fascist bastard near broke my arm," the man protested. "I wanna make a complaint."

The constable's face darkened and Carver spoke up before he lost patience and arrested the little nuisance.

"Thanks," Carver said. "I'll take it from here."

The cop let go at the same moment the man gave a fierce jerk of his arm, nearly landing him on his face. Carver steadied him, then stepped back, hands up.

Dismissing the constable with a nod of thanks, he drew the injured party to one side. "Why were you trying to get inside that building?" Carver asked.

"What's it to you?" The man glared at him, his eyes red-rimmed, fingers twitching.

"D'you know another way in there?"

"I don't know what you're on about."

"What if I said we want the same thing?" Carver said, lowering his voice.

The man seemed at a loss, and Carver turned and walked back to the cordon, then raised the blue-and-white police tape, inviting the other man inside to join him.

He hesitated, then moved at a dash as if someone might stop him at the last moment. He glanced nervously over his shoulder before dipping under the tape.

Carver moved away from the crowd, turning his back to it.

"I think you're right about the risk," he said.

"Aw, shit." The man rubbed his chin fiercely and his eyes bugged.

"Look," Carver said. "I know you're concerned about your projects, your security."

"So what?"

"I think *they* got it wrong." Carver jerked his head, indicating the uniform police controlling the crowd.

The man looked past him, regarding the police presence with impotent hostility.

"I shouldn't be telling you this," Carver said, deliberately putting himself in the wrong. "But that mad bastard has barricaded the door into Adam's studio. He's already torched one building—and I swear he's looking to go out in a blaze of glory."

He could see the man was torn, so he pushed harder. "The fire at the warehouse in the North Docks is still blazing."

The man passed a trembling hand over his brow and stared at the sweat on his palm for a good ten seconds. Finally, he looked Carver in the eyes.

"No awkward questions? No comeback?"

"I just want to get in there," Carver said. "I don't care how."

The man nodded. "Follow me."

86

I'll need to improvise. *Yin-Yang* is going to be special: art as performance; performance as art.

I face the screen and look into the laptop camera, not afraid to be seen anymore.

"I want to incorporate the S-shape into the design, but I'll have to break bones to make it work."

A flurry of comments comes in—some horrified, but many encouraging, telling me to "go for it," as if I need their approval.

"I've already decided on the representation of the seed of *Yin-Yang*." I'm so amped, I have to steady myself before I tell them: "I'll dissect out the hearts of the two subjects and swap them over."

Adam groans.

Ruth Lake is harder to read.

I turn the laptop to allow my followers to see them, and the comments go wild! So many coming in I can't keep pace.

I'm *loving* the Q&A element of Facebook Live.

"Adam," Ruth murmured, keeping a careful eye on Milner as he greedily bashed out responses to his fans on the laptop keyboard.

Adam was weeping silently.

"Adam, come on." Ruth shifted slightly and grunted as a muscle spasm ripped through her side, sending shafts of pain through her injured ribs.

Suddenly, a voice boomed into the room and Milner jumped like a cat.

"Mr. Milner. Can we talk?"

The negotiator.

"You can end this now, with no more bloodshed. It's in your hands."

Milner had reached instinctively for the length of wood on the table next to the laptop, but now he set it down and sucked his teeth, that snarl of contempt appearing again for an instant. He typed a few words into the computer, then closed the lid.

He looked at Ruth and Adam and winked. "Wouldn't want any interruptions for this," he said. Then he walked calmly to the tarp rumpled against the wall and extracted a petrol can.

Ruth's mouth dried. "Don't—"

She coughed, tried again. "Don't do this, Milner."

He smiled. In a matter of moments, he'd gathered a glass jar and rags. He poured petrol into the jar and stuffed a rag inside.

"Don't," Ruth said, holding Adam close, tears blinding her. "Please."

He took out a lighter, lit the rag; she heard the growl of flame and air as he turned fast, moving to the window.

Too late, she roared, "FIRE! Look out below!"

People started screaming.

"I don't think we'll be hearing from the negotiator again," Milner said.

"Bastard . . . You bastard," Ruth gasped.

He grasped her chin and tilted her face to him. "Tears?" he said.

His expression was flat, dead. Like there was nothing behind the eyes.

"One more reply, then I think we should make a start."

He stepped up to the laptop again.

Ruth held her breath, waiting for sound of the tactical unit breaching the building, *willing* the whistle of rappel ropes as they made their way from the roof. But all she heard were screams and frightened sobbing from the crowd; urgent shouting as the police pushed the crowd back.

DC Ivey, shielded inside one of the Matrix vans, was thumb-typing comments to Milner's Facebook Live session on his phone.

"Is it true you got banned off the Alderson Bank comp because UR too OLD???"

A female PCSO sat next to him, tapping the keyboard on her own smartphone, her face intent. Ivey knew that in the Scientific Support Unit, everyone available—from CSIs to office staff—was doing the same thing. Merseyside Police had not asked for the page to be taken down because they needed to see what was happening inside the room, but that didn't mean Milner should get things all his own way.

"You had your chance for FORTY YEARS," Ivey typed. "Isn't it time you gave the next generation their go?"

"And what about the victims? Why pick on the young guys? What did they ever do 2 U?"

"Heard you had a grudge against Adam Black. Wanna Xplain?"

"Hey—anyone out there know MadAdaM? THAT'S who this OLD FART's gonna kill next. Me I LIKE Ad's stuff." To this one, Ivey added an image of one of Adam's trompe l'oeils.

He paged down to the comments following on from his. He was getting a response. Comments were coming in fast, condemning the Ferryman, calling him a fraud. A bitter old failure.

He scrolled to the top of the page. People were "unliking."

Nudging the PCSO, he tilted the phone for her to see. "It's working," he said.

Ruth watched as Milner picked up the length of the two-by-four and began tapping it absently against his leg, his eyes still on the laptop screen.

Help was not coming. She blinked tears from her eyes. *This bas-*

tard isn't going to get it all his own way. The knife she'd taken from Adam lay on the floor a good ten feet away from them; if she could get to it . . .

"He's going to move in," she whispered to her brother. "I'll go for the knife, but . . . Adam—I need your help."

His eyes closed.

"*Listen* to me," she hissed, forcing back tears of rage and helplessness. "Do not give up on me."

"What's the point, Ruth?" His voice was no more than a whisper. "What's the . . . ?"

Oh, God, she thought, *he's dying—my brother is dying, and he doesn't know the truth!*

She leaned in close, speaking urgently into her brother's ear: "Remember when Dad came to the house that day? The day his girlfriend was murdered?"

Adam roused a little. Sick heat came off him in waves.

"*Adam.* Dad didn't kill Mum. I swear—that's the truth."

He nodded, his eyes hooded, almost closed.

"Did you hear me?"

"Mmph."

She estimated the distance from their position to the knife. She might never make it, but she couldn't see any other way; Adam couldn't last much longer.

Milner was poised to turn the laptop around, put the two of them in the frame.

Ruth gathered all her strength.

A muffled exclamation. Milner took a step back, distancing himself from the screen.

"Fuckers," Milner spat. "Intellectual pygmies." It seemed his followers weren't reacting well to his new "artwork."

Milner cast about, and his eyes lit on the knife. He bared his teeth and in three long strides snatched it up and was on them in a second.

"Adam, MOVE!" Ruth yelled.

Adam screamed in agony, but he rolled, kicking his legs out, catching Milner on the ankle.

Milner yelled, darting out of reach, and even as Ruth launched herself forward, she knew she wouldn't make it.

A panicked hammering at the door signaled that the Matrix team had finally made a decision.

Too late! Ruth saw the blade flash.

Darkness shadowed her vision.

It's over, she thought.

The shape took form and bulk.

Carver?

He hit the killer at hip level in a flying rugby tackle.

The knife sailed across the room, embedding itself in a picture frame. The two men grappled, moving perilously close to what was left of the shattered window.

Carver, not yet at full strength, was losing. He stumbled backward, ending at the shattered window. Ruth sprang up but fell to one knee, feeling a piercing shock as the broken rib stabbed into muscles and tendons. Cold sweat broke out on her face and neck and she panted, fighting the pain.

Seizing him by the lapels, the killer forced Carver back, back, back into the gaping space.

Carver scrambled for a hold of what was left of the window frame and gasps and shrieks rose from the crowd below. Ruth crawled to them, her breath coming in short, painful coughs. She wrapped her arms around Carver's legs and held on, digging her nails into the cloth of his suit pants as rappel ropes snaked past the window from the rooftop.

Milner let go with his right hand and swung a punch at Carver. Carver twisted left to avoid it, letting go of the window frame, relying on Ruth to anchor him, and shoved Milner's right shoulder with the flat of his hand, using the killer's momentum to catch him off-balance.

Milner spun, his momentum carrying him forward into empty air.

He snatched at Carver, a look of terror on his face, caught a handful of shirt fabric.

Carver felt himself slipping from Ruth's grasp, but she dug in, roaring against the pain in her rib cage. Carver's shirt tore in Milner's hands and with a cry of surprise, he clutched at the sagging remains of the rotten window—frame, plaster, splintered glass, but could not save himself.

Screams from the street. Cries of "Stay back!"

Then the whistling sound of a Matrix team rappeler sliding down the rope. A second later, Rayburn was inside the room, prying Ruth's fingers from around Carver's legs.

"You can let go, Ruth," he murmured. "I've got him—he's safe now."

87

Carver arrived at his office three hours later, deflated and exhausted after a bollocking from Detective Superintendent Wilshire. When he sought Ruth out at the hospital, she was snoozing in a chair in the waiting area, dressed in surgical scrubs, shivering with cold and the aftereffects of the attack. Her own bloody clothes had been taken by Scientific Support. He draped his jacket over her.

"I hear you refused a lift home."

She didn't answer.

"Adam will be in surgery for another two hours, according to the surgical staff," Carver went on. "Why don't you go home, take a shower, get some sleep—or at least rest up while you can?"

She looked at her hands; they were stained red with Adam's blood, and Carver saw that the rope burns on her wrists were seeping.

"I can't leave him, Greg." Her eyes filled with tears and she dashed them away. "Bloody hell," she muttered. Then, "How did you get into Adam's studio? I mean, I know you've got these mad superpowers now, but . . ."

"Rayburn asked the same question," Carver said.

In fact, the Matrix team leader had said, *How the bloody hell did you get in here? What are you, Spider-Man?*

"I came in the old-fashioned way—through a door."

"The door was barred," Ruth said. "I heard them pounding on it."

"Different door."

Ruth's brow furrowed. "Greg, I'm too tired for this."

"If I tell you, will you promise to go home?"

She took her time thinking about it. Finally, she gave a single nod.

He told her about his encounter with the paranoid businessman, whose name, it turned out, was Unwin. Mr. Unwin had taken Carver to the building next door, where a police officer stood guard.

"If you get in, go up to the third floor," Unwin said. "There's an office with the name 'Springer' on the door." Catching Carver's look, he added, "Well, I wasn't gonna use me own name, was I?"

He'd shown Carver a keyring with two keys on it. "The Yale will get you into the office. This one"—he lifted the mortice key—"gets you into my office—the one next to Adam's. This used to be all one building, like. There's a filing cabinet in front of a door. The door is bolted top and bottom."

"It leads to Adam's studio?" Carver asked.

A brief nod.

"What if it's locked on the other side?"

"It isn't."

Carver took a breath.

"Don't ask," Unwin warned.

"Okay." Carver reached for the keys, but Unwin snatched them away.

"And don't be sending no one asking questions on your behalf, after."

"You have my word," Carver said.

"What the hell is he up to?" Ruth asked.

Carver shrugged. "I didn't ask, and I didn't send anyone to inquire—a promise is a promise."

She nodded, but he could see that her mind was elsewhere. "So how'd you get past the bobbies guarding the place?"

"Mr. Unwin provided a distraction," Carver said, smiling at the memory.

Everything had been as Unwin had described. The office desk was piled with papers, schematics, what looked like plans for bunkers or saferooms, but Carver didn't give those a second glance.

He had a few moments of anxiety over the filing cabinet, but it turned out that Unwin had left it empty, no doubt to make for easier access or escape through Adam's studio.

"If you hadn't come in when you did . . ." Her voice trailed off.

"You were right about how he found his victims, by the way," he said, as a way to change the subject. "They'd all been featured on local news in the weeks before they vanished. We think we've identified three more."

"So what set Milner off?" she asked.

"Ivey had a word with Milner's head of department at Fairfield: things didn't go quite as smoothly for him as he tried to make out. Adam's complaint to the ethics committee was time-consuming, and Milner missed the deadline for Alderson Bank's Art Awards last year. When he applied again *this* year, the age criterion had been changed—he was refused entry."

"And Adam won a Street Art Award—in the Young Talent category, no less." Ruth sighed and shook her head. "That was the trigger, wasn't it?"

Carver nodded. "All the victims were around Adam's age. All blessed with good fortune. But Yi thinks Adam was the primary target all along. Milner just didn't have the emotional insight to see it."

She sat deep in thought for some time. Suddenly, she roused, her eyes wide. "The negotiator—I should've asked—"

"He's fine," Carver said. "His pride's a bit singed, but he's okay."

"I heard Bill Naylor didn't make it."

"Extensive internal injuries," Carver said. "Pathologist says it was instant."

She nodded and he said, "Okay. Now you know everything I know—and it's time you went home."

It would be several more days to process the scenes: the warehouse;

the van; Adam's studio; to identify the remains they'd found in freezers and preserved in blocks of plexiglass.

Ruth allowed him to guide her to a waiting police car, but she insisted, in true Ruth Lake style, on handing his jacket back.

Now, at headquarters, his head still full of the craziness of the day, Carver felt flat. The corridors were empty—everyone with any sense having clocked off for the night—tomorrow would be a busy day. The building had taken on its nighttime dullness, giving itself up to sighs and creaks, and then he became aware of the hum of the air-conditioning.

He unlocked his office door, shucked off his jacket, and flicked on the light.

A bright red-and-blue Spider-Man model had been placed square in the middle of his desk. Next to it, a card, signed by Sergeant Rayburn and what looked like every member of the Matrix team.

He took out his phone and tapped in a reply to Rayburn. "Apology accepted."

88

Ruth told the cop who dropped her at home not to wait—she would call for a cab when she was ready to go back to the hospital. She turned the key in the lock thinking she would fix things with Adam. It wouldn't be easy while she was still lying to him about their parents' deaths, but she would find a way.

The stairs had never seemed so steep. She hauled herself up them step by aching step, pausing at the turn to catch her breath. The front bedroom door stood open. But she always closed interior doors before leaving the house.

Ruth reached for her Casco baton and realized it was in evidence, along with her clothing. The other doors were all shut.

With the image of Karl Obrazki's mutilated body imprinted on her mind, she took a breath and pressed the door lightly with her finger-tips. The wardrobe was ransacked—every item of clothing dumped on the floor—shoeboxes, shoes, the lot. Stepping over them, she looked inside and felt a stab of horror.

The album was missing.

Adam?

Ruth searched every room upstairs before heading below. The front and TV rooms were untouched, which left only the kitchen.

The blue leatherette album lay closed on the kitchen table. On top of it, the house key Adam had returned to her; he must have borrowed it from old Peggy again. It was almost funny: all the time she'd been searching the city for him, Adam was here, sitting in their family home, refreshing his memory. She turned the pages.

He had added press clippings, filling in some of the details she had so carefully kept hidden, populating the timeline around her mother's death—and after. She found printed clippings from the *Liverpool Echo* announcing the double murders of Dave Ryan's son and his daughter-in-law. She had expected this much, but she hadn't thought that Adam would make the connection to the other, much later double murder of John and Millie Garrod. He had photocopied a series of features from the national press, reporting on the elderly couple, battered to death with a hammer in their retirement bungalow. They were key witnesses two days away from testifying in a drug trial against Alan Jones. Without their testimony, the trial foundered and the Crown Prosecution Service had reluctantly dropped charges.

But Adam had been thorough: he included a story about an evidence review that had resulted in the rearrest of Jones some months later, charged with the murders of John and Millie Garrod. He was convicted and sentenced to life.

The final press report was one short paragraph, headlined: "Double Murderer Beaten to Death in Prison Attack."

Adam had penned handwritten notes on a sheet of sketch paper.

Fact 1: Mum and Ffion; Damien and Naomi Ryan; John and Millie Garrod—all murdered with a clawhammer. All beaten about the head.

Fact 2: Dad confessed to murdering Mum and his girlfriend.

Fact 3: Dad was dead when the other murders (same MO) happened.

Fact 4: You said you believed Dad when he said he didn't kill Naomi.

Question 1: Why? You didn't think so at the time. So what changed?

Question 2: If Dad WAS innocent, why did he confess?

Question 3: Why did Dave Ryan say justice was done? (See Fact 1)

Question 4: If Jones murdered the Garrods, how come it took an evidence review to get the conviction?

Question 5: Did Ryan have Jones murdered in prison?

Question 6: Why does Ryan "owe" you, Ruth?

He had doodled in the margins: graphic-novel-style ink drawings of a clawhammer, dripping blood; of Jones wielding a hammer, teeth bared, eyes bulging, the whites shot with blood.

At the bottom of the page, Adam had scrawled, "Fact 5: We need to talk."

ACKNOWLEDGMENTS

My love and gratitude to Murf, my anchor through life's storms, my first auditor, champion, and gentle critic. To Felicity Blunt and Lucy Morris at Curtis Brown, and Emily Krump at William Morrow, I am deeply grateful for your editorial insights and guidance in crafting and honing this book—it has been greatly enhanced by your input. Julia Elliott, thanks for efficiently and cheerfully keeping the wheels turning so smoothly during the hiatus. Over the years, I've learned to appreciate the importance of great copyediting, and I feel blessed to have worked with Laurie McGee on both *Splinter in the Blood* and *The Cutting Room*. Huge thanks also to Melissa Pimentel at Curtis Brown and Jenn Joel at ICM for bringing the book to the wider world.

To Ann Cleeves, Mo Hayder, and AJ Finn—all brilliant writers—my thanks for your kind words of support, and my admiration, always.

I will be forever in the debt of those who put my books into the hands of readers—publicity, sales, and marketing experts who work behind the scenes, and booksellers who stock, display, and recommend the novels to their customers. In this regard, I owe special thanks to Kaitlin Hari, Gena Lanzi, and Mary Ann Petyak at William Morrow, for their enthusiasm and expertise. To the Goodreads reviewers and podcasters and book bloggers who have taken time to read, comment on, and champion my work, my heartfelt thanks. I hope this new tale pleases you.

ASHLEY DYER is a writing duo based in the UK.

Margaret Murphy was a longstanding Writing Fellow and Reading Round Lector for the Royal Literary Fund, and is a past chair of the Crime Writers' Association (CWA) and founder of Murder Squad. A CWA Short Story Dagger winner, she has been shortlisted for the First Blood critics' award for crime fiction as well as the CWA Dagger in the Library. Under her own name she has published nine psychological suspense and police procedural novels.

Helen Pepper is a senior lecturer in policing at Teesside University. She has been an analyst, forensic scientist, scene of crime officer, CSI, and crime scene manager. She has coauthored, as well as contributed to, professional policing texts. Her expertise is in great demand with crime writers: she is a judge for the CWA's Non-Fiction Dagger Award and is Forensic Consultant on both the *Vera* and *Shetland* TV series.

MORE FROM ASHLEY DYER

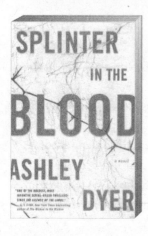

Splinter in the Blood

A propulsive debut suspense novel, filled with secrets, nerve-jangling tension, perplexing mystery, and cold-blooded murder, in which a police officer on the hunt for a macabre serial killer is brutally attacked, and only his partner knows the truth about what happened—and who did it.

"One of the boldest, most inventive serial-killer thrillers since *The Silence of the Lambs* . . . Perfect for fans of Jeffery Deaver and Lisa Gardner."

—A. J. Finn, #1 *New York Times* bestselling author

"A taut and compelling thriller, as sharp as the thorns that feature in the plot."

—Ann Cleeves, Internationally bestselling author of the Vera Stanhope and Shetland series

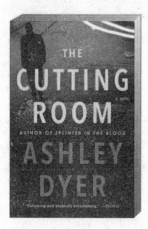

The Cutting Room

Detectives Ruth Lake and Greg Carver, introduced in the electrifying *Splinter in the Blood*, must stop a serial killer whose victims are the centerpiece of his macabre works of art.

In this utterly engrossing and thrilling tale of suspense, the pair of seasoned detectives face off against a wickedly smart and inventive psychopath in a tense, bloody game that leads to a shocking end.

"Disturbing and wickedly entertaining." —*People* Magazine